HUSBANDS AND LOVERS

What Rhea Sheridan—Santa Fe's wealthy culture countess—wanted, she usually got. What she wanted was to have Mona Gallagher's handsome husband, Terry, become the latest of her lovers—and she would use every weapon in her arsenal of seduction to get him.

Mona knew that Rhea had the savage sting of a Queen Bee with an insatiable appetite for honeyed pleasure. And that Terry would be very responsive to Rhea's beauty and brains, money and social power. But now that Mona was being forced into a fight for him, she tried to imagine what her life would be like without Terry . . . and then again, what it *could* be like in the arms of someone else—the passionate Sylvester, perhaps the mysterious Nigel. . .

SANTA FE

Santa Fe

Melinda Snodgrass

A SIGNET BOOK

NEW AMERICAN LIBRARY

NAL BOOKS ARE AVAILABLE AT QUANTITY DISCOUNTS
WHEN USED TO PROMOTE PRODUCTS OR SERVICES.
FOR INFORMATION PLEASE WRITE TO PREMIUM
MARKETING DIVISION,
NEW AMERICAN LIBRARY, 1633 BROADWAY,
NEW YORK, NEW YORK 10019.

SIGNET TRADEMARK REG.U.S.PAT.OFF. AND FOREIGN COUNTRIES
REGISTERED TRADEMARK—MARCA REGISTRADA
HECHO EN CHICAGO, U.S.A.

SIGNET, SIGNET CLASSIC, MENTOR, ONYX, PLUME,
MERIDIAN and NAL BOOKS are published by NAL PENGUIN
INC., 1633 Broadway, New York, New York 10019

First Printing, December, 1988

1 2 3 4 5 6 7 8 9

PRINTED IN THE UNITED STATES OF AMERICA

Occasionally life is kind enough to provide a person with a circle of friends who become almost a family. One of those friends is Jim Moore—archaeologist, writer, gamer, shooting buddy, and dear friend. Thank you, James, for all the help.

Acknowledgments

A number of people helped me create this book. I'd like to single out for special thanks Maureen Barron at NAL, who suggested that I write a book about New Mexico. That this little effort has a life at all is completely her doing. I would also like to thank Fred Ragsdale, who advised me on Indian law matters, and guided me to several very helpful law-review articles. Jim Moore, who loaned me a stack of books on Pueblo culture, suggested I use the Cruzate grant for the climax of the book, and reduced me to giggles at the notion of fry-bread stands outside an expensive residential area. Thanks also to Victor Milán, Walter Jon Williams, and Joseph Reichart for allowing me to steal some of their better lines, and allowing me to repeat a few of the spellbinding stories which have arisen out of New Mexico's unique culture. For any people interested in reading further about the Pueblo culture, I recommend the mesmerizing and beautiful book *The Tewa World,* by Alfonso Ortiz; *The Pueblo Indians of North America,* by Edward P. Dozier; and *Handbook of North American Indians: Southwest,* edited by Alfonso Ortiz. And finally, many thanks to Laura Mixon, who read the proposal for this book and reassured me that there really was a story here.

Author's Note

As knowledgeable people will tell you, there is no San Jose Pueblo. San Jose is a figment born of a fertile imagination, but based on two actual Pueblos—San Juan and Taos. I would like to thank the Pueblo people for allowing me to present even a fraction of their admirable and fascinating culture to readers. Any mistakes are mine alone, and I humbly apologize for them in advance.

1

There is a mystical rhythm to riding a horse. The surge
of muscles between the knees, the thrust from powerful hindquarters rocking the body in a motion rem-
iniscent of cradles or waves. Pure magic.

Or pure Freud. Terry's teasing words returned to
her, and Mona Gallagher smiled as she recalled the
last time they were together. *"Masturbation and dom-
ination fantasies all rolled into one."* Appreciative
giggles all around, and Terry—face flushed with wine,
and the heat of too many bodies wedged into their
small New York loft—throwing back his beautiful head
and laughing. She had stared at the hollows formed by
the tendons in his neck, the sparkle of a spilled drop
of wine on his lower lip, white teeth gleaming in a
tanned face. Her love had formed a painful vise about
her heart, and she wondered if she were mad to love
so intensely.

Lord knows, she and Terry knew all about Freud
and sexual fantasies. From the moment of their first
meeting, when he had rescued her from a New York
traffic snarl and guided her to the Garden, their bodies
had dictated their relationship.

Allegro tossed his big head, jerking the reins in
Mona's hands as she fought to hold him. He was more
attentive than she. Robert Smith and Lucy in the Sky
were lifting into the final fence, the big chestnut mare
giving her distinctive tail flip as she hit the apex of her
jump. Mona settled deeper into the saddle. They were
almost on. Robert had racked up two faults on this

11

round. If she and Allegro had a clean go, they would have the championship.

She pushed aside thoughts of Terry, of the move, of the home to come, and the baby to follow, and concentrated on the business at hand—to ride an internationally acclaimed show jumper to his ninth Grand Prix victory. This might be her final ride before her retirement from the circuit, but Allegro had a long career before him, and deserved her total attention.

Removing her black velvet hard hat, she saluted the judges, gathered up the reins, and cued him with a touch, and he rocketed into a long, ground-eating canter. They took the first four jumps with ease. The course had been designed for that, to lure the unwary horse and rider into overconfidence that would send them into the final fences with too much speed. Mona took up on the reins, felt the bite of leather even through her gloves, and the ache in her shoulders as thirteen hundred pounds of horse tried to ride through the pressure. She dug deep into the saddle and tightened her legs, driving him onto the bit, forcing his compliance. His ears flicked back, forward, back again. He was once more listening to her.

The run grew trickier here because he had to gather himself and change leads while still airborne. When he veered a little too sharp on the angle as they came off the second fence, Mona realized she had overcued. Allegro landed and bobbled as he tried to twist his body to follow his forelegs. Beyond, an enormous oxer looked horrifyingly solid as Allegro scramble to sort out his feet and regain his long, fluid stride.

For two paces she let him be, her hands, seat, and legs quiet as she let him find his balance. He too saw the fence coming up, and hesitation rippled through his big body. But Mona communicated calm as she held him steady with her hands and carried him fearlessly into the fence with her leg. And he responded to her call with that indefinable something that old-timers call ''heart.'' A combination of nerve, guts, and competitive spirit that marks the great horse.

Raw power thrusting them into the air, back arching

beneath her, and for one timeless moment the sensation of flight. . . .

Like being on a runaway elevator dropping a hundred floors, skydiving without a parachute. (A horrible sensation, this riding in a dream.) *A bone-jarring landing which seemed to drive his spine through the top of his head. No contact with the mouth, and The Third Man seizing the moment, pounding for the next fence, almost out of control. He grabbed for the bit, fought the restive head shaking as The Man tried to relieve the pressure on his mouth.*

The next fence loomed ever larger between The Man's pricked ears. But the jump itself was nothing when compared with the approach. And this one had all the grace of a three-legged man on stilts. Tension turned his belly into a hard knot, and fear licked at the edges of his mind, tightening his scalp, shortening breath. Please God, I don't want to fall—again.

The reins, like sensitive telegraph wires, transmitted his fear to his horse. Both of them were jittery now, eager to have it over with.

The takeoff.

Too far! Too far back!

Desperation as The Man tried to claw his way over. His hindquarters slammed into the fence in a tangle of wooden bricks and delicate legs. Twenty thousand gasps rose like a moaning wind. Explosions of agony through the hip and back, and that soul-deep sound as broken bones ground past each other. And somewhere deep within the murky grayness the shrill screams of an animal in agony.

Silvestre C. deBaca jerked upright in bed and ran his hands across his face, wiping away the film of tears and sweat. He stripped off his clammy pajama top, balled it, and flung it into the darkness.

He lay back, but the sheets were soaked. With a sigh that verged on a groan, he pushed aside the handwoven Navajo blanket that served as a quilt, and staggered away from the looming bulk of the massive wooden canopy bed.

The brick floor was cool beneath his bare feet, but he felt dizzy and abandoned in the center of his darkened bedroom. He tottered forward and came up against the whitewashed adobe wall. Two feet thick, the mud-and-straw bricks held the chill of the high desert night and breathed it back into the house. It acted as a compress for his burning cheek. His knees began to feel less like rubber, and he pushed off, making for the square of silver formed by the wide picture window.

It was near dawn. In the west, a quarter-moon was sinking toward the piñon-covered hills, touching the granite outcroppings with silver, and forming pools of darkness in the lee of boulders. The piñon, squat and gnarled, threw long grotesque shadows in the milky light and looked like twisted old men gathered on the hillsides to talk of demons.

Silvestre remembered how Grandfather Teofilo had been said to go alone into the mountains to wrestle with demons. And always returned triumphant from these encounters with evil. Sil wished the old man were alive now to do battle with his grandson's demons. But Sil had a feeling that these phantasms from his own soul would not respond well to Penitente prayers and curses. The Devil himself could not have created more terrifying monsters than those that sprang from his own mind each night. Born of fears and memories, they haunted and ultimately banished sleep.

Far off in the foothills of the Sangre de Cristo Mountains came the high, mournful yip of a coyote. The lonely sound seemed to ricochet off the distant stars. The yipping trailed away in a long sad howl, and all the dogs in the area sent up a chorus of hysterical barking. A door slammed, the sound unnaturally sharp in the clear mountain air, and a basso voice shouted imprecations at the dogs. The chorus yapped fitfully into silence. A few moments later there came one last puzzled "woof," and then silence.

Silvestre unlatched the window and pushed it open. The night was quiet, the only sound the sighing of the

wind through the sagebrush. It hissed across the stiff
blades of the buffalo grass, and set the branches on the
piñons to creaking. Then it, too, was gone, racing back
to the home of the winds.

A horse whinnied.

Sensing the morning, it called for food and company, and the distant neighing struck Sil like a blow.
They had had to put The Man down. And he'd never
even gotten to see him again. The memory brought a
sting of tears, and Silvestre brushed them away. The
men of his family, of his culture, did not cry.

He became aware of the room's chill when his toes
began to feel like tiny numb blocks. He shut the window, and crawled back into bed, the heavy weight of
the Indian blanket quickly driving back the cold.

It was only four-thirty, but he knew from ten weary
months of experience that he would never get back to
sleep. The nightmare marked the beginning of the cycle, and his basement demons wouldn't be satisfied
until he had played the cycle to its end.

He fumbled for the package of cigarettes on the bed
side table and snapped on his lighter. The yellow-blue
flame brought his narrow face into sharp relief, deepening the hollows in his cheeks and intensifying the
sunken eyes. His high cheekbones were chiseled
wedges, and they hadn't come from any hidalgo fore-
bears, but from some Indian far back in his pedigree,
though his father and grandmother would vehemently
deny any such admixture. The C. deBacas prided
themselves on their purity of blood and line. Thick
curling black hair formed a touseled halo about his
head, and his skin was a warm gold with highlights of
rose at the cheeks and lips. By anyone's standards he
was a handsome man.

The lighter clicked shut, and the end of the cigarette
burned like a tiny red eye in the darkness. Sil exhaled
a long stream of smoke and eyed that tiny glowing
point.

Where to start? *Men at some time are masters of
their fates: the fault is not in our stars, but in ourselves, that we are underlings.*

Wish I could be the master of mine. He hadn't felt truly in control for almost two years now. It had started in Aachen when he and Sweet Love had gone head-over-heels after the water jump. It had been a minor injury—a broken collarbone—but it seemed to eat at his confidence, eroding that state of sublime fearlessness which is so essential to a world-class rider. Another fall in England had left his ego like a rotten honeycomb, and he had gone searching for a solution.

He couldn't tell anyone. Fear was not a thing that you admitted even to yourself, much less to outsiders. *That* lesson Dad had succeeded in pounding into him. *The fault . . . the fault.*

He gave his head an angry shake and took another long drag on the cigarette. The fault was his. No good trying to push it off on Dad, or whining about his childhood. Nobody had held him down and shoved that crap up his nose the first time. No, he'd walked right into it, eyes open, brain disengaged.

Hell, the stuff was everywhere. You can't have a profession that involves so much money, and so much glamour, and all those endless parties, and not find cocaine.

At first it seemed a wonder drug. The fear vanished, replaced by a sense of invincibility. But the duration was short, and each time he used it, it seemed shorter still. Bobby Smith, over drinks one night, had tried to tell him . . . warn him that its effects were illusory. Only one reality existed when cocaine was in use: it impaired judgment.

He hadn't listened. Instead he'd branded Bobby a nervous old woman. The drug might affect *him* that way, but not Silvestre C. deBaca. A real man was in control of his mind and spirit. He could handle it.

Paris. One spectacular horse dead. One formerly great rider reduced to uselessness.

Yeah, he'd really handled it. Terrified to ride, and even more terrified to admit the truth. He couldn't face the pity or the smug, self-righteous expressions from his friends and acquaintances on the circuit. And at home? No help there. Nothing was more damning to a Hispanic male than to be marked a coward. Assault, rape, even murder could be explained, excused, tolerated, even applauded under the right circumstances, but not cowardice. His father wouldn't turn a hair if Sil were to confess his drug addiction, but to face those dark eyes and tell him that the reason he had skulked miserably about the house for the past eight months was that he was afraid to climb on a horse . . . ? Impossible!

No, he was trapped by nature and upbringing. The only thing to do was provide some plausible excuse for his continued stay in Santa Fe.

And that thought brought him squarely around to Franklin Delano Pierce. Loud, fat, red-faced, cunning, vulgar, and sentimental by turns, a man of large appetites and towering passions, Pierce might have been named after a whole gallery of presidents, kings, and emperors. He was now locked in a fight with the U.S. Equestrian Team over his attempt to construct a world-class riding center in Santa Fe. The USET jealously tried to maintain control over the locations of world-cup shows, and they disapproved of Santa Fe as a location, and of Franklin Pierce as an individual. Five months ago Pierce had approached Silvestre for help. And Sil had turned him down flat. He had hoped that he might ride again, and the last thing he wanted was to piss off the USET. But that was then, and this was now: the sharp looks from his father, and sharper words from his grandmother, told him he was out of time. He had to have an excuse, and Franklin Pierce's crazy dream to build a world-class equestrian center in Santa Fe, New Mexico, would do as well as any other.

The light pouring in the window had shifted by subtle degrees from silver to gray to a breathtaking rose and gold as the sun sailed over the edge of the eastern mesas. A door slammed, and from this Sil

concluded it was five-thirty. He could set his watch
by his brother, Jorge, preparing for his damn daily
run. As the tantalizing smells of brewing coffee,
frying eggs, and chili crept through the house, Sil
climbed wearily from the bed. If he wasn't precisely
ready to face a new morning, at least he had enough
interest in the day's doings that the bed seemed less
of a haven than usual.

First, breakfast, then to Ernie to buy another gram,
and finally a call to Pierce for the chance to twist the
tail of the USET and to hide for another day from the
consequences of fear.

Sheet lightning hung like a curtain across the sky,
and the upswept roof of the Santa Fe Opera—with its
fingerlike rafters—lay exposed in the stark light like
the rib cage of some alien monster. Thunder followed,
snarling around the peaks of the mountains that formed
such a spectacular backdrop for this outdoor opera
house.

Nigel Vallis stripped quickly from his dress jacket
and held it protectively over his wife's head. But there
was no answering spatter of rain, just a sharp breeze
redolent with the scent of moisture and pine sliding
gaily off those distant peaks.

"Whew, what a night."

"God's timing is a little off. We needed this display
last week for *Oedipus*. It's a little too vigorous for
Magic Flute."

Lexa Vallis hung over the low parapet that sur-
rounded the bar area and stared down into the rocky
bed of dry arroyo. On either side of the theater, small
extrusions held a surging crowd of operagoers, and the
one lone bar looked like a tiny fortress in the midst of
a besieging army.

"Do you want a drink?"

"Please." She didn't look up from her rapt contemplation of the arroyo.

Nigel was small and deft, and not above being
rude, for he didn't want to spend the entire intermission standing in line for a drink. He wished for

perhaps the thousandth useless time that Lexa could
tolerate cognac. *That* he had in a silver hip flask,
and he could have dispensed with this football skir-
mishing.

He ignored the angry looks thrown his direction,
placed his order for a glass of white wine and a shot
of scotch and went weaving back to Lexa, the small
plastic glasses held protectively over his head.

He paused, arrested as he always was by the line
of her profile. Neat, upturned nose, the network of
fine lines about her elongated eyes, the flow of jaw
into a swanlike throat. The corner of her mouth was
pulled down, but whether it was caused by sadness
or vexation, he couldn't say. He wanted to go on
studying her for a few more seconds, but with that
sixth sense that had marked their relationship from
the beginning, she felt his presence and turned to
face him.

Judged objectively, she was better in profile. Her
face was a shade too long for real beauty, mouth too
wide and jaw far too square and strong. But Nigel
loved her for that very strength. She exuded calm and
confidence, from the tip of her blunt-fingered hands
with their short (and sometimes dirty) nails to the top
of her head, crowned with that mane of black hair.
But not really black—under the brilliant New Mexico
sun, it could blaze with a patina of red that was both
beautiful and disconcerting. She was a bit more wrinkled than one would expect a thirty-two-year-old
woman to be, but years of digging at archaeological
sites throughout the Southwest had dried her milk-
white Black Irish skin. Rhea was always harping at her
to wear a hat lest she dry up like an old prune, but
Lexa, with a sublime disregard for such vanity, had
said simply it was too much trouble. And that was
something else Nigel loved about her—she knew that
there were many things more important in life than
one's physical appearance.

When Lexa turned to face him, Nigel felt a surge of
satisfaction. At least their telepathy was still in oper-
ation. She sipped at the wine and made a face.

"Bad?"

"Not good." She eyed the pale liquid. "In fact it tastes rather like horse piss."

"I thought that epithet was reserved for American beer."

"I'm expanding the definition."

He laughed, a little longer and a little louder than the moment warranted.

"I think Merlik sounds very good," Lexa said.

"Yes, it's a deceptively difficult part. Of course, we've still got to endure the ultimate absurdity as she and Tamino become Freemasons."

"You sound a trifle jaundiced," she observed wryly.

"Do I? I don't mean to. Frankly, I'm just delighted that Monsieur Crosby has seen fit to treat us to some real music instead of that cat-in-a-packing-factory tripe that passes for music in so many modern operas."

Nigel was talking to her profile again. Lexa had returned to her contemplation of the arroyo.

"End of August," she sighed. "Only two more months of digs left. Then boredom."

"Thank you," he heard himself say, and immediately wished the words back.

She turned the full force of her amazing blue eyes on him, but remained silent. She was more mature than he was, Nigel decided. Or maybe it was mere avoidance. Perhaps they'd be better off if they could just get down and really fight. These meaningless little exchanges—marriage babble, he'd dubbed them—were killing him. Through eleven years of marriage they had shared everything. Communicating totally, not only with their bodies but also in a constant stream of words. But for the last year . . .

God damn you, Santa Fe, God damn you, Benny Aragon, and God damn Rhea!

An awesome fork of lightning cut the sky, leaving behind a lingering scent of ozone and raised neck hairs. Seconds later, the thunder came, and several people gasped as the sound crashed overhead. As the

lights flickered, then came back up, there stood Rhea.
It was like the arrival of Maleficent, or the Queen of
the Night. Pure theater, and trust Rhea to take full
advantage of it, Nigel thought sourly.

After that kind of introduction there should stand
revealed a tall, willowy beauty with midnight hair,
but the woman who joined them was a tiny kitten-
faced blond. There was a strong resemblance between Nigel and his half-sister. Both were small, and
they shared the same tipped-up eyes that gave them
the look of some woodland creature. The effect of
those eyes in Nigel's narrow face was rather fey, but
on Rhea it was pure mischief. Pointed chin, high
cheekbones, a Cupid's-bow mouth, and high, arched
brows that gave her a look of constant surprise. Dark
honey-gold hair lay in waves across her shoulders,
and a fringe of bangs just brushed the top of her
brows. She used those bangs, and a set of impossibly
long eyelashes, the way an eighteenth-century courtesan used her fan. To tease, to tempt, to allure. Her
effect on men was electric, and tonight was no exception. They turned, momentarily abandoning wives
and lovers, as Rhea glided to Nigel and gave him a
peck on the lips.

She slid into her sister-in-law's embrace, and the
women touched cheeks. Lexa was taller than either
Nigel or Rhea, and she seemed rustic and a little
gawky next to the delicate siblings. Whereas Rhea
wore a shimmering evening gown of amber silk, Lexa
was dressed in what she and Nigel had dubbed
"Santa Fe chic"—tight designer blue jeans, boots,
lots of turquoise jewelry, and a handwoven wool se-
rape.

"Darlings. Enjoying the opera?"

"Yes," Lexa answered in that cool, unruffled way
she had. Her deep, husky, and slightly hesitant voice
set an interesting counterpoint to Rhea's light bell-like
tones. "Nigel is relieved to have some real music to
listen to."

"Poor darling, so old-fashioned."

"Yep."

A vise seemed to tighten about his chest, driving the breath into his throat and sending pain flashing from his breast into his head. It happened every time his wife and his sister occupied the same space. And that was an event that took place with distressing regularity, because for the past three years they had all been living in Santa Fe. Just one big, happy family.

Rhea caught her lower lip between her teeth and peeped up at her brother from beneath those long lashes. "Nigel, we must speak."

"Isn't that what we've been doing?"

"Seriously," she insisted.

"Oh, Rhea, please. Not now, not here."

"When, then? You promised me you were going to take some action when this co-op was proposed. You didn't, you haven't, and now they're moving in display cases. You have got to organize the Plaza merchants before it's too late."

"It's already too late," Lexa spoke up. "The fox is well and truly among the hens. Indians selling their own works with no Anglo middleman. Shocking."

Rhea shot her a poisonous glance. "This is going to hurt Nigel, too, you know."

"Not that much," Lexa said. "We have discussed it."

"Whose side are you on? Your husband's, or that awful little toad's?"

"Benny's hardly a toad. He's a very bright, very ambitious young man who, unlike most educated Indians, wants to use his education to benefit the Pueblo."

"Things have worked just fine in Santa Fe for years."

"Worked for whom?" Lexa asked. "The Anglo merchants? I'll agree with that. They pay the Indian artisans a pittance, and then mark up the wares to a fantastic level. Why shouldn't the Indians sell direct, and keep that markup?"

"Lexa, they don't have any head for business, you

SANTA FE

know that, the co-op is going to be run into the ground in no time—''

Lexa cut off her sister-in-law's unconsciously racist remark. "So why the worry if they're going to go belly-up next week?"

"Because it won't happen that fast, and in the meantime Nigel is going to be hurt. And lest you forget, it's *my* money that opened that store, and I like a return on my money."

"Oh, we could never forget that, Rhea . . . dear," Lexa said grimly.

Nigel dug into his hip pocket, pulled out his flask, and poured a liberal dollop of cognac into his empty glass. It burned on the way down, and seemed to ease the steel bands somewhat.

"Nigel, I want to see some action from you. Some stand," said Rhea.

Lexa's eyes, accusing and pleading, were on him. Two nights before, *she* had asked him for action, a stand. Unfortunately, what she wanted was diametrically opposed to what Rhea wanted. He writhed like a bug on a pin, took another swallow of the brandy, and remained silent.

Rhea didn't. "Benny Aragon is a dangerous little troublemaker whose only interest is in agitating his people and making enough noise to launch his political career. Then he'll abandon them, and there they'll be, stuck with a shop they can't run and having earned the ire of the legitimate shopowners."

"How do you know this?" Lexa demanded. "You've never even talked to him."

"I've lived in Santa Fe long enough to know the type."

"Rhea, you don't know the first thing about this city. You live up at Rancho de Palabra in splendid, wealthy, Anglo isolation, and prattle away about what the Spanish and the Indians *really* want. Aside from your maid and your gardener, do you know any Hispanics? And the only Indians you talk to are the artisans who bring their work to Nigel to sell. Oh, yes, and you know John Cheykaychi because you commis-

sioned him to make that fetish necklace for you.''
Lexa's hand described a disgusted arc in the air between them.

''It's people like you who are out to destroy the Indian culture,'' Rhea accused.

''No. We're not talking about culture, we're talking
about power,'' Lexa said. Nigel refilled the plastic cup
and downed the liquor in one long swallow. ''And I
don't happen to think poverty, and alcoholism, and the
highest suicide rate among any ethnic group in the
state are a very good cultural heritage,'' she continued.

''It's because of the inroads of white values that
they're in that predicament,'' Rhea shot back.

''Initially, maybe, but you can't turn back time, and
a return to 'traditional ways' is going to accomplish
nothing! And personally, I think it's pretty racist to
wish that on anyone. I don't want to have to scratch a
living out of the ground, you don't want to hoe beans
ten hours a day and pray for rain the other fourteen,
and people get pretty damn hungry when it doesn't
come and the beans don't grow. Education and economic growth are the only solutions.''

Nigel's flask was almost empty, and the faces of
the crowd seemed to be ballooning and receding
about him. He had lost the thread of the women's
argument. It was just sound, muffled by several layers of alcohol. The warning bell chimed, silencing
the two combatants and leaving them eyeing each
other like angry prizefighters too bellicose to return
to their corners.

For one wild moment Nigel contemplated the chaos
he could produce if he simply voiced what really lay
between them. It held them all in a shadowy web of
lies and fear and guilt and lust. He and Rhea knew,
but Lexa was blind, fumbling against the hate that
flowed off her half-sister-in-law and the cowardice she
sensed in her husband.

To hell with Benny Aragon, and Indians, and Hispanics, and the clash of cultures, and power and politics, he thought. What's at work here is pure lust,

and the hate that forms the other side of that nasty coin.

My half-sister is still in love with me, Lexa, and that's why she hates you. Because you have me, and she can't.

But of course he would never say that. Shame had its uses.

2

"Hey, Silvestre! Over here. You know, you greasers are never gonna amount to a damn until you develop a sense of time."

Half the patrons and a number of waiters in the Compound stiffened with outrage as the foghorn cut through the polite murmur of conversation, the clink of silver on china, and the ring of ice in crystal goblets.

Sil forced a smile to his lips. He reminded himself that Pierce really didn't mean anything by the use of the offensive label. He wished he could wipe the smirk off Benny Aragon's moon face, then decided that it was only a matter of time until Pierce referred to the Pueblo man as a "blanket-assed Indian" or a "lazy redskin." And then the shoe would be on the other foot, and the smirk on the other face.

Franklin Pierce was a big man. Six and a half feet tall, he was built like an ambulatory beer keg, with a great barrel chest and a belly of truly monumental proportions that hung down over his belt. As he hitched up his pants, Sil saw he was wearing a six-by-four-inch hammered-silver belt buckle, and he wondered how the man could stand to have the scalloped edge digging into his gut. Just tough, he guessed. The older man's long, pear-shaped head was adorned by a narrow fringe of hair just above his ears, and both face and pate were bright red. He grinned, displaying teeth proportionate to the rest of him, and Sil decided he was an unlovely sight. On the other hand, there was something very charismatic about the man despite his

ugliness. Maybe it was the patina of money. God knew
Pierce had a lot of it.

"Franklin." His hand disappeared into Pierce's
hamlike grasp. "You are a heathen, also a redneck and
a shit-kicker." A bellow of laughter carried the scent
of bourbon. "Haven't you learned that in these en-
lightened times we do not fling about racial slurs? You
will have us thrown out of the restaurant."

"Not a chance. I spend too goddamn much money
in here. Though Christ knows it's overpriced," he hol-
lered at the maître d', who gave him a sick smile.
"You know Benny Aragon?" Pierce threw an offhand
wave toward the silent Indian.

"Only by reputation."

"Glad to know I'm making an impression on the
hidalgo class." They shook.

"We notice, even though you're pulling the tail of
the Anglos. Not many Hispanic shopkeepers around
the Plaza."

"Hey, forget that pissant little shop," Pierce said.
Benny's face darkened briefly. He had worked too hard
for the co-op to now have it summarily dismissed. "I
got Benny hooked in on my center, and now we're
gonna see something."

Silvestre shot a startled glance at the young Indian.

"Yes, Franklin speaks a language I understand—
money," Benny explained. Then he and Pierce exchanged smiles, and Sil discovered there was an
uncanny resemblance between the two men.

Benny was a squatter version of the big Anglo. Same
barrel chest, but only a kettle belly pooching out the
vest of his suit. A round head that seemed to spring
directly from broad, powerful shoulders, without benefit of a neck. He presented an odd juxtaposition of
traditional Pueblo and modern western businessman,
with his long black hair wrapped *chongo*-style at the
nape of his neck, several large turquoise rings on each
hand, and an intricate squash-blossom necklace hanging down over tie and vest.

It was always tough to guess with Indians, but Sil
put him at no more than twenty-seven or eight, which

was unusual. Pueblo culture put a premium on age, so for Benny to attain this much notoriety this quickly meant he was a very special individual. Silvestre tried to remember something of the *New Mexico* magazine article that had profiled the young Pueblo, but he drew a blank. Still, if he was going to be working with Aragon, it would do no harm to show some interest in him.

He gave him a smile. "Unlike my father and brother, I don't pay much attention to business," Sil said. "So aside from hearing about the rumpus you're causing with the Plaza merchants, I really don't know much about you." He made an encouraging gesture.

"Not too much to tell," Benny explained. Pierce let out a sarcastic snort. "Went to school at UNM for three years, won a scholarship to Wharton. Got my MBA. Came home and set to work."

Pierce cracked Aragon on the knee, his small brown eyes bright with pride. "He's a hell of a kid, Silvestre. If I'd had a son—" The older man broke off suddenly, pulled out a handkerchief, and gave his nose a defiant blow.

Sil and Benny exchanged glances, then Sil busied himself by attempting to flag down one of the supercilious Compound waiters. Benny watched for several moments while Silvestre ineffectually waved and stared. Then the young Indian gave a single sharp snap of the fingers. A waiter came to a quivering halt, and Benny reeled him in with a single glance. Sil shot him an admiring and envious glance, and placed his order for a margarita.

"Damn sissy drink," Pierce declared, giving his nose one final vigorous wipe. "Another bourbon, boy. Benny?"

"Soda water with a twist."

"Rot your insides. Let's get some grub ordered, so we can get down to business."

"Grub" for Pierce meant shaved slices of prosciutto, *coquilles St. Jacques,* and an artichoke with drawn-butter sauce.

Silvestre, placing his order for a simple rack of

lamb, eyed Pierce quizzically. "Franklin, you disappoint me. Is this a meal for a real man? Where's the thirty-six-ounce steak running with blood?"

"Hey, I'm a complex personality."

"That you are," murmured Benny, but affectionately.

"Okay, let's get down to it." Pierce snapped open a battered old stand-up briefcase and pulled out a sheaf of topographical maps. "But first . . ." He pinned Sil with a glance. "Five months ago you told me to get fucked when I talked to you about this project. What changed your mind?"

A shrug, carefully nonchalant. "Five months ago I thought I might ride again—"

"And you were scared to upset the United States Equestrian Team," Pierce interrupted in a mocking singsong voice.

"Yes. You're goddamn right I was!"

"So what's changed?"

"I've begun to realize that my injuries might in fact keep me out of international competition. But I can't spend the rest of my life living off my parents. I've got to find something else to do, and since horses are all I know . . ." He spread his hands.

"Fair enough. Five months ago I told you the biggest barrier to my center was land. Well, my man, Benny here has just solved that."

The Indian pulled a mechanical pencil from a breast pocket, and there was a frenzied rattle of paper as he shuffled through the maps. "It's not precisely the location Franklin had in mind, but the Pueblo has two thousand acres here." The pencil circled a section. "It's reasonably flat, level land because in the past it was farmed."

"So there's water," Sil said.

"Yes, a small stream, and a fairly shallow water table. It's not used for agriculture anymore, because our economy's been turning more toward wage jobs, minimum though they may be." He gave a thin smile at the bitter joke. "I've talked with the governor—"

"Who just happens to be Benny's uncle," Franklin put in.

"Convenient." Silvestre acknowledged.

Benny ignored both of them. "—and Ernesto thinks the council would agree to a ninety-nine-year lease with an option for another ninety-nine. And in addition to annual rents and royalties—"

"Sweet Mary and Jesus, Benny, you drive a hard bargain."

Again Benny ignored Pierce's interruption. "—Franklin has agreed that most of the workers will be drawn from the San Jose population."

"So everybody wins," Pierce concluded, pleased.

Silvestre had lost track of their words. Picking up two of the maps, he glanced from one to the other.

"So what do you think?" Benny asked.

"Pretty slick, huh?" Pierce looked pleased with himself.

Slowly Sil lowered the maps. "I think it will be a miracle if you ever get this thing built," he said.

"What the fuck?" Pierce looked less pleased.

"Look—" Sil began.

"At what?" growled Pierce.

"Right here." They both followed the line of his slender brown forefinger. "You know what that is?"

"Can't say as I . . . Oh, shit."

"What? What?" Benny demanded.

"Rancho de Palabra," Sil told him.

The Indian fell back in his chair and took a large swallow of soda water. But he recovered quickly. Giving a sharp shake of his big head, he hunched forward in the chair and slammed the glass onto the table. "So there are a bunch of rich honkys next door. So what? Rich honkys have horses."

"Not in Rancho de Palabra they don't," Sil said quietly. "They're excluded by restrictive covenant. They draw flies, remember."

For a moment Benny frowned, then gave a quick shrug. "So let them scream. It's all they can do. We're a protected people with the feds on our side. Nobody can mess with Indian land-leasing except the Secretary of the Interior, and he's not going to care that a bunch of wealthy white pricks don't like horseshit.''

Silvestre's hand tightened about the stem of his margarita glass. Slowly he raised it, licked salt from the rim and took a long swallow. He tried to quiet the anger that had flared at the Indian's words. The C. de-Baca family had been one of the founding families of New Mexico, and until the advent of the Anglos they had enjoyed both wealth and prestige. Then they had been drowned in a sea of white Protestant Americans, and though they maintained the wealth, they had lost any shred of prestige.

For two centuries, the masses of Hispanos and Pueblos had shared virtually identical life-styles; tilling the same fields, planting the same crops, building houses out of the same desert clay. Then the Indians had come in for special and preferential treatment, leaving their poorer Hispanic neighbors fighting for a subsistence living. And to add insult to injury, the Pueblos had absorbed the negative Anglo-American attitudes toward Hispanics.

What surprised Sil almost more than his anger was how, despite his years away from the insular Hispanic culture of Santa Fe, he was still carrying the seeds of resentment.

Franklin leaned over and cracked Benny on the knee.

''That's the attitude,'' he said. ''Hey, I got as many millions as any of those faggot playwrights and sleaze-ball actors.''

''Yes, Franklin, but there's only one of you, and several hundred of them,'' Sil replied. ''If they band together on this—and they will—they might find a way to block you.''

Pierce's face suffused with blood. ''I don't need any goddamn nay-sayers on my team,'' he bellowed. ''Now, you either get with the program, or you can just butt out of here!''

Silvestre hated to be yelled at. Some of his earliest memories were of his father screaming at him in Spanish, and the sick, loose feeling that filled his bowels.

He had learned early on not to cry. That brought only a blow and more yelling. The optimum response was to strike back with equal volume and equal anger, the way Jorge had, but he had never been able to manage it.

So now he clasped his hands tightly between his thighs and bent his head under the assault, waiting for Franklin to wind down. Then he spoke quietly.

"I didn't think you'd welcome a yes-man on your team either, Franklin." His voice sounded small even to his own ears.

Surprisingly, Benny came to his defense. "Silvestre's right, Franklin. It's better to be prepared for trouble than surprised when it jumps up and hits you in the face. He's not advocating that we give up, he's just advising us to do our homework, lay the groundwork, make sure we've got all our ducks in a row."

"I'm sorry, son. Didn't mean to holler at you." Franklin wiped a hand across the high dome of his forehead. "Got a mean temper and a real short fuse. Also, this project means so goddamn much to me." He looked Sil in the eyes, and the younger man read the pain that lay shadowed there. "You know why too."

"Yes, sir, I know," Sil agreed.

"Now, you figurin' to invest?"

"I don't know. I'll have to talk with my father and brother. I'm actually more interested in having a position after the center is built. I need something to do."

"Well, I've already hired somebody as trainer."

"That's fine," Sil rushed in. "I doubt I'd be much good riding, but I do know how to run a barn. It's the one place where business and money don't give me a headache. And several people have said I'm one of the best course designers in the business. We might be able to expand the center, and have it also provide jump-course design for shows in neighboring states."

"And then when I'm ready to host a world-cup show at *my* center, I'll have a world-class designer to set the course." Franklin grinned and winked at the two younger men. "Always dreamin', always lookin' to the future. You gotta think big if you're ever gonna amount to a damn." He gave an expansive sigh and rolled an eye about the crowded restaurant. "That's how I've lived my life."

"And you're an inspiration to us all," murmured Benny in a sweet, tiny voice. He clasped his hands primly on the table in front of him, and cast his eyes toward heaven.

"And you're one smart-alecky redskin. We should have broken you people up and scattered you through society."

"Ah, but then you would have just hastened the red man's revenge." Benny glanced to Sil. "You've heard of the red man's revenge?"

"No."

Another sly glance back to Pierce. "We marry your women until sooner or later every white man in the world has a drop of Indian blood."

The big Anglo gave a shout of laughter again, earning frowns from the more decorous diners at the Compound. He snatched up his tumbler of bourbon.

"Here's to us! By God, we'll kick anybody's butt who gets in our way!"

Rhea stood in her copper-and-tile kitchen, phone tucked beneath her chin. Behind her, Maria slipped silently about the gleaming room, preparing *biscochitos* for the Tuesday bridge club. The sharp scent of ground anise filled the air as the muted sound of rock-and-roll spilled out of a portable radio set in a corner.

Absently Rhea flipped through her appointment book, noting upcoming events. *Opera Guild meeting, Monday 7:00 p.m.* She would have Maria prepare several dozen of those melt-in-your-mouth cheese sticks. Suddenly Averell Prescott's fluting, lisping tones penetrated.

"I'm sorry, Averell, what was that again?"

"Wellll, I wouldn't think I'd have to repeat myself with something as upsetting as this!"

She glanced through the broad picture window. All

she could see of Prescott's house was the tip of the chimney and a small thin stream of blue-gray smoke standing ruler straight in the sultry air. She wondered how he could stand a fire in this mid-September heat.

"I was out at San Jose buying a couple of pots from Philomina, a nice big melon pot for me in that scrumptious orangy-red color, and a couple of miniature seed pots for Stan and Roger. They may think I'm tight, but frankly I'm not about to spend three hundred dollars on them. And those miniatures don't come for cheap anymore. Seventy dollars—"

"Yes, yes, Averell, but what did she tell you?"

"She said there's been a big meeting to propose a lease of Pueblo property to Franklin Pierce for that equestrian center. Now, as you know, darling, we blocked him not five months ago when he wanted to plop that eyesore out on the west side."

"Yes, Averell, I do know. I was involved in the commission meetings."

A brittle laugh. "Oh, yes, so you were," he said. "You just have your finger in so many pies, Rhea I can scarcely keep track. But the point is, he's trying it again. *And right next door!*"

"Next door? What do you mean?"

"Take a look north, that big beautiful mesa that runs right up to the foot of our fence. That's where he's planning to put it. Oh, this is such a nightmare. It's like the creature that wouldn't die, and every time it raises its ugly head, it's moved closer to *us!*"

"I'm glad you told me, Averell, and for keeping your ears open. I've been in Santa Fe thirteen years now, and it's just amazing to me how we have to keep fighting and fighting to maintain the city. You'd think people would realize that it's the lack of development that makes Santa Fe, Santa Fe. But greed is a constant. As long as these people get theirs, they don't care if they ruin it for everyone else."

She drew a careful line through her Wednesday exercise class. Morning was always a good time to gather the residents. "What about Wednesday?"

"What about it?"

"Could you meet then?"

"You haven't been listening," he said peevishly. "I'm off to Los Angeles tomorrow, that's why I bought those presents for Stan and Roger."

"So as always, other people raise the alarm, but it's up to *me* to do something."

"But we know you'll do it so well, Rhea dear."

Her strange tipped-up eyes narrowed with amusement.

"Everybody flatters me so I'll work myself ragged. I don't think I'm appreciated."

"Oh, you are, sweet. You are. By the way, how's that gorgeous half-brother of yours?"

"Fine. And why don't you go buy your presents in our shop instead of from Philomina?"

"Because it's more than flesh and blood can bear to be around him when he's so uninterested. Also, I can Jew down Philomina. Nigel's too much of a businessman."

"If only that were true."

"Well, toodles, love. Call you when I return from the land of the lotus eaters."

"And I'll bring you up-to-date on our progress. You've brought me this news, Averell, but that's not going to be enough. This time you're going to have to do some work."

"Oh, horrors."

Chuckling, she dropped the receiver back into its cradle and crossed the polished brick floor to snap off the radio. She turned to Maria, who was busily beating dough in a large porcelain bowl.

"Maria, I'll be in my office making some calls. I need you to prepare a brunch menu for Wednesday."

"For how many, *señora?*"

"Probably a hundred."

A quick head bob made the Spanish woman's long heavy braid slap against her back. "*Sí, señora,* I will do it."

The heels of her low pumps clicked on the brick floors as Rhea hurried from the back of the sprawling adobe house toward her study. She cut quickly through the sun-filled atrium, filled with droop-limbed cypress pines and a profusion of orchids about a tiny pool and waterfall. The intricate stained-glass window, set in a hand-carved oak door, threw red and amber fire across the floor and shattered on the needles of the trees.

She was proud of this house. It held her soul. She had worked with Diege Delgado, the Southwest's most famous adobe builder, on every aspect of its design. It combined the best of the modern school with Spanish traditional elements, and she wasn't going to let Franklin Pierce ruin her happiness. This was her refuge, her haven. Granted, she was alone now, but someday she would find the right partner. The perfect person to share her world.

Rhea entered the study with its thick Chinese flower carpet covering the bare bricks. Built-in bookcases, with their leather-bound volumes gleaming richly, added warmth to the room. A Queen Anne desk nestled into a bay window. It faced inward, but with a quick spin of the chair, she could gaze out across a panorama of tan and ocher desert to the towering purple Sangre de Cristo Mountains.

She picked up the receiver, pulled her address book closer to hand, then hesitated and dialed the store.

"Wenima, may I help you?"

"Nigel, where's Caroline?"

"Sick again."

"You really ought to fire that girl."

"She's not a bad kid."

"No, just lazy."

"Young. It does seem unfair that we have to work when we're young, and then maybe get to enjoy ourselves when we're too old to enjoy ourselves."

"Are you busy?"

"Couple of lookers. What's up?"

"Oh, Nigel, I'm so upset." Agitation put a quiver in the soft voice.

"What's wrong?"

"Franklin Pierce is planning to put that equestrian center right next to Rancho de Palabra, so now I have to start fighting and organizing all over again. And I get so tired. Everyone is always *behind me all the way,* but I'm the one who has to do all the work.''

''Whoa. I'm lost. What equestrian center?''

''Nigel, don't you pay any attention to what goes on in this town?''

''No,'' he admitted, but there was a hint of a chuckle in his voice. ''It's all so farcical.''

''You've got to start taking a greater interest. But you procrastinate . . . like this situation with the Indian Artists Cooperative—''

''Rhea, are you going to pick at me again about that, or am I going to comfort you?''

His tone made her angry, but she bit back the sharp words and cooed instead, ''What you could do is help me.''

''Okay. If I can, I will, but since I don't live out in millionaire row . . .''

''I just meant to be there for me. When I'm tired, and worn out from the fighting.''

She could sense his frigid withdrawal even over the phone. But he didn't pull back very far. He knew too well the threat she held over him if he truly abandoned her.

''Have dinner with me Thursday night?'' she coaxed.

''That's the night Lexa teaches,'' Nigel said.

Rhea was silent. Finally he sighed and agreed.

''Good, I'll have Maria make something special, or maybe I'll do it myself.'' She gave her musical laugh. ''It'll do you good to have a decent meal. After being married for ten years to a woman who prides herself on her inability to cook, you need some fattening up.''

''Cooks you can hire. Life companions are tough to find.''

His words were a cold lash across her skin.

Tears gathered on her lashes and spilled slowly over and down her cheeks. ''Oh, Nigel, don't be mean to me. If Burton hadn't died . . . I think I keep marrying in the hope of replacing him.''

''What can I bring Thursday?'' he said brightly in an effort to change the subject.

"Just your darling self." The crisis averted, she wiped away the tears and straightened in her chair.

"And don't worry, Rhea, I'm sure you'll once again bring confusion to your enemies."

"Oh, Nigel." A quick giggle. "You make me sound so formidable."

"You are."

The man stood on the side of the rutted dirt road. At the headlights of Nigel's car washed across the broad figure, he noted the dollar bill held out to pay for the ride. It was one in the morning. What the hell was this man doing on the side of the road in the middle of the Navajo reservation at one in the morning?

Nigel put the New Yorker onto the shoulder. He heard cactus and sage crunch beneath the tires, and watched in the rearview mirror as the Navajo ran to the car. He rather welcomed this proof of another human presence in the vast emptiness of western New Mexico. It had been a relief to flee the suffocating confines of Santa Fe, and Rhea's almost daily calls, but too much aloneness was conducive to too much thought. Thoughts of escape, and the impossibility of ever achieving it. And Thursday. Thursday was coming far too soon.

"*Ha'at'iish baa nanina?*" Nigel said in greeting as the man climbed in.

"Been workin'. Goin' home now."

"Nigel Vallis."

"Sammy Begay."

"You're out late."

"Yeah."

Nigel suddenly wished he had the P-7 a little closer to hand. Hitchhikers on the res were usually harmless, but all it took was one exception.

They drove in silence for several miles. Moonlight washed across the desert, throwing the shadows of the towering rock formations into sharp relief.

Begay glanced back several times. Then he noticed the pile of handwoven rugs in the backseat. "Them are the people's rugs."

"Yes. I have a shop in Santa, and I come out here a couple of times a year to buy."

"You know the people's talk."

"Only a little. It's a very difficult language for whites to learn."

That admission seemed to please Begay. He covered his mouth as he smiled. A few moments later he had lapsed back into a frowning reverie. Again he glanced out the back window.

"Is something wrong? Are you in trouble?"

"Got a skinwalker after me."

"Oh."

Skinwalkers. Navajo witches. People capable of taking the form of animals—usually wolves or coyotes—in order to wreak vengeance, or to gain wealth, or simply to injure wantonly. Another classic Witchery Way technique was the preparation of poison made from the flesh of corpses. It was not surprising that the legends would present this as the method for gaining power, given the Navajo Indians' horror of the dead. Nigel also recalled that witches were closely associated with incest.

That struck him as grimly humorous under the present circumstance.

Rhea.

Lexa.

Begay was nodding off at his side. Nigel glanced into the rearview mirror and started at the sight of a long gray form loping behind the car. The vast clouds of dust thrown up by the wheels seemed to inconvenience the animal not at all. Nigel pressed down on the gas, nudging the car up to forty. The creature kept pace.

Fifty.

They struck a pothole. The seat belt snapped tight across Nigel's belly, and Begay's head bounced off the roof of the car. Instantly awake, he gripped the back of the seat and stared back through the dust.

"Skinwalker," he said with an almost wry pleasure.

They were at sixty, careening through the night, the car shaking and vibrating as the washboard road beat

at its tires and frame. They skidded into a curve. The
coyote was still keeping up.

Nuts. I must be nuts. We're going to be killed.

And Nigel remembered something else about Skinwalkers. They liked to force a person into harming
himself. A wreck in the vast waste between Tohatchi
and Newcomb would certainly qualify as harm. Lifting his foot from the gas, Nigel allowed the car to slow
down.

He leaned across Begay, and opening the glove box,
pulled out his pistol. The Indian's black eyes reflected
the moonlight like twin dark mirrors. Nigel glanced
out the window and saw a shaggy gray hand, almost
more paw than anything human, close about the door
handle. He jabbed for the electric window button, realized it would take too long, and slammed the butt of
the pistol against the glass, shattering it with a loud
report. Shifting the butt back into his hand, he laid
the barrel of the P-7 against the disembodied paw. It
melted away. Nigel didn't lean out the window to see
what lay behind the car. He didn't want to know.

The stink of his own sweat was strong in his nostrils.

Begay was staring at him impassively. "My hogan
not too far now. I can walk from here."

"That . . . thing?"

"Him not come back. You scared him good." Nigel
stopped the car. Begay climbed out, paused, and
leaned back in. "I do a sing for you. A Blessing Way."

"Thank you. I could use it."

Begay nodded wisely and vanished into the desert.

3

"Mi pobrecito, so you have come home at last." Her soft voice still sang with a strong Spanish accent, despite the two years she had spent at an exclusive Catholic women's college on the West Coast.

Sil hung his soft brown fedora on the coat rack in the entrance hall and embraced his mother.

"I'm sorry. Am I horribly late? I was with Franklin and Benny, helping them prepare the papers for the Secretary. Not that I was much help. All these buzz words that have to be hit. It's a wonder anything ever gets done in this country with—"

She laid a slim brown hand across his mouth. *"Querido,* you chatter too much. Which is not a good thing when your father is tired, hungry, and angry."

The years had dealt kindly with Doña Mercedes de Vargas de C. deBaca. The birth of three children had not affected her slender girlish figure, or the ingenuous doe-eyed beauty that had made her the toast of Santa Fe society. But she no longer took part in that society. Having been raised strictly and traditionally, she had strong notions about the proper role for a Spanish wife and mother, and after her marriage she had devoted herself to church and family. She had bequeathed her delicate beauty to her two younger children, and though she tried to deny it even to herself, Silvestre was her favorite.

Her son tucked her arm formally beneath his, and asked, "What's got him upset?"

Her free hand fluttered in the air. "I don't know, something with bonds, or stocks, or margins, or something. I don't concern myself. But it is too bad, for I invited Father Conroy to dinner in the hope your father would be feeling expansive—'' She cut herself off when she saw her son's expression, and gave his arm a shake. "Now, you must be nice, Silvestre. He is a priest."

"Mama, he reminds me of a sleek, overfed cat, and frankly, he reeks of piety. Give me Martin anytime."

She made a moue of disgust. "I know he is your cousin, but he is too radical for my taste. And Father Conroy is assistant to Archbishop Sanchez."

"Whoopie."

Mercedes paused in the doorway, and added in an undertone, "But you have your wish about Father Martin. Paloma invited him."

Good, and not so good, thought Sil. He had a feeling that his sister's interest in her priestly cousin partook less of piety than of lust. With a sigh he stepped into the great circular living room of Hacienda C. deBaca.

Everyone was assembled there finishing off cocktails. Sil noticed that Father Conroy's piety didn't extend to the fruit of the vine. His plump face gleamed a bit under the track lighting as he busily swilled down the sherry. Nearby sat Father Martin de Vargas, tall and lanky. His face wore signs of the years he had spent in Central America: lined, too thin, passion burning in the brown eyes, but behind the fire, sadness. At his feet sat Paloma C. deBaca. She gazed up into his handsome face with the look of a pilgrim witnessing an epiphany.

Sil's brother, Jorge, was propped against the massive oak mantelpiece, a cocktail glass all but swallowed up by his big fist. At the opposite end was propped the senior C. deBaca. They were like two massive, silent stone figures, twin Titans, each an Ozymandias. The resemblance between Benito C. deBaca and his elder son was startling. Big-boned, they both had wide, square faces and silver-touched black hair springing thickly back from high foreheads. The elder C. deBaca was running to fat, but Jorge's early-

morning regimen had so far kept his powerful body
rock-hard.

Jorge's wife, Consuela, heavily pregnant with her
fourth child, sat meekly beside the real power in the
deBaca family—Alejandra Cortez de C. deBaca.

At eighty-two, Grandmother Alejandra sat imperi-
ously in a high-backed chair. Her long hair was a startling river of black-and-silver stripes. Tonight it was
confined in a proper chignon, perhaps in deference to
their priestly visitors. She had also changed from her
usual slacks and ruffled shirt into the standard uniform
of the elderly Spanish woman, a black dress. But this
dress was Paris-designed, fashioned from the finest
silk, and embellished with jet beads that rang coldly
each time she shifted.

The gnarled hand which was thrust out to her grandson blazed with a single giant marquise-cut diamond.
She had promised it to the bride of the first of the
grandsons to marry, but after evaluating Consuela she
had termed her a wretched little nothing, and refused
to bestow the ring. Sil wondered, if and when he ever
found a lady, what his grandmother would say about
her. He had no illusions that she might actually like
this mythical bride.

Her parchmentlike skin was cool and dry as Alejandra touched him in greeting, first against his palm and
then his cheek. She had a horror of randomly bestowed kisses.

"So, you finally decided to join us," she said in
Spanish.

"I lost track of the time," he explained, in what he
hoped was a humble tone.

"Hmm, this business with the equestrian center?"
grunted his father.

"Yes, sir."

"Well, as long as it was something legitimate. God
knows you've been dragging around the house long
enough."

"Silvestre was badly hurt," cried Mercedes.

"Well, be that as it may, it's time for him to be
doing something," Benito grunted.

A flare of pain shot through Sil's jaw, and he relaxed his gritted teeth. "I agree, sir. That's why I'm working with Pierce."

"Hmm, well, if you want a drink, get one, but hurry with it. I'm damned hungry."

The cocaine he had snorted just after parting from Pierce and Aragon was still singing in his veins, and Sil wasn't such a fool as to risk mixing the drug with a highball. He gave his head a small shake.

Then he found his cousin's eyes upon him. Sil forced a smile, and gave Martin a slap on the shoulder. They exchanged handshakes. "Well, Padre, how's the man of God?"

Father Martin, still holding Sil's hand, replied lightly in English, "Suffering from the slings and darts of lesser men."

That pulled Father Conroy's attention out of the sherry glass. He stiffened. "I know you would like to be reassigned back to El Salvador, Father Martin, but the church is concerned for your health."

Father Martin's and Sil's eyes met, and then the priest mouthed a single word. *Bullshit.*

"Also, a priest can learn humility and obedience serving in a—if you will—somewhat duller parish."

"Father, forgive my plain speaking, but neither concern for my health nor concern for my soul is at the root of this. The church hierarchy is pissing in its pants over my political activism. But how is a priest to avoid becoming involved when goons are killing and starving his parishioners?"

"We are to minister to their souls."

"Oh, crap on that! How can they possibly think of God when they're—"

"Please," cried Mercedes.

Doña Alejandra's sharp barking laugh filled the room. "Don't be so precious, Mercedes. Martin is only returning to his historical antecedents. The fathers of the Inquisition often rode with armies. So instead of a sword, our Martin carries a Kalashnikov."

Sil stared quizzically at his amazing grandmother,

wondering where and why she had learned the name of the Soviet machine gun.

The priest's voice quivered with laughter. "No, you awful old beldam, that is *not* what I'm advocating. Though I do agree with you that modern priests are far too mealymouthed."

Jorge's glass hit the mantel with a dull clink. "All this philosophy. Can we eat?" he asked in his basso grunt.

Benito hurried to Alejandra's side and tenderly helped her from the chair. The meekness of this powerful man when in the presence of his mother did not disturb Alejandra; it was all her due. She also had no resentment for his solicitude. It showed he was still under her thumb.

The cherrywood dining table glowed beneath the light from a heavy wrought-iron chandelier. Silvestre hid a smile. Mother really had gone all-out to fete the archbishop's assistant. Though beautiful, the Nambe place settings were really not terribly practical for day-to-day use. They resembled finely polished silver, but were really a secret mixture of eight different metals, and the acids in certain foods could pit their mirrorlike surfaces.

Sil settled in next to Paloma and shook out his napkin. "How's school?" he asked. She was a second-year law student, and each day she commuted the sixty miles down to Albuquerque for classes.

"Fine." Her eyes remained locked on Father Martin, seated across the table.

"Hmm, so, tell me about the center," Benito called down the table as Rosita came trudging into the dining room with a tray of covered dishes. The sharp, pungent odor of roast chicken and lime juice set Sil's mouth to watering.

"Not a lot to tell. Basically the Pueblo decides to do it, they request permission from the Secretary of the Interior, who gives it—"

"You're sure about that?" asked Jorge, his mouth full of seasoned rice.

Sil looked startled. "Benny says they never say no."

"The government sure as fuck says no to us," Jorge grunted, surprising his family with this show of loquaciousness.

"Ah . . . well, *they* do get everything." Benito ladled half a chicken onto his plate and sniffed appreciatively at the spicy odor. "Health clinics, special schools, everything."

"They have their own problems," put in Father Martin, trying to inject some balance into the conversation.

"Brought on by themselves, though they try to blame us," said Benito.

"The history of our early treatment of the Indians doesn't bear very close scrutiny." Father Martin had never been intimidated by his uncle.

"We used to be better neighbors," interjected Alejandra. "When I was a girl I used to ride out with my father to check on the tenants. Everyone shared the same ditches, and worked together in the fields."

"Now they're special, and we're just dirty Mexicans," said Jorge.

"Not when you've got as much money as the C. deBacas," replied Father Martin with a grin. "Then you're just uppity Mexicans."

"If I hear about the 'charm' of Santa Fe or the 'mystique' of Taos one more time, I'll scream," flared Paloma. "All these pasty-faced Anglos running out to the Pueblos, spending vast amounts of money to take pictures of pagan rituals, and prating on about how meaningful and symbolic and majestic the Indian culture is. What's wrong with *our* culture?" She flung out her arms, nearly knocking Sil's fork from his hand.

"Well, you must admit that to your average Anglo there's a good deal more charm, and a great deal less threat, in a *tablita* dance than in the weekly low-rider parade in downtown Española." Silvestre grinned.

"Don't be flippant." She cast him a haughty sideways glance. "At base this is really a bias against our faith."

"Oh, Paloma, please. You're going to be a lawyer, not a nun." Sil sighed.

He noticed that his mother kept her eyes strictly on her plate, and he realized that while he had been traveling the world pursuing his career, life might not have been so easy for his sister. Her decision to become a lawyer probably did not sit well with their traditional mother. Mercedes held the rather outmoded view that a family owed one child to God. If she had been pushing Paloma to be that child . . . So maybe there was a reason his little sister sometimes acted like a schizophrenic.

"Paloma, I'm a priest, and even I find that a little too strong," Father Martin said softly. "To some extent I think you're right. There is a strong anti-Hispanic bias in this country. We're Catholic in a predominantly Protestant society, and as some Anglo politico pointed out, we can marry with white folks and have children who are indistinguishable from *real* white people. We're the largest-growing minority in the country, and that's scary."

"So are we damning the Indians or the Anglos?" asked Alejandra.

"Both, I guess," Sil answered.

"All this talk is bullshit," Benito said. "You can either deal with people, and make money with them—or off them—or you can't. Who cares if the *turistas* think the Indian culture is superior to ours? Frankly, I don't want to be selling pots on the Plaza. I'd rather do business, and you rarely see an Indian doing that."

"Except for Benny Aragon," put in Sil.

"So he's unique."

"But speaking of making money, Dad," Sil asked, "should I ask for a share in the center, or should I just take a salaried job?"

"I'd say that depends on you. Are you going to return to the Grand Prix circuit, or aren't you? If you aren't, I'd prefer not to have to support you for the rest of your life. So take an interest. If you are, then work on salary until your health returns."

"But which do you think is best?" Sil insisted.

"Ah, well, I'd have to take a look at the prospectus," Benito replied. "Personally, I think it sounds like a cheese-headed idea. There's not enough money in New Mexico to support this kind of enterprise. Unless Pierce is planning to support it entirely on his own?''

"I think he might be. This project has less to do with making money than with allowing Franklin to spit in the eye of the U.S. Equestrian Team.''

Silvestre suddenly remembered Father Conroy, his ears out like antennae, and cursed himself for being indiscreet.

"Take a salary,'' advised Jorge, mumbling around a mouthful of chicken.

"What's the Indian angle in all this?'' asked Benito.

"Jobs, income. Even if Franklin gets bored with the project after a few years, they'll still have their ninety-nine-year lease.''

"When is this project supposed to get under way?'' inquired Father Martin.

"Franklin plans to start breaking ground by the end of the month.''

"Mr. Pierce said they would start building the first port-a-stall barn this week. So by the time I get there it will be finished, and Fav will have a home.''

"And so will we.'' Terry wrapped his arms around Mona's waist and nuzzled the nape of her neck. Shivering, she pressed her body to his and devoured his mouth. He tasted wonderful, of coffee and the lingering flavor of cinnamon roll, and the overall taste that was Terry.

His hands cupped her small breasts, thumbs flicking across the nipples, and she moaned and pushed him away.

"No, no, no, no, no. I'm only half-packed. I still have to drive up to Vermont to collect horsey-fu, and I don't want to start this trip in the dark.''

"All right, crush my manhood.''

Mona eyed his crotch. "Your manhood looks like it's doing just fine.''

Terry pressed the back of his hand to his forehead. "Oh, where is the shy little dove I married?''

"Five years in the past.''

The loft reflected Terry's personality. Modern fur-
niture, piles of books, an easel propped against one
wall with a welter of canvases stacked about its legs.
A nude bronze of Mona which he had cast during his
sculpturing phase. Baby grand piano. A word proces-
sor humming on the desk. Only in one small corner
of the room was Mona's presence felt. Pictures hung
on the wall. Horses climbing, flying, leaping over
fences, Mona stretched out along their necks, small
face tight with concentration. On a shelf below rested
a blinding array of silver trophies.

Terry perched cross-legged on the bed and watched
as she crammed sweaters, rat-catcher shirts, breeches,
and blue jeans into the case. Shook his head.

"What a mess. Let me."

Reaching up, she massaged his neck. "I always start
out a trip impeccably packed. If only I had my neatnik
husband to travel with me."

"I'm sorry about the drive to Santa Fe, but I really
should be here for the editors/writers party."

"Agreed."

A large mirror hung over the bed's headboard, re-
flecting an image of the windows and the New York
skyline beyond. Mona studied their images—Terry six-
foot-three, with broad shoulders and narrow hips. Her
at five-foot-nothing. Only in coloring did they match.
They were both brown-haired, but Terry's hair held a
wealth of gold and red highlights. Hers was like dark
sable falling in a river to her shoulders. She wore it
brushed back, displaying her deep widow's peak and
high forehead. His eyes were a sparkling hazel, while
hers were a warm pansy brown. At twenty-five, Mona
still had smooth white skin, though a few wrinkles
were beginning to pucker around her eyes. She
frowned, which only intensified the straight heavy
brows. No amount of plucking could coax an arch from
those dark slashes. She had given up trying, and resigned herself to looking serious.

"I suppose your dad isn't going to miss this opportunity to trash me," Terry said suddenly.

"Terry, it doesn't matter what he thinks." She laid

a hand against his cheek. "Darling, not everyone is
going to love you."

He bit down on his full lower lip. "He's a lawyer.
He doesn't understand artists. He thinks I'm a bum for
living off you all these years."

"Terry, if I hadn't wanted to do it, I wouldn't have
done it. Your career, your happiness, are the most important things in the world for me."

"Oh, Moni, I love you. But you better not let dear
old dad hear you running on about happiness. God
forbid anybody should have some happiness in this
life."

She turned away. "Don't make fun of him, please.
I think he's a very bitter, unhappy man, and that makes
me feel guilty. Maybe there was something I could
have done to lighten his life."

"You dad loves to be miserable." He picked up a
nightgown, ran it between his hands, frowned sternly
down at her. "You call me *every time* you stop."

"Terry . . ."

"I worry."

"Don't." She pulled her nine-millimeter Beretta
from its holster, dropped the clip, noted it was fully
loaded, and slammed it home.

"And your coming across like Dirty Harry doesn't
reassure me. Those things are dangerous: you're just
as likely to have it taken away and used against you."

"I used to feel the same, good liberal upbringing
and all, but it makes me feel better to have it when
I'm in the middle of nowhere with a broken-down
truck. Most of the women on the circuit carry one—
at least the ones who do any solo driving."

"Just be careful."

"You're always rescuing me. Do you remember that
first time?"

"God, how could I forget?" Terry laughed. "Traffic backed up for twenty blocks while you tried to figure out how to wheel that eight-horse rig to the
Garden. You were in tears. I've never seen such a miserable puppy."

"And you just hopped up on the running board and

told me to scoot over, and took over. Why on earth I ever opened that door . . . You could have been a mad killer.''

"No, just a mad sex fiend." He caught her around the waist and tossed her onto the bed.

"Terry, I've got to go."

"Which would you rather do? Drive while there's still daylight, or screw while there's still daylight?''

"That's no choice." And arching against him, she let him pull off her jeans.

With its round tower and position high atop a hill, the house looked like a fortress against the night sky. And no knight ever approached a fortress with greater reluctance than did Nigel on Thursday night. But no monster waited to greet him. Only Rhea, dressed in a foaming creation of lace and silk. The dusty rose of the . . . caftan? . . . lounging robe? . . . peignoir? . . . set off her golden looks to perfection.

Nigel had fortified himself at the house with several snifters of brandy, so the world seemed to be ballooning about him in a strange pulsing motion. Perhaps it was the effects of the liquor coursing through his system that released the errant thought.

Fairy-tale princess, fairy-tale house, fairy-tale prince, but nightmare story. Grimm, very Grimm.

He giggled.

Rhea slipped his arm companionably beneath hers and led him into the house. "My, you're in a good humor." She smiled.

"Just feeling no pain," he corrected.

Her rather full lower lip protruded in a delectable pout. "Ni, I wish you wouldn't. You've been drinking so much recently, and it worries me.''

He waved her aside, and freed his arm from her soft grip. "Mid-life crisis.''

"I decided to dispense with formality," she said, leading him into the kitchen. "It seems so cold for the two of us to eat in solitary splendor in the dining room. I gave Maria the night off. I wanted to cook for you.''

He swallowed, and the saliva hit his stomach like a

ball bearing dropped into a deep and empty can.
"Fine. Lexa and I usually eat in the kitchen."

"I made all your favorites: veal Oscar, pilaf, raspberry soufflé."

"You shouldn't have gone to so much trouble."

"It's no trouble for my baby brother." She slid him
a roguish glance out of those uptilted eyes.

He helped her fill the plates, but when he started to
seat himself at the big hand-hewn table, she stopped
him with a glance and led him into the luxurious sit-
ting room off her bedroom.

The CD player was spilling the lushly romantic final
act of *Lucia di Lammermoor* across the room. The
small glass-topped table was set with a pair of Waterford crystal candlesticks and Rhea's best Wedgwood
china. An ice bucket held a bottle of champagne.

Nigel laughed, a rusty sound like a grinding of stone
on metal. "Such elegance."

"It's an occasion." Rhea looked faintly hurt. "I
scarcely see you anymore, and yet we live in the same
city."

"That's because you're always jetting off to the
Cannes Film Festival or the Edinburgh Festival, or to
Paris for a little shopping," he teased.

Nigel cut into the golden-brown veal cutlet. He
added a bite of asparagus, and a piece of crab, and
chewed experimentally.

"Delicious."

"I do cook well," Rhea replied in an injured tone,
as if implying there was little else she did well.

Nigel obligingly rose to the bait. "One of many
things you do well, sister mine."

The food *was* excellent, but it was landing like jagged lumps in his stomach. Desperately he grabbed for
the champagne and filled their glasses. He emptied his
in a few frenzied swallows, then refilled.

"Do you find it hot in here?"

She shook her head, the golden hair brushing at her
cheeks. "No, but if you like, I'll open a window."

"Sit still, I'll do it." He pushed open the French

doors that gave out onto a small private patio, and
sucked in great lungfuls of air.

"Nigel."

"Hmm?" He returned to the table.

"Are you all right?" One of Rhea's great gifts was
her ability to be completely in the moment. When she
turned her eyes full onto a person, he knew that all of
her concentration was upon him. It could be very flat-
tering. Or terrifying.

"Yes, yes, I'm fine."

He gulped down more champagne, and chewed doggedly through the large cutlet, the rice, the green beans
swimming in a delicate but very rich butter sauce.
Rhea set down a crystal bowl filled to the brim with
raspberry souffle and topped with gobs of whipped
cream. Then coffee, also topped with whipped cream,
and a liberal dollop of brandy.

It was more food than Nigel normally ate in two
days. Eleven years with Lexa—who viewed meals as
something that interfered with the interesting business
of life—and a naturally small appetite had combined
to make him a very abstemious eater. But to refuse
Rhea was to reflect upon her ability. Besides, as long
as he lingered at the table, they could continue to talk
idly of this and that. No personal little tête-à-têtes.

Finally it could be delayed no longer. With a sigh
that was almost a groan, Nigel leaned back and surreptitiously loosened his belt. His head was spinning
from the alcohol he had consumed.

"Come, sit here." Rhea patted at the love seat. Nigel settled onto the ottoman. "No, here!" Sharp, a
command.

Reluctantly he settled down next to her.

"Now, talk to me."

"What about? The shop? We're doing well. Had a
good summer. It'll be a little slow until Christmas."

"It may be slow at Christmas too."

"How so?"

"That co-op," said Rhea.

"I think you're making way too much of that co-op.
It's only one store."

"It's a trend."

"Maybe a healthy one."

"You're sounding like Lexa."

"Married couples frequently do."

"Nigel, I'm not blind. I can see that you and Lexa are having problems, and that it's hurting you, and that hurts me."

"How did we get to this? We were discussing Indian self-determination." His tone was light.

"Stop it! Just stop it! Nigel, I *care!*"

"I know you do, but it's really not your problem."

"Don't tell me to mind my own business in that cold, distant way." She sniffled, and he hurriedly pulled out his handkerchief. "Ni, I only want to see you happy. If you're having trouble, I want to help. That's what big sisters are for."

He carefully withdrew his hand from her frenzied clasp. "First, I don't like to burden you, and second, I have no respect for men who discuss their wives with outsiders."

"There, you've done it again. I am *not* an outsider."

He was being manipulated. He knew it, and resented it. Turning, he stared down into her tiny kitten's face. "Rhea, I'm not trying to hurt you. All I'm saying is that there are some things which are uniquely private to a married couple. You know, or you should; you've been married."

She looked away. "But never in love. Oh, there was Burton, but he died so soon, before I had a chance to see if what we had was real." She spun to face him, throwing open her arms. "I *want* to be loved, Ni. I need it so badly."

"I love you, Rhea."

She clutched at his shoulders. "Really? Truly?"

"Yes, yes."

She laid her head on his breast, rubbing her cheek against his shirt. "Oh, Ni, I'm so glad fate brought you to Santa Fe. It gives me a chance to make up for all those years. All those lost years when you were so alone."

"I had Lexa for most of them." He set her aside
and paced to the table, where he shook the empty
champagne bottle and dropped it with a resounding
crash back into the bucket. Then he whirled to face
her, using the table for support. "Look, I'd really
rather not talk about this. Okay?"

Rhea arched tensely toward him, and the position
forced up her breasts and etched the tendons in her
swan's throat. "What's wrong between you and
Lexa?" The tip of her tongue shot out and moistened
her upper lip. "What!"

"You're both putting demands on me, and unfortunately they're a little contradictory right now."

"You have an obligation . . . to me." Her eyes
darkened with memory.

Nigel shuddered, wondering what she had seen in
that brief introspective moment. He forcibly reburied
his own memory, which had fought its way to freedom.

"Lexa must learn that a wife's obligation is to her
husband," Rhea said.

"No."

"No, what?"

"That's not the kind of marriage we have. We're
partners, equals."

"Not true. She dominates you."

"And you'd like to!"

"*Nigel!* That's not true!" She rose and rustled toward him with outstretched arms. "I want to *help*. I
want *you* to understand that *I* understand."

He thrust his hands behind his back, retreated, and
glanced desperately at his watch. "I've got to go."
His bright social mask slid back into place. "Thank
you so much for dinner, sister mine."

She stood silent for several moments, chewing on
her lower lip, and finally spoke. "My pleasure. Come
again soon."

"Ah!" He snapped his fingers. "We never did talk
about the equestrian center."

"Then we'll just have to get together again and do
so." It was more an order than an invitation.

"Uh . . . right. Thanks again, Rhea. G'night."

Nigel fled from the house. As he staggered down the long redstone steps, he nearly fell from haste . . . and alcohol. Beating his fists on the steering wheel, he cursed them all, and himself most fiercely.

There had to be a way out.

Short of death.

4

Waves of heat bounced off the sidewalk and crept through the wide front windows of the Wenima Indian Arts Shop. From his vantage point behind the counter, Nigel could see a flock of dispirited pigeons pecking at the dust and weeds of the Plaza. Some equally dispirited tourists slumped on a metal bench and stared glassy-eyed at the Indians squatting beneath the portico of the Palace of the Governors. The sidewalk sellers were a historic sight in Santa Fe—stone-faced, impassive, usually wrapped in blankets, with their wares lying before them.

The Plaza merchants hated them. Their prices were always substantially lower than those in the elegant shops, they would bargain, and, of more interest to the tourists, they were *real* Indians. During the 1960's, when Santa Fe was a mecca for flower power, various communes had tried selling their wares on the sidewalk in front of the palace. And they had gotten sued by the Indians. It was still an ongoing problem.

Real big-time trouble, thought Nigel, fanning himself with a rolled-up magazine. *Ranks right up there with world hunger and nuclear disarmament. God, how I hate this town.* He tossed aside the magazine.

There was an illusion of coolness inside the store because of the dark wood-beamed ceiling, the Navajo rugs forming muted splashes of color on the whitewashed walls, and the soft lighting. But he continued to frown at the beauty around him.

Nigel felt worn down by this tail end of summer. There were still a few ninety-degree days lurking in

the wings, and because of the recently ended monsoon
season, the humidity was very high. He enjoyed fall
in New Mexico, and looked forward to crisp nights,
the smell of piñon burning in fireplaces, the aspens
forming gold fire on the mountainsides, and most important, a break between the summer tourists and the
winter skiers. It was a time of slow business at Wenima. A time to pull in a supply of good books and
relax.

The bell over the door tinkled wildly as Linda Car-
rio thrust it vigorously open. A large box was balanced
precariously on one broad hip, and her shapeless
blouse and skirt made her seem wider than she really
was. She looked tired, hot, dusty, and irritable, and
Nigel couldn't blame her. It was a long drive from
Hopi, across the Arizona border, to Santa Fe. Especially when you made it in an un-air-conditioned
pickup truck.

Nigel quit propping up the lighted glass display case
and walked into his office. He pulled out a couple of
frosty cans of Coke and sauntered back into the shop.
Crumpled newspaper littered the floor at Linda's feet,
and she was busily pulling pots out of the dilapidated
cardboard box.

They were beautiful smooth pots in shades of pale
tan and blush rose. Unique pots appliquéd with a single ear of corn. Works of art. And she carried them in
a trashed-out box with only a modicum of paper to
protect them. Nigel shuddered and touched one tiny
pale rose pot with a forefinger. It was cool to the touch,
yet it seemed to hold an inner warmth. He cupped it
in both hands and laid it against one cheek.

"You love the clay like an Indian," she said in her
deep husky voice. Like many Indians Linda spoke so
low that Nigel had to strain to hear her.

"No, I love what you put in the clay, Linda. It's like
holding a piece of your soul."

Her mouth split in a wide grin. "Good, then you
give me lots of money for these little bits of my soul."

A cold line seemed to trace down the back of his
neck, and he shivered, then cursed himself for being

an overly emotional idiot, reading significance into every statement.

They haggled for a bit, occasionally breaking off for gossipy asides about the upcoming gubernatorial race, Pueblo rivalries, the latest idiocy of the BIA. A final figure was agree upon, and Nigel wrote a check for some and pulled cash from the drawer to cover the rest. He had no problem with Linda cheating the IRS. It seemed only fair, considering how the Indians had been screwed by the BIA for so many years.

She was shuffling out when suddenly she was arrested by an arrangement of sgraffito pottery in one case. "Oh, Joe Mondragon is dead."

"What?"

"Yeah, him and his old lady, and four of the six kids."

"My God, what happened?"

"He'd been into Albuquerque with some pottery. Had a few drinks to celebrate, and headed home. Went head-on into a big truck on I-25."

"Oh, shit."

"Yeah, one dumb fucker."

The door slammed behind her, and Nigel regretfully recalled the lean-faced Indian with the wild sense of humor who had done such phenomenal work. Walking over, he carefully pulled out the three pieces of sgraffito and arranged them on a piece of black velvet. Then, resting his elbows on the counter, he hunkered down until his eyes were level with the fragile pieces.

Sgraffito was created by treating the clay with many layers of different slips. The mineral content caused them to fire in different colors; then the artist, using a tiny pin, scraped out the design. Joe Mondragon was acknowledged as one of the finest sgraffito artisans in the Southwest. Now he was dead. Leaving behind three bits of his soul.

One had a black background with an antelope design picked out in brilliant turquoise. The second was red and tan and black, but the third . . . It was unique. On a deep green background, spiraling about the tiny oval of clay, was the figure of a flute player in a strange bone white. The little figure seemed unearthly as he vigorously blew on his long flute. Nigel gathered it into his hand, and his fingers closed about the two-inch piece. This one he would take home, to honor the memory of its creator.

He had been so deep in his thoughts that he had missed the tremulous ring of the bell. Now a voice intruded.

"That's beautiful, how much is it?"

"Huh?" His head snapped up, and he looked into a narrow face framed by curling black hair. A strangely familiar face, but he was too disoriented to place it. "Oh, it's . . ." He checked the bottom, where Joe's initials were stroked into the clay. "Four hundred dollars. But it's not for sale," he hurried on. "I'm going to keep it." Then, feeling as if some explanation were required, he added, "Joe was killed."

The man lifted the sgraffito from Nigel's fingers, said softly, " 'Any man's death diminishes me, because I am involved in mankind; and therefore never send to know for whom the bell tolls; it tolls for thee.' "

The sad patter of rain turning the ground to a mixture of mud and ash. The stink of burned vegetation now that the mortar attack was past. Eight men squatting in the muck, haunted faces dark with stubble listening as Jonas Washington read Donne's Devotions XII in his rich deep voice. The sharp crack of a sniper's rifle, the bullet spinning the black man in a complete circle, dropping him to the ground with half his head shot away.

Going absolutely berserk. Snatching up his M16 and plunging into the jungle.

"Sarge, you're fucking crazy!"

Only one man following him in. Private First Class "Silly" deBaca. Guarding his back while he found and iced the gook who had killed Jonas and silenced that mellifluous voice, stilled the poet's soul.

"Sergeant! Nigel!" Sil's hands gripped his shoulders.

"My God, Silly, I can't believe it."

"Neither can I," said Silvestre. "How long has it been?"

They paused, counting.

"Holy shit, nineteen years," whispered Nigel.

"Goddamn, it's good to see you again! But, Nigel, how, by all that's holy, did you fetch up in Santa Fe?"

"My wife. She runs the Cummings Museum and heads up their archaeological digs. We've been here for three years." He cuffed Sil lightly. "But how did I miss you until now? Unless you just moved here?"

"No, I'm one of those rarities, a true native New Mexican, but—"

Nigel held up a forefinger. "Wait, hold this story while I get us a couple of beers."

They settled back with bottles of Dos Equis, and Sil resumed.

"My parents live in Santa Fe, but I haven't been home much during the past ten years. I ride . . . used to ride on the international Grand Prix circuit, but I took a bad spill last fall, spent a month in the hospital, then came home to recuperate."

"Grand Prix." Nigel lipped at the foam around the neck of his bottle. "A lot of years ago I drove some Formula Three in Europe, but I never heard . . . I have a feeling I'm being ignorant."

"No. Most people don't associate horse shows with the term 'grand prix.' But on the world-class level that's what it's called."

"And you're on that world-class level."

"Was," Silvestre answered shortly, goaded by Nigel's admiring tone.

"What, then, other than synchronicity, brought you into my shop today?"

"My grandmother's birthday. She has everything, but still expects to tear open gifts like any five-year-old."

"What did you have in mind."

"None of that *Indian trash,*" Sil said, giving a credible imitation of Alejandra.

Nigel propped his chin in his hands, his eyes nar-

rowing with amusement. ''Then why the hell did you
come into an Indian-trash store?''

''You had nice merchandise, and I figured I could
find something that's not too overtly Indian.''

Nigel tugged at his upper lip. ''Has she got long
hair?''

''Of course. We're talking heavy-duty Spanish
grande dame here.''

''So how about a silver comb?''

They paced over to the counter, still nursing their
beers. Sil seriously considered the combs, finally se-
lecting one which had no turquoise, but instead an
intricate shadow-box pattern carved deep into the polished silver.

That out of the way, Nigel brought out two more
beers, and they settled into the cane-and-leather chairs
in the rug section of the store.

Sil puffed music out of the neck of the bottle while
Nigel looked at him fondly.

''You know, you haven't changed much. You still get
that terribly intense look when you're searching for a
way to say something . . .'' He groped for the correct
word.

''Rude?'' suggested Sil. ''Tactless, nosy?''

''All of the above.'' The chair creaked as Nigel settled deeper into its depths. ''So say it.''

''It's this shop. I'm having a hard time picturing you
here, and yet here you are.''

''Truth be told, it isn't what I would have chosen
for myself, but . . .'' He shrugged.

''So why do it?''

''I've got no skills, and my résumé is a mess. I've
done a lot of interesting things in my life, but they
don't add up to much. At least not as the world meas-
ures such things.''

Sil shook his head. ''I don't know, you were always
a real people person. Babying the kids, bullying the
brass when you thought they were being unfair to our
unit. Tough and tender, Nigel, that's what I remember
best about you.''

''I'd like to work with kids, like in the police-department juvenile division, but my wife has the typical sixties attitude toward the cops, and my sister . . . insisted on the shop. They were both so busy manufacturing a job for me, they didn't bother to ask me what I wanted.''

Sil stared consideringly at his old commander. Tried to reconcile this self-effacing man with the one who had led him safely through the jungles and rice paddies of Vietnam. He decided not to push.

"So when did you leave 'Nam?"

"Couple of years after you did," Nigel said. "I left reluctantly too. I would happily have been career military, but the Marine medical corps seemed to think it was best.''

"Shit! What happened?"

"A poor bastard hit a mine. I was unlucky enough to be next to him. Anyway, I rambled around Europe for a few years. God, I had fun, but it was all short-term stuff."

"Like what?" Sil asked.

"This is boring."

"No, it's not. Stop being a modest ass."

Nigel shrugged. "Okay. I modeled in Paris." The mobile upper lip curled ironically. "They seemed to think I was pretty. Did a few bit parts in some movies in Spain. Race-car mechanic, and I drove a little. After I married Lexa I worked on digs with her. See, just a collection of useless experiences."

He shot a quick grin at Silvestre, and the Spaniard again sensed that Nigel wasn't being entirely candid with him. Maybe not even candid with himself. Nineteen years ago they had sat in a smoky Saigon bar getting drunk and maudlin and exchanging life stories. Nigel had presented himself as a useless wastrel whose father had finally reached the end of his tether and tossed him out on his ass. It hadn't rung true then. And it didn't ring true now.

"Now it's your turn," Nigel said.

"Not a lot to tell. Got back from Vietnam when I was twenty. Tried a semester at the university. Believe me, that did not appeal. I'd been horse crazy all my

life, and it suddenly occurred to me I might be able
to make a career with that. Studied riding all over the
world. Daddy bought me fine horses, I started to win."
He shrugged. "End of story."

And now it was the older man's turn to realize that
what was not being said was far more important than
the bloodless rendition of this little story. Something
was eating at Sil's soul. But this wasn't an eighteen-
year-old private. This was a man, and a man Nigel
didn't know.

"Are you married?" Nigel asked suddenly.

"No, still looking."

"You'll have to meet Lexa. She'll be fascinated with
you. What are you doing tomorrow night?"

"Nothing." Silvestre's mouth twisted. "I seem to
say that a lot. Oh, no, wait. I have a meeting." He
rose.

"Damn. Lexa's going into the field on Monday. Can
you break it?"

"No, Franklin would give birth to puppies."

"Franklin? Not Franklin Pierce, by chance?"

"Yes? Do you know him?"

"Nooo, not exactly. But he's got my half-sister giving birth to puppies."

Sil sank slowly back into the chair. "I don't want
to ask this, because I have a horrible feeling I already
know the answer. *Why* is your half-sister having puppies?"

"Because of this equestrian—"

"Oh, hell!" Sil hammered at his chest. "I'm working with Franklin trying to get that center built."

"Silvestre, I don't live in Rancho de Palabra. I don't
care a good goddamn if you build an equestrian center."

"You Anglos, you got no sense of family." He allowed his accent to deepen.

"Families," Nigel snorted. "Frankly, I sometimes
wish I had been born an orphink."

"You know something?" Sil confided with a little
laugh, "sometimes I do too."

Nigel rose and walked Sil to the door.

They gripped each other by the forearms. "God, it's good to see you again," Sil said.

"I feel the same. I'll call you as soon as Lexa's in from the field. Ought to be about ten days."

"Hey, let's not wait that long. If you're going to be a bachelor, let's take advantage of it."

"Sounds good." Nigel leaned on the doorjamb and watched Sil weaving his way through the few window-shoppers. "Hey . . ."

"Yeah?"

"I hope your grandmother likes the comb."

Sil grimaced. "She won't. But that's all part of the game."

It was only ten after five, but Nigel couldn't stand another twenty minutes in the shop. Seeing Silvestre again after all these years had filled him with a restless excitement, and he wanted to tell Lexa about their meeting.

As he locked the doors and turned the key to switch on the alarm, he wondered briefly if he was rushing to see her because of a guilty conscience. He knew he had a tendency to look for trouble, to overanalyze every word and action, to assume that people would read significance where he did. So the fact that all the players in the drama of Rancho de Palabra were gathering in his life seemed significant and troubling.

He jammed his hands deep into his pockets and left the Plaza, heading up East Palace Avenue. Listened to the click of his loafer heels on the sidewalk. Listened to an inner voice matching those steady footfalls as it repeated over and over: *liar, liar.* Was he really guilty of deception? Yes. But the deception of silence—he hadn't told Lexa he had spent Thursday evening with Rhea.

Not that Lexa would care. There was nothing odd or unusual in siblings dining together. Or so the world would say. Unfortunately, the world didn't know what he knew. Fortunately, Lexa didn't either.

His thoughts beat against the confines of his skull like frightened birds. He walked past the courtyard containing the Shed, one of Santa Fe's most popular Mexican restaurants. There was only a faint odor of chili, for the establishment only served lunch, but it was enough to remind him he was hungry. Two doors down, and a wave of chocolate came floating out the door of Señor Murphy's Candy Sellers. It was too much to be resisted. He pulled open the screen door and plunged in.

It had begun on their second date. Nigel had brought the young archaeology student a small gift, and he had continued the practice all through the eleven years of their marriage. Until recently. Recently he had waited for the special occasion. It was a dangerous sign. As dangerous as their conversations, which were either meaningless or politically profound. What didn't seem to be happening anymore was just *talking*.

He accepted the white-wrapped box of piñon toffee and continued toward the Cummings Museum. Unlike the museum in the Palace of the Governors, which could enjoy the prestige of a centuries-old adobe building, the Cummings had to make do with an ugly red-brick monstrosity that would have looked more at home in Missouri. Erected somewhere around the turn of the century, before the citizens of Santa Fe had fully realized the potential of their "City Different" and begun to insist upon southwestern styling, it squatted like a self-conscious hippo in a herd of impalas.

Still, it was large and rambling, with plenty of room for displays and for workshops, and Lexa's upstairs office enjoyed a spectacular view of the mountains to the north. She was so engrossed in her work that she didn't notice his entrance, so he spent a few minutes leaning against the doorjamb, admiring her.

A sheen of sweat left a glow on her golden skin, and her hair, carelessly piled into a knot on top of her head, was starting to droop tendrils down her neck and around her cheeks. She sighed, brushed back hair with her free hand, and continued writing. Nigel tiptoed into the room, bent, and bestowed a soft kiss on the nape of her neck. She squeaked, and the fountain pen left a streamer of ink across her neat list.

"Oh, Jesus Christ! You scared me half to death."

"I'm sorry. You just sounded so tired when you gave that little sigh, and I wanted to kiss you."

She arched back in the chair, cracking her back. "Not tired—bored. I hate the detail work."

He fished in his pocket and laid the box on the desk in front of her.

She cast him a long sideways glance and reached for it. "What's this? Have you been doing something naughty, and are appeasing me before confessing the fact?"

"No." Irritation and guilt made the word sharper than he intended. "I always used to bring you little presents, and when I realized I'd gotten out of the habit, I was ashamed." The words tumbled out, perhaps a little overly soft and appeasing.

"I suppose the romance goes out of any marriage."

He settled onto the corner of the desk. "Is that a general observation or is there something profound and specific that I'm supposed to get out of it?"

Her mobile eyebrows sprang up in surprise. "Just a general remark."

"You relieve me. On the other hand, I do think maybe it's time we took a look—"

"At what? At our marriage?"

"No, no. At the direction of our marriage. I'm forty, Lexa."

"So?"

"Well, maybe it's time we thought about starting a family." He forced a smile. "Otherwise I'll be this old crock trying to relate to my teenagers, and probably making a mess of it."

Her face had closed down. It was an expression that was unfortunately becoming all too familiar. This subject had arisen with greater and greater frequency during the past year, and he bitterly wondered what excuse she would give him this time to avoid the discussion. A dinner date he didn't know about? The imminent arrival of an appointment?

Lexa carefully capped the fountain pen, laid it precisely in the center of the pad, shifted to face him.

"You should have asked me sooner." The tone was gentle, regretful, but it also contained something he couldn't place. "My career has become so important now. It would be difficult to . . . arrange."

"Lexa, you're the most efficient and organized person I know. You could arrange anything if you really wanted it."

"It would be such a change . . . in our life. I'm in the field so much."

"Of course, some compromises would have to be made. Cummings has offered to hire an assistant for you, and there's no reason why I couldn't pick up some of the slack. Take the baby to the shop with me."

"We'd have to have day care," she said a little desperately.

"Sure, sometimes."

"Well, we really can't afford it."

Nigel slid off the desk and stared down at her. "What are you really saying, Lexa?"

"I'm just saying that there's a lot to think about. About starting a family."

"God knows we've been evading each other for the past year, Lexa. I didn't realize we'd also gotten around to out-and-out lying."

Pain seemed to explode in her chest, and Lexa pressed the heel of her hand hard against her breastbone. She listened to his retreating footsteps clattering down the stairs. Far below, a door slammed. She laid her head on her desk, and a few tears leaked out.

How could she tell him that it had nothing to do with the goddamn career, and everything to do with the gulf that was inexorably widening between them? He had changed when they came to Santa Fe. Lost his strength, his sense of control and command. He had become like a frightened deer. Starting at shadows, increasingly nervous, as if anticipating a blow. *From her?* Was she the problem? Did he fear her?

It was too horrible to contemplate. She loved him, and wanted not a shadow on his life. Had she changed? Had the power and responsibility of running one of the finest private museums in the world made her less

caring? But he had the shop. And the very ludicrous-
ness of the situation struck her again. His life had been
filled with romance, in the old sense of the world. Had
marriage to her removed the romance? Caged her
wonderful, free-living hawk?

They had met during the Albuquerque balloon fi-
esta. She had risen at the ungodly hour of four A.M.
to watch the filling of the great hot-air balloons and
the mass ascension from a mesa north of town. She
could still remember his face highlighted by the flicker
of a flame through the silken material of the French
entry. The face of a saint or an ancient king. She had
walked right over, asked him to explain the process of
filling one of the giant bags.

They had talked and talked, and she had forgotten
her chilled fingers and frostbitten toes, and the fact
she was starving, and as the sun crept over the crest
of Sandia Peak, the balloons had launched. The roaring of the propane heaters was like the cry of dragons,
and the balloons were fantastic, shuddering, multicolored creatures etched against a turquoise sky. Nigel
had wrapped his arms about her, and she hadn't
minded. It had all seemed so natural.

He was supposed to have left, but instead he hustled
and found a job with Whizzer Baker, who was running
the Arabian Nationals in October. Soon they were
spending every available moment together, and her
grades would have gone all to hell except Nigel had
forced her to be disciplined, speaking gently as he
placed a textbook in her hands.

"I never had a chance for an education, and I'm too
old and too undisciplined to start now. But you have
it all before you, and I'm not going to let you risk it
because of a ne'er-do-well like me." Then he would
smile. "And I'll be so proud of you when you have
that degree. You're going to be a famous archaeologist."

And now she was. And sadly, it tasted of ash and
sulfur, for her best friend, lover, and companion was
drifting farther and farther away from her.

It was ten P.M. at an all-night convenience store on the outskirts of Tulsa, Oklahoma, and Mona was huddled in the small box that passed for a phone booth in this modern age. Hoping the five shit-kickers lounging around the front of the store would stop preening, pile into their big-foot pickup, and drive away. Listening to the lonely *ring ring ring* of a phone sounding in an obviously empty loft in the Village. Wondering. *Wondering*.

There was an ache in the back of her throat, and her eyes felt hot and gritty. Tiredness. She would *not* cry. Mona carefully hung the receiver on its cradle and shambled stiffly toward her truck.

They had arranged that she would call him tonight. She had been so looking forward to hearing his voice. It would have washed the weariness from her bones. And now he wasn't home.

Oh, Terry!

"Hey, little lady!"

She plowed doggedly on toward her truck, ignoring the adolescent bellows from behind.

"Hey, lady. Cutie."

Suddenly they were all around her, a rash of pimples and nervous bravado spread across their young faces. Dangerous, however, because they were in a pack. She drew herself up to her full height and pinned them with a cold, adult glance.

"Let me by."

"Hey, it's too dark and late for a little thing like you to be out all alone."

"Come on, we'll buy you a drink," piped up another.

"I doubt you're old enough to buy a drink legally," Mona snapped. And instantly she regretted the words. Attacking their budding manhood was not going to help.

A pebble in the parking lot crunched beneath a boot heel. One of them was advancing on her unprotected back. A pulse was beginning to hammer in Mona's throat, and her stomach had become a small knot. She shrugged slightly, allowing her denim jacket to fall open.

"You think we're not old enough. You gonna find out different," brayed the ringleader.

Mona's hand plunged into her coat and closed about the butt of her Beretta in its shoulder holster. She drew the gun in a smooth motion as her father's voice ran a litany in her head: *Stance, sight, prepare, squeeze, recover.* When the inner voice reached *squeeze* there was a crashing explosion, and a bullet dug up asphalt between the spokesman's feet.

There were yells and curses, an opening appeared, and Mona plunged through, got her back against the cab of her truck. Recovered. But it was all over. All she saw were asses and elbows heading for the ludicrous truck.

The shot had brought the clerk at a run.

"Jesus! Are you okay?"

"Yes." She was starting to tremble. Carefully she thumbed on the safety, and returned the pistol to its holster. "I handled it badly. It shouldn't have been necessary to use this."

"You want to call the police?"

"No! Good heavens, no. I'm sure they received a sufficient scare." A bleak little smile touched her lips. "And no doubt they'll think twice or even four or five times before they hit on a woman alone again."

Turning, she climbed into her truck, fired up the engine, and headed back out to the thoroughbred farm where she and Favory were bunking for the night.

She forced her thoughts to Terry in an effort to calm herself. And found to her chagrin that she was becoming angry. As if her difficulties in the parking lot were his fault. Which was completely unreasonable of her. Terry was out. Okay. No big deal. Undoubtedly something had come up, and he'd been forced to leave the apartment. He was probably worrying even now. Concerned because he hadn't been there to take her call.

She would just phone again in the morning. But she wouldn't tell him about the incident tonight. Terry disapproved of all guns in general, and handguns in particular. No sense upsetting him because she'd drawn down on a gaggle of teenagers. And if they did get into it, the discussion would just end in a stalemate, as it always did. Because Mona was not about to stop carrying a weapon when she traveled alone. As a policeman friend had once said, "Better to be tried by twelve than carried by six."

She drew in a deep breath as she watched the headlights play across the dirt road. She seemed to taste grit, and longed for a long hot soak in a tub. Then she pulled in the main gates and drove back to the barn. A chorus of whickers welcomed her as she climbed down from the cab. Lifting the latch on the stall door, she entered, and propping herself against one wall, pulled off her tennis shoes. Next the jacket and the pistol, the gun laid close by her sleeping bag. Favory, her old gray hunter, had his nose buried deep in his hay net. He rolled one liquid brown eye toward her. Slipping in under his head, she wrapped her arms around his neck and breathed in the rich horse scent.

The groom had shaken her head when she saw that Mona intended to spread her sleeping bag in the stall with the big jumper. Mona had tried to explain that she had delivered this horse, and slept with him for the first week of his life because he had been so premature. There was no way he was going to step on her. But it was obvious the girl was unconvinced, so Mona had stuttered into silence and simply gone on with her preparations. A few minutes later the groom had returned with a release form. Mona had gladly signed it. Anything to be allowed to get out of here and call Terry. And . . .

Well, and then the rest had happened.

She gave the big horse a slap on his heavily muscled rump and slid into her bag. Tomorrow she was going to try to cover the seven-hundred-odd miles that lay between Tulsa and Santa Fe in one long marathon push. Unfortunately, the way she felt now, she didn't think that was going to happen. . . .

Could it have been a meeting?

A dinner, perhaps, with some potential publisher?

Maybe something with the family. His grandmother hadn't been well for some months. She only hoped it wouldn't delay him joining her in New Mexico.

And she instantly felt guilty for the thought. Mona murmured a quick prayer asking for forgiveness, then began her normal evening devotionals. Terry sometimes teased her a little, calling it her "now-I-lay-me-down-to-sleep" ritual. But never to hurt. Deep down, he had a very strong faith. It just took a different form. After all, he hadn't been raised within a church the way she had.

And perhaps he was more honest than she was. Maybe she was just going through the motions. Trying to hedge her bets by a slavish performance of ritual. God knows Dad had made the proper observances throughout the years, and he was the most miserable human—

She broke off the ugly traitorous thought and wrapped an arm about her head. Wondered what on earth was the matter with her that she could be so uncharitable, so mean-spirited twice in one night. But the truth was, she was angry with Terry. *So we've been married for five years. That's supposed to be the dangerous hump. Get over that, and you're home-free.*

That's why the move to New Mexico was so important. A new direction for their life and their marriage. But it was going to be a real change. Instead of brief flying visits home, a week or two snatched out of her schedule, they were going to be together every day. Nodding at each other over the coffee. Kissing each other good night.

Five years.

She had been like the sleeping princess in a fairy tale, and had literally been awakened by his kiss. Sex. It formed the foundation of their relationship. But it wasn't all they had. Mona was also fascinated with the breadth of his interests. His ability to talk on any subject. *Knowledge a mile wide and an inch deep,* had been her father's dismissive remark. Well, since her knowledge—apart from horses—was two feet wide and a quarter-inch deep, Terry's facile chatter and humorous lectures bothered her not at all.

But now she was twenty-five, and no longer the same little girl who had married Terence Palmer Gallagher. Did he understand that she had grown up? That she had needs that couldn't be filled by the magic of his body alone?

She was doing it again, whipping up anger to no good purpose.

Tired.

It was the only explanation.

Or was she only making excuses?

Thoroughly miserable now, she burrowed deeper into the bag and tried to sleep. Tried not to hurt. Tried not to worry. Tried not to be afraid.

5

"Personally, I think this covenant banning horses in Rancho de Palabra is just so much horseshit. If you'll forgive the pun."

Rhea glared at Jason Reiner. "It isn't, and I don't. And if you feel that way, what are you doing at this meeting?"

"Being a troublemaker."

"I don't need this, Jason. It's taken a full week longer than it should have to organize this meeting. You'd think people don't care."

"Well, I admit this doesn't rank right high on my list of important issues."

Rhea turned her back on him and surveyed the crowd. Women, mostly, their chatter like the trillings of birds filling the enormous living room. The men *always* had something more important to do. As if preserving their homes and the investment represented by those homes wasn't important. But maybe it was just as well; in her experience, men seemed to excel at strutting, and beating their breasts, and getting the *big picture*, but they were frankly useless when it came to the tiny drudging details that really got things accomplished.

It looked as if some hundred people were present. A large crowd, but the vast living room was capable of containing it—forty feet long and thirty wide, with whitewashed adobe walls that formed a canvas against which the colorful clothing splashed like bits of animated paint. Thirty feet overhead, the sloping ceiling, punctuated at intervals with great sheets of glass, gathered the morning light and flung it down onto the heads of her guests. Last year Rhea had had a local stained-glass artist fashion small jewellike bits of glass and hang them just below the skylights. The result was spectacular.

At the far end of the room, bulging majestically in its corner, was an enormous kiva fireplace. Eloy, who helped Maria with the heavy ·work, had arranged gnarled piñon logs and cut evergreen branches in the gaping mouth of the fireplace. In a niche above it hung a large kachina painted in outrageous shades of pastel pink, blue, and tan. He was hardly traditional, but Rhea had loved the colors, and the comical little O of his mouth, and the upthrust feathers of his headdress.

Maria slipped about carrying a plate of cheese straws, looking tense and nervous. Rhea sighed, and wished that the local Spanish help could acquire the kind of invisible panache she had found in European help. From the other door Eloy came mooching in, a chair clutched in each hand, and his long drooping Zapata mustache quivering as if embodied with a life of its own. Rhea frowned. He was supposed to have done the setting up long before the guests arrived. You just couldn't depend on these people.

The front doorbell rang, a series of falling tones like a Gothic clock tower striking the hour. Maria looked harried, Rhea waved reassuringly to her, and went to answer the door. Glancing through the peephole, she saw John Greer pursing his lips in that unconscious kissing action which he did when he was deep in thought.

"Hello, John," Rhea said, throwing open the door. "Late, as usual."

He stopped polishing his shoe against the back of his pant leg. "Oh, Christ, Rhea, if I told you everything that's gone wrong today—"

"And it's only eleven-twenty. You have more crises in a single day than most people endure in a lifetime, John dearest." He grinned in response to her teasing.

They entered the living room, and Maria stepped forward, basket outthrust. John seized a handful of cheese straws and stuffed them greedily into his mouth. Flakes of pastry spilled over his tie and came to rest on the shelf of his rapidly developing paunch.

"*Señora.*"

"Yes, Maria, what is it?"

"Telephone for you, *señora.*"

"Maria, I've told you repeatedly that when I'm entertaining I am not to be disturbed. Now, take their name and number, and say I'll call back. Then put on the answering machine so we won't be interrupted again."

"But, *señora,* it is your daughter."

Rhea started. "Elani! What on earth . . . ? John, excuse me for one moment. Go be entertaining so the ladies don't lose patience with me."

"Right, entertaining. See a man walk the legal highwire. Death-defying acts of assumpsit. Have your quantum merit checked today," he muttered as he walked away.

Rhea hurried to her office and picked up the receiver. It was a bad connection, as if the waves of the Atlantic Ocean, which separated her from her child, were hissing and popping on the lines.

"Elani," she said in her soft trilling voice.

"What? What? I can't hear you," came back an aggrieved voice.

"Elani," Rhea bawled, and felt a surge of unreasoning irritation with her daughter. "What is it? I'm very busy."

"I don't like this school!"

There was a long pause as Rhea absorbed this statement and considered her response.

Elani continued petulantly, "I don't like being in a school with only girls. I don't like being away from Em. And he feels the same way."

"How do you know? He's miles away in another city."

"I just know," came the stubborn reply. "We're twins."

"Elani, I'm getting very tired of this twin game.

You have far too active an imagination, and you do *not* have a psychic link to your brother.''

"Have you ever heard of letters?" The tone was barely polite. "I want to be with my brother. I hate this place, it's like living in a chicken coop. All hens.''

"Elani, you're fourteen years old. It's time for you to acquire some polish. And I don't believe in coeducational education for teenagers. You're going to make contacts at school that will help you for the rest of your life.''

"Big deal! I hate it here.''

"Elani, I don't have time to argue with you. I have a number of guests, and a very important meeting to chair—''

"What is it this time? Saving the endangered pigeon? Well, what about your endangered children?'' the girl yelled.

"I am not going to listen to this kind of nonsense, and you'd better moderate your tone when you talk to me, young lady! I want to talk to your headmistress.''

"Well, you can't because I'm not at school.''

"Not at . . .'' gasped Rhea. She knew that the exclusive boarding school was fifteen miles out of Lucerne.

"I'm at the main post office.''

"How on earth did you get there?''

"I hitchhiked.''

"Oh, Elani! And you're absent without permission! I am *not* amused by this, young lady.''

"Mother, don't you care that I'm miserable? And that Em's miserable too?'' Her voice rose with childish hysteria.

"Things that seem vastly unfair when you're fourteen will make sense when you're twenty. Now, you get back to school—''

"I'll run away.''

"Now, you stop this right now!'' She was shouting, and the receiver slipped in her sweat-slick hand. "I don't have time to come to Switzerland right now. For once in your life think about somebody other than yourself, Elani.''

Sobs were the only reply, then a click as the phone was hung up at the other end. Still trembling, Rhea quickly flipped through her address book, located the number of the school, and rang the office. Frau Schattinger was soothing, and very efficient, and promised to send a car at once into Lucerne to collect the truant.

John was standing by the fireplace, a glass of lemonade in one hand and cheese sticks in the other. He raised his eyebrows inquiringly, and Rhea laid her fingertips against her forehead and gave her head a tiny shake.

"Children. My daughter is turning into an unmanageable little hoyden."

He finished off the last cheese stick, wiped his hand on his trousers, and gripped her hand tightly in his. "I can't believe that. Any daughter of yours would be sugar and spice, and as soft as moonbeams."

"Unfortunately, her father had some input into the genetic stew," Rhea retorted sharply; then her bright smile returned and she tipped her head back to look up at him. "Well, shall we get down to business?"

"Oh . . . oh, yes." He awkwardly released her hand.

Rhea floated away, her soft chiffon dress clinging to her thighs. The layers were woven in different but complementing pastel colors, and the entire effect was very girlish and utterly charming. But there was nothing immature about the still-firm bosom accentuated by the tight bodice, and John swallowed hard.

A silver spoon rang on a crystal goblet, and the busy chatter died away. "Ladies and gentlemen . . ." Rhea twinkled, and gave a slight bow to Averell. "And my darling in-between." He smirked back at her. "My attorney, Mr. John Greer, has arrived, and is ready to tell us all about stopping this dreadful center. John." She graciously surrendered the floor, and found a chair.

The lawyer fiddled with the knot on his tie, then stroked a hand down his incipient paunch. "First, let me thank you all for having me over. And if any of you have attorneys who are experts on Indian law, I

certainly wouldn't mind talking to them.'' He paused
and took a sip of lemonade. ''When Rhea called me
last week, I took some time to run down to Albuquerque and do a bit of reading at the law school. And
what I found isn't terribly encouraging.'' He smiled
at Rhea, but it died as his brown eyes met her blazing
blue gaze.

The clearing of his throat echoed explosively through
the room, and he groped nervously in his suit pockets
for his notebook. ''Uh . . . well, to start with . . .''
He slid his eyes back to Rhea, and what he saw there
brought a line of sweat to his upper lip. Quickly he
flipped through the pages, and began again.

''I think we need to begin with some history and
background, so if you'll all bear with me . . .'' His
tone was brisk now and businesslike. ''In 1846, General Kearny took possession of New Mexico from the
government of Mexico. The Pueblo Indians were guaranteed all rights that they had enjoyed under Mexican
rule, and their land holdings were affirmed. The attitude was that while the Pueblos could never hope to
attain the level of white people, they were better than
most redskins, and because of this, they didn't need
to be protected in the way the 'savage nomadic tribes'
were protected. Therefore they could sell their land
just like white folks.

''By the early 1920's this had caused a land-title snarl
that had to be resolved. In 1924 Congress passed the
Pueblo Lands Act, which effectively placed the Pueblo
Indians on the same level as other Indian tribes, and
placed their land in trust to be overseen by the federal
government.''

Greer glanced up at some subdued shifting. ''Bear
with me, we're almost to the point of all this. The
most pertinent section of this bill states: 'and no sale,
grant, lease of any character, or other conveyance of
lands, or title or claim thereto, made by any Pueblo as
a community, or any Pueblo Indian living in a community of Pueblo Indians, in the State of New Mexico,
shall be of any validity in law or in equity unless the
same be first approved by the Secretary of the Inte-

rior.' And that's the crux of the matter. Because, while San Jose Pueblo must receive the Secretary's okay to lease the land to Franklin Pierce, it is under no obligation to consider any other interests, and in fact no other party can set forward an interest. The disposition of Indian lands is a matter solely between the Secretary and the tribe.''

There was a rustle and movement from the hundred-odd people in the room. One woman, her plump baby face screwed up with concentration and confusion, leaned in to Averell and moaned, ''I don't understand.''

''But Rhea does.'' The little homosexual indicated their hostess with a jerk of the head. ''You just listen, and she'll put it all in perspective for you.''

Rhea unclenched her hands, noting the impressions left by her nails on the palms. ''What you're saying is that we're helpless. We can do nothing to stop this terrible invasion. Nothing to preserve our homes and life-style. Because they're Indians.''

Greer, surveying the room, saw on those beautiful tanned faces an inner battle being waged. Liberal guilt and love for the Indian versus an unholy anger that the kind of preferential treatment allotted to that beloved minority was now going to hurt *them!*

Yup, a conservative is a liberal who's been mugged, thought Greer snidely.

The pandemonium died, and Rhea pinned John with a cold glance. ''Thank you so much for not telling me this days ago. Before I interrupted everyone's life with this now pointless meeting—''

''Wait, wait, just hold the phone. I don't think I said that. I indicated that our prospects aren't good, but they're by no means hopeless.''

''Go on.'' She reseated herself and primly arranged the hem of her skirt over her knees.

''What we can do is petition the Secretary, indicate that this is a major federal action, and hence requires the preparation of an environmental-impact statement. Those things take years to prepare, and cost thousands. That ought to discourage Franklin Pierce.''

"Why an environmental-impact statement? What's more natural than horses, and that which is excreted by horses?" asked Reiner with a pointed glance to Rhea.

"Actually you've hit the nail right on the head. There's a whole section of the Clean Water Act dealing with effluent waste." John gave a little smile. "I call them the duck-poop cases from when I was researching all this for a racetrack down in the southern part of the state."

"Very funny," Rhea drawled.

"Anyway, animal manure is a major problem. It's a hazard to ground water. If we can show that without careful planning this facility might endanger Santa Fe's water supply, we would be cooking. God knows we've got enough water problems up here already."

"All right, so how do we establish this?" Rhea asked.

"Hire an expert." Rhea glanced about, and John handed her his notebook and pen from his breast pocket. She made a note.

"All right, what else? Or is that our only recourse?"

"Well, there is one other approach, but it's not precisely a remedy in the traditional legal sense. You can try to divide the Pueblo on this issue. Find some group that opposes the project, and tie it up at that level. The Secretary can't approve if the Pueblo doesn't ask, and there's no law saying the Pueblo can't change its mind."

A woman in the front spoke up. "Will there be such a group?"

"In a Pueblo? You're damn right there will be."

Rhea smiled brightly out over her assembled neighbors. "Then we find that group, and give them all our support and encouragement."

"And bribes, don't forget bribes," Averell sang out.

"Averell, you're such a philistine. What a dreadful thing to say."

"But true," Greer muttered to himself. After twenty

years practicing law he had no illusions about people—Indians included.

The meeting was being held in Governor Ernesto Barela's modern split-level house on the edge of the San Jose Pueblo. Out front, six mangy, skinny Pueblo dogs lay in the dust scratching fleas and setting up a hunting-pack call each time a car or truck pulled in.

Ernesto kept slipping to the front window to nervously check on his new GMC four-wheel-drive pickup with top cab lights, chrome running boards, front grillwork, translucent window cover. All he needed was some asshole scratching the dark blue paint job, and by god he'd kick some butt.

The lieutenant governor, George Sena, popped open a can of Pepsi, and grinned at him. "Relax, Ernie, nobody's gonna hit your damn truck." There was a laugh from the other assembled men.

A Lincoln Continental pulled into the front yard, and out climbed Benny with the big Anglo. Ernesto hurried to the front door to usher them in.

"Welcome to my home, Mr. Pierce." Franklin and the Indian shook hands and sized each other up. "We have a good crowd."

"Never liked doing business with a crowd."

"This is a Pueblo, Mr. Pierce, there is no other way to do business."

Pierce grunted.

The front room contained fifteen men ranging in age from the mid-thirties to late seventies. Or so Franklin guessed. The old geezer leaning back in the recliner looked more like a mummy than a person, so *old* was about the best one could do.

Dress also varied widely. The governor was in a pair of Levi's with work boots, and a flannel workshirt. Benny looked like a punk yuppie in his dark business suit, long hair worn loose over his shoulders. Then there was the old hooter in his smocklike shirt, high moccasins, and leggings. His hair—an amazing snow white mane—was wrapped *chongo*-style with a traditional woven band.

A large woman with a dirty-faced toddler clinging to her skirts traveled back and forth between kitchen and dining-room table, setting out refreshments for the guests. Franklin's stomach let out a loud rumble, reminding him it was close to noon and definitely time to eat, so he chugged over to the table to check out the grub: a big pot of simmering green-chili stew and beside it an equally large pot of posole, its white hominy floating in a thick red-chili sauce spotted here and there with fist-sized chunks of pork. A plate of flour tortillas, potato chips, and a large bowl of Jell-O-fruit-and-whipped-cream salad completed the feast.

"Go ahead, help yourself. My aunt's a wonderful cook," said Benny, ladling out some posole.

The Pueblo men circled the table like dropping vultures, but unlike a similar gathering in a white house, there was almost no conversation. Franklin wondered if the cliché of the "silent red man" was in fact true or if the presence of a white man was inhibiting them.

One of the youngest men filled up a bowl and hurried back to the oldster still entrenched in the recliner. His expression and attitude were reverential as the knotted old hands closed about the bowl. Nowhere could Franklin discern any of the impatience or pity one so often saw when young Anglos were forced to wait on an elderly person.

For a few minutes everyone paid close attention to the business of shoveling in spoonfuls of the spicy stews. Franklin was soon sweating, his eyes watering from the heat of the chili. He caught Benny's eye, grinned, and mopped his face with a paper napkin.

"Oohh, God, I'm sufferin' so good."

Ernesto set aside his bowl, and, staring down at the floor, began to make introductions. "George Sena, my lieutenant governor, Jesus Mendoza, our sheriff." He proceeded through the ditch bosses and war captains, and finally indicated the ancient in the chair. "And one of our village chiefs, Joe Martinez of the Oyikentunyo Moiety."

The old chief raised heavy lids and pinned Franklin with a reptilian glance. And in that instant the Anglo realized who was the real power in this room. And it wasn't any of the men with their political titles bestowed by the conquering Spaniards four hundred years before.

"Excuse me, I'm ignorant. What's this Oy . . . Oy—"

"Oyikentunyo. It means 'winter.' Tewa people have a dual division between Summer people and Winter people. Joe's our Winter chief," explained Ernesto.

"Oh," Franklin responded weakly, feeling overwhelmed by a sea of unfamiliar words. *Tewa, moiety, Oy . . .* Shit!

"But you don't want to hear about cultural anthropology," Benny said. "And *we* know *all* about anthropologists."

There was a ripple of quiet laughter from the assembled men, startling because it was so sudden and because it seemed to arise for no reason. Benny's remark sure didn't strike Franklin as a knee-slapper.

"But to business," snapped Benny.

There was a flicker of irritation from the old geezer at the commanding note in the younger man's voice, and Franklin, who hadn't become a multimillionaire by being obtuse, stepped into the conversation. He might know squat about Indians, but he sure as hell knew human nature.

"Chief."

"Joe," the old man corrected in a surprisingly strong voice.

"Joe, I'm damn impressed with this young fella." He waved a shovel-size hand in Benny's direction. "If your Pueblo has more like him, you aren't gonna have no troubles at all."

"Unfortunately, we do not have a long line of Bennys waiting in the wings." Martinez laughed at the white man's expression. "Forgive me my little joke, Mr. Pierce. I do so look the part of 'ancient red man, long on wisdom, short on words,' that I sometimes surrender to the urge and play it. I spent twenty years in Hollywood falling off horses and pretending to be shot by cowboys before returning to the Pueblo. I know

the white world—its dangers and also its benefits to
my people.''

''So you approve of my project?''

''With certain reservations. The main reason I'm
present for this meeting is that I'll be running the
Pueblo for the next six months.''

Franklin glanced at Ernesto.

''You have to understand, there are levels upon levels in a Pueblo,'' said the governor. ''Those of us with
the Spanish titles generally deal with the Pueblo's re-
lations with the outside world. But within the Pueblo
there are other, more traditional duties, handled by the
chiefs.''

''Uuuh,'' Pierce groaned. That drew another laugh.
''So who do I deal with?''

''All of us,'' piped up George Sena.

''Aaaw, I was afraid you were gonna say that.''

''Not to worry, we're not going to be too hard on
you,'' Benny chuckled.

Joe leaned forward slightly. ''I'll be frank with you,
Mr. Pierce. There is some rumbling from certain seg-
ments of the Pueblo about our proposed lease of this
land. Traditional elements who feel we're losing sight
of our own history and culture, and becoming white
men.''

Franklin opened his mouth, then shut it again at an
urgent gesture from Benny.

The old man went on, ''I think that this project will
probably be approved by the village, and our request
sent on to the Secretary of the Interior, but remember
that that approval can be withdrawn at any time prior
to the signing of the lease agreement.''

''Can you prevent that? 'Cause I'm sure as hell not
going to go to all this trouble just to get fucked at the
last minute.''

''I think I can outargue the Summer chief, Ralph
Quintana, but I need some answers so I can formulate
those arguments and reassure our more conservative
people.''

''Ask away.''

"You've pitched this equestrian center as a way to provide jobs for Indian workers," said Joe.

"Well, yeah—"

"Just what kind of jobs did you have in mind?" Ernesto asked sharply.

Pierce opened and closed his mouth several times, reminding Joe of a large bass he'd caught at Fenton Lake just last month.

"I thought so. We're talking about shoveling horse-shit, aren't we?" the old man said grimly.

Franklin muttered about unskilled labor and minimum-wage glut, then rumbled into silence.

"Sorry to be so aggressive, but this is the kind of thing we're going to face from Ralph Quintana."

"He's also got his own slate of secular officials he'd like to get on the ballot next election and kick my butt out," Ernesto added. "So this goes deeper than just your center, and we've got to have the answers."

"So what do you want? Lay out your cards, and let's deal."

"We want you to guarantee that the bulk of the construction crews will be drawn from this Pueblo, and that you start some kind of training program so our people can stop driving shovels and learn some skills," the chief said.

"Sounds fair. You got any problems with that, Benny?"

"No."

"I'll even talk with Silvestre C. deBaca about riding lessons for interested kids. A world-class Indian rider, that would sure make those mongoloids on the USET sit up and take notice." Pierce's big laugh boomed out, and he slapped at one fat thigh.

"What else can you offer us?" asked Sena.

"Management training for running a center like this," offered Benny. "Jump-course design. Apprenticing to veterinarians and farriers. And I'm sure we can think of more opportunities."

"That will do for now. All of this should be included in the lease agreement, and that will take negotiation."

"Shit, you did learn some nasty habits in Hollywood. *Negotiation!*" Franklin snorted.

"Yes, I also learned about lawyers, and how useful they are."

"Damn, you don't miss a trick. Well, you send your shysters, and I'll gather mine, and they can beat each other to death with verbiage. But meantime you'll get things moving with the Secretary?"

"Yes."

"How soon do you think we can break ground?"

Ernesto and Joe exchanged glances. "This is Washington we're talking about here. Perhaps by the end of October, if things move quickly."

"Hell! And then we hit winter and can't do a damn thing. Well, I better get one barn up or there'll be hell to pay."

"Why?" asked Benny.

"That trainer. She's gonna arrive any day, and I promised her a place to stow her horse." Franklin heaved out of his chair. "Now, don't you let me forget to attend to that, Benny." He waggled a sausage-size finger beneath the young Indian's nose. "Ernesto, I want to thank you for your hospitality, and you be sure to tell your wife she's one hell of a cook." His broad, gum-revealing grin encompassed all the men. "What a tale. Came to powwow with the redskins, and emerged with a whole skin."

"For now." Joe's black eyes twinkled. "Wait until our lawyers start flaying you."

Hands were shaken all around, and Benny and Franklin headed out to the Lincoln.

"That went well, Franklin. They like you."

"Shit, boy, everybody likes me."

He paused by the door of the car, shaded his eyes, and peered off toward the towering bulk of the Pueblo proper. The sun glinting off the adobe gave it a golden sheen, and he understood why Cortez thought he had found the fabled Cities of Gold.

"How come your uncle lives away over here in this here split-level ranch house?" he asked Benny.

"We're progressives. He got tired of climbing ladders, and Minnie got tired of carrying water cans on her head.''

They jounced down the dirt road pursued by the pack of barking dogs. A stand of cottonwoods partly obscured the view of the Pueblo, but it was still a very pretty sight. The remaining three-story section loomed like a monolith over its single-level brethren.

''It's not as impressive as Taos,'' Franklin noted.

''We know. We hear that all the time. One of the few Pueblos left with a multilevel dwelling, and all we hear is 'it's not as nice as Taos.' Causes a lot of rivalry, let me tell you.''

''Well, look at it this way. They ain't gonna have no world-class equestrian center.''

Benny took his gaze from the road and eyed his companion. ''Why is it, Franklin, that when you are at your most smug and self-satisfied, you lose command of the English language and sound like an ignorant shit-kicker?''

The big red face became even redder as Pierce vibrated with suppressed chuckles. ''Why, shit, boy, you know the answer to that. I got my start in shit.''

6

Seven days, seven hideous days to drive across the country. A near-gang-rape in Tulsa, a broken axle in Amarillo, a traffic ticket for a broken taillight outside of Tucumcari. So far the West was not treating her kindly. Mona glanced down at the scrawled map that lay beside her on the seat. It was almost too dark to discern the lines, and none of these unfamiliar Spanish names seemed to correspond to anything around her. Santa Fe was a glowing blob to the south and west of her, the mountains a dark blue looming presence ahead. The sun broke through a line of purple clouds and threw one last fitful golden stream across the high desert before plunging behind the distant rim of mountains to the west.

That last fire touched on a plume of dust traveling roughly parallel with her, but instead of having a reassuring effect, this sign of another human presence in the vast emptiness brought tears to her eyes.

Mona drove past an elaborate electronic gate complete with spotlights and a guardhouse, and wondered *what* or *who* on earth lived behind those forbidding walls. The momentary flash of curiosity allowed her to regain control of her emotions. She wiped her sleeve across her face. She might be forced to present Franklin Pierce with a dirty face, but she was damned if she was going to show him a tearstained one.

Somewhere around here there was supposed to be a big boulder with a piñon growing in its lee. She spotted it, and slowed to a near-crawl in order to swing her rig down the narrow, rutted dirt road. Little better than a cow path, it made the rough dirt road she had just left seem like a superhighway.

Mona tried to tell herself that these deep ruts and potholes had been dug by large trucks passing to and fro to build the center. And didn't believe it for a second. So she wasn't terribly surprised when an expanse of weeds and dirt met her tired gaze. No barn, no fences, not even a shed. Surprised, no . . . heartbroken, yes. Her spine slumped as if it had been snapped, and she rested her forehead on the top of the steering wheel.

A shadowy figure pushed off from a parked car. She had missed the silver-gray Porsche in the twilight. Mona tensed. With her elbow she pressed down the lock, and laid a hand on her Beretta.

"Good evening."

Gaping like a fool, she cranked down the window and stared incredulously into the narrow face of Silvestre C. deBaca, one of the premier riders of the eighties. She had watched him at a party in London one night. Watched, and later dreamed of him, and had felt an agony of guilt. A woman who had Terry Gallagher had no business allowing the intrusion of another man—even into her dreams.

"Mr. C. deBaca."

"Silvestre, please, since we're going to be working together." His smiled seemed to gleam in the twilight.

"Working?" she parroted, then with greater strength repeated, "Working? Where? And at what? Where's the barn I was promised? And where's Mr. Pierce?"

"Down in Hobbs solving a labor dispute. He deputized me to meet you and explain what's been going on."

"Obviously not very much."

He laughed, the clear sound echoing in the desert night. "You surprise me. I thought you were too shy to say boo."

"Normally I am," she replied, incurably honest. "But I'm very tired, and very hungry, and I've been on the road for seven days, and I'm feeling rather abused and as if I've been lied to."

"Now, that would hurt Franklin. He's certainly an old horse trader, but fair dealing is his god."

"Then why was I promised a barn, and there is no barn?"

"Why don't you hop down from the truck, take a stretch, and I'll explain everything."

She popped the lock and pushed at the door. It released with a shrieking moan, and Favory let out a loud whinny. "Not yet, baby. Just a little longer," she called.

C. deBaca held up a hand, and she laid hers into it. Though she wanted to deny it, that strong support was welcome as she slid from the cab to the ground. He led her away, and his arm swept in an arc to the north and west.

"We'll have a beautiful view when it's all finished."

"Yes."

"You sound bemused. Don't. You'll learn before you've been in Santa Fe more than a month that a view is something over which court battles are fought."

"Is there a point to this?"

"Actually, yes. You see, much of Santa Fe is a myth. The ambience, the life-style, the charm—all myth. But myth or not, people will fight like badgers to preserve this vision. Over there"—he jerked a thumb over his shoulder—"is Rancho de Palabra, the most exclusive residential area in Santa Fe. Captains of industry, and movie moguls, and Hollywood stars have homes over there—"

"The big gates!"

"Yes, that's it. And over there"—this time his arm pointed north to a distant spot of light—"is San Jose Pueblo. There are no captains of industry or movie moguls or Hollywood stars there. Just six hundred or so Pueblo Indians who own the land we're standing on."

Silvestre continued, "Franklin is planning to lease this land to build his center, but nothing moves quickly when you're dealing with the federal bureaucracy, and without that bureaucracy's approval we can't put up a barn. Also, the residents of Rancho de Palabra are gearing up to wage war. There have been shrill editorials in the daily *Dispatch* decrying this rape of the environment, and it seems likely that these people are going to carry the fight to the Secretary of the Interior. For all I know, one of them may *own* the Secretary of the Interior. So before Franklin goes blindly rushing in, he's testing the water and getting a lay of the land—''

"Which must be difficult to do in one and the same spot." Mona dusted off a small rock and seated herself.

"Beg pardon?" He hunkered down next to her.

"You're mixing your metaphors."

"Oh." They stared at each other in silence for a few moments. "Anyway, Franklin's going slow, so nothing is built, so that's why I was sent to meet you and bring you up-to-date on the situation."

"Mr. C.—"

"Silvestre."

"Silvestre, I was promised a house too. Has that also fallen through?"

"No, I can take you to the house."

"And does it have someplace where I can stash Favory?"

"No, but I do. My parents' house has a large stable where we keep a few riding horses. There's plenty of room, and you can leave your horse for as long as you like."

She rose, brisk and energetic now that she had something affirmative to do. "That should be satisfactory for tonight. Then I'll have to see your board schedule to see if there's someplace more—"

"What are you running on about? Board? There won't be any board. You'll stay as my guest."

Her oval face tightened. "No, Mr. . . . Silvestre. I pay my own way. I'm not a charity case."

He stared down at her, exasperated. "I'm not implying you are. I'm simply trying to show hospitality to a fellow professional."

She pressed a hand to her forehead, and he noticed how tiny her wrists were. "I'm sorry, I'm not trying to offend you, and I'm trying not to become offended. I just have a horror of owing people favors.''

''Look, this can wait. You're tired and hungry. Your horse is tired and hungry. Accept my offer for one night, and we can renegotiate in the morning.''

She gave a little half-laugh. ''Sounds fair. Now, how do I get to your parents' house?''

''Follow me.''

She followed the lurching taillights of the Porsche back down the rutted track, past the guarded gate, back to the blacktop road, and once more north toward the looming mountains. Down a gravel drive, through wrought-iron gates set in the midst of a seemingly endless and very high adobe wall. Mona only had an impression of the house—mud, like everything else in this strange city—low and sprawling, and ablaze with lights.

The Porsche continued to the left and went behind the house. Nestled at the foot of a hill was the stable. It, too, was built of mud, with a red-tiled roof. The white rails of an arena glimmered in the half-light.

Silvestre climbed stiffly from the sports car and hurried into the barn. Favory was bellowing and the horses in the stable were answering. The back door of the house was opened, and a curious face poked out. Mona blushed with embarrassment, and busied herself with the latch on the trailer door. The thud of nervous hooves muffled by the deep bedding of sawdust filled the air as Favory shifted from foot to foot. But he was a gentleman, and stayed close up to the feeder. Darting forward, Mona swung open the escape hatch and unclipped him. Then, hurrying to the rear of the rig, she held his tail to give him confidence. He lurched down the long step to the ground, shook himself, and blew softly into the palm of her hand. There was a faint mist about his muzzle, and Mona realized that she was cold.

Silvestre beckoned from the doorway, and she led Favory into the warm, fragrant interior. A tiny golden palomino pony regarded the big hunter with disapprobation and curled back his upper lip in the "you-stink" expression.

"Be careful, little monster. He could eat you for breakfast," Mona laughed.

"He is the most awful little cretin. My nieces and nephews ride him, but about once a week I have to get on him, just to get his head right."

Laughter bubbled up. "The image of you bouncing along on this tiny pony."

"Actually, I like to ride ponies. Makes me feel like Sancho Panza as we go trotting along." The small Spaniard stepped back and critically appraised the big thoroughbred. "But this big fellow is very nice. Long sloping shoulders, good powerful loin."

He slapped the horse on his round, heavily muscled butt, and Mona led him into a stall. Several bags of sawdust had been dumped over the concrete and rubber mat that formed the floor, the water bucket had been filled, a hay net hung with hay, and a handful of sweet-feed liberally laced with bran lay in the bottom of the feeder.

"I figured he might need a little laxative after so many hours in a trailer," Silvestre explained, leaning on the wooden door.

"That's fine. In fact, I include bran at every feeding."

"I never saw you ride this horse, did I?"

"No. Favory got me to the world-class level, but he wasn't quite good enough to compete there. Besides, there's no money in riding your own horses."

"Favory?"

"Favory Capriola, actually." Color washed into her cheeks, and she bit down on her lower lip.

"I'm not going to laugh."

"Everybody usually does. I was fifteen when he was born, and had just seen the *Legend of the White Horses*. You remember that?"

"Very well."

"So I had Lipizzaner on the brain, and here came Favory, who was going to turn out to be a gray." She

twisted her hand into the short three inches that remained of his mane after her careful pulling.

"Don't regret something you did in the enthusiasm
of youth. I sometimes think what we do then is stronger
and more honest than what follows in the rest of our
lives."

"That's a very bitter thing to say." She stepped out
of the stall and looked up at him. "Is that because of
what happened in Paris?"

"No, I have no right to be bitter about that. I know
who was at fault." His boot heels were loud on the
brick floor as he left the barn.

Mona rushed after him. "I'm sorry, that was a truly
thoughtless, nosy thing for me to say. I had no right."

"It happened. I'd respect you less if you had ignored it." He walked a few steps, and paused, staring
at the glow of moonrise just washing the tops of the
mountains.

Mona jammed her hands into her pockets and
scuffed at the dirt. "I've always admired you tremen-
dously."

He turned back, his teeth white in his face as he
grinned. "Thank you."

"Are you . . . ? I mean, will you . . . ?"

"No, I won't ride again. That's why I'm working for
Franklin. But why are you leaving the circuit?"

"Personal reasons," she said firmly and unencour-
agingly.

"I see. May I buy you dinner?"

"That's not necessary. If you'll just show me where
my house is, I can buy a few groceries and—"

"Don't be silly."

She bristled slightly.

"Let me amend that. Don't push yourself so hard.
You've been on the road for hours. Let someone else
worry about cooking and washing the dishes."

Her mouth twisted comically. "I hadn't even thought
about that. Besides, my dishes are packed in a box in
the back of the truck. All right, why not?"

"Just let me nip into the house, and tell them I won't
be eating at home, and alert them to a new horse.

There's no reason for you to come in," he added and she visibly relaxed. "Why don't you pull the trailer in beside the barn and leave it? No sense hauling it around Santa Fe."

By the time he returned she had the rig unhitched. "Look, there's a saying that the streets of Santa Fe were laid out by a drunken monk riding on a drunken donkey on a moonless night. Why don't you ride with me, and we'll come back after the truck."

"All right."

The Porsche's computerized dashboard looked like an instrument panel for the Space Shuttle. The smell of leather filled Mona's nostrils as she settled into the deep bucket seat. She wondered just how much this car had cost. Silvestre C. deBaca was obviously not one of those riders who had come up the hard way. Maybe it wouldn't be so awful if she didn't pay any board—

She nipped off the thought like a careful gardener pulling a particularly noxious weed.

"I've made a decision," Silvestre announced suddenly.

She laughed, a bit startled by his intensity. "Okay."

"You're a gringa, and you're tired, so no Mexican food."

"I've had Mexican food."

"Where?"

"In California."

"Then you have *not* had Mexican food. You've had corn tortillas covered with tomato sauce and catsup. Trust me."

"I suppose I have no choice." They were whipping down a busy six-lane road. A green sign flashed by, ST. FRANCIS DRIVE. "We're moving too fast for me to jump. So what are we going to eat?"

"I'll take you to the Bull Ring. That will also allow me to give you a quick tour of Santa Fe."

They were crossing a multiple-light intersection. In the center was a large yellow sign with an ear, and the red circle and line mark across it.

"What on earth?" asked Mona.

"The school for the deaf is on that corner." Silvestre indicated a number of large yellow-brick buildings. "That quaint picture is how one communicates that fact to illiterates."

"Oh, I see."

"Off to our left is the downtown area of Santa Fe. The Plaza, and all the shops. We'll take a turn through here after dinner. Ahead of us is the government district. The Merry Round House."

"Beg pardon?"

"Our state capitol is a big round brick building, and since New Mexico politics are filled with so many fools and buffoons, it's become known as the Merry Round House." He spun the wheel, and they turned right up a narrow winding road. "This is Canyon Road. It's filled with quaint and expensive little shops and galleries, but it's well worth a walking tour. You can do all your Christmas shopping here and on the Plaza. Since it's a one-way street we'll have to do some interesting maneuvers to get back to the restaurant, but better you should learn now that there is no logic to our roads."

They were passing through a residential area. Most of the houses were hidden behind thick adobe walls or behind fences constructed of rough tree limbs. The bark still remained on these bundled sticks, giving them a gray-silver sheen. It seemed a very odd way to construct a fence.

They shot down another street, and took a quick left. "Down there is the Plaza." Mona peered, but there wasn't much to see. "And now we're driving past the Cathedral."

A big gray-stone building loomed up on their left, the double bell towers thrust like spears against the night sky. "Interesting bit of trivia, there's a Hebrew character set in a triangle on the keystone of the arch above the main doors. The character means God, and the triangle indicates the Trinity. A number of charming stories have arisen about this symbol. Back when the Cathedral was built, some Jewish businessmen lent money to the archdiocese to pay for the construction.

And later, quite a few of the loans were canceled, so some say that the Hebrew character went up as a thank-you to these men. How am I doing as a tour guide?''

"Very well, but my head's in a whirl.''

Up yet another winding street, and past a small chapel. It seemed to be cringing away from the large modern adobe hotel that loomed beside it.

"Another interesting, touristy place to visit. The Miraculous Stairway.''

"And is it?''

"What? Miraculous or a stairway?''

"Miraculous, of course.''

"I guess so. At any rate it's a great story, and a very pretty chapel. You should see it.''

"All right. So what's the story?''

"Oh, that the nuns had no way to reach their choir loft except by a rickety ladder, so they prayed to St. Joseph, and lo and behold, an itinerant carpenter arrived and built them a spiral staircase to the loft without benefit of nail or support. It's supposed to be a miracle that it stands at all. And of course the man vanished after completing the work, and without accepting payment.''

"You do seem to have a lot of miracles.''

"This is a magical land. Kachinas, skinwalkers, saints, and demons all walk here.''

Sil spun the wheel, and they drove down a tiny alley into a back parking lot. "And here we are. The Bull Ring. The bar is the main watering hole when the legislature's in session. It's one of our chief winter amusements to hang out and watch our state senators and representatives get drunk and try to pick up women. Which takes us from the miraculous to the absurd.''

"Oh." She sounded so dubious that he laughed as he held the car door for her.

"Don't worry. The particular form of madness doesn't start until January, so we're safe.''

They made their way to the front door, and Mona recoiled at the sight of a superior maître d' impeccably attired in a tuxedo.

"If you'll follow me, Mr. C. deBaca.''

"I think I'm a little underdressed," Mona said in an undertone as they walked into the dining room.

"Nonsense. All you need is ten pounds of turquoise jewelry and you will have achieved Santa Fe chic."

As she took her seat, Mona had to admit the truth in what Silvestre had said. Attire ranged from expensive knit suits to crushed peasant skirts to blue jeans.

"Enjoy your meal, Mr. C." The languid young maître d' smirked a bit and pranced away.

"You must be a regular."

"No, but I do think I've made a hit," Silvestre replied a little sourly. "Of course, it could be that my father is a big tipper. He lunches here three or four times a week, and maybe his glory and manna are spilling over onto his undeserving children."

"You sound half-serious."

"I suppose I am." He slid onto the low cushioned adobe bench, shook out his napkin, and regarded the white square of linen fixedly. "Jorge's a real chip off the old block. God knows he looks like he was chiseled off the old man, but my sister's . . . unusual, and I'm . . ."

"What?" she asked softly.

The golden-brown eyes raised to hers were filled with pain. "A failure."

For a long moment their eyes held. Then the arrival of a waiter offered an escape. Mona snatched the enormous leather-bound menu from his hands and immersed herself in a bewildering array of dishes. Later she stole a glance at Silvestre, but he was still buried behind the menu. Perhaps he was as disturbed as she.

Emotions were such slippery, treacherous things, and good manners dictated that a person keep them well-concealed. Silvestre had violated that tenet of her upbringing, but though it made her uncomfortable, she felt an undeniable pull to the man. Dining tête-à-tête with her hero, her idol. A man she had even dared to fantasize about. As a not very good substitute for Terry in the flesh.

To love and be wise.

Perhaps it was impossible.

"Mona. Mona?"

"What?"

"I've been calling you for about three minutes."

"Oh, come now."

"Well, one minute."

"Well, I'm back now. What was the question?"

"It's about Franklin Pierce. I just wondered when and how you got drawn into all this madness."

"Is that how you'd describe the center?"

"Yes."

"Then why work on it?"

"You first, then me."

Mona twirled her water glass. "I knew Denise Pierce on the circuit, not well, of course—she was a few years older. But it hit hard when she was killed by that drunk driver."

"Yeah, Franklin almost lost his mind. Did you know he put the driver in the hospital?"

"What?"

"Yeah, really. Since the kid was only seventeen, he couldn't be punished like an adult, and his daddy had plenty of bucks, so he didn't even spend one night in jail. Franklin found the boy and beat the holy crap out of him. The lawsuits are still pending in both directions."

"Good heavens! It's been three years."

"Franklin has a long, long memory. You'd do well to remember that."

"You sound like you don't like him."

"I do and I don't. He's a disturbing contradiction. Warm, kind, and generous one minute, and a crude redneck the next. After a month of working with him, I'm getting to the point where I answer to 'beaner' and 'greaser' and 'chili belly.' "

"Silvestre! How terrible. Why do you put up with it?"

"Because at heart I don't think he really means it. You know how some people use profanity so often that it just becomes sounds? Well, that's Franklin, only with racial slurs. Benny gets off a lot easier than I do because Franklin can't think of any really scurrilous and bigoted phrases for Indians.''

"Benny?"

"Benny Aragon. He's the young Indian who's wedded his dream to Franklin's.''

"And his dream is?''

"A better standard of living for his Pueblo. Jobs for the young men.''

The waiter arrived, and they placed their orders. Sil spent a few moments discussing various wines, and when he looked back at Mona she was again frowning down at the tablecloth.

"What's wrong now?''

"I'm sorry. I don't mean to be so gloomy." She began to chatter brightly about the trout amandine they had both ordered. Silvestre reached across and caught her hand. She stared, panicked at the long slender fingers wrapped firmly about hers. Her skin was very white against his.

"Mona, don't. Don't make bright cocktail conversation with me. We're going to be working together.''

"But does that necessarily make us friends?''

He drew back his hand.

"I'm sorry. That wasn't meant to be as harsh as it sounded. I suppose I'm just tired, and a little peeved with Mr. Pierce that he didn't tell me about the delay with the center. What am I supposed to do now?''

"Sit back and wait for us to get a few buildings up.''

"And live on what?''

"Franklin will pay your salary.''

"I can't take money I haven't earned.''

"Mona, putting up with Franklin is job enough.''

"Don't try to jolly me, Silvestre. I'm serious.''

He fell back in his chair and regarded her in exasperation. "You're the oddest girl. Can't you just settle back and enjoy an unexpected vacation? New Mexico in the autumn is at its peak.''

"You men! You always assume that a woman will be just delighted to sit back and do her nails, watch the soaps, and read romances. Well, I *like* to work.''

"It's highly overrated.''

"What?" she cried.

"Work!" It took her off guard, and that sweet delicate smile peeped out again. "You have the most beautiful smile," Sil said impulsively. "Like a Madonna."

"Please." Embarrassed, she glanced away. "Well, since I won't be working for a few weeks, tell me what New Mexico has to offer. What I should see."

Eagerly he began outlining a sightseeing tour that sounded as if it would take until April to accomplish. Through it all Mona smiled, and ate, and nodded, and thought how much his ingenuous conversation reminded her of Terry. Her husband loved to talk, and it was relaxing to be with a man who didn't throw the entire conversational burden upon the woman's shoulders. Suddenly Silvestre laughed and pushed aside his dessert plate.

"You look like a drowsy kitten. Your eyes are wide, trying to deny how tired you are, but you have this stunned, somnolent expression."

"That's not very nice."

"Come on, I'll take you home."

"Home." She savored the word, then sighed. "Except it doesn't feel very much like going home. It's a strange house, and I'll be all alone in it."

Their eyes met and held. Hers broke under his intense gaze, and fluttered down to stare at the floor. Sil stared down at the top of her head. The sable-brown hair sweeping back from that incredible widow's peak, brushing softly at her cheeks, cascading to her shoulders. He allowed his eyes to slide down until his gaze rested on her hips flaring softly in the faded jeans and the taut curve of her buttocks. There was an answering tautness in his groin, and he swallowed hard several times.

He took her hand as they walked out of the restaurant. There was no encouraging pressure, but she didn't pull away either. They didn't talk during the walk to the car, or the winding drive back to the small rented house resting on its piñon-and-rock-covered hillside.

Silvestre handed Mona the keys and allowed her to open the door to her new home. Franklin had done a good job, or rather he had hired people who had done a good job. A chocolate-brown sectional sofa curved about the kiva fireplace. There was a carved oak table in the dining nook, a bay window, and a view of the now invisible mountains. Mexican rugs were thrown onto the adobe window seats, and a sheepskin rug rested before the fireplace.

The master bedroom held a gaily painted armoire and a king-size four-poster bed. Sil eyed the bed, and drew his thumbnail thoughtfully across his lower lip. His groin stirred. It was a good feeling. For four months after the accident he had been too ill and in too much pain to coax any sexual reaction from his body. Then depression and cocaine had sapped him. Now finally he was coming back to life.

How had he missed Mona on the circuit? he wondered as he watched her explore the room. Lithe, strong body. Brown hair, brown eyes. She wasn't flashy, not like the groupies who routinely followed the riders—rich and beautiful because the rich could afford to be beautiful. But she had a genuine glow. And then there were those absurdly straight brows, which gave her a frowning intensity. Sil pictured the two of them naked together, rolling in that big bed, and his mouth went dry.

Mona lightly touched the top of a pillow, and suddenly realized what she had done. So how to emerge from this sexual morass gracefully? It couldn't be done. The best she could hope for was total alienation. An enemy where she could have had a chance for a friend. She gritted her teeth, turned to face him, and held out her hand in a stiff dismissive gesture.

"Well, thank you for dinner, Silvestre. I'm afraid I'm going to have to be rude and throw you out now. I have to drive down to Albuquerque tomorrow to pick up my husband."

His glance flew to her hand. "You don't wear a ring." It emerged as an accusation.

"No, not when I'm handling horses. It's too dangerous. You know that."

"I'm surprised you didn't mention him earlier."

"I should have." It was as close as she would come to an apology. She hoped he understood.

They reached the front door.

"Oh, Jesus, my truck . . . it's still at your house."

"Not to worry," he forced out brightly. "I'll bring it to you in the morning, and you can drop me off back at home or at my father's office, where I can hitch a ride home."

"Thank you again, Silvestre."

"Good night, Mrs. Gallagher, I'm glad I could rescue you and Favory. Until tomorrow."

"Wait." She ran after him. "My keys, you'll need those to bring the truck."

"Oh, yeah, yeah." She could sense that he was desperate to be away from her. She felt the same. And she had managed to drag out this painful and embarrassing parting.

He took the keys and stalked back to the Porsche. Mona slunk into the house and closed the door.

Estúpido!

Sil rested his forehead against the steering wheel and cringed as he considered what she must think of him. Groaning and clucking like an oversexed duck. Shit! Christ, she'd get a good laugh at his expense tonight.

Well, soon he would be home, and he could lose his disappointment, anger, and embarrassment in the white-hot fire of the drug's power. Forget at least briefly what a dick he had been. Would she ever forgive him?

7

Would he ever forgive her?

Mona dropped her face into her hands, nails digging deep into her scalp. Then she threw back her hair, a violent gesture that expressed all the self-loathing she was feeling.

She could have mentioned Terry much earlier to defuse her and Sil's very real sexual attraction. But she had waited, and now he was angry. And who could blame him? Call him and apologize? Impossible. They were going to have to work together. Had she also made that impossible?

A shiver ran through her, and Mona realized that the house was very cold. Straightening, she set aside her guilt like a woman shaking dust from a mop. Efficiently she went hunting for the thermostat, and while she searched she took a closer and more critical look at the fifteen hundred square feet that were to be her home. *Hers and Terry's. Hers and Terry's and the baby's.* She critically studied the small guest bedroom, considering its distance from the master. How clearly would sound carry? Enough to alert her. Not enough to disturb Terry. Good.

Back in the living room, she sat in one of the window seats and regarded the twisted shadows of the piñon trees. *Would Terry like this house? This place?* He'd spent his adult life in large metropolitan areas— New York, Los Angeles, San Francisco—what would he make of this tiny city? Mona knew from reading various travel magazines that Santa Fe (the City Different) was considered quaintly charming, with its adobe architecture and three cultures. Terry, however, might think otherwise. He had a wicked and acerbic tongue, and she could just image his description of the city. Some comparison to the Sumerian underworld, no doubt. Souls of the dead eating mud in a city made of mud.

Agitated, she sprang to her feet. Was this a mistake? Had she been thinking more of herself and her aching need for a child than of her husband? Pierce's salary was generous, but it would not match what she had earned on the circuit. And Terry was extravagant. She so hated having to play the exchequer. Lecturing him on his spending.

The shrill cry of a dog pack cut the night. Mona jumped, her stomach fluttering with fear, and ran to the window. The spill of yellow light illuminated a hellish scene. A kitten, eyes wide with terror, being tumbled by five pursuing dogs. Screaming with fury, Mona raced out the front door and into the milling pack. The kitten gave a scream of agony as a dog's jaws closed about its front leg. Mona kicked out, her toe hitting the mongrel in the chest and flipping it backward. Startled by this unexpected assault, it released the cat, and Mona scooped him up and thrust him inside her shirt. Claws raked at her soft skin, but she hardly noticed, for she was locked in combat with the circling dogs.

One of them leapt, jaws closing about her ankle, but her high-top tennis shoes took the worst of the bite. She snatched up a large rock and pitched it. There was a satisfying *thwap* as it smashed into the dog's mangy side. Yelping, it jumped away, and she backed for the door, slipped through, and freed the kitten, who still had a frenzied grip on her flesh.

Like most farm-raised children, Mona had a horror of roving dog packs, and if the Beretta had been handy she would have cheerfully shot them all. Her breathing slowed, and she regarded the tiny, bony creature she had rescued: jet black with emerald-green eyes, a torn ear that gave him a pugnacious look, and the mangled front leg. Carrying him into the bathroom, she washed the leg, and decided that it looked worse than it was. No bones appeared to be broken. She searched for a first-aid kit, but that seemed to have been overlooked, so she settled for soap and water on her own claw marks and hoped this feisty stray was not carrying any really horrible diseases.

Fortunately he was not feral. He seemed to sense he had found a friend. When she carried him in to bed, he curled up against the bare skin of her stomach, purred for a few minutes, and fell into exhausted sleep. Mona touched him gently.

"At least I did something right tonight," she whispered thickly.

Then she realized that placing such emotional significance on one battered stray cat was stupid. *Sleep,* she ordered, and tense muscles slowly began to relax. Everything was heightened tonight. Even the rub of the sheet across her breasts was drawing a response from her nipples and groin.

"Tomorrow," she whispered, and the cat let out a sleepy chirp. "Tomorrow Terry will be here."

"Well."

He had a funny little habit of wiggling his upper lip just before he laughed, and now the ginger-colored hairs of his mustache were dancing.

"It looks rather like broken brown teeth protruding from dun-colored gums." Terry Gallagher chuckled.

Mona's hands tightened on the wheel of the truck, but the laughter wasn't disguising anger. He did seem genuinely amused.

"That was a pretty good metaphor, wasn't it?" he asked.

"Yes."

Mona wasn't a great reader, so Terry's discussions of his novel—whether to use a flashback to indicate Granger's turmoil, if he could get away with three points of view in the party scene—left her feeling stupid and inadequate. He was really having discussions with himself, and she was just there as a Greek chorus (*that* she had absorbed from him) to supply the exclamations.

"Pity the book's set in Paris and I can't use it."

"Maybe you could do some articles for *New Mexico* magazine." She fumbled beneath the Albuquerque city map and pulled out the glossy magazine. This month's cover was a photographic still life of three Indian pots and a bundle of multicolored Indian corn, all resting on a Navajo blanket. "I bought one for you. The man at the bookstore said it's a very prestigious magazine, and they're often looking for articles." She turned her attention briefly from the dark ribbon of road unrolling before her, and smiled at him.

Their hands met as he accepted the magazine, and from his widening smile she knew he had sensed the physical storm rising within her. He was leaning nonchalantly against the door of the truck, an elbow propped on the open window. The breeze ruffled his heavy brown hair, throwing a tangled forelock across his high forehead. Suddenly she reached out and lightly touched the deep cleft in his chin.

His thin white linen shirt was open at the neck, revealing a tangled mat of dark hair, and he had rolled back his sleeves to the elbows. Mona had this thing about forearms. There was something unbelievably sexy about watching the play of tendons and muscles beneath the skin of a man's arm. Terry grinned and pushed back the sleeves a little farther. Mona stifled a giggle.

She jerked her attention back to the road, realizing she had almost missed the turn. They went rattling up the long hill, and finally Mona spoke, with a small jump in her voice. "Well, here it is. Home."

Terry eyed the little house. "Oh, my." His brows arched comically toward his hairline.

"It's quite charming inside, really. And I think you'll like—"

"Sweetheart." He caught her flying hand. "Am I such a terrible, crabby old husband that you have to be this nervous around me?"

"I've asked you to make such a big change, and I

want you to be happy. Also . . .'' She cleared her throat. "There's something I have to tell you, and I've been putting it off.''

"Is it unpleasant?''

"Yes.'' The truck jerked to a halt before the front door.

"Then please,'' Terry said as he swung down from the cab, "keep putting it off.'' He fished two suitcases from the back of the truck and strode toward the door.

Mona, staggering after with two more, called, "This is not something that can be joked away, Terry. We have to talk.''

"Key.''

"Huh?''

"Key,'' he repeated patiently. She dropped the ring onto his outstretched palm, and he opened the door. Stepped in, dumped the suitcases, eyed the curving living room. Smiled. "Charming. Absolutely charming.'' He walked to the small Santo in its wall niche and lifted down the hand-hewn wooden statue. Whichever saint he represented had obviously come to a bad end, for he was drenched in blood, and the square primitive face was twisted in agony. "And what's this little horror?''

"A Santo. Silvestre''—her throat closed momentarily—"says they're religious figures.''

"Could have fooled me.''

He replaced the little saint and paced to a bay window. "Beautiful view. Almost makes me want to pull out my easel rather than the lap-top. Fortunately, the easel's being shipped, and the lap-top's already here, so I'll be a good boy and work on the novel.''

"Terry, there's trouble with the equestrian center,'' she blurted.

"Oh, what kind?'' He continued to roam.

"Apparently some people don't want it built, and Mr. Pierce doesn't really own the land.'' She trailed after him, the words beginning to trip over each other in her haste to get it all out. "He's trying to lease it from this Indian tribe—''

"Indians!'' He bounced experimentally on the bed.

"That's right, there are Indians out here. I'll have to get a look at them."

"This could end up delaying things for months, maybe even as long as a year."

That did catch his attention, and he paused in his scrutiny of the gaily painted Talavera tiles in the bathroom. "What are we going to do for money? Babs says that Phil is really interested in my script, but you know how long things take in Hollywood."

"Silvestre says that Mr. Pierce will keep paying me."

"Oh, well then."

"But I'm not comfortable with that, Terry. It feels like charity."

"Sweetheart," he threw back over his shoulder as he darted off to explore the second bedroom, "if you don't let him pay you, we really *will* be needing charity. What a great room. I'll put my desk in the bay window. That view ought to be inspirational."

Mona hung in the doorway. "I'd sort of planned on this room as the nursery."

"Well, we'll have to talk about that. I have to have a place to work." He gave her another encouraging buffet on the shoulder as he passed by.

She heard cabinet doors slamming as he examined the kitchen. "A gas stove!" he cried. "Bless your Mr. Pierce, he's a man of taste."

"Terry!" She placed herself in front of him, halting his busy perambulations. "If things go completely wrong, and the center doesn't get built, I won't have a job!"

"Don't worry. You can always go back to the circuit."

Mona spun and left the kitchen. The sound of pots crashing onto tile countertops pursued her down the hall.

"Hey, Mona love." He was grinning around the corner like a mischievous ten-year-old. "When you unpack my cases, you'll find a little something for you in one of them."

"Oh, Terry."

"How about an omelet for lunch?"

"Fine."

"You know, I think this is going to work out great."

"Thank you for picking me up. I hope it's not too much trouble. I usually don't ask for . . ."

There were tiny furrows between her brows, and her brown eyes seemed tired and faded. Sil felt an irrational surge of anger, and apparently it showed, for Mona took a slight step backward. Her fingers tightened on the edge of the front door, driving the blood from her nails. He smiled, trying to calm her.

"It's fine, my pleasure."

"You see," she continued, "my husband needs the truck. He's going down to Albuquerque to research. There just isn't an adequate library in Santa Fe."

Sil wondered why she was babbling like this. Was she still discomfited by what had almost happened between them? But they had seen each other several times since that disastrous evening, and maintained civilized facades. Proved that a disastrous beginning was not necessarily a permanent impediment to friendship. But something had left shadows in her eyes. Sil would have liked to remove the something.

Mona plunged out of the front door as if pursued.

"You should take a jacket."

"Huh?" She stared out at the brilliant sunshine drawing sparks from the mica chips in the driveway.

"It's deceptively warm today. The wind can get really nippy. It is October, you know."

"Yes," Mona agreed mournfully, and stepped back into the house. She hesitated for a moment, as if debating whether to leave him on the front stoop like an irksome magazine salesman, then invited him in with a curt nod of the head.

The smell of brewing coffee hung in the still air. The stereo was spilling Mozart across the room, and from the back bedroom Silvestre heard the distinctive hum of a computer. A man stepped out of the kitchen, coffee mug clutched in his hand, and a Jovian frown wrinkling his high forehead.

A pair of smoke-gray slacks, a silk sweater knotted by the sleeves around his neck, a pale blue shirt. He looked like an advertisement for *Gentlemen's Quarterly*. The only discordant note was set by his stocking feet shooshing softly across the brick floor. It seemed like excessive elegance for a man who was going to the library.

"Terry." Mona's voice was soft, tremulous. "This is Silvestre C. deBaca."

"Oh. How do you do? Moni's mentioned you."

Sil accepted the outstretched hand. Wondered if he and Terry Gallagher were going to play macho handshake games. But his hand was released after the briefest of pressure. Obviously whatever Mona had said, it hadn't aroused her husband's jealousy. Or his interest either. He was already heading back to the bedroom.

"I should be back by two." Mona glanced to Sil for confirmation. He nodded.

"Well, I can't say when I'll be back. I've got to get this chapter finished, and then there's that damned hour drive, and then I have to find this cow college that at least has the virtue of being a bigger cow college than the ones up here."

Gallagher's face had taken on a sulky, petulant expression. It was at odds with the deep baritone voice that caressed each complaint like a polished gem before laying it out before his unhappy wife.

Silvestre said quietly, "St. John's would resent that. They take intellectualism very seriously."

"Oh, them." A dismissive shrug. "I hate intellectual snobs."

Sil's lips twisted wryly, but he forced down his irritation with the man. Gave him the benefit of the doubt. He might not be seeing Terry at his best. He tried another overture.

"You might want to stop in at one of the public libraries for a joint-use card. Unless you're a student, you can't check books out of the UNM library."

"Oh, terrific! Well, add another hour to this little jaunt," he shot at Mona.

Sil forgot about trying to be friendly and helpful and

decided to add to the burdens that the world was obviously conspiring to lay on Gallagher's shoulders.

"Oh, one more thing."

"Yes." Terry bit off the word so hard that it must have left a taste between his perfect white teeth.

"The parking situation at UNM is really atrocious. My sister's a law student down there, and if you don't have a pass you'll be ticketed and towed. Guaranteed."

"So what do I do?"

"Try parking in the free lot and riding the bus onto campus." Sil paused to consider, head tipped slightly to one side. "Assuming of course there still is a free lot. I seem to remember something about them closing it. Well, I guess you'll just have to park on a street somewhere and walk."

"Thank you so very much."

"Glad to be of help." Broad smile.

Then he looked down into Mona's rigid face, and his enjoyment died. For he wasn't going to be the one who had to listen to Terry Gallagher's displeasure when he returned from Albuquerque. Sil checked his watch.

"We better go. The Rotaries wait on no one, not even their featured speakers, and Franklin will be pissed if we're late."

Mona slid to her husband and wrapped her arms fiercely about his shoulders. "Oh, God, I'm scared. I've never done anything like this before."

Terry gave her a long, lingering kiss, his hands sliding lightly across her hips. Sil looked away. "You'll do fine. See you tonight." Suddenly charm was washing off the man like the aroma of his expensive aftershave. He grinned at Silvestre. "Maybe *late* tonight after all the horror stories Mr. Baca has told me."

"It's C. deBaca."

"It makes a difference?"

"Oh, yes."

As they shot down St. Michael's Drive, Sil glanced at his silent companion. Mona's eyes were focused sightlessly on the road before them, and she chewed nervously at her lower lip.

"It won't be that bad, honestly."

"I just don't know why I have to be there."

"You're Franklin's trainer."

"With nothing to train."

"That's why Franklin's having us speak to the Rotary Club."

"Why? They can't do anything. Only the Secretary of the Interior can okay the lease."

"It doesn't hurt to have public opinion on your side."

"I should think it's almost impossible to know public opinion in this town. It's so hard to meet and get to know people."

"Oh?"

She shot him an aggressive glance. "Yes."

"Ter . . . Mr. Gallagher finding our little city too slow?"

"He had hoped I'd be able to introduce him around."

Silvestre turned partway around and stared at her incredulously. "How? You only arrived here a day before he did."

"Well, Mr. Pierce—"

"Had to go back to Hobbs and then to Washington so that we'll have a center."

Mona was looking slightly sick, and the hand that she raised to her forehead was trembling. "I'm not trying . . . I mean, I don't want to argue."

"I'm not angry."

She reached out, clasped his arm. "How do we meet people, Sil? Terry isn't like me. He needs people . . . interesting people around him. Part of the reason for coming here was the artistic . . ." She groped for a word.

"Scene? Atmosphere? Ambience? We're real big on ambience around here."

"You sound bitter."

"Mona, remember what I told you the first time we met? This city's a myth. Well, maybe not a myth, but

it certainly has two faces. There's the face that attracts
your husband, and gets written up in *The New Yorker,*
and then there are the real people who live in this
town.''

"Meaning *you,* I take it.''

"No. My family's the right ethnic group, but too
rich to really fit in. And by the standards of the beautiful people, we're the wrong race, and my father's a
businessman rather than an artist, so they don't particularly like us.''

"Are you saying we're bigoted?''

"Some people are. A sad-but-true fact of life. But
we're way off the subject,'' he continued as she
frowned down at her hands. "I don't know the artistic
community, but Franklin does—''

"Mr. Pierce?''

Sil gave a tight little smile. "He is very rich.''

"What made you so cynical?''

"Cynical?'' He rolled the word around in his mouth.
"I've never thought of myself as cynical.'' Her eyes
were on him, focused and intense, with no hint of the
shyness that usually afflicted her. " 'Alienated'?
Maybe that's a better, if somewhat pompous, description. Sometimes I don't feel like I fit in anywhere.''

"Why?''

"Because . . . You don't want to hear this.''

She didn't argue with him, making protestations of
heartfelt interest, and he respected her for it. Because
she wasn't interested. All of her attention was centered
on Gallagher: his loneliness, his alienation, his disappointment. Personally Sil thought a stint in basic
training would have had a very salutary effect on Mr.
Gallagher, but Mona's function in life was obviously
to protect and pander to Terry, and since Sil liked
Mona, he would see what he could do to help.

They pulled into the public parking lot on Water
Street and walked quickly down the block to the La
Fonda Hotel. One of Santa Fe's oldest, it squatted in
adobe splendor on one corner of the Plaza, and held
within its thick walls an international dress shop, a

French pastry shop, the requisite Indian arts shop, and an antique jewelry store.

The Rotary luncheon meeting was being held in an upstairs conference room. As the couple paced past the jewelry store, Silvestre saw Mona's eyes slid surreptitiously to the glittering displays, only to be yanked firmly and resolutely away. It struck him again, what an odd woman she was. What would it have hurt to have devoured the glittering beauty in those windows?

They took the stairs to the second floor, Mona looking sicker and whiter with each step. Sil gripped her by the elbow and drew her to a halt.

"You've never done any public speaking." She shook her head. "Okay, rather than have you lose your lunch—"

"I'm not going to eat."

"Well, so you can eat your lunch, and not lose it, how about I just introduce you, and talk about the exciting partnership that we're forming, and you can smile and nod and look beautiful."

"What if I don't agree with something you say?"

"Then you'll just have to pipe up and disagree with me, won't you?" He grinned.

"Thanks so much," came the ironic reply, but her color was better.

The ancient elevator opened and disgorged a knot of murmuring businessmen. Sil gave a start.

"What?" Mona asked.

"My father's here."

"Oh, Lord," she said.

"What's wrong?" Sil asked.

"I don't know. That makes it worse somehow."

"For whom? You or me?"

"Does he always come?"

"No, hardly ever."

"See?" She started into the room.

Sil plunged after. "See what?"

She made no reply.

"Does fear always make you irrational?" he demanded.

She pivoted slowly, and faced him with some dignity. "I'm fine on a horse."

He stood watching her vanish into the throng of businessmen, head up, searching for Franklin Pierce.

And I'm fine nowhere.

It was a very depressing thought. So depressing that he decided he couldn't face the next hour without a little help. He bolted for the john.

8

"I wish you hadn't done that," Nigel said softly.

The rattle of the sack and the thunder of the charcoal briquettes falling into the grill seemed to echo off the high adobe wall surrounding the backyard.

"Why?" Lexa asked aggressively. "It's my house too. One might argue *more*—" She folded her lips together, cutting off the words.

Nigel concentrated on carefully folding the empty sack in half, then into quarters, twisting it into a tight screw of paper, pacing across the patio, dropping it precisely into the center of the garbage can. By the time he turned to face his wife, his anger was under control.

She stared back, expressionless. In Lexa this *lack* of expression was an expression of guilt. It was also as close as she would come to an apology. It had taken him several years to accustom himself to this habit. With Rhea, "I'm sorry" came tripping easily and frequently off her tongue. For Lexa, the words would not be spoken, but the actions would change. After years of marriage Nigel realized that Lexa's way was preferable. It was so damn easy to murmur "I'm sorry." So much harder to make a change.

"Our annual autumn fete has always been a treat, but this year it's going to look like an armed camp, a nuclear-arms negotiation, a British soccer match," Nigel said quietly. "We're going to have Rhea and Stash and the rest of the beautiful people lined up on one side of the yard, and Benny and Silvestre and Pierce and these Gallagher people on the other."

"I'm not going to take the full blame for this," said Lexa. "I invited Benny because he's *my* friend, and I have that right. *You* invited C. deBaca because he's your friend. He's the one who brought in the Gallaghers."

"And Pierce? How did he get into this?"

"He invited himself."

"Terrific."

Lexa gave a gurgle of laughter. "Oh, I don't know. You sort of have to admire that kind of gall."

He smiled back at her. "No you don't. You deplore it, or are shocked by it, or irritated." He drew her arm through his and pinched at the slender, roughened fingertips. "Only if you're my wife are you amused. Need help mixing the sangria?"

"Yes."

It was a lie, but a nice one. It was her apology. And he accepted it.

The big cut-crystal punch bowl was awash with Chianti. Nigel poured in the orange and lemon juice, soda, brandy, and Cointreau while Lexa measured out the sugar. He then took another bag of ice back into the bathroom and dumped it over the cans of pop and bottles of Corona beer that lay cooling in the tub. He hated beer snobs almost as much as he hated wine snobs, and he had been sorely tempted to buy Coors or Budweiser for his guests. It had become just so chic to drink Mexican beer.

Back out to the patio with its split-pole riata and heavy grape vines forming a golden roof overhead. Nigel poured a splash of lighter fluid onto the coals, tossed a match, and padded back into the house to check on the food. Piles of carefully flattened hamburger patties, hot dogs, bratwurst, chicken, steaks. In the old days it had been BYOM (bring your own meat), BYOB, and he and Lexa had provided the side dishes and condiments. Now Lexa was a world-renowned archaeologist and curator, he was—slight shudder—a prosperous shopowner, and they provided it all. It had been more fun somehow when they were poor. Cheaper too.

The big picnic table beneath the riata had been covered with a cloth, and the plates, tableware, and side
dishes were arranged for easy serving. Around the yard
were dotted card tables set with bug-repellent candles,
and folding chairs.

Everything was ready, and New Mexico had obliged
with a spectacularly beautiful fall evening. Which was
not always the case. The Southwest's weather was un-
predictable. Some years it had been broiling on this
third weekend in October, and once he had been flipping hamburgers in the snow. This year the weather
would be perfect. Nigel wasn't so sure about the
guests.

There was the distant ring of the doorbell, heralding
the first arrival. With a sigh, he put on his party face
and went to help Lexa greet the first of their guests.

The young woman on the front stoop stared up at
Lexa like a frightened fawn. Took a tighter grip on her
companion's arm. Despite eleven years of marriage,
Lexa had a healthy interest in gorgeous men, and the
specimen on her front step was a real knockout. He
and the tiny lady were also total strangers, so Lexa
gazed at them with a furrowed brow but with a smile
of welcome on her lips. Finally she spotted Silvestre C.
deBaca trotting up the sidewalk, and it fell into place.
The mysterious Gallaghers. She said as much, and was
treated to a flash of white teeth from the male.

Sil arrived, dipped his head, and shot her that secret
little smile that made him look like a mischievous
eight-year-old. He then thrust a bouquet of three rose-
buds into her hands.

"How sweet you are."

"*Sí.*"

Sil had become a fairly regular visitor since his and
Nigel's reunion. Lexa was happy that Nigel had at last
found a pal, but her husband's pleasure in the company
of this old Vietnam buddy only seemed to point up
their own problems, so she found herself ambivalent
about Sil.

"Lexa, this is Mona Gallagher, and her husband,

Terry. Terry's looking for the beautiful people, and had trouble finding them. I knew that scarce breed would have emerged from their artistic hazes to attend tonight, and he would at last find his own, so I imposed on Nigel.''

Behind the joking words Lexa heard the yowlings of jungle cats. The background music hadn't been missed by Mona Gallagher either. The young woman was white-faced, and Lexa roundly cursed all males and their inopportune testosterone attacks.

"Well, we've got a carload of beautiful people. Enough talent and IQ to attain critical mass. All in the backyard stuffing their faces. So come on back and join the munching throng.''

Terry Gallagher stepped eagerly forward, unceremoniously dropping his wife's arm. Lexa noticed that Sil lost no time in appropriating the abandoned arm.

Major-league testosterone.

"Silvestre tells me you work with Indians," said Gallagher.

Amusement edged Lexa's words. "Yes. Also with the state highway department, and coal companies, and uranium mines. But I admit those lack the romance of Indians.''

"Oh, romance." A dismissive jerk of one shoulder. "I just hoped there might be some here tonight that I could meet. Moni and I walked around the Plaza last weekend, but you can't imagine talking to the people that line the wall of the Palace. They just sit there like they've been stuffed.''

"What did you want to talk to them about?" Lexa asked, honestly intrigued.

"I wanted to ask them about their lives, their hopes, dreams, fears.''

She gave a bark of laughter. "You don't want much. And why should they tell you anyway? A stranger, an Anglo asking them impertinent questions. They'll think you're as bad as an anthropologist.''

Gallagher was looking sulky. "Everybody down here lectures me.'' He sent a smoldering glance back at Sil. "And besides, I didn't ask them anything anyway."

"Well, I can provide you with one honest-to-Christ Indian, and Benny is anything but stuffed. But he won't want to talk about art and nature, and how he's in touch with both. He'll want to talk business, with maybe a little politics thrown in for leavening."

"And writers?" he urged. "Will there be any writers here? You see, I'm a novelist."

"How exciting." They were at the sliding glass door leading onto the patio by now. Lexa smiled up at him. "And as for writers, there's a whole knot of science-fiction writers in that corner."

She led him out into the noisy murmur of fifty-odd people all talking at once. The spattering of grease onto hot coals provided an energetic counterpoint to the voices. She indicated a very loud, very exuberant group of people. There would be a quick spate of conversation followed by uproarious laughter, a few insulting gestures exchanged, followed by more talk and more laughter. The group seemed to be young, mid-thirties, proud, and aggressive.

Terry pulled a face and shook his head.

"Problem?"

"Science fiction."

"Oh. Well, let's see, serious literature." She drew out the final word as she turned in a slow circle about herself and scanned the crowd. "The best I can do is a New Mexican poet—in Spanish, I'm afraid—and of course Benny, my token Indian. But I'll leave you to plunge in."

"I'd prefer an introduction."

"Sink or swim, Mr. Gallagher," Lexa replied shortly, and walked away.

Wandering past Nigel, busy flipping hamburgers on the big green grill, she slipped an arm around him, pinched his waist.

"I've been bad," she confessed.

He pressed a kiss onto the corner of her mouth. "Oh?"

"Rude," she elaborated.

''Past fixing?''

''Probably not. He's too self-absorbed to notice when people find him offensive.''

''Sounds like a real charmer. Do I know him?''

''No.''

''Do I want to?''

''No.''

''Then I think I'll stay here and be a hamburger chef.''

''You don't have any choice.'' She worried at her lower lip with her teeth. ''I feel sorry for his little bride. I think I could quite like her.''

''Another of your wounded ducks?''

''Don't be snide.''

''I wasn't. Just amused.''

They both sheared away, sensing a fight narrowly avoided.

''I think I'll go find out,'' said Lexa.

''Do that.''

''Here's my filly,'' Franklin Pierce bellowed.

Mona stiffened, endured the hearty embrace. She had little taste for casual hugs and kisses. It had always been one of her problems with Terry's friends. According to him, they thought she was aloof, a snob.

''My kids did good at the Rotary,'' he boomed to Benny Aragon. He slid that crafty gaze to Sil. ''Even though C. deB. here was about to shit his pants 'cause his daddy was there.''

''Franklin, you're the most horrible old man.'' Sil smiled.

Pierce ignored Silvestre. ''Mona, what are you doing with this Dago Don Juan? Where's that husband of yours? I haven't met him yet.''

Benny pulled the beer bottle from his lips. ''What a lucky man he is.''

''Watch it, Redskin.''

''Paleface.''

''Blanket-ass.''

Mona was looking uncomfortable again.

Terry wandered up, and Mona brightened appreciably. Sil concentrated on popping the cap off his Corona. Then Mona registered her husband's sulky expression, and seemed to shrink in on herself.

"You're not having fun?" she asked anxiously.

"Oh, yeah, some party. Met a bunch of *sci-fi* writers. The only thing they could tell me about was the Chamisa writers workshop—which, by the way, *they* don't attend. Probably do them some good if they would—so I guess it isn't a completely wasted evening."

"Terry," Mona murmured, embarrassed. "This is Mr. Pierce."

"Pleased to meet you."

Pierce smiled up at the young man. He liked the strength of him, the greedy smile, the arrogant ease with which he took center stage. Didn't even really mind the sulky carping. So he was a little spoiled—time would take care of that.

"How are you settling in?" the older man asked.

"Just fine. The house is great. The view out that back-bedroom window is both inspiring and distracting. Still, I think I'm going to do some good work back there."

"That's right, you're a writing fellah."

"Among other things," Mona said with a flash of pride. "He's also a very fine painter, sculptor, and actor."

Sil walked away. Only Benny noticed.

"Well, that's just great. Sit on down and talk a minute." Pierce shifted his bulk on the flower-garden retaining wall, formed of stacked railroad ties.

"I have to ask you something."

"Ask away. Can't promise I'll answer—"

"Oh, you will," interrupted Benny. "The concept of privacy means nothing to you."

Pierce laughed.

Finally Terry got to his question: "Is your name really Franklin Pierce?"

"No."

"Aha!" shouted Terry triumphantly, and pointed a finger at Mona.

"That's the shortened version. My full name is Franklin Delano Lincoln Pierce."

Everyone gave a shout of laughter.

"You have *got* to be making that up," Benny gasped, wiping his eyes.

"No, God's truth, that's my name. My momma was a patriotic lady."

"Hey, Moni," said Terry abruptly, "I'm starved. How about bringing us something to eat?"

"Okay, what do you want?"

Terry waggled his brows. "Steak. Rare."

Benny slid off the wall. "I'll come along and help."

"No, sit. I was hoping to visit with you. Mona can manage."

"Really I can," she agreed. "Stay."

Benny sank back down.

Sil was nowhere in sight, and Mona felt somewhat cast adrift as she pushed through the crowd. A small blond man was busy brushing barbecue sauce over chicken, pausing every now and then to blot at his sweaty brow with a forearm.

Mona gathered up a plate and shyly approached.

"And what would you like?" His smile was one of the warmest and sweetest she had ever seen.

Silently she pointed to one of the largest porterhouses on the grill, then blushed at his startled look.

"Oh, it's not for *me*. It's for my husband."

"You reassure me. If it had been for you I was going to demand that you sit right next to me so I could watch where you stowed that amount of beef. Of course, you ladies can be deceptive," he continued as he speared the meat. "My wife can eat like a stevedore and never gain a pound. Now, what would you like?"

"I'm not hungry just yet. I'll come back a little later."

"Okay."

She paused by the picnic table, glanced back over her shoulder at him. "Do you ever get to eat, or do you have to cook all night?"

"How nice of you to ask. But like you, I'm not very

hungry. When you cook something, you seem to lose your appetite.''

She ducked her head and sidestepped to the table. It wasn't the most elegant way to end a conversation, but Nigel recognized chronic shyness when he saw it and wasn't offended.

''Business can too be creative,'' Franklin Pierce was objecting when she returned. ''You got to have the imagination to see a need and fill it. Take me, for example—''

''But who else?'' Benny murmured, but affectionately.

''I got my start in septic tanks. Not very romantic maybe, but a definite necessity.'' His big face screwed up into delighted lines. ''You know, there's a shitload of money to be made in shit.'' A deep laugh rumbled out, setting his enormous belly to shaking. Mona could tell that this was a line he delivered often, and each time enjoyed it with the gusto of the first.

''Yeah, I did it all. Borrowed the money to buy myself a pump tank. Drove all around Hobbs diggin' out the tanks, pumpin', haulin'. Came home dead tired after a fourteen-hour day smellin' like a shithouse myself. My wife would always tell me not to pick up the baby until I'd washed, but Denise would always cry and crow and reach up for me. She didn't care how her old dad smelled.'' He pulled a big handkerchief from his back pocket, gave his nose a hard blow. Blinked several times, then thrust it away.

Silvestre was back, his amber eyes overly bright.

Terry sawed into his steak. ''That's too much work for me. Far too hard.'' He cast a comic glance around the group. ''I personally think inherited wealth is the only way to go.''

''Or letting your wife earn it,'' came quietly out of the darkness.

Knuckles went white around the blade of the steak knife, but Gallagher's tone was placid when he replied, ''Mona understands that until I have my career up and running, the burden's going to fall on her.''

"It's great when a couple can be that supportive,"
Pierce rushed in.

"But which career?" Sil asked in a flat cold tone.

"What?" Gallagher asked.

"Which career? Are you going to try the writing,
and if that doesn't work, try a little art, and if that
fails, move on to acting? At that rate the burden's going to be on Mona until she retires."

Terry came to his feet. Set aside the plate. "All of
that is presupposing that I'll fail. I don't fail."

"Now, that's the spirit," Franklin called out heart-
ily, and slapped his knee.

But the bluff remark did nothing to ease the tension.
Instead it seemed to disturb the heavy, sullen anger
like a stone thrown into a still pond.

Benny Aragon glanced at Mona. White-faced, she
looked on the verge of fainting. Suddenly she turned
and bolted. Gallagher didn't notice. He kept his attention locked on Silvestre, who was making a convulsive
movement as if to follow Mona. Benny checked him
with a touch to the arm.

"Hello."

Small forest animal, thought Lexa as she studied the
delicate oval face and wide-set eyes, filled now with
alarm.

"Excuse me, I'm sorry. I shouldn't be in your bedroom," Mona apologized.

"It's quite all right. You couldn't very well sit on
all those coats in the guestroom."

"Still, it was rude . . ." Mona's voice trailed away,
and she eyed Lexa warily as the older woman stepped
into the room and pushed the door closed.

Mona moved to rise from the bed, but Lexa stopped
her with a gesture.

"Please, sit down. It's all right. You seem upset.
Can I help?" It wasn't her most graceful approach.
Enough to frighten any wounded bird back into cov-
er. Mona gave a mute shake of her head, which set
her long hair swinging. "I'm a very good listener,"
Lexa coaxed, stepping closer.

"But I don't know you. At all." Those comically straight brows snapped together in a pugnacious frown. "And I don't like to burden people with my problems."

"Like to handle things yourself?"

"Yes."

"Me too." Lexa perched on the water-bed rail. "But I'm also the most inveterate tinkerer. I have this terrible need to *fix* things." She made a droll face. "My husband says it's because I'm so good at it. I think it just comes from a meddling nature."

A fleeting smile lit Mona's delicate face. She drew a handful of hair forward, then back, and, as if the movement freed her, she suddenly said, "I don't do well in crowds."

Lexa nodded sympathetically. "I think there are people who are emotional empaths. Get them around too many people, and they just absorb all the woes and worries."

"Oh, that's not me. I'm really very self-absorbed. I don't notice the people around me except as a faceless throng. Terry says I'm very insensitive. He's probably right. But I do notice the people I care about."

"Very healthy and sensible. Otherwise you'd be squandering vast amounts of energy on people that you don't know from the pope."

"I'm taking you away from your guests."

"I don't think they'll miss me. We're starting to get to the 'feeling-no-pain' stage." Lexa gave a sudden bark of laughter. "But poor Nigel, diligently doing his duty at the barbecue, pointing a line of lushes toward the booze bath, and trying to fend off the advances of lonely widows, misunderstood wives, and predatory teenagers."

"Oh, the man cooking the food. He's *very* handsome."

"Yep. A little on the short side, but quality, every inch of him. But you didn't exactly strike out. Mr. Gallagher is a hunk."

Mona sat up and wrapped her arms around her knees. "Are you natives?"

"Ah, so you've learned that bit of regional cachet. No, Nigel and I are relative newcomers to New Mexico. Well, on-again, off-again New Mexicans. I went to the university down in Albuquerque, and that's where I met Nigel. He was just passing through, picking up odd jobs. But I wasn't about to let him go drifting on. I grabbed him good." She smiled faintly as she considered that whirlwind three-day courtship, then sobered. Maybe it was true that marriage was hell on romance.

"Anyway, we stayed in Albuquerque until I got my bachelor's. Then off to Arizona for postgrad, worked on digs in Mexico and Central America. Then I got offered the job at the Cummings Museum. So here we are back in New Mexico."

"And you like it?"

"Love it. You will too. It just takes a while for green girls like us to adjust to all the brown."

"Green girls?"

"You're from back east somewhere. Vermont, New Hampshire?"

"Vermont."

"Massachusetts for me. See, green girls."

"I'm not sure I like that. I feel *too* green most of the time. Half-trained, nervous, flighty—as in green-broke horse."

"How old are you?"

"Twenty-five."

"Plenty of time before you have to start worrying about settling down."

"But I want to settle down. That's why I left the circuit and took the job with Mr. Pierce. I want a home and a family. I want to stop living out of a suitcase."

"This center sure has caused a rumpus," Lexa said.

"You know about it?"

"You'd have to be deaf, drunk, or dead not to have heard about it. This house also represents a veritable war zone." She smiled, but it never reached her eyes. "Benny Aragon's a very good friend of mine. I think he's right-on to be looking for new directions for the

Pueblo. Not everybody can make pots, beat silver, and
grow chilies.'' She folded her hands and pressed them
firmly against her lips, as if holding something back.
''Unfortunately, Nigel's half-sister, Rhea, lives in
Rancho de Palabra and is the leader of the opposition.
Sounds like that old sixties song. 'The leader of the
pack,' '' she sang, again trying to make light of something that obviously affected her deeply.

''God, how awful for you. And your husband . . .''

''Oh, Nigel's being a real sweetie. Having Benny
over, and you over, and Silvestre over. And allowing
Rhea to moan on one shoulder while I weep on the
other. In short, not taking . . . sides.'' The words
trailed away.

''And it's driving you crazy, isn't it?'' Mona offered.

''Yes.''

''I think I'd feel betrayed.''

''Oh, no. Nigel and I have always granted each other
the right to disagree. This house is a testament to our
diversity, if you will. Nigel's really not very big on
what he calls 'Indian Gothic'—pots, rugs, beads, and
so on. He likes a slick, modern look. Lots of chrome
and crystal. But because of my work, I *do* like Indian
Gothic, and my lace-curtain-Irish background also
makes me a sucker for antiques. So we assigned rooms
that are totally ours, and in the main traffic areas we've
created this interior decorator's nightmare.''

Mona glanced about from the modern pedestal
water bed on which they sat to the Victorian marble-
topped side tables. There was an abstract crystal-and-
silver wind chime hung before the window, an antique
dressing table in the corner, and a collection of Indian
pots arranged in front of the corner fireplace.

''I see what you mean.''

''So what would you call this? Healthy compromise,
or some sort of weird covert warfare?''

''I don't know,'' Mona said honestly. ''I don't know
the two of you well enough.''

Lexa sat up abruptly, setting the bed to sloshing.

"Personally, I'd like to change that. What are you doing tomorrow?"

"Church, then ride Favory, then . . . nothing. Which seems to sum up my days recently."

"So how about brunch, and then riding . . . Favory?"

"I'd like that."

"Well, I'd best get out there and rescue Nigel so he can have something to eat."

"Then it will be your turn to fend off lonely widowers, misunderstood husbands, and predatory teenagers."

Lexa bent and peered at herself in the glass of the dressing table. "How sweet you are. Thank you."

9

Nine o'clock, and no Rhea. Good news? Bad news?
Nigel, slumped on his tailbone in the canvas chair,
nursed a beer (his tenth or his eleventh, couldn't remember which) and stared blankly into the dying
coals. Better that she didn't come. Then she wouldn't
spot Pierce and Benny and accuse him of disloyalty.
But her absence might mean she was angry. And he
couldn't afford to have her angry.

He watched with detached interest as the big red-
wood gate swung open. It seemed strange that someone would enter so casually through the back gate.
Rhea stepped lightly through, her high heels clicking
on the flagstone walk. John Greer was in tow. With
his tumbled mop of hair, burly build, and the way he
hovered so hopefully at Rhea's shoulder, Nigel had a
disconcerting image of the man as a large, willing
sheep dog.

Rhea was dressed absurdly for a New Mexico autumn evening. She was wearing a filmy bit of black
material shot through with gold and ruby threads,
draped like a sari. Surely she and Greer had been out
to dinner. Nigel couldn't believe that even Rhea would
need to make such an entrance at her half-brother's
barbecue.

And an entrance it had been. Despite the coy little
slip through the gate, virtually every eye was now upon
her. She lifted her head in a queenly gesture, as if
greeting and welcoming all of the assembled guests.
Nigel knew he ought to move, to rise and say hello,

but he was held by the strange playlike quality of the entire scene.

Women shifted, hoping to recall the wandering attention of their stunned male companions. Franklin Pierce was staring slack-jawed at this tiny vision, and even Benny Aragon seemed mesmerized.

Then there was movement. A tall young Adonis setting his beer on the top of the wall and striding forward to stop directly in front of Rhea. He stood at arrogant ease, hands hanging loosely at sides, legs slightly straddled, back erect. And Rhea, lifting her delicate kitten's face, held out her hands.

When his hands closed over hers, she felt something very akin to a shock. Rhea instantly chided herself. Such things occurred only in cheap romances, and even if she secretly believed in such a power, it was something that she did *to* men. Not vice versa. Behind her she could sense Greer, a large unhappy presence as this beautiful man stared down at her with obvious admiration. His velvet gaze held a frank invitation.

She studied him from beneath her lashes as she contemplated an opening gambit. He removed the initiative from her by pulling her hand through his arm and leading her away.

"You're going to be cold. My jacket's just over here. I'll give it to you."

She felt as if she owed something to Greer. He had just taken her to dinner. "Why don't you find us something to drink, John, dear," she tossed back over her shoulder, "while this gentleman plays knight-errant and shields me from the cold." The lawyer slunk away.

"Poor dube," the delicious man said as he placed his jacket about her shoulders. It smelled of tobacco and after-shave, and she rubbed her cheek against the rough tweed.

"That's not very kind," said Rhea severely, but the final word quivered on a giggle. The stranger smiled approvingly. "Who are you?" she finally demanded.

"Terry Gallagher at your service. And you?"

"Rhea Sheridan."

"What are you doing at this stultifying gathering?"

"That's not very nice. Especially since my brother and his wife are hosting it."

"I notice you came late," came the quick, laughing response.

She covered her face with a hand, peeped through the fingers at him. "You're not very gallant to point that out. But who are you? You *can't* have been in Santa Fe long, or I would have spotted you . . . instantly."

His teeth shone very white beneath the mustache. "In fact I've only been here a few weeks. My wife has a job out here."

"And you?"

"I'm a writer."

"How lovely. I can introduce you to people . . . other writers."

"Real writers, I hope," he said, his mouth forming a moue as he glanced to the science-fiction crowd.

"Of course. Is that why you came tonight? To try to meet people?" He nodded. "Then I'm afraid you picked the wrong party. My brother is a very talented and sensitive man, but his wife . . ." An expressive little shrug. "And she does seem to call the tune. Most of the people here are her friends. It doesn't seem fair to poor Nigel. But all that aside, I host a little luncheon once a month for the writers and artists. John Rankin calls them my *salons*. But I don't really aspire to such heights. Still, people seem to enjoy them. Manuscripts are exchanged, publishing news traded—"

"John Rankin, the man who's written those wonderfully satiric novels about developers and politicians?"

"Yes, the same." She laid a hand on his arm. "Don't worry, you'll meet him. You must come to my little coffee klatch." Her eyes wandered about the yard and fell upon Franklin Pierce and Benny Aragon. "Oh, my God!"

"What's wrong?"

"How could he? How *could* he? How could Nigel

have those people here when he knows how I feel? But I know who's behind this. I just wish Nigel would have the courage . . . But I suppose I can't expect him to develop the balls to stand up to Lexa at this late date," she concluded bitterly.

"What's the problem with those people?" Terry asked in a strangled voice.

"Oh, they're just trying to ruin my life by building a stinking eyesore just down the hill from my house."

"You don't mean the equestrian center?" he asked faintly.

"Yes. How do you know about that?"

"Oh, this is great! Just terrific! Well, another perfect friendship strangled at birth. I'll just take my jacket and get out of your way."

"Why?"

"Because my wife's been hired to train at the new center. So I guess I'm in the enemy camp."

"Oh, no!"

"Not that I give a fuck about this center. I didn't really want her to leave the circuit, but she insisted."

She laid her hands against his chest. "I'm not petty enough to hold you to blame for your wife's job. You didn't know."

"Yeah, but this is going to be a little awkward."

"Why?"

"It might look a little disloyal for me to be coming to your house when you're trying to block the center."

"Everyone knows artists are apolitical. And we'll just keep those two parts of our lives separate. When I meet with you, I'll be meeting with a very talented young writer, not with a man who's married to . . . well, who's peripherally involved with the center."

"Mona may not be so understanding," he said slowly.

"She's working while you get your career up and running, correct?"

"Yes."

"Then put it to her this way. With my help, that just might happen a lot sooner, and then she doesn't have to work for Pierce, and the problem will be solved."

"I think you're stretching for that." His teeth flashed again in the darkness. "But what the hell, I'll buy any amount of convoluted reasoning if it gets me what I want. So when is the first meeting of this *salon*?"

"You've missed this month's, alas, but why don't I have a little dinner just to introduce you around. Do you have an agent?"

"Just a Hollywood agent."

"My, a man of many talents. Well, let's see if we can't find you one in New York. We'll talk to John."

"Sounds great." He lifted her hand and gave it a squeeze. "Maybe we'll set a new standard for dé-tente."

"Have you eaten?" Lexa asked.

"No."

"Well then, let me fix you something." She lifted the half-empty bottle from her husband's slack fingers and set it well away. "I met the little bride, and we're having brunch tomorrow. Why don't you come too."

He looked blank for a moment. "Oh, right, your new wounded duck. Okay, I'll come."

A hamburger hissed as it hit the hot grill. "What's been going on out here? Anything interesting?"

"Rhea's made a new conquest. Probably a good thing. A little distraction to keep her from rumbling with Pierce and Benny in the middle of our back-yard."

"Oh. She came, then."

"Yeah. Dumped poor old John Greer and took up with some young stud in a turtleneck sweater and tweed." Lexa followed Nigel's gaze, and dropped the hamburger bun through the wire of the grill.

"Nigel, that's the bride's husband!"

"Oops."

"Is that all you have to say?"

"Lexa, they're just talking."

"There's no such thing as *just talking* with your sister. She puts claws into people." Her lips compressed into a thin line, and she unwrapped the sack and pulled out another bun with a sharp jagged motion.

"I wish you two could like each other."

"It's not required that I like her. I'm married to you, not to her."

Nigel stretched, recovered the beer and stared bleakly into its golden depths. "I'm afraid we come as a package."

"We're out of plates. I'll get some."

Standard married person's way out of an uncomfortable conversation. Fall back on the mundane.

Late that night Nigel stepped into the master bath. He unzipped and sighed with relief as he relieved himself of a load of beer. Lexa was still poking about the yard recovering cups, plates, and bottles from behind bushes and out of the crooks of trees.

He glanced idly over at the basin, and frowned at the spill of white powder across the deep blue tiles. Their bedroom and bath had been strictly off limits to their guests, but someone had obviously ignored the closed doors.

Zipping himself, he washed his hands, and then ran a long forefinger through the powder. It felt grainy. Talc? A sudden suspicion flared. Wetting a finger, he dipped it lightly and tasted.

Cocaine.

It wasn't entirely surprising. After all, it was the drug of choice for the upwardly mobile. Nigel was acutely uncomfortable with the witch-hunt mentality that currently gripped the country, but he also personally disapproved of drugs.

Unless it's your drug of choice, he thought acidly.

But all that aside, he didn't like people using illegal substances in his house. In a private area. It showed contempt, and a disregard for the feelings of others. Unfortunately, it was impossible to tell who of some sixty-odd people had used several hundred dollars worth of dope.

Reaching beneath the sink, he seized a sponge, dampened it, and wiped away the offending smear. He and Lexa would have a field day analyzing their various friends and trying to figure out who was using coke.

He stepped into the bedroom as Lexa was sliding out of her jeans. "That Mona Gallagher is really a beautiful woman," she said, "but I don't think she knows it."

"What brought her to mind?"

"This was where I found her." Her voice became muffled as she pulled the sweater over her head. "Huddled on the bed like a terrified fawn. Too nervy by half, that girl."

Nigel, tossing back the down comforter, decided that maybe he wouldn't mention the cocaine.

"Have you had Mexican food yet?" asked Lexa as she poured coffee from an antique silver coffee set.

"No, everyone keeps saying it's too soon yet. 'You're not ready.' Makes it sound as awesome as having sex for the first time." Mona clapped a hand over her mouth and blushed.

Nigel Vallis was just pulling a Red Zinger tea bag out of his mug, and the remark startled him so that he dropped the bag with a soggy splat onto the floor.

"My unflappable husband has just been flapped."

"I'm sorry."

"Never mind." Nigel swept up the bag and tossed it. "It just seemed incongruous coming out of your mouth."

"Why?"

"You don't give a very earthy appearance."

"But I am. I'm a farmgirl."

Nigel leaned back against the counter and framed her face with his hands. "In a museum in Florence there's a Renaissance Nativity. The Madonna in that painting looks exactly like you."

Mona pressed her hands to her cheeks. "Hush, I think it's bad luck to be compared to saints and angels. We always fall so short."

"Well, thank God for that." Lexa rose and hitched up her tailored green fatigue pants with a decided tug. "I've always considered Mary to be just too mealy-

mouthed for words. Hey, baby, says some angel. How'd
you like to have a kid? Of course you aren't going to
have any fun conceiving it, and your fiancé is going to
be pissed, but just tell him God did it. I would have
told them to take a hike until I got some serious answers to some serious questions.''

"My wife is something of a pagan."

Lexa shrugged into a photojournalist's vest, its myr-
iad pockets filled with unidentifiable bulges. Nigel
gathered up the car keys from the hall table and
checked for his wallet.

"These men, they have it so lucky. No purses."
Lexa linked an arm through Mona's. "You see, I have
this theory that purses are a male invention designed
to keep women subjugated."

"And I, tired of listening to her howl every time
she picked up her purse, bought her that vest, and
liberated her," Nigel said.

"Isn't he a sweetie?"

Mona studied the slim, narrow-hipped form silhouetted by the garage door. Vallis wore an intricately
patterned Icelandic pullover sweater, faded Levi's and
boots. The light from the rising garage door touched
on his silver-gilt hair and accentuated the high, wide
cheekbones and pointed chin. Thinking about the
males of her acquaintance, Mona decided that a person would have to look long and far to find three men
as gorgeous as Terry, Silvestre, and Nigel. For an instant she thought of that silly cocktail-party game: If
they had been animals, which animals would they be?
Terry was clearly a Great Dane or a Lipizzaner—big,
powerful, beautiful. Silvestre was a saluki . . . or as
a horse, of course he would be a thoroughbred. Nigel
was a whippet or an Italian greyhound or a delicate
Arabian—all fire and nerves.

"You're looking intense."

"Sorry, just being silly. Do you ever compare people to animals?"

"All the time," came Lexa's dry reply.

"Yes, and Lexa's a porcupine," Nigel teased. "Let
me back the car out. It will be easier to get in."

"What a gentleman I married."

Once they were settled and on the road, Nigel glanced to his wife and asked, "We never did resolve the question of brunch." A wink to Mona. "Do we devirginate Mona or leave it to a more intimate partner?"

"I think we do it. Silvestre will be too solicitous and find her some gringo food or else burn out her intestines. And if we leave her and Terry to wander as innocents alone, they'll never find the good restaurants."

"Molly's."

"Molly's."

"Molly's?"

"One of the best Mexican restaurants in Santa Fe. It has all the ambience of a bus station, but great inexpensive food."

"I miss the old Molly's," Lexa sighed.

"It looked like a Victorian whorehouse," Nigel explained. "Each room was papered with this incredibly tasteless flocked velvet wallpaper. And each room was a different color."

"And the green beer and green sopaipillas on St. Patrick's Day, do you remember?" Lexa asked.

"How could I forget." He made a gagging noise.

"Reminiscences of eleven years ago," she told Mona.

Molly's was jumping, and they had to wait in the bar for almost twenty minutes, but eventually they were seated and Mona puzzled over the unfamiliar names: *Carne Adovada. Chiles Rellenos. Chimichanga. Huevos Rancheros.*

"I'm totally confused. Please help."

"Try the chiles rellenos. That always has a green chili sauce, so Lexa or I will get something with red sauce and you can try bites."

"Carne adovada! I need meat!" Lexa growled.

Nigel selected the combination plate, placed an order for chile con queso, and leaned back in his chair, surveying Mona over the top of his beer glass. "So what do you think of New Mexico?"

"I don't know. It seems to defy opinion. Not that I've seen much. Terry's been too busy researching for us to do much sightseeing."

"That must be remedied while you've still got some free time," Lexa stated firmly.

"Then you think the center will be built?"

"I'm confident of it. Franklin Pierce is one tough son of a bitch."

Nigel stared down at the table. "Don't underestimate Rhea."

"I don't."

Mona looked uncomfortably from husband to wife. "How would you describe New Mexico?" she blurted.

"As a paradox wrapped in a contradiction—with a nod to Churchill for cribbing and altering his phrase," Nigel replied.

"How so?"

"Well, think about it. Just up the hill we have Los Alamos, where the atomic bomb was developed. At that lab and at Sandia in Albuquerque, people are unraveling the mysteries of fusion power and designing ever-more-efficient bombs—and the superconducting supercollider may end up in New Mexico. Then set that against one of the highest dropout rates in the nation, a per-capita income that's one of the lowest in the country, and a sense of magic—in the nonpejorative sense of the word—and spirituality that's unequaled elsewhere."

"Nigel calls it magic. I call it superstition," Lexa said.

"No, that's not true. You have a great respect for the Indian religions. It's the more aberrant Catholicism that you consider superstition."

"Touché. But, Nigel, you have to admit the Sacred Tortilla did a lot to prove my hypothesis."

"It's a fetish just like the ones in the Pueblos," he replied.

"Sacred Tortilla?" asked Mona faintly.

Lexa seemed surprised. "You haven't heard this story?"

Mona shook her head.

"Well, a few years back, a woman was frying flour tortillas for dinner when suddenly the burn marks formed the face of Jesus on a tortilla. She framed and hung the thing, and people came from miles around to witness this miracle, and miraculous things were attributed to the tortilla. The church hierarchy was about to shit a brick, let me promise you." Lexa laughed.

"My practical wife scorns this, but she'll buy the idea that a Navajo sand painting can cure illness. I submit there's no difference. It's all magical. It's . . . New Mexico."

"You're not just making this up to confuse the gullible little newcomer?"

"Oh, no. We need to take you to some dances at the Pueblo," Lexa said, "so you can soak up some of these things firsthand."

"And to witness the Easter pilgrimage to the Santuario de Guadalupe," offered Nigel.

"And maybe even arrange for a UFO."

"Now you *are* getting silly," Mona objected.

Nigel spread his hands before him. "Maybe not. New Mexico's one of the premier places for saucer sightings."

When their meals arrived, Mona stared fascinated at the long finger-shaped green chili pod lightly breaded and fried, swimming in a sea of green-chili sauce. She cut into it, and melted cheese spilled across the plate. With a swallow, she gathered her nerve and forked the bite into her mouth. It was *hot*. Tears started into her eyes, but she chewed bravely on, and soon the heat faded and the flavor came through.

"Are you on fire?" Nigel asked solicitously.

"A little."

He caught her hand before she could lift her water glass. "That just makes it worse. Try this." He tore open a sopaipilla and poured honey into its hollow interior. She tried a bite of the puffed bread and found that the fire did die.

"These are wonderful."

Nigel and Lexa exchanged glances. "Everybody loves sopas."

"What are they?"

"Sopaipillas—little pillows," Lexa explained.

"Ah, I see. I'll have to bring Terry here. If I had known you were going to bring your husband, I would have invited him along."

"Well, next time we'll do a foursome."

Nigel withdrew from the conversation, and watched Lexa draw out Mona. They talked of horses and Grand Prix competition, and archaeology, and homes and babies. He noted with a twinge of pain that this last subject seemed to agitate Lexa. He took a deep swallow of beer and tried to banish the sense of age that had crept over him. Mona, and even Lexa, seemed too young today.

Watching Mona's delicate face, the emotions that rippled lightly across her gentle features, he thought again what a shame it was that she was a doper. Well, maybe Lexa could be a help. Generally the people she took an interest in prospered.

He only wished she would take an interest in him again.

10

Rhea glanced about. She'd never been in the private living quarters of an Indian before. Though she'd made a number of trips out to San Jose to buy from Philomina and the other Pueblo artisans, their hospitality ended at the door of their workshops. It hadn't been easy to draw out the quiet Pueblo woman. It had taken four visits, and purchases amounting to almost three thousand dollars, before she'd elicited that Benny Aragon's family had made some enemies after twelve years of Pueblo rule. And that Ralph Quintana did not like the equestrian project, but, not having any really good reason to oppose it, had allowed the request to be sent to the Secretary of the Interior. Then she had set about to wangle an invitation to talk with Mr. Quintana.

Now she was seated on a rug-covered adobe bench that was an extrusion of the wall itself. The wool of her cherry-colored suit pricked through her hose and into her thighs. Thank heaven Philomina's home was on the ground level of the Pueblo. Rhea hadn't thought when she'd selected her outfit, but climbing one of the long wooden ladders to the upper levels would have been hell in high heels.

There wasn't much in the room, by Anglo standards. A religious picture hung on one wall, a wooden straight-backed chair, a simple sofa. Though a virtual thicket of TV antennae littered the roof of the stairstep Pueblo, Philomina didn't appear to own an idiot box, and that pleased Rhea. The modern technological boom might have made life easier, but it was certainly

145

making it duller. Everyone was becoming the same. Supermarkets in Rome, McDonald's in Paris, televisions in ancient Pueblos.

The chair was still empty, though the sofa, and much of the narrow floor space, had been filled by eight men. Most were from late middle to old age, but there was one young man who looked to be in his late twenties. As Rhea faced eight pairs of expressionless black eyes, she began to wish she'd brought John. Or even better, Nigel. He was used to dealing with Indians.

There was a brush of leather moccasins on the floor, and an old, old man came hobbling in. Philomina escorted him to the chair, then vanished. Obviously women's liberation was an alien concept within a Pueblo. Rhea recalled that even one of the most progressive southern Pueblos had almost had a riot when a woman ran for governor and won. The silence lengthened, and Rhea nervously decided that perhaps her kittenish pose—legs folded demurely beneath her— was a touch too cute. She placed her feet neatly side by side on the floor and stared at Ralph Quintana.

"Philomina says you wanted to talk to me," Quintana said.

"Yes—"

"Why? What do you want?"

Rhea bit down on her lower lip. "I'm a very close friend of Philomina's"—something perilously close to a snort whispered from one corner—"and . . . and she said you were upset about this equestrian center. And since I'd fought Franklin Pierce before on just this issue, I thought I could be . . . well, offer my help." Silence. "If you want to oppose it, of course." Rhea was beginning to see why some people didn't like Indians.

"I am against this center." Quintana had the hesitant, rhythmic speech patterns of the traditional Pueblo. "But not because I want to preserve your land values or protect your investments."

Rhea gaped. "Oh, no. That's not the issue. We love this land the same way you do. We want to see it preserved."

"For more million-dollar condos?" the young man asked.

"That's not fair," she cried, stung. "New Mexico has a unique culture, a unique life-style. We don't want to see it ruined."

The old man held up a hand. "Say that we want to stop this center, for *our* reasons. How can you help?"

"I'll place my attorney at your disposal. We'll help you draft petitions, or whatever has to be done. If you need money—for whatever reason—we can back you. We'll help. And if we succeed, Governor Barela will have a black eye. It might break the hold the Aragon and Barela families have on San Jose." She was proud of that bit of gossip she'd managed to unearth. And at Lexa and Nigel's party, of all places. *That* would put Lexa into a slow burn. "While it's true that I can't fully understand your reasons for opposing this project, I can tell you that we're fighting for our homes, and I know you can understand that because your people have loved this land, and your place on it, for thousands of years."

She could sense that something had happened. Amidst all the shifting and eye contact, some decision had been reached. Ralph Quintana pushed himself out of the chair with palsied hands.

"We'll take the help. You work with Gilbert Gonzales." His rheumy eyes fell upon the young man who was looking eagerly up at him like a coursing hound. "And Ramon Dominguez."

Six of the men left with Quintana, leaving only Gilbert and Ramon. Rhea shifted uncomfortably under their flat stares. "My attorney, Mr. Greer, said there were strong traditional factions in this Pueblo. I'm glad to see he was right. It's good to know that not all people are abandoning—"

"White lady, cut the crap," Ramon interrupted. "Tradition's great, and stomping on that asshole Benny Aragon is a bonus, but let's get real. What's in it for us?"

"Well, you'll stop the center—"

"What's in it for us?" echoed Gilbert.

"What do you mean?"

"Come on, lady. You got money. Three grand just to get a chance to talk to Ralph?" Ramon scoffed. "You got influence. Use it."

"For what?"

"We need a health clinic," Gilbert stated bluntly.

"I can't afford to fund something like that." She was on her feet, purse clutched protectively to her chest.

"Some new wells, both irrigation and drinking," Gilbert went on as if she hadn't spoken.

"I'm not going to adopt a Pueblo," she snapped in a voice gone shrill with tension and outrage.

Gilbert remained impassive. "We've already been adopted by the great white fathers in the form of the BIA. You go to the Agency for the Nine Northern Pueblos. You ask for Natal Otero. He's in charge of a lot of shit. Welfare, scholarships. He wants to be a senator. Maybe you guys can work something out."

Rhea knuckled her chin and studied them speculatively. "I think I understand."

Ramon nodded. "Of course you do, if you've lived more than three months in New Mexico."

Mona, seated cross-legged on the bed, was busily towel-drying her hair. Terry squatted on bare haunches and fed twigs into the tiny tongue of flame dancing fitfully in the kiva fireplace. She could count the knobs of his vertebrae, watch the play of muscles across his shoulders as he lifted a piñon log, the way his hair whorled in an unruly cowlick at the base of his neck. Her breath went a little short, and tossing aside the towel, she ran her hands through the wealth of her hair.

"Brush out the tangles for me?" she asked softly.

He looked up, his face ruddy from the heat of the fire. Mona leaned back, allowing the beige silk of her teddy to cling more closely to her small breasts.

"Sure."

The bed squeaked under his weight. The brush of his hands against the nape of her neck felt like a caress as he gently worked the brush through the damp, silky strands. Then he pushed the hair aside and bent to press a kiss onto the back of her neck.

Mona slithered around and wrapped her arms about him. He fell back against the pillows, reached out, and snapped off the light. Red shadows danced on the whitewashed walls. Reaching down, he snagged the tiny teddy and gently pulled it over her head, cupped her breasts in either hand, and massaged the nipples with his thumbs.

Her breath exploded from her throat in tiny, gusting moans, and she straddled him, gripping with her powerful legs. She reached down and wrapped her hands protectively about his cock while his hand crept into the hair of her mons and a forefinger flicked tantalizingly across her.

She arched back, guiding his penis toward her. Suddenly he held her off.

"Diaphragm," he whispered hoarsely.

"I thought . . . I hoped we could start trying for a baby."

"Not yet."

"Why not?" Her arousal had drained away.

"The novel is just starting to work. I need my office, and I can't have the distraction of a baby around the house. Not right now."

"It won't be for nine months."

"I'm not a hack. I don't just crank out books." His face was mulish in the firelight. "And things are so iffy with the center. What if it doesn't get built? You'd have to go back to the circuit, and who'd take care of the kid?"

"It's going to get built. Mr. Pierce is one tough operator."

"So's Rhea Sheridan."

"You'd know. You see enough of her." She scrambled off him, and sat hugging herself by the edge of the bed.

"What's that supposed to mean?"

"It means what it means. I'm not subtle." She looked back at him over a bare shoulder. "It just seems

wrong to me that you should be spending time with
an enemy."

"Oh, God, how melodramatic."

"She is against us."

"Against the center, not against me. She's intelligent enough to separate the cause from the people."

"Meaning I'm not?"

"It means what it means," he mimicked cruelly.
"She went to a lot of trouble to set up that party last
week."

"Yes."

"Look how many people we met."

"You met. They hardly talked to me."

"And whose fault is that? This happened in New
York too, Mona. You just don't promote yourself."

"I'm not comfortable in crowds. And they don't talk
about anything I'm interested in."

"There is more to the world than horses."

"Not for us, there's not, because horses pay the
damn bills."

"Now you sound like your boyfriend Silvestre taking a swipe at me."

"He is *not* my boyfriend."

"He's got the biggest hard-on in the world for you.
Everybody can see it."

"That's not my fault. I've never, never given him
any encouragement."

"Okay, then stop accusing me about Rhea."

"I'm not. The loyalty I'm talking about is toward
the center."

"Mona, frankly I don't give a fuck about the center.
Things are finally starting to happen for me. Stop be-
grudging me."

"I'm not. Really." She placed her face in her hands,
drew in a deep breath, looked up. "I'm sorry. The last
thing I want is to be unsupportive. And I was being
selfish. I just want a baby so badly."

He gripped her hand. "And we'll have one, but just
not yet."

She gave him a somewhat watery smile. "I'll get
my diaphragm."

"Good girl." He slapped her on the rump as she rose. " 'Cause I'm really anxious to pick things up where we left off."

Cerrillos Road. Probably the ugliest stretch of real estate in Santa Fe. Bumper-to-bumper traffic consisting almost entirely of Santa Fe's legendary bad drivers. Fast-food joints marching shoulder to shoulder down the length of its six lanes. Gas stations and cheap motels. Liquor stores, lots of liquor stores, and therefore lots of drunks on any Friday or Saturday night.

On this Tuesday morning in November it wasn't too bad. Silvestre drove the Porsche through a narrow opening between two cars, and went bouncing into the parking lot of the A Ace High bar and package liquor store. Its owner, Ernie Mondragon, was a shirttail relative to the C. deBacas. He was useful, though rarely acknowledged, when they were catering a party, because he always supplied the booze wholesale.

Sil liked him. Though older by some six years, Ernie had always been a good friend to his young cousin. He had taken the excited twelve-year-old for rides in his awesome red Chevy, given him his first taste of beer, provided him with his first woman.

Ernie was the other face of Santa Fe, an ordinary joe. He played in a softball league in the summer, coached Little League, had never been to the opera or an art gallery. He ran his bar and liquor store, fought with his old lady, and was a generally good father, though like most Hispanic males he was more interested in his four sons than in the three big-eyed girls.

In addition to the bar, Ernie ran a discreet escort service, providing girls for the civil servants who lay battened like leeches on the body of Santa Fe year-round, and for the legislators who afflicted the city for only a few months out of each year. He always knew where you could find a hit of prime grass, and most important for Sil, he was keeping him supplied with cocaine.

One of his two employees, a hard-faced woman of fifty, was in the liquor store, so Sil passed on into the bar. Ernie, in blue jeans and a T-shirt advertising the latest salsa rock band, was shuffling around emptying ashtrays into a dustpan, a cigarette dangling from his lips. Red flocked wallpaper and mirrors behind the bar gave the dark room the look of a Victorian whorehouse. The only light was provided by the flickering TV above the bar, the Tiffany lamp over the pool table, and the illuminated Coors sign.

"Hola!"

"Eeeh, qué pasa, Sil?"

"Oh, things aren't too bad." Sil swung out a red-leather-topped bar stool and sat down. "How's it going?"

"It's a crapper, man. Business is lousy, and Rita, that *perra,* she bought a new washer and dryer yesterday."

"Had something else in mind for the money?"

"Yeah, no fucking kidding, a stereo for the car. Mine got ripped off. You can't depend on anything anymore, this town's going to hell." He popped the cap off a Miller's, and leaned on the bar.

"Anything new and interesting?"

"Depends on what you want to know. Our self-righteous redneck attorney general got his rocks off with one of my girls Saturday night."

"Big deal."

"Yeah, maybe, but it really pisses me off. He's got a fucking Bible in one hand and a handful of subpoenas in the other. Go after the real big-time criminals— prostitutes, fags, and junkies. You'd think they'd have something better to do. I'm tempted to blow the fucking whistle." He crammed some stale pretzels into his mouth and washed them down with a swallow of beer. "But I won't, 'cause it would get Conchita in trouble, and I look after my girls." He belched, and thumped himself on the breastbone. "Oh, yeah, there was something. Word is that Natal Otero has got himself an expensive white woman."

"He's some shirttail relative of ours, isn't he? Works for the BIA?"

"Yeah. Anyway, word is she's gonna make him a senator if he comes through for her."

Sil felt a prickling at the back of his neck. "You didn't happen to get her name."

"No, sorry."

"Know what he's supposed to do?"

"Uh-uh."

"Then why bring it up if you don't know anything?"

"Hey, gossip's slow today," Ernie said. "Besides, it's about Indians, and I thought you were fucking hooked on Indians. Thought you'd want to know everything there was to know."

"If it's my Indians. Look, try to find out, will you? It may be nothing, but things are getting hot out at San Jose. The Pueblo's split right down the middle over the equestrian center, with a couple of extra splinter groups just to keep things interesting."

They fell silent, Sil compulsively trying to fit broken pretzels together. Ernie lipped thoughtfully at the neck of his Miller's and studied his cousin.

"You need some more?"

"Yes." The reply was scarcely audible.

"Shit, man! What are you doing with the stuff? Sticking it up your nose twelve hundred times a day?"

"Don't preach, Ernie."

"Hey, I do a hit now and then, smoke a joint at a party, but shit, Sil, you can't live without this shit. Where are you gettin' the money? Even with me supplying you at cut rate, it ain't cheap."

"Are you going to give it to me or not? If not, I'll go out and find somebody else."

"Yeah, and then you get busted, because you ain't got no brains, Sil. It's different buying on the street, *mi primo*. And you'll pay through the nose." Silvestre gave a sharp laugh at the unintentional pun. Ernie glared at him. "And you may get shit, and burn out your brains 'cause you're sniffing Drano. Smart, Sil. Real smart."

"Okay, I'm an idiot, I admit it. I'm naive. I'm a weak son of a bitch who'll never amount to a damn."

He ran down the list in a bored, sarcastic tone. "Now, may I please have some coke?"

"I don't have any right now. I didn't know you were going to snort it with a vacuum cleaner. It'll take me a few days to get some."

A sickly gray pallor replaced the usual warm gold tone of Silvestre's face. He stared stricken into the bar mirror.

Ernie gripped his shoulder, his plump face wrinkled with concern. "Hey, easy, man, easy."

"I haven't got much left. I don't think I can face . . ."

"I'll find you some stuff. I'll get it fast."

"Thank you," he whispered, sliding off the stool.

Ernie stroked at his fat cheeks with both hands and worriedly watched his narrow-hipped cousin as he left the bar.

"You gotta get some help, man," he said in a loud, aggressive tone, and then hunched his shoulders up around his ears and wished he'd had the courage to say it to Sil's face.

Terry was bubbling. Dancing about the kitchen. Mixing waffle batter, setting the table with a clash of silverware. He rushed back to the stove and flicked several fingertips' worth of water onto the antique cast-iron waffle iron. Droplets danced hysterically, and died in an evil hiss.

Mona, standing glumly in the door, surveyed all this boundless energy and made a face. She chewed experimentally on the taste in her mouth, grimaced, crossed to the refrigerator, and poured herself an orange juice. Last night Terry had written until four A.M., and Mona, in the mood for a little romance, had lain awake hour after endless hour willing him to come to bed and make love to her. Now he was whistling like a tree full of tone-deaf birds and raising cain in the kitchen.

"It's only ten o'clock in the morning."

"Look, Moni, it snowed."

Mona peered out at the thin dusting of white that

clung tenaciously to the sharp blades of the tall yucca plant and cowered about the granite boulders.

"Impressive."

"Hey, maybe there'll be more by Christmas."

Terry poured batter onto the iron, dropped the lid with a spat and a hiss, and broke two eggs into a skillet.

Mona rumpled her hair and padded to the kitchen table. She stared with burning eyes at the local Santa Fe newspaper.

"God, that's a useless rag, isn't it?"

"What?"

"That so-called newspaper. And the boy didn't even deliver the Albuquerque paper. Not that it's much better."

Mona started for the phone. "I'll call and—"

"Oh, don't bother. It'll be afternoon before he gets off his dead butt and gets out here, and by then who cares?" He grinned.

She stared at him. Why was he so manically cheerful? "I don't get it. Usually when you bitch, you really mean it. Why so happy?"

"I had a great night. I wrote *seventeen* fucking pages. Can you believe that?"

"Great." She sat back down, rested her head in her hands. "God, I'm so tired. How can you have so much energy?"

"Excited about tonight."

"Yeah, me too, but I'm going to have to take a nap or I'll never make it."

"Maybe I better too." He flipped a waffle onto her plate. "The last thing I need is to look like an idiot in front of Malcolm Adnett."

"Who?"

"You know, the editor."

"Editor . . . ?" She faltered. "But, Terry, we're going to Shalako tonight."

"What?"

"Don't you remember? Lexa and Nigel invited us to go to Zuni with them to see the Shalako dance."

"Oh, shit! Is that *this* weekend? Well, I can't do it."

Mona mechanically broke the eggs with her fork, and jabbed bacon into the yolk.

"Rhea's having a reception for me. One of her friends is a senior editor at Houghton Mifflin. He came out for a vacation, and she roped him for tonight. I can talk to him about my book. I told you about this."

"I know, you just didn't tell me when." She lifted her head and shook back the brown veil of her hair. "Well, that's the way it goes. We'll just do Shalako another year. I'll call Lexa and explain what happened."

Terry poured more batter on the griddle and stared at the steam rising from the sides. "There's no reason why you can't just go," he said in a too-casual tone.

There was a shriek of wood on brick as she slewed the chair around. "I don't want to go without you. No, I'll be happy to come with you tonight."

"There's really no reason."

"Terry, do you not want me to come? Is that what you're saying?"

"I'm just thinking of you. This is going to be just like the last party—mostly writers. You'd be bored."

"I don't read much."

"I know. You made it a point to tell everybody." He put an edge on the words to pay her back for the hurt-puppy routine she was pulling on him.

"They kept talking about all these books I hadn't read. I felt silly constantly saying 'I haven't read it.' I just thought it would be simpler if I was honest. I didn't mean to embarrass you."

"Well, you did."

"I'm sorry."

"So you may as well go on to this Indian jimjam. That way I won't feel guilty for denying you something you wanted to do." He gave her a smile.

"You don't want me to come to the reception with you."

"I didn't say that."

"You don't have to."

A curious expression passed over her face, but it was gone before Terry could decide what it had meant. It made him nervous when he didn't know what Mona was thinking. She had always been such an open book to him.

"Hey, you're not eating."

"I've lost my appetite."

"You're not coming down with something, are you?"

She seized gratefully at this explanation. "I might be. My head's hurting . . ." She seemed unable to go on, but he picked up eagerly for her.

"Hey, look, I'll call Lexa and make our excuses, and then I'll tuck you up with some aspirin, tea, and a good . . ." His face suffused with blood.

"Thank you." There was no sarcasm in the words.

She was so humble, so grateful for every act of affection. For a moment he struggled with guilt. It was an emotion neither familiar nor comfortable.

Phone tucked beneath his chin, he washed up the dishes and listened to the distant ringing.

"Hello, Lexa, Terry Gallagher here. . . . Well, that's what I'm calling about. I'm afraid we're not going to be able to go. I've got this important meeting tonight. Might be a chance to get my book sold. I guess Mona forgot about it. . . . Have her come without me? Well, I suggested that, but she seems to be feeling a little punk this morning. I made her go back to bed. In fact she probably won't even come with me tonight." Tight little laugh. "It's really not her scene . . . books and all. . . . Yeah, I'm sorry too. Well, have a good time, and think of me. Keep your fingers crossed. 'Bye."

Lexa replaced the receiver and returned to the table with a truly indescribable expression on her face. Nigel dropped his reading glasses down his nose and peered inquiringly over the top at her.

"That man is slime. Pure, unadulterated slime."

"That doesn't appear to be a remark to which there is any reply."

"Just agreement. Is your sister by chance hosting a soiree tonight?"

"I don't . . . no . . . well, yes I think she is."

"Hmmmm."

"I take it the Gallaghers won't be joining us at Shalako?"

"You take it right. And here we are with enough food to feed an army."

"Let's invite Silvestre."

"An excellent notion."

Nigel returned to his paper while Lexa sipped thoughtfully at her coffee and stared off into space.

"I don't believe she's sick."

"Hmm?"

"Mona. She was fine when I talked to her last night. Really looking forward to the trip."

"The flu can hit suddenly."

"Yeah, maybe."

"Okay, agreeing for the moment that Terry Gallagher is slime, that doesn't necessarily make him a bluebeard. . . . *What?* You really think he's got her locked up in there?"

"No, I think he's upset her."

"These things happen between married people." They eyed each other in silence for several moments. "I'll call Sil and see if he can come."

"Ummmm."

She was once more frowning abstractedly at the far wall.

Silvestre was not the most punctual of humans. So it was nearly seven before the hamper was stowed, blankets and pillows tucked in the backseat of the New Yorker, tapes selected to while away the travel time.

Lexa had insisted on driving the first leg, so it wasn't until they turned left instead of right on St. Francis Drive that Nigel twigged.

"This isn't the way to I-25."

"Nope. We're making a stop."

"Can I guess where it is?"

"Yes, if our telepathy has decided to start working again."

" 'Married-people' talk," Nigel explained to Sil, who was looking confused in the backseat. "We're about to attempt to collect Mona."

"I thought she was sick."

"Lexa doesn't believe that."

Fifteen minutes later they pulled up in front of the small adobe house. The pickup was gone, but a wisp of smoke curled up from the chimney.

"You fellows wait here."

"Fine."

There was a nervous scuffing in response to Lexa's imperative knock. Then Mona's voice asking huskily, "Who is it?"

"Lexa."

"Oh, gosh, just a minute."

The scuffing retreated. A few minutes later the door opened. Lexa peered closely at the younger woman's face. Noticed the signs of a hastily scrubbed face. It had probably helped, but it couldn't hide the puffy eyes or the reddened whites.

"Terry called you . . ."

"Yes, he called me. Is he here?"

"No, he gone to Rhea's."

"Good."

"Wh-why?"

"You're being kidnapped. It'll be easier if I don't have to walk over him."

"Lexa, I've got the flu."

"No, what you've got is a bad case of the dumps," she threw over her shoulder as she strode down the hall. Mona followed helplessly behind as Lexa went on, "Okay, so you and Terry got your signals crossed about the availability of the date. So he can't come." She was busy hauling jeans and a cable-knit sweater from the wardrobe. "No reason why you shouldn't. And don't worry about being a third wheel. We invited Sil. As a matter of fact, he's got something he wants to discuss with you."

"Something about the center?"

"No, something to fill in the days while you people wait for the Secretary of the Interior to get off his butt and approve the lease request."

"Oh." Interest flared briefly, then died. Mona sank down on the edge of her bed as if her legs had lost all strength. "No, Lexa, thanks for coming by, but I really don't feel like going."

"I won't take no for an answer."

Mona touched her fingers to her forehead. "Oh, please, why are you doing this?"

"Mona, look, you're upset because you wanted to come with us, turns out Terry can't go. For some reason, you don't want to go with him, or . . . whatever." She eyed the slumped figure closely. "Well, for God's sake, don't sit here and mope. Just because you're married to someone doesn't mean you've been grafted to him."

"I can't just go off without a word to Terry," protested Mona, but clearly beginning to weaken.

"Then leave him a note." Lexa thrust pants and sweater into the younger woman's arms. "Now, come on, girl, time's a-wasting. This is going to be fun. Tonight the gods are going to appear on the earth. You can't miss that."

They arrived at Zuni near eleven P.M. Mona, already exhausted from an emotionally upsetting day, sat propped in the corner of the backseat inhabiting that interesting state between waking and sleeping.

Nigel nosed the dark gray New Yorker sedan in next to a large Sanchez tour bus. The engine died, and in the sudden silence, borne on the back of the sharp December wind, came the murmur of hundreds of voices.

"Now we wander over to the Chavez house, settle down, and wait for the Shalakos to appear," Lexa said, thrusting open the door. A knife blade of wind thrust into the car, and Mona shivered.

"Probably be two hours," her husband remarked, checking his watch. Their voices faded as they moved to the back of the car and opened the trunk.

Silvestre leaned in. "Are you awake?"

"Barely."

"You'll come back to life. This is really quite interesting."

"Then you've been before."

"Yes, but not for many years."

"What exactly is Shalako?" Mona asked as she slid out of the car and slammed and locked the door.

"Better ask Lexa. She can give you a far more complete answer than I can."

The Vallises were waiting with coats, gloves, mufflers, and hats.

"Mona's confused," Sil said to Lexa. "Want to give her a quick lecture on kachina ceremonies?"

"Shalako," the older woman began as she wrapped a muffler about Mona's neck, "is a house blessing. Seven houses can be created during the year. Tonight the gods will come to bless these new homes. In fact the design of a Zuni house is dictated by this ceremony. One enormous room where the gods can be entertained."

Nigel and Lexa walked on ahead, about two feet apart. Their body language made it seem a chasm.

Sil was walking with his hands thrust deep into the pockets of his sheepskin coat, and Mona, suddenly needing human contact, linked her arm through his. She called after Lexa, "But it really doesn't have any importance anymore—it's just done for tourists, right?"

"By no means," Lexa corrected. "In the days preceding the ceremony, the various societies have had their secret rites conducted in the different kivas. No outsiders see that. This may be the public face of Shalako, but it still has meaning."

Mona glanced toward the shadowed bulk of the church. "But the Indians are Christians now."

Nigel joined in. "Oh, no, what they have achieved is an interesting blend of traditional Indian religion and Catholicism. The Christianity they practice on Sundays, the older religion they live. Of course, I'm making a broad generalization: you could find Pueblos and Navajos who have completely accepted our cosmological view. But most are loyal to their own faiths."

Sil gave her arm a squeeze. "The fact that they've managed to survive two separate waves of suppression gives you a pretty good idea of how devoted they are to their own religion. My forefathers made a truly heroic attempt to stamp out paganism throughout the sixteenth and seventeenth centuries. The Indians responded by massacring the Spanish colonists in the Pueblo uprising of 1680, and driving us out of New Mexico for about twelve years. I guess maybe the dons learned their lesson, because when they returned they stopped messing with the native ceremonies. As long as the Indians came to Mass on Sunday, they could dance for rain or corn, and the priests turned a blind eye.''

Lexa picked up the story. ''Then the Protestant Anglo settlers took up cudgels on behalf of religious intolerance, and once more drove the Indian religion underground. Fortunately, we have a constitution that can defend against that sort of thing, and the situation eased in the 1950's. Each Pueblo deals with these assaults on its customs in a slightly different way. The eastern Pueblos have opted for what all of us bright anthropologists and archaeologists call compartmentalization. In the west, Hopi and Zuni have chosen virtual rejection of the white faiths.''

''So they really believe—''

''Oh, yes,'' Nigel replied firmly.

''We're lucky this year,'' Lexa said, smiling back over her shoulder. ''One of Nigel's artists has built a new house. We're guaranteed a good view, and they'll save our place if we want to wander off to see the mudheads later.''

Mona felt terribly awkward as Nigel led them quickly through the village to a brilliantly lit adobe house. She tried to tell herself that this was nothing more than a housewarming party, but where she came from, people didn't allow dozens of strangers to enter their homes.

Inside, trestle tables sagged under a veritable feast: plates of tortillas, great crocks of stew, posole, chili.

They queued up for food, and Mona tried to release her sense of embarrassment. If Nigel and Lexa and Silvestre could casually enter a stranger's house and eat his food, then she guessed she could too.

They inched through the crowd into the kitchen. A large window had been cut in the wall, giving an excellent view of the great Shalako room that Lexa had described. Chairs had been arranged along the walls, and these were occupied by the Chavez family. The whitewashed walls themselves had been hung with jewelry, blankets, baskets.

Sil followed Mona's gaze and explained, "They're displaying their wealth for the gods."

"I thought it was best not to make the gods jealous."

"That's the western view."

"It's the only view I have."

"Dare to be a little daring."

"I'm not sure I want to." She stared down at her plate and toyed with the plump white hominy in its red-chili sauce. "This place scares me."

"Zuni?"

"No, New Mexico. Since I've come here I've felt like I'm losing my footing."

"You want to talk about it?" Sil asked. "We could go for a walk."

"Wouldn't that be rude?"

"Nigel and Lexa won't mind. They'll expect you to explore. And you won't miss anything. The Shalakos probably won't arrive for another hour."

Zuni, unlike San Jose or Taos, was not a stairstep Pueblo. The adobe houses were all one-story. Despite the lights and the people, the overall impression was one of dusty poverty. Still, there was a feeling of pride and dignity and solidarity surrounding the village. Mona sniffed deeply, drawing in the scents of roasting chili, freshly baked bread, piñon smoke, manure, and overall, the fresh sharp air of New Mexico.

They strolled toward the small river, where bare-branched cottonwoods seemed to be reaching up to tangle the stars in their twiggy fingertips. The gurgle and chuckle of the water was like the voice of an old friend, and Mona squatted on her haunches and tossed twigs into the dark, almost unseen water.

Silvestre leaned against the trunk of a tree and watched her. "Mona . . ."

"Yes?"

"There's something we need to discuss." Her face was a white mask of alarm in the darkness. "What happened between us that first night is still . . . well, between us. I can sense it. So I think we should clear the air. You are very beautiful and desirable, and

because I'm a male I'm very attracted to you. I also
understand and accept that you're married, and very
much in love with your husband. But beyond that,
Mona, I like you. It's not something I'm used to.
'Women' and 'friendship' are two words I somehow
never thought of in conjunction. And . . . well, I
guess I just wanted you to know that you can trust
me. And as trite as it sounds, I'd like to be your
friend."

She came carefully to her feet, bridged the two feet
that separated them, and laid her head on his shoulder.
He wrapped his arms about her and stood breathing in
the spicy scent of her perfume, the wool of her stocking cap pricking his nose.

"What's wrong?" he finally whispered after minutes had elapsed.

"Do you think it's possible to become someone
else?"

"Depends on how you mean 'someone else.' I overcame—or I'd like to think I overcame—my upbringing.
That's one kind of change, but if you're talking about
satisfying someone else's expectations . . . well, that
can be dangerous."

She faced him. "Why?"

"Because you can never live up to the image that
person has in his mind, and if things fall apart, you're
left not knowing who *you* are. You've spent years being a reflection of another person. It's tough to find
your own reality after being a simulacrum."

She slipped from his grasp and stared out into the
darkness. "I've defined myself by Terry and by my
work," she said in a distant voice. "Now I have no
work, and Terry . . ."

He remained silent.

"Not going to take the opportunity to trash him?"
she asked.

"No."

"You don't like him."

"No."

"Why not?"

"Do you really want to know?"

"Yes, I think I do."

"Okay. I can neither like nor respect a man who allows his wife to support him. It's his job to be protector and provider." A quick, not very humorous grin. "I guess to that extent I haven't overcome my traditional Spanish heritage. I also don't like the way he takes you for granted."

Fingertips to forehead, a jerky motion as she spun away, Mona said, "Please stop. I should never have—"

He caught her by the arms. "You asked. That means you're wondering about his treatment of you. You're a wonderful person, Mona, I care for you." They were separated by inches, eyes searching the other's face. Finally, slowly he bent and pressed his lips to hers. Guilt and panic began to flare, but the comfort the kiss brought her was too great to be denied.

He set her gently aside. "I don't know how to act," he said quietly. "I don't know what it is between us." He turned away and his footfalls faded into the darkness.

She gaped after him, then began to pick her way back toward the Pueblo. Suddenly she froze in wonder as an impossibly tall figure came swaying up out of the darkness. More followed. Etched against the star-strewn sky were tall feather headdresses surmounted by curving horns and sharp beaks. Bells rang with each step they took. Humans were escorting these fantastic figures.

Mona turned to bolt, and came up hard against Sil.

"I'm back."

"So I see."

"I shouldn't have left."

"No," she agreed, and wondering if the sight of the alien gods had driven her mad, she cupped his face in her hands and pressed a soft kiss onto the corner of his mouth.

The night passed with a dreamlike slowness. Shalakos blessed, and the mudheads—attired only in pinkish clay smeared over their bodies, ragged kilts, and

pieces of dark fabric tied around their necks—capered
and clowned. These amazing figures with their distinctive masks added to Mona's dislocation, her sense
of having stepped out of her own time and place.
Somehow what she did this night would have no consequences in the real world. So she held Sil's hand and
rested her head on his shoulder as she took tiny cat-
naps.

But now it was a new day, and the Shalakos were
preparing to run their footrace. It was difficult to
see. The crowds were kept well away from the race-
course. As she watched the looming seven-foot figures, Mona wondered how the men supporting the
frames of the kachinas had stayed on their feet for
so long. Perhaps, as Lexa had said at one point in
the predawn hours, they had truly taken on the aspect of the gods.

Nigel, gazing through a pair of binoculars, said,
"There they go." He passed the glasses to Lexa, who
waved them away and indicated Mona.

"Let our newcomer have the best look."

The Shalakos sprang closer. Mona swayed exhaust-
edly in time with the lurching figures. Suddenly one
stumbled and went down. A moan like a rising wind
shook the crowd. Nigel gripped her wrist and urged
her into a run.

"Come on, let's go."

And they were all racing for the car.

"What . . . why?" gasped Mona, stumbling along
behind him like a clumsy puppy on a leash.

"It's *very* bad luck when a Shalako falls," Lexa
panted. "You saw those fellows with the yucca
whips?" Mona nodded, having no wind for a reply.
"Well, they have been known to use those whips on
the observers. Usually they bypass the tourists, but not
always. Better to get out of the way. You noticed how
the natives all melted away."

"Well, that's an unfortunate ending to an otherwise
outstanding Shalako," panted Nigel, fishing out the
car key.

"A bad omen," Lexa sighed.

Mona, watching Sil open the door for her, had to
agree. She had looked at her marriage in a new and
uncomfortable light, and found a void not filled by her
husband. She had allowed another man to hold her and
kiss her. *Those they would destroy, the gods first make
mad.* Now the madness of the night had passed, leaving only the consequences, like shattered glass shards
all about her.

Terry was waiting.
When Mona saw his tall, powerful figure, all the
evils of her situation rushed in. White-faced, she
folded Lexa's muffler and cap and laid them on the car
seat.
"Thank you for taking me. I really enjoyed it."
"I'll see you in," offered Sil.
"No!"
Lexa did join her. Drawing close, Mona could see
the pinched white nostrils, the deep lines etched on
either side of Terry's wide mouth. She raised her eyes
to her husband's, read the anger there, and quickly
looked away.
"Hi," Lexa called easily. "Hope your evening was
as outstanding as ours, though I doubt it."
"Did you sell your book?" Mona asked in a small
voice.
"You don't sell a book at a cocktail party. Any idiot
knows that."
Mona blanched, ducked her head, and fled into the
house.
Lexa, gasping with outrage, stared up into Terry's
sulky face. "Well, what an absolutely *shitty* thing to
say!"
But she was addressing a closed door.
Sil was hanging tensely over the backseat. "What
happened?" he demanded as Lexa slid into the front
seat of the car. "What did he say to Mona?"
"Don't be an agitator," Nigel warned his wife in a
low voice. Lexa pressed her lips together.
Sil glanced from one to the other. Then, in a voice

shaking with anger, he said, "Then I'll find out for myself."

"Hold it right there!" Nigel rapped out in his sergeant-major voice. Silvestre froze, with one foot out of the car. "You can't go charging in there like Don Quixote. They are man and wife."

"Sometimes I'm not at all sure that this 'peace-at-any-price' attitude is necessarily the correct one," Lexa said.

Nigel cranked around to face his wife. "And just what the *hell* do you mean by that?"

Sil became small, melting into the corner of the car.

"Why are you getting so upset? I wasn't referring to you."

"Oh, really?"

"Yes, really."

It was a very uncomfortable ride back to the house.

"Mona, honey, I'm sorry."

"Go away."

She was huddled on the toilet seat, Kleenexes wadded against her streaming eyes. Barnaby, finding himself trapped, sent up several gentle *twerrks*, and when that failed to elicit any response, passed on to loud yowlings.

"I overreacted. But only because I was worried about you. I didn't realize you'd be gone all night."

Yeeeeow!

"Barnaby, shut up!" Mona screamed, and launched a hairbrush at him. With his fur standing on end in shock, the cat dived for cover in the bathtub.

Terry's deep chuckle sounded beyond the door. Mona found herself laughing, and hiccuping a bit as fresh sobs strove with giggles.

"Don't terrify the poor cat, Moni darling."

"All right, I won't." She opened the door. "Were you really worried?"

He wrapped his arms around her. "Horribly. I didn't sleep at all. I kept picturing all these terrible accidents." He tipped up her chin with a forefinger. "And

no, I didn't sell the book, but Mr. Adnett wants to see
it just as soon as it's finished."

"Oh, Terry . . ."

"So it wasn't a wasted evening."

She rested her head against his chest. Reassured
herself that he would never learn what had passed between her and Sil. It could only be misunderstood.
How to explain that a kiss could be a seal of friendship? He would never understand. *A night of madness.*

Resting his cheek on the top of her head, he decided that he had to keep her well clear of Rhea's
friends. Someone might talk about what was happening between him and Rhea. *Careful. He had to
be careful.*

The currycomb swept in ever-widening circles across
the sleek gray back. Favory stretched his neck and
curled his upper lip in ecstasy as the sharp tines of the
comb reached those inaccessible itches.

"Good morning," called Silvestre.

"Good morning," Mona replied.

He carefully searched her face, but there was no
sign of the injured fawn. Her slug of a husband had
apparently not been a bastard. A real step out of character, that.

"We never did talk this weekend."

She dropped her hand to her side, and Favory pushed
his nose urgently into her back. "I think we *talked*
quite a bit." She bit down on her lip, guilt clouding
her brown eyes, then turned her back and resumed
brushing.

Nettled, Sil replied rather too sharply, "This is
business."

The hard rubber curry fell into the tack box with a
crash, and Mona continued with the soft dandy brush.

Sil went on more calmly, "My friend Linda Gallegos is a physical therapist at St. Joe's. She wants
to start a riding-therapy class for her disabled children, and she asked if I could find horses and work-

ers. I offered ours, and then I thought of you and
Favory. He's as gentle as a kiss, and would be perfect.''

Much of Mona's tension had leached away, and in a
far less prickly tone she asked, ''What would we have
to do?''

''Just show up at the racetrack three days a week for
one hour. We'll lead the kids around on the horses, or
ride behind them while Linda and her assistants ma-
nipulate their arms, legs, and backs.''

''Sounds good. God knows I've got to find something to fill my days.'' Now that he had once more
proved himself to be safe, she added generously,
''Would you like to come for a ride with me?''

''No, I'd better not. I should call Linda back and
tell her we're set up. See you later.''

Lexa, looking like a particularly careless housewife
who had shattered all her china, hunched over the big
table and pushed at the pottery shards with a forefinger. She hated this job, and usually had graduate students handle the labeling, but today no grad assistants
were handy. They were all studying for finals. The site
report was due at the highway department on Monday,
and she hadn't even started it.

''Knock, knock,'' said Benny, poking his head
around the corner. ''Ah, you look busy.''

Lexa threw open her arms. ''Oh, my prince, my
white knight, come to rescue me.''

''That bored, huh?''

''Yes.'' She spun around on the stool and smiled up
at him. ''What's up?''

''Oh, not much.''

''Liar.'' She indicated a chair, and he slumped into
it, hands clasped between his thighs.

''May I snivel?''

''Snivel away.''

''I don't know what's wrong with my people. You
offer them a choice between something for free, just
another handout, and a chance to earn a living, learn
a trade, and what do you think they choose?''

"That's not necessarily an Indian trait. I think that's just good old lazy human nature manifesting itself."

"Yeah, maybe. The point is that from having a solid majority of the Pueblo behind us, we're now split evenly on the equestrian center. It just doesn't seem fair that Ralph Quintana has your sister-in-law and John Greer and Natal Otero on his side, while all we have—"

"Is you, summa cum laude, valedictorian of Wharton College's class of 1982, and Franklin Pierce, self-made millionaire."

"Well, thanks, but I don't feel like we're very tough right now. And I haven't told you the worst yet."

"So tell."

"Greer has managed to postpone the hearing before the Secretary of the Interior until we've prepared an environmental-impact statement. Do you know how much those things *cost*?"

"Yes, dear heart, I do. As one oil executive complained to me, 'You people find a broken pot, and we have to add another thousand pages to the EIS.' "

"I'm just afraid Franklin's going to pull out. And I wouldn't blame him if he did. This thing isn't likely to make any money for years."

"Benny"—Lexa crossed to him, and gathered his hands in hers—"Franklin's not doing this for money. It's a memorial to his daughter, and a way to pull the nose of the USET. And now that Rhea's roused the troops at Rancho de Palabra, he's really not going to back down."

"Yeah? Why not?"

"Because if there's one thing Franklin Pierce hates worse than bureaucrats, it's rich snobs. He's got the traditional chip on his shoulder carried by all poor boys who've made good."

"Um, maybe you're right. I've just sunk so much of myself into this project that to have it fail would almost kill me."

"That's stupid. At the risk of sounding pompous,

Benny: you've got to find your serenity within you. Looking for happiness outside yourself is no answer because sooner or later you are going to bump your nose, and you've got to have the inner resources to deal with it.''

"Umm."

"But that doesn't mean you have to do it all yourself. So, what can I do to help?"

"You already have—you let me snivel."

Lexa rocked back on her heels and nibbled thoughtfully at a cuticle. "Maybe there *is* something we can do.''

"What?"

"Politicians are notoriously sensitive to public opinion. Maybe we can try to swing it your way."

"Fat chance. Rhea's got the paper firmly in hand."

"The *Dispatch* is not a newspaper. As we used to say back home in Boston, it's something in which to wrap fish. Also, I seriously doubt that the Secretary of the Interior even reads it. What we need is a series of articles by a big-name journalist that will get picked up by the big eastern papers."

"They're never going to support my side. They're going to take one look at Quintana, and assume that we *are* trying to destroy our traditional culture."

"In the first place, Chief Martinez looks just as quaint and traditional as Ralph, and he's a lot more articulate. And where we need to put the focus is on the honkies at Rancho de Palabra. How their devotion to your cultural heritage is just a pose covering their basic selfishness and racism.'' Lexa was on her feet, pacing excitedly about the office. "We can bring out all these great things. Like how rich Anglos continue to block the installation of indoor plumbing at San Jose because it would spoil the ambience. Ambience to them maybe, but a hell of a lot of work for those poor women who have to carry water from the river.''

"Sounds pretty good," said Benny cautiously. "But where do we find this journalist?"

"I actually have one in mind. Over the years, Nigel and I have met the most amazing assortment of peo-

ple. Dan Bryant served with my husband in Vietnam,
and they've stayed close. He free-lances for a number
of newspapers.''

''Will he help?''

''I think he just might. Nigel and I will call him
tonight.''

''Lexa, I don't mean to be pushy, but, uh . . . well,
isn't this a little awkward for Nigel?''

''What? Because of Rhea and me?''

''Yeah.''

''I'm his wife.''

''And he's got to choose, is that it?''

''That's not how I meant it.''

''That's how it sounded.''

''All right, I'll call Danny myself. I won't even involve Nigel.''

''A subtle distinction that may be lost on Rhea.''

''Why are you so obsessed with her?'' Lexa asked.

''I'm not, it just seems that Nigel's afraid of her.''

''*Nigel?*''

''Yes.''

''Well, you're wrong!''

''Okay, I'm wrong.''

Linda Gallegos reached for the tubby little boy, who
instantly sent up a howl.

''No, no, ride more! Kiss, Mona.'' Because of his
physical and mental infirmities the words were thick
and slurred.

''Toby, Favory's tired. He needs a carrot before he
can go around again. Would you like to give him the
carrot?''

Toby, eyes swimming behind thick-lensed glasses,
nodded eagerly. Mona pressed a kiss onto his chill
cheek and handed him down to the therapist.

Her assistant carried him back to his wheelchair,
and Mona slid off Favory's broad rump.

''You're really wonderful with the children,'' Linda
remarked as Mona pulled a carrot from her tote bag.

''I think they're great. And you are too.''

''Well, as long as we're having a mutual-admiration

society, allow me to add that I can't thank you and Sil enough for helping out. These kids have made greater strides in a few weeks than in months of traditional therapy.''

Mona slapped Favory's neck as he craned for the carrot. ''Just proves what I've always believed—horses are magic.''

Linda led Favory over to Toby, who eagerly gripped the carrot in both hands and poked it toward the big gray muzzle. As an added precaution, Linda laid her hands over the boy's, but the big hunter seemed to sense that he needed to be careful. The carrot disappeared in tiny careful bites, the horse didn't nose after the final bite enfolded in Toby's pudgy fingers.

Mona watched. ''He's getting a little restless with all the walking. I think I'll take him out onto the track and let him shake the fidgets out.''

''Okay. It's Kool-Aid time anyway.''

Silvestre trotted up on Ragtime. ''Where you headed?''

''Onto the track. Care to come?''

''Sure.''

They clopped out of the paddock area, swaying lightly in their saddles, knees almost touching. The snow had melted, but the sandy loam of the track was still wet.

Sil eyed it with disfavor. ''Footing might not be too safe.''

Mona shot him a startled glance. ''Not safe? It's barely damp.''

''You've got to be careful out here. This caliche clay turns to glass when it's wet.''

''But this isn't caliche. It's a maintained track.''

''Nonetheless. And my hip is still like glass.''

''Sil, don't be a chicken.'' She nudged Favory into a trot, glanced down at his shoulder to pick up the correct diagonal, and missed the brick-red flush that spread over Sil's thin face.

As they hit the turn into the backstretch, Mona sat the trot, cued for the canter. Favory was doing his dressage-horse act. Rocking-horse canter, so slow, so comfortable that it barely tipped her in the saddle. He was being a gentleman about it, but he wanted to run. That was clear from his flicking ears, his tongue testing the bit. She lifted into two-point, seat raised out of the saddle, holding with her knees and upper thighs, and gave him his head. His stride lengthened slowly. He was an old horse, and not a racer so there wasn't that explosion of power one found in racing horses. But though his acceleration might be slow, it was sure, and soon they were running flat-out.

A bay head came nosing up on her left. It was Ragtime challenging. Favory tossed his head and gave a trumpeting cry. But he had no more to give, and in two strides the younger horse was alongside.

Mona laughed, feeling the wind snatch it from her teeth and fling it behind her. Then she shot a look to Sil, and her enjoyment died. His face was rigid, eyes staring in panic at the muddy track just in front of Ragtime's flying hooves. The tendons in hands and wrists were etched beneath the skin from his death grip on the reins.

At least he hadn't begun to saw on his horse's mouth. Despite his fear, he was enough of a horseman not to want to ruin such a fine animal.

Contradictory emotions roiled within Mona. Disgust and disbelief that someone could actually be afraid on a horse. Pity and embarrassment for placing him in this position and forcing him to reveal his terror. A desperate desire to help, to make him whole again.

Favory, with that equine telepathy that is common to all good horses, read Mona's confusion and slowed to a hand gallop, canter, trot, walk, without waiting for her signal. Ragtime, seeing his buddy fall behind, also checked in his headlong run.

The scent of sweating horse hung strong in the cold air. There was a creak of leather and a jingle of a chin chain, the blowing horses loud in the quiet afternoon as Mona rode to Sil. Their mounts stood nose to tail as they regarded each other, one flushed and sad, the other pale and wary.

Somehow Mona got the horses into the trailer, and Sil into the truck. Linda didn't argue about breaking early. She seemed to sense that something had occurred out on that lonely track. Silvestre hadn't spoken a word since they'd reined in. Mona risked a quick glance at him, felt an inward flinch at the naked despair on his face. She silently cursed the big stock trailer rumbling along behind them with its load of horses and ponies. She didn't dare drag it through town and leave it parked someplace. No, the horses had to come first. Sil understood that.

They bypassed the town to make the seemingly endless drive to the C. deBacas'. The clop of hooves was loud as the horses came down the ramp and were led one by one into the barn. Still nothing out of Silvestre. Mona tried to still the nervous fluttering in her gut. This silence was brooding and uncanny. It reminded her of her father's cold angers. Terry, by contrast, was very vocal about whatever concerned him. She had always thought open anger was the worst. Now she knew better. It was *all* unpleasant. And she was ill-equipped to deal with any of it.

She looked to where Sil stood hunched wretchedly over the bottom half of a stall. Squaring her shoulders with determination, Mona moved to him.

"Come on, I'm buying you dinner."

"Not hungry, and besides, it's too early."

"Then I'm buying you a drink."

He turned at the unaccustomed sharpness in her voice. "You're not going to take no for an answer, are you?"

"No. We have to talk, and either we can do it here or we can do it with some alcohol to help lubricate matters."

"Why?"

She was already walking toward the truck. "Because you don't have anyone else who'll understand.''

He stared down at the toes of his boots, shrugged. ''You know . . . you're right.''

12

Mona turned on Sil angrily. "I can't deal with this."

He had taken over driving after their third abortive stop and was now huddled over the wheel in the Pizza Hut parking lot.

"Look, Mona, I don't want to talk about this, and I sure as hell don't want to talk about it when there are people in the next booth with their ears flapping."

"They probably don't even care."

"But I do!" he shouted.

Mona was irritated. "Can we at least get something to drink?" she asked. "I'm parched."

"Yeah, why not?"

He spun the wheel, misjudged the narrow drive. The left tires crashed off the curb, and they went bouncing out into the street. Mona gingerly touched the sore spot where her teeth had snapped shut on her tongue, hoping that Silvestre would interpret "drink" as soft drink and pull into a McDonald's. Instead he turned in at the A Ace High bar and braked in front of the drive-up window.

The round-faced man at the window grinned, leaned on the small counter. *"Eh, Sil, comó estás?"*

"Muy bien, y tu?"

"Friend?" murmured Mona.

"My cousin Ernie Mondragon." Then, to Ernie: "How about a six-pack of Miller's." And to Mona: "You?"

"Uh, wine cooler," she said.

"Hard drinker, aren't you?"

"Hey, I only suggested this because I thought it

might help." Ernie had mooched away, so Mona added
in a sharp whisper, "And I'm not too wild about sit-
ting in the hills in a pickup truck filled with booze.
All we'd need is to be stopped by the police."

"Yeah, they might find this." He pulled a small
packet from his shirt pocket and tossed it onto the seat
between them.

"You idiot!"

"So, you're not as innocent as you seem."

"I've seen too much of this poison on the circuit."
She yanked open the door, grabbed the tiny plastic
sack, and stormed to the dumpster.

"Hey!"

Mona walked back to the truck, fastidiously dusting
her fingertips on her breeches.

"That was one hundred and fifty bucks."

"So, some wino is going to get a nice surprise."

"I don't know you in this mood."

"That'll be six and a quarter," Ernie said, pushing
across the liquor.

"I ought to make you pay for it."

"My pleasure." Mona dug bills from her purse.

" 'Bye," Ernie called as the truck clashed into gear
and peeled away. He pulled down his waving hand as
if embarrassed to find it flapping up over his head, and
smoothed down his hair. He hoped he wouldn't have
to bail Sil out of jail before the night was out.

The muted mutterings of Tom Brokaw blended with
the sharp hiss of chopped vegetables hitting the hot
sesame oil and Lexa humming as she set the tiny table
in its window nook. Nigel, briskly stirring the mixture
in the wok, wondered how to open the conversation.
Fortunately, she did it for him.

"I think it'll be great having Dan here for Christmas. You two haven't seen each other in ages, and this
will give you a chance to catch up."

Her too-casual, too-bright, too-cheerful tone an-
gered him more than defensiveness would have. He
slammed the wooden spatula onto the counter and
whirled to face her.

"Why don't you just level with me. You didn't invite
Dan out here for my sake, but for yours!"

Her straight brows snapped down in a thunderous
frown. "That's not fair. Okay, I was hoping that Dan
would take an interest in the San Jose problem, but I
looked at it more as killing two birds with one stone."

"No, what you were doing was looking for a sop to
keep me quiet and happy. Why are you putting us in
the middle of this thing, Lexa? It's not our concern."

"I think that's a pretty shallow attitude. The world's
in a mess right now because most people don't want
to be bothered, won't take a stand. I *care* about the
people at San Jose, and I want to help."

"Careful, you're starting to sound like one of those
eastern liberals you despise so much. You're talking
about the Indians like they're pets or retarded children.
They're bright people, they can handle their own af-
fairs without interference from us."

"Rhea's interfering."

"And, I would argue, with more justification than
you have."

"How can you say that?"

"Because she believes—rightly or wrongly—that
she's fighting to protect her home. Why are you fighting, Lexa?"

"All right, I'll make it personal. I'm involved because I care about Benny."

"How about making it a little *more* personal?"

"I don't know what you mean."

"I think you do. I think the real reason you're em-
broiling us in this mess is that you want to take a slap
at Rhea."

"No! I'm doing it because I want *you* to make a
goddamn choice, to take a stand and commit to something."

"I am committed. To you . . . to us."

"I wish I could believe that," Lexa said sadly, "but
I can't. We're not a partnership, we're some kind of
weird gimping trio. Rhea is twined in everything we
do."

Turning away, Nigel gathered up the pork and flung

it blindly into the wok. "That's silly—we hardly ever see her."

"We, yes. But you—*you* see her quite a lot."

"She looks to me for advice."

"I can't imagine why."

"Thank you so very much." He headed stiffly for the door.

"Nigel, wait, I didn't mean it that way."

She listened to his retreating footsteps, and moments later heard the engine of the car turn over. Helplessly she stood in the kitchen while tears streamed down her face and the stir-fry became a burned, indigestible mess.

"I'm so glad you came."

Backlit by the foyer chandelier, Rhea seemed a creature out of Greek mythology. Silver and gold ribbons were twined through her hair and cinched in the white satin peignoir tight beneath her breasts.

"I'm just glad you'd have me. I feel like an orphan."

"Poor baby." She reached up and stroked back Gallagher's unruly forelock. "You have no idea where she's gone?"

"None. I called that Linda person, and she said Mona left the track around four. I then called the C. deBacas', and got that surly father. He grunted out that the horses were back in the barn, but he couldn't say where my wife might be. He suggested I call the state police if I was really worried."

"Um," murmured Rhea, wishing she hadn't asked. Terry's careful listing of the steps he'd taken in search of his wife was boring. "Could you close the door, love? I'm freezing to death."

"God, and here I am babbling away like an idiot." He marched her into the living room, briskly chafing the chill skin of her upper arms.

Rhea sank gracefully into an armchair by the fire. "Have you written any more since Sunday?"

"Two chapters."

"Do I get to hear them?"

He ruffled his hair, scanned the room, then said with a bashful grin, "I was sort of hoping you'd ask, so I put them in the car."

"Well, go and get them. I'll have Maria prepare some eggnog. Don't make a face, naughty boy. This is not that dreadful yellow stuff from the supermarket, but my grandfather's *secret* recipe."

"Sounds sinful."

"It is, and decadent."

"Perfect for us."

"Do you think you'd ever make love with me?" Sil asked.

"No. I feel far too ambivalent about you."

Sil didn't insult her by pretending not to understand. Just sighed and said, "The cocaine."

"Yes."

"It's common enough."

"That doesn't make it right."

The pickup, its engine slowly cooling in the icy December night, let out a series of sharp metallic pings. The wind was scudding streamers of gray cloud across the sky and pulling a deep rushing sound from the limbs of the great pine trees. On a nearby slope Mona could see the shapely, slender aspens with their beautiful white trunks thrusting up from an icing of snow. A carload of tired, happy skiers passed the couple parked on the side of the road, heading down the mountain to light and warmth. But there was no warmth in the silent truck.

"Why did you quit riding?" she asked him soberly. "Was it your injuries, or was it fear?"

"What do you think?"

"I think you're afraid. I also think you're using the center as a way to hide, to never have to confront that fear."

Sil sucked down beer. "Shit, what is this? Cheap psychoanalysis?"

"No, it's free," she shot back tartly. "And besides, you asked."

"Where have you been hiding these claws?"

A tiny frown puckered the skin between her brows. "I'm not a total shrinking violet. I fight for things that matter."

"Do I matter?"

"Yes."

"To you?"

"Yes."

"Personally or professionally?"

"Both. Sil, you should stop the cocaine."

He rolled the cold bottle across his cheek. "Tell me something I don't know."

"If you quit, you could get back on the circuit."

"It's not that simple." His hand shot out, gripping her tightly around the wrist. "My little friend is the only thing that takes away the fear. Which makes it hopeless for me to consider a return to the circuit. You know our business—if fear is riding with you, you can't make it. Look at what happened in Paris."

He almost flung aside her hand, and Mona stared at the white bands left by the pressure of his fingers. She drew in a deep breath to steady herself. "That had a little bit to do with fear, but it had a hell of a lot more to do with bad judgment. Brought on, I would say, by your *little friend.* I've seen tapes of the accident. I could never understand why it happened. Now I do."

"So you think I should quit?" he asked.

"Yes."

"Just like that?"

"Just like that."

"Do you have any idea how difficult that is?"

"Nobody promised you life was going to be easy." She hefted her wine cooler, and eyed the bottle as if it were an alien artifact.

"You're not very sympathetic," Sil said.

"I don't understand addiction."

"I don't agree."

"What are you trying to say?" Mona asked warily.

"Oh, no. Uh-uh! This area is far too touchy."

"You think I'm obsessed with Terry," she challenged.

"I think maybe too much of your own self-worth

hangs on his approval. I also think you spend too much time shunning the limelight so he can be center-stage.''

''He's a much more interesting person than I am.''

''Says who?''

''Says him.'' She froze, cranked down the window of the truck, and threw her half-empty bottle against a boulder. Glass shards flew glittering in all directions. ''God damn you!''

''Me?''

''All right, so it's not the best marriage in the world. Whose is? But at least I'm working for what I want. Not like you.''

''Mona, it's not a sin to admit you might have made a mistake. People change.''

''May I submit that that little homily could be applied to you too.''

''Give me a break!'' he demanded.

''No.''

'' 'The darkness seemed to have a texture. Velvet and incense. Was it only memory, or did the soul leave bits of itself like tiny shining facets in each place and time that a person lived? Had Donald, by returning to this childhood place, somehow been reunited with that younger, stronger, more innocent part of himself?' ''

Terry turned the final page, glanced at Rhea with an appealing little-boy look, and shrugged. ''And that's as far as I've gone.''

She clapped her hands, the sound sharp and unnatural in the quiet room. Even the fire had died to slow-burning embers. Suddenly the wind returned with redoubled fury, driving the thin snow against the windows with an eerie sound. Rhea jumped and shivered. Instantly Terry crossed over to her, dropped gracefully to one knee, and put his arms around her waist.

The strands of his hair were soft against her fingers. ''It's beautiful, brilliant,'' she murmured. ''You've evoked this man's soul so beautifully.'' A coy smile. ''Is it, perhaps, just the tiniest bit autobiographical?''

"Well . . ." A self-deprecating little cough. "Maybe just a little."

It was a difficult moment, and for the first time in more years than Rhea cared to remember, she was at a loss. Carefully she slid from his grasp and glided to the table.

"A little more wine?"

He sank all the way down to sit cross-legged on the cold brick floor. "I'd better not."

"Why?"

"I think you can guess why."

"*I* wouldn't mind, but I don't want to upset you . . ."

The way he moved! Rhea's breath caught short. A jittering danced down her nerve endings. She was almost frightened by his advance. Hunting predator. Four husbands, two children, yet to feel so innocent. She giggled, and he froze, a display of male outrage.

She ran to him, her tiny hands gripping the lapels of his coat. "Oh, darling, darling. I'm not laughing at you, but at *me*. I feel like a blushing virgin. You're quite terrifying."

His lips pressed frenziedly against her throat. "I don't want to frighten you," he mumbled.

She pushed him gently away, laid a hand against his cheek. "Oh, please do."

A sharp bark of laughter, and he had her up and into his arms. Carried her swiftly through the house.

"You know the way," she accused. A slipper fell from her foot and hit the floor with a clash.

"Yes, I scouted out the territory."

"You were planning for this."

"I was hoping . . . praying for it."

"Oh, Terry . . ."

Mona had climbed out of the truck and was picking up glass shards with numb fingers.

"Here, let me help you . . . pick up the pieces."

They were separated by inches, Sil's hand clasped lightly about hers. A sudden blast of wind came shrieking down the mountains, stinging their faces with icy snowflakes.

"And I want to do the same for you."

"*What?*" screamed Sil over the crying of the wind.

"*The same. I want to do the same for you.*"

"*Why?*"

"*You must ride again. You were the best in the world.*"

"*That's no answer!*" he yelled.

"*I care for you.*"

"*More than Terry?*"

"No." She didn't shout this last word, hardly said it at all, but he could read her lips.

Silvestre lurched to the truck, bent almost double by the force of the wind. Mona stumbled after, gasping for air. The wind seemed to snatch the breath from her lips. The truck was shaking under the assault of wind and snow. Panting, Mona touched her eyes, and discovered that tears had frozen on her lashes.

"You're crying," said Sil.

"A little."

"Why?"

"Because I've hurt you, and I wish I didn't have to."

"You don't love me."

"Not that way."

He thrust the key into the ignition. The engine turned over with a growl.

Mona lightly touched his cheek. "Sil, are you going to quit?"

"I don't know. I'll try."

"Trying gets you trying."

"Huh?"

"Something I heard once. From the editor of *Bon Vivant* magazine. Seemed to make sense."

"Trying is the best I can offer you right now," Sil said.

"Don't offer *me* a damn thing! Do it for yourself! And if you don't want to quit, that's fine too."

"Would it really be all right?" he asked.

She stared into his golden eyes. Scraped back her

sodden, snow-matted hair. "No. I'd hate to think you're a coward."

"But I am."

The darkened room filled with the sibilant thrash of limbs on bedsheets, the atmosphere redolent of the musky scent of sweat and sex. Terry lifted his head and grinned at her. His face was wet with her juices, and milky droplets clung to his mustache. With a growl he slid up the length of her, and kissed her. She could taste coffee, brandy, and herself.

Shivering, Rhea clung to him, pulling him closer, closer. Using him as a talisman, a buffer, a shield. She lay silent while he, tiny groaning pants punctuating each breath, penetrated her.

Suddenly she came to life. Arching violently, she matched each powerful thrust, tangled her fingers in his flying sweat-slick hair, pulled him closer . . . closer! Terror warred with passion. Regret with pleasure. Tears flowed.

Terry groaned, long and desperate.

She felt him flooding her. His head fell forward onto her breasts. Rhea stroked the damp hair, listened to their matched breaths. The darkness and the loneliness receded.

"Rhea, I love you."

She briefly considered the image of the only man she had ever truly loved, that perfect boy, so slim and beautiful, but now a distant glass image, a shadowy form blurred by years and suspicions. That hazy image couldn't sustain itself against Terry—a warm, solid, comforting, passionate presence at her side. She buried her head against his chest, the sheer size and power of him making her safe.

"Oh, Terry, I love you too."

13

TRADITIONALISM OR RACISM?

Rhea lifted hooded eyes from the page and met the cool gaze of Dan Bryant. His dark face was impassive, but behind the ebony facade she sensed dislike. It was certainly reciprocated on her part. Laying the papers on the table, she pushed them away with fastidious fingertips.

"Why are you showing me this?"

"Thought you might want to comment before I send it. I wanted to give you one last chance to talk with me. If not, this story goes in as written. Talk to me, and I'll include your side."

"Interesting how you have suddenly developed journalistic ethics. You come out here at the behest of my sister-in-law, write this blatantly slanted and biased piece of yellow journalism, and then stand here pious and self-complacent and tell me how you *might* include my side," Rhea hissed. Silverware clattered on stoneware plates, and the hum of conversation filled the restaurant like a swarm of cicadas on a summer evening.

"Lady, there's no question of *might*. You talk, and I'll put it in, and let my readers judge."

Rhea skimmed the sheets he handed back to her, and glanced through them again. "I see that you've interviewed Benny Aragon, and Chief Martinez, and Franklin Pierce, and Silvestre C. deBaca, and even my unspeakable sister-in-law, and for an opposing view you're going to interview me. Very balanced reporting, Mr. Bryant."

"Look, Mrs. Sheridan, your lawyer won't discuss a client's business with me, and I can't get past the fucking guard gates to talk to your neighbors, and Chief Ralph Quintana—who, by the way, really strikes me as a pompous old crank—won't discuss tribal business with an outsider, so that leaves *you*. Now, you take it or leave it, because I'm getting damn tired of blocking traffic in this restaurant."

Rhea's luncheon companion, Louise Marshall, stared uncomfortably down at her plate, then put aside her fork and asked in a nervous whisper, "Do you want me to leave?"

"No, Louise, we've planned this day for two weeks. I'm not going to have it spoiled by a rude boor who—"

"Okay." Dan swept up his story.

"I will meet with you, Mr. Bryant, at my home this evening. I was raised to believe that one's prior commitments take precedence, and I do not intend to be rude to my luncheon guest. Good day."

"Sho, I just be shufflin' 'long, li'l missy," Dan drawled in a heavy Stepin Fetchit accent.

"At seven, Mr. Bryant," Rhea forced from between clenched teeth.

"See you then."

Rhea leaned solicitously toward Louise. "Would you like some dessert?"

"I'm afraid I've rather lost my appetite."

"I perfectly understand. Well, let's go to Suzanne's and chase away the bad taste by buying something expensive."

Louise didn't speak again until they had stepped out into the tiny courtyard that fronted the restaurant. She then tucked a hand beneath Rhea's arm and gave a quick squeeze.

"I don't know if anybody's said it, but we really do appreciate all your efforts. And not only on this center mess, but all the other times too. You're a real powerhouse, Rhea."

"Thank you, Louise. Sometimes I do get a little

tired. It's rather frustrating when everybody's always *totally behind you*, but won't do a damn thing to help."

"I know." The words oozed concern.

"But tell me, how does Gina like Vassar?"

Louise prattled along in her high soprano voice, and Rhea allowed the bright chatter to form a backdrop to her turbulent thoughts. Anger churned within her. What should have been a lovely day . . . completely ruined.

A sharp ringing of bells made Rhea realize they were passing Wenima. She skidded to a stop.

"Louise, would you mind going ahead without me? I'll catch up in a minute, but I just remembered I need to talk to Nigel."

"Oh, of course. Tell him hi for me. He's so gorgeous. Makes me wish I were single."

Nigel was huddled over the counter and didn't look up at the ringing of the bell. A tiny frown narrowed his eyes and puckered the skin between his brows. Nibbling nervously on the tip of a pen, he occasionally scribbled in a notebook. Rhea thought he looked tired and rather sad. She pushed aside concern and sympathy and allowed anger to harden her will.

Reaching up, she flipped the sign from Open to Closed. Nigel looked up.

"Rhea." He then noticed the sign. "We aren't going to do much business that way. Not that we've been doing so well anyway. Worst Christmas I've ever seen."

"I didn't come to talk about the business."

His eyes flared with alarm, and he said neutrally, "Oh?"

"How dare you bring in this journalist to harass and annoy me?"

"I didn't."

"He's your friend."

"Yes, and he came to visit me."

Her purse slammed onto the counter. "Don't patronize me! You *never* involve outsiders in Christmas. You're so damned private about holidays that you won't even come to the house for Christmas dinner."

"I think Christmas should be a family holiday."

"And I'm not family?"

"Yes, of course, but you always surround yourself with . . ."

"With what?" Her voice was dangerously low.

"With all of these people I don't know."

"But you're having Dan Bryant in."

"Well, he's been through a bad patch recently. Just got a divorce . . ." He floundered into silence.

"Why don't you just tell me the truth?"

"Because you're trying to put me in the middle between you and Lexa. And I refuse to be placed there. I'm a neutral bystander in this mess."

He gathered up his papers and rose from the stool, only to be held in place when Rhea's fingers locked around his wrist like talons.

"There's no such thing as *neutral* in this. You should be supporting me. I'm your sister."

His gray eyes flicked up to her implacable face, then away. "That's what Lexa says. But of course she doesn't say 'sister'." The tiny sally drew no answering response, and his nervous smile died by agonizing degrees.

"Nigel, you owe me . . . a lot."

Anger crashed in, driving the breath from his throat, leaving his head swimming.

Not quite sixteen years old—terrified and homeless. Sixty-seven cents in his pocket. He'd been hitchhiking west, desperate to put as much distance between himself and Rhode Island as was humanly possible. Now he was up against it—broke and a minor. He had turned to the Marines, and after lying long enough and hard enough, he'd found a recruiting sergeant willing to go for it. Or perhaps the man had realized that the frightened boy huddled in the chair before him truly had no place else to turn.

Five years of hell in Vietnam followed by the long and painful convalescence.

The aimless years in Europe.

Oh, yeah, he certainly owed her!

He was horrified at his reaction. Blame flowed both ways in this situation. She too had suffered.

When Nigel refocused on the present, he discovered that Rhea had retreated several steps. What had she read in those few violent seconds?

Humbly, contritely, he murmured, "I know."

She rushed toward him like a diving raptor. And from her glittering eyes he knew that her anger had grown, perhaps fueled by the scare he had given her.

"Without me, and my money to set you up in this shop, you'd be a lapdog for your wife, or some kind of common laborer."

"That's true."

"But none of that matters. I know you didn't call in Bryant—"

"Then why accuse me?"

"Because you won't hear a word against Lexa."

"I still won't," he warned.

"But she did send for him?"

"What does it matter? Done is done."

"I want to know."

"All right, yes."

"I want him gone, and I want his story quashed."

"And just how am I supposed to do that?"

"For once in your life, Nigel, would you get some balls in your pants." He flushed. "For eleven years you've let this woman rule your life. Well, now she's interfering in mine, and I want her stopped. You'll do it?"

"If I don't?"

"You'll do it, Nigel . . . because of what lies between us."

A vise closed on his windpipe. "You wouldn't," he forced out.

"Just try me."

"But it would smear you too," he cried desperately.

She clasped small hands to her bosom, her kitten's face falling into lines of shattered innocence. "I was very young. You took advantage."

"Lexa would never believe you."

She dropped the pose. "You want to risk it?"

"Rhea, please!" he begged in an agonized whisper.

"Do it, Nigel. I expect your support."

His eyes closed briefly in a spasm of anguish. "All right."

"Eh, Padre."

"Hi, Ernie."

The proprietor set aside his push broom and dusted his plump hands on his thighs. "Damn kids," he said with a nod to the broom. "Nobody wants to work anymore. So what can I do you for?"

"A case of beer."

"Hey, I didn't know you priests had that much fun."

"It's not for the rectory," Father Martin said. "I'm going out to San Jose to help with some repairs on the church. The entire north wall is crumbling, and with all the snow we've had, it can't keep till spring. If we waited, there'd be a big pile of mud in the center of the Pueblo."

"Hey, I thought you were a big administrator now. Second left wheel to the archbishop, or something."

The priest grimaced. "Truth is, I'm playing hooky. I can't take the bullshit level at the Cathedral, so I'm fleeing to find some real people."

"Hey, you ain't gonna find it with no Indians."

"Ernie . . ." Father Martin warned.

"Sorry. You just sort of breathe it in with the air up here, or drink it in the water."

"Interesting explanation for bigotry."

"Well, it ain't exactly bigotry," Ernie said. "Just sort of human nature. In Santa Fe the Chicanos hate the Indians, the Indians hate the Chicanos, the Anglos hate the Chicanos . . ." He paused and considered. "So I guess the bottom line is that everybody hates us spics."

"Oh, our Anglo patrones can whip up some good old-fashioned hate against the Indians too."

"Yeah." Ernie sniggered, then sobered as thoughts of Rancho de Palabra brought to mind Silvestre. "Hey, Martin, you got a few minutes?"

"Is this dog-collar business?"

"Yeah, I guess it is."

"Then I've got a few minutes."

"Great." Ernie bawled into the bar proper, and his sad-faced bartender came in. His long face got even longer when he learned that he had to oversee both bar and package liquor store. Ernie ignored his distress and led the priest into his office.

The chair creaked as Ernie canted it back and dropped his tennis shoes onto the littered desktop with a thump.

"You seen much of Silvestre recently?"

"Some," Martin replied. "Why?"

"Anything strike you about him?"

"Ernie, cut the crap and get to the point."

"That's hard," the barkeep complained.

"Try."

The older man eyed the priest warily. "You know I do some . . . some . . . business on the side?"

"Yes, Ernie."

"And you don't mind?" came the eager query.

"Let's just say I'm not enthralled by it. But what's this got to do with Sil?"

"I got contacts on the street."

"Yes! The point, Ernie, the point."

"Well, a year ago, right after Sil got home, some of my friends told me that he was burning up the sidewalks looking for coke."

"Oh crap."

"Well, he's family, and you know how bad the street stuff can be, so I . . . I—"

"So you started supplying for him."

"Yeah. You know I'm not a dealer. The escort service is as far as I'll go, but I've got contacts—"

"You said that."

"So I could supply him with something that isn't cut with Drano. But now I'm worried. I've been after him to get some help, but he hasn't listened, and the past week he's really been burning through the stuff. He's going to be smoking it next, and, well, you know what that means."

"Is this in the nature of a confession, or are you asking for advice?"

"Advice, please."

"Okay. Next time Sil turns up—"

"That won't be long," Ernie said moodily.

"You tell him you're cutting him off."

"Huh?"

"My poor-little-rich-boy cousin's been having it too easy for too long. I assume you've been supplying him at cost?"

"Of course," Ernie cried, stung.

"Then let him see just how much more expensive it gets and how bad the street variety can be."

"There's a lot of bad stuff mixed in—"

"I'm not planning on letting him blow out his septum. I'll confront him in a day or two. Any idea what suddenly upped his intake?"

"Just the nature of that shit."

"No, I don't think so. Silvestre had himself well in hand. *I* didn't notice he was using, and I lived in Central America, for Christ's sake. Something's changed."

"If you say so."

Martin rose, and laid a hand on Ernie's shoulder. "And by the way, thank you for telling me."

"I care about Sil. He's family. And frankly, I wasn't too comfortable . . ."

"With your role in all this?"

"Yeah."

"Don't worry. I'll see to it he gets help."

"Thanks, Father."

A pair of teenagers, as fair and beautiful as elves, slithered onto the top of the lichen-covered boulder and surveyed the fat old man standing in the open desert. An enormous red flannel cap with earflaps was pulled down low on his forehead, and it looked perfectly ridiculous with his black overcoat, cowboy boots, and walking stick. That stick was punching neat round holes in the frozen earth, but the man's focus seemed to be turned inward.

The twins eyed each other.

"Do you think he's a derelict?" whispered Elani. She had heard much of America's destitute street people in Europe.

"I doubt it, the coat's too expensive."

"He might have stolen it."

"True." Em's blue eyes narrowed with determination. "Still, we'd better check it out. This mesa's right below Mama's house. He might be . . ."

"Casing the joint," supplied Elani, whose current taste in fiction ran to hard-boiled detective novels.

Cat quick, they jumped down from their rock eyrie and circled around to blindside the mysterious stranger. But surprisingly, when they topped the ridge, he had turned and was staring at them. The small eyes enfolded in their layers of fat twinkled merrily, and the twins relaxed. It was hard to be concerned about a man who looked so much like Santa Claus in mufti.

"Well, hello there," Franklin Pierce drawled.

"Hello," they said in chorus.

Then they lapsed into silence, and the little trio again eyed each other.

The teenagers made a pretty sight in their matching maroon ski jackets, knee-high leather boots, and faded blue jeans. The cold wind off the Sangre de Cristos whipped Elani's hair into a long silver-gold pennant, ruffled Em's, and painted bright color in their pale cheeks.

Em finally spoke in a tone that struggled for firmness, and ended up sounding rather defiant. "What are you doing on my mother's property?"

The big man eyed the tall walls of the eight palatial houses that backed up against the mesa. "I'm afraid you're a little off there. This here is Indian land." They followed the line of his pointing arm.

San Jose Pueblo looked as if it were huddling in on itself to escape the cold, and blue-gray smoke lay like a lid on the adobe buildings.

"Then what are you doing here?" asked Elani, chewing on the end of a strand of hair.

"Dreaming, and hoping."

"What about?" she asked.

"For what?" Em chorused.

With a grunt, Pierce lowered himself onto the ground. The twins squatted before him. "I'm picturing it springtime with the Russian olives along that creekbed all pale green and silver in the sun, and the yuccas just starting to blossom. And right here"—his arm executed a circle—"there'll be a big oval arena all shiny white with jumps in the middle. And over there will be a big barn with a brick floor, and out there the pasture grass will just be starting to seed, and I'll be looking ahead to when it's tall and the horses are munching on it."

This burst of loquacity seemed to stun the twins. Elani fell back with a plop onto her bottom, and Em frowned and scratched at one pale eyebrow.

"That's weird," he said.

"What's weird about it? You don't like horses?"

"Don't mind him," put in Elani. "He always says that when he doesn't know what else to say. And yes, we both like horses. In fact, I love horses. We've had riding lessons, and we've even been to Aachen. Our father took us."

"When was that?"

"Umm, four or five years ago." She looked to her brother for confirmation.

"Five years," he said promptly.

"Em remembers things better than I do. He has a very precise mind."

"Does he now." The old man eyed the blushing youth. "Well, if you were in Aachen five years ago, you saw my daughter ride."

"Really?"

"Uh-huh, Denise Pierce." Franklin paused and gazed off across the desert, but Elani sensed that this jolly old man was not seeing scrub, dirt, and rock. She shifted uneasily, for the sorrow that dragged his face into sagging folds gave her a brief and uncomfortable glimpse of the world beyond childhood.

The man resumed. "I'm building this center for her. In memory."

"What happened to her?" Em's voice was low.

"She was killed in a car wreck three years ago. Seems so senseless. *Was* so senseless."

"I'm sorry."

"That's kind of you, boy." Pierce gave a massive shake, like a bear rousing from hibernation, and beamed at the pair. "What are your names?"

"I'm Emmerich Richter, and this is my sister, Elani."

"Emmerich? Is that some kind of Kraut name?"

"Yes, sir. Our father's Dietrich Richter. He's a major industrialist."

"Oh, is he now." Pierce laughed. "Well, I'm a major septic-tank mogul."

Elani giggled.

The beat of hooves brought all three heads up like questing hunting dogs. Favory burst over the hill with Mona huddled high on his withers. She reined in, and stared surprised at the odd gathering.

"What are you doing out here?" she demanded, slapping Favory's sweating neck.

"I might ask you the same," Pierce retorted.

"I always ride out this way."

"Dreamin' and hopin'?" Pierce suggested with a wink to the twins.

"What?" Mona asked.

"Never mind."

Elani drifted over and laid a timid hand on Favory's nose. The big hunter wuffed and dropped his muzzle into her palm.

"Do you like him?" Mona asked with a kind smile. She had seen that horse-struck look on too many girls' faces not to recognize it.

"Yes, he's beautiful."

Em was taking a more analytical approach, carefully evaluating the horse's points.

"Mona, this here is Elani and Emmerich Richter. Mona Gallagher. Trainer for my center."

"We saw you too," cried Elani with excitement.

"Whoa, what?"

"At Aachen."

"Five years ago," Em added.

"I'm surprised you'd remember. I didn't win."

"I know, but I remember anyway. You had such a great horse." Em's shoulders suddenly hunched up about his ears.

"Who did win?" Franklin abruptly asked.

"Silvestre."

"Speaking of our boy Silly, where is that chili-belly?"

Mona busied herself with straightening Favory's mane. "I haven't seen him for a few days."

"Ooooooh?"

"There's nothing very significant in that."

"No, of course not," Franklin said.

"Stop looking like a fat, smug old cat!"

"Are my trainer and my manager fighting?"

"No," Mona insisted, too sharply. "Stop being nosy."

The twins stood forgotten as the adults eyed each other with demanding and wary intensity.

"If something's going on, I want to know about it."

"There's such a thing as respecting a person's confidences."

"I don't buy that bullshit."

"Okay, it's your right not to." She bent and repositioned her foot in the stirrup.

"Well, are you going to tell me?" It was a warning rumble, but the woman didn't flinch.

"No."

"Mona Louise Gallagher!"

Elani jumped, and Favory shied.

"Now look, you've reduced yourself to frightening children and animals!"

Pierce glared at her like a baffled boar; then suddenly his features lightened and he grinned and slapped his thigh. "You little devil. I was worried I'd got the wrong person for the job. You were so shy and demure. Glad to know you got some gumption."

Mona was blushing. "There's something cockeyed about a world that regards me with approbation for acting like a snippy witch."

Franklin rounded on the twins. "Hey, it's colder than

a whore's . . . than a heifer's hind tit out here,'' he
boomed. "What say we go off and get some hot chocolate or chili?''

"I don't know,'' Elani began, casting a glance back
toward the houses.

"She won't mind,'' was Em's firm response. "She
probably won't even notice. Not when she's *entertaining,*" he added with a significant roll of the eyes.

Elani pulled off a glove and flipped open the top of
her watch ring. "Em, Maria's going to start dinner
soon.''

"Yeah, I guess we really don't have time.''

"But perhaps another time?'' suggested Elani hopefully.

"Why, sure, little honey. I'll take you down to the
French pastry shop.''

"That may be a little like taking coals to Newcas-
tle,'' murmured Mona, having noted the twins' Continental accents.

Elani gave Favory one final, regretful pat.

"Where are you two headed?'' Mona asked.

Em pointed. "Over that wall.''

"My, you are athletic. That must be a good mile
away. What say you two hop up on Favory, and I'll
take you over there.''

"Really?''

"Really.''

"But you'll have to walk in those heavy boots,
ma'am,'' said Em solicitously.

"I've done it before.''

Em turned to Pierce and held out a hand. They
shook. "I'll look forward to seeing you again, Mr.
Pierce.''

"We got a date now,'' he replied with a careless
flick of a finger to Elani's wind-chapped cheek.

"But can we always find you . . . out standing in
your field,'' said the girl, her voice catching on a
laugh.

The old man guffawed. "Well, maybe we can arrange a more certain meetin'.''

Mona stood ready to offer help, but Em swung easily into the saddle. His sister placed a foot on his, gripped his wrist, and swung up behind him. Mona released her grip on the reins and allowed the boy to gather up the double bridle. There was clearly no need to lead these children.

"He's a nice man," said Elani, swaying to the rock of Favory's powerful haunches.

"Yes, he is. He has a kind heart. And he will take you out for chocolate. He always does what he says he will."

"Will *you* be there, ma'am?" asked Em.

"Well . . ."

"Oh, please," cried Elani.

"Well, if I can."

They reached the wall.

"Thank you so much for the ride. My new school doesn't have horses." A small moue. "I guess they don't think riding is something young ladies need to know how to do."

Mona looked at her, arrested by a novel thought. "Would you be interested in taking riding lessons?"

"Oh, yes."

"And so would I," Em added as he slid to the ground.

"Well, maybe I'll just teach you. With all the delays on the center, I've been going stir-crazy. I could use Sil's horses. God knows *he* doesn't use them. Why don't you ask around and see if there are any of your friends who'd be interested."

"We really don't know any children. We're only here for a month."

"Oh, that's too bad."

Elani looked at Mona anxiously. "Will that make a difference?"

"No, not at all. I'd be happy to teach you for a month."

There was another round of formal handshakes, then Em boosted Elani up the wall. He then took a running jump, and Elani caught his wrists and hauled him up. A final wave.

Dusting off his knees, Em led them at a trot back to the house.

" 'Montmartre . . . on Assumption Day in 1534, Ignatius of Loyola and six of his companions met, and swore solemnly to fight against the enemies of religion, and by this act created the Society of Jesus. Donald wondered—' "

"Ma mère, we met the nicest old man. He's going to take us for cocoa."

"Shhh, Terry's reading his new chapter."

"Oh, well, we wouldn't want to interrupt *that,"* Em said, rolling his eyes toward his twin.

Rhea, not missing the significant look, decided to take the focus off Terry. "Elani, you know I've warned you against talking with strangers."

"It's all right. He was perfectly safe," Em replied for his sister, lifting a small sugar cake from the tea tray. His eyes flicked briefly across Terry, who sat with the pages of his manuscript clutched in one hand. Terry flushed and looked away.

"Was he a neighbor?" Rhea demanded.

"I don't think so. He was out on the mesa." Em pointed off to the northeast.

"Mama, may I take riding lessons?" Elani asked in a rush.

"What?"

"We met a woman too. Mona Gallagher—"

"Oh, Lord." Terry fell back in his chair with a laugh.

"What was this man's name," Rhea demanded sharply.

"Franklin Pierce."

"I forbid it! I absolutely forbid you to have anything to do with him. With either of them!" Her voice rose stridently.

"Rhea, that's going to be a little . . . difficult."

"Oh, Terry, I'm sorry." She flew to him and wrapped her arms around his shoulders. He reassured her with a pat and another chuckle.

Em frowned. "I don't understand."

Terry grinned. "That's because this is grown-up stuff."

The boy flushed at the amused, condescending tone. "Are you hoping to be number five?" Rhea's head snapped up, but Em continued, "Don't you think my mother's a little old for you?"

"Emmerich!"

Terry reared up out of the chair. "You little jackass. Your mother's the most beautiful woman I've ever seen. If you don't like me, or resent me, that's fine, but don't you *ever* take that tone with your mother again in my presence."

"I'm not afraid of you," the boy said shrilly.

"You fuckin' well better be!"

"Emmerich, go to your room," rapped out Rhea. Two bright spots of color burned on her cheeks.

Em bolted from the room, and Elani followed quickly after. But she paused on the stairs listening, trying to understand.

"Oh, Terry, this is killing me."

"Hush, love, we'll work it out."

"But you're *married* to her!"

"That can be fixed."

"I'm not too old. I'm not!"

"No, no, of course you're not. You're beautiful, and passionate . . ."

Elani slipped the rest of the way up the stairs to the tower room.

"Make way for number five."

Em threw his book across the room.

14

The big dump truck from Montoya's Sand and Gravel roared, whined, and farted, and with a sigh the load of sand shooshed onto the concrete apron in front of the garage. The two East Coast gringos eyed the pile with wary, puzzled expressions, and Martin, hiding a grin, strolled up.

"Hi, I don't think we've met. I'm Father Martin, Silvestre's cousin."

"How do you do. Terry Gallagher. My wife, Mona."

Hands were shaken all around. Mona's glance slid back to Grandmother Alejandra, seated in regal dignity in one of the big dining-room chairs. It was a startling sight, the aged, elegant woman in a chic rose pantsuit seated in a garage next to a stack of small brown paper bags. Alejandra unfolded a sack with a loud snap, and with quick, sure movements, her gnarled beringed fingers quickly folded down the top to form a neat one-inch hem.

Nearby, Benny Aragon was ripping the tops off cases of votive candles, Jorge was handing out shovels, Paloma and Mercedes were setting out snacks on a long table, and Benito was barking out orders like a D-day general.

"Do you have an idea what's going on here?" Father Martin asked with a smile.

Mona eyed the turned collar and opened her mouth to reply, but her husband was before her. "No, Padre, all the invitation said was a *fa . . . farolito* party. What the hell's a *farolito?*"

"Well, they're also called *luminarias.*"

"Gosh, that really clears things right up." Terry laughed, with a droll glance to Mona. She didn't smile back. She was embarrassed by his casual use of "Padre." She felt it had little to do with respect for the priest, but a lot to do with the fact that he was Hispanic.

"But that's the gringo phrase," continued the priest. "And let it never be said the C. deBacas aren't traditionalists first, last, and always."

"But whatever they're called, what are they?" asked Mona.

"They're a peculiarly New Mexican Christmas decoration. *Farolitos* are little lights set out to guide the Christ Child to earth. We line the walls and roofs and walks of our houses with them on Christmas Eve, and again on New Year's Eve. It's really a spectacular sight, particularly if you get an entire block decorating. It is, however, a pain in the butt to prepare them and set them out, so my family has taken to turning it into a party. It's worked very well."

"That's charming. Did the custom originate in Spain?" Gallagher asked.

"In a manner of speaking. There's some rather strong evidence indicating that the tradition arises out of the Jewish Hanukkah."

"How can that be?"

"Little-known fact. A great many of the families who settled in New Mexico were Sephardic Jews. Spain was not the safest place to be, no matter how secretly you practiced your faith. The Inquisition was always on the hunt for people whose conversions lacked sincerity."

"But everyone's Catholic now," said Mona.

"Oh, yes, with some odd quirks. For almost two hundred years this territory was isolated from Rome. We developed some odd variations."

"Like those crank Penitentes." Terry laughed.

"I don't know if I'd call them cranks," replied Father Martin.

"What else can you call them? Crucifixions, flagellations."

"I have a hunch that a lot of the real horror stories were fabricated by outraged Anglos. And even if they were true, so what? Those villagers weren't forcing people to take part. It's their faith, and their customs."

Terry wagged a finger under Martin's nose. "We'll have to argue this in greater depth sometime, Father."

"I'd enjoy that."

Franklin Pierce chugged into the garage and bore down on Mona. Terry pulled a face and pointedly walked away.

Pierce's small eyes apparently missed little, for after a hug he asked, "Have I pissed him off?"

"No," came Lexa's clear voice. "He's just feeling a little ambivalent about you, and his wife's job, even though it puts food on the table. You see, Rhea has been busy whispering in his left ear that he's the greatest American writer since Hemingway, so naturally he feels like he ought to take her side in the fight over the center. The fact that it's Mona's career doesn't count for much. *Art* is, after all, everything."

"Lexa!" The word snapped out like a whip crack as Nigel glared at his wife.

Mona had gone white, and shrank into the shelter of Pierce's arm. But the archaeologist's attention was fixed on her husband. She didn't seem to care about the effect her words were having.

"You must admit that Rhea seems to have an uncanny knack for destroying loyalties," Lexa said tightly.

"Don't." Nigel tried to make it sound like a warning, but it came out more like a plea.

"Why not, Nigel? Ashamed to have Franklin and Benny and Mona and Silvestre hear how you betrayed them?"

"Hey, whoa now, Lexa," Pierce said soothingly. "What's all this?"

She spun on him. "I brought Dan Bryant to town. You know, Dan Bryant, syndicated columnist with the

Washington *Post.* He had prepared a scathing article on the efforts to block the equestrian center. Then my husband and Dan went off for some secret *boy* talk, and suddenly Dan declines to file the story and heads back to Washington on the first plane. I just hope Rhea doesn't get any ideas from this. Like bringing in her own journalists and portraying us as rapers of the environment.''

Nigel Vallis was looking sick. His mouth had compressed into a tight line, and he turned and walked from the garage. As he passed, Father Martin caught a brief glance of his eyes. He thought he'd never seen a man in greater pain or filled with such absolute despair.

The priest took Mona's arm. "Tell me, do you want to be on the bag brigade, the sand brigade, or the candle brigade?'' he asked, jerking the conversation to safer ground.

"What?'' The word burst out stretched and tight. "Oh, I don't really know. What do they involve?''

Martin walked her toward Alejandra. "Well, you can either fold sacks if you've got dexterous fingers, or you can fill them halfway with sand, or you can stick candles into the sand, or you can load them into a wheelbarrow and trundle them out to us poor fools who'll be dancing on the roofs and walls like Hottentots.''

"Well, I guess I'll fold.''

"A good choice.''

"Why?''

"Because our revered matriarch has an uncanny ability to make people feel safe.''

Mona reared back.

"As I obviously do not,'' the priest added ruefully. "I'm sorry, but I couldn't miss what was going on back there.''

"It's embarrassing.'' Her face was canted away. "This is the most incestuous little town. Everything that happens instantly becomes everybody's business.''

"Mrs. Gallagher, I'm not just being nosy, really. As trite as it sounds, I do care."

She lifted her lashes, and her gaze when it met his was steady. "I would expect you to. That's the province of men of God."

"Good heavens, someone who's not a cynic in this questioning modern age?"

"Yes, I'm a dinosaur. I even go to church."

"Ah, but are you one of those dirty Proddies?" he teased.

"Yes, you popish devil."

"Who is a devil?" demanded Alejandra.

"I am, *abuela.*"

"Quite true," she replied placidly. "But at least you have passion, unlike that mealymouthed Father Conroy, whom I cannot abide. He gives me *un dolor de cabeza.*"

Father Martin gave his whinny of a laugh. "Well, I suppose that's a compliment. *Abuela,* I give you Mona Gallagher."

"Ah, the young lady who keeps her horse in the barn and works with Silvestre, and of whom he speaks so highly. I am pleased to meet you. But why haven't you come up to the house before, instead of hiding in the stable?"

"She'd heard about you," suggested Father Martin.

"Go!" She drove him away with an imperious wave.

"Sil tried," said Mona. "But I don't like to impose, and you've already been so nice about letting me keep Favory here."

"You pay, don't you?"

"Yes."

"Then there's nothing nice about it. Now, tell me about the center. . . ."

Terry was busy shoveling sand with Benny. Lexa, still looking like an avenging fury, was bearing down on him. Father Martin shifted direction toward what looked to be another interesting eruption.

"Don't you feel the least bit odd about being here?" Lexa flared.

Terry leaned on his shovel. "What *is* your problem?

Early menopause?'' The look he raked her with
brought the blood to her cheeks.

"You, among others, are my problem. How can you
just drift along like this?''

"A natural disinclination to take part in unpleasant
psychodramas.''

"You're absolutely self-absorbed, aren't you?''

"Naturally. I'm an artist.'' He grinned at Benny,
who responded by deepening his already impassive Indian expression.

Lexa gestured helplessly, frustrated by his slick
smile. "Do you even understand what I'm driving at?''

"Sure, you think I'm a slimeball because I won't be
childish, and stamp and pout, and take sides. I also
have a very real ability to remain neutral, not to put
people's backs up, and that really pisses you off because you can't say the same. You've managed to totally alienate your sister-in-law, and now you're
working hard on your husband.''

"My, Rhea does gossip, doesn't she?'' Lexa said in
a tight voice.

Terry smiled sweetly, seized the handles of a loaded
wheelbarrow, and pushed out the door.

Benny looked sympathetic, and a little rueful.
"Didn't come out of that one too well, did you?''

"No.''

"You know, there are times when I wish Franklin
and I had never cooked this up.''

Lexa grabbed Benny's arm and gave a hard shake.
"Don't *you* wimp out on me! Your instincts are right.
The center *is* important. The co-op's important.''

"Lexa, it's not just *your* family that's being torn
apart,'' Benny said.

"Oh.'' She bit down hard on her lower lip.

The priest slipped quietly away.

New Mexico had served up one of those crystal winter days when the clouds rolled back, the sun came out
sparkling, and each scent and sight seemed as new and
sharp-edged as if just created.

But Father Martin, crunching up and down on the
flat gravel-coated roof placing *farolitos,* had little time

to spare for scenery. He was watching Sil mop constantly at his streaming nose, the slight shivering of those fine long hands, the overall sense of malaise that hung about him. When Sil suddenly bolted down the ladder, Martin decided that Silvestre's travails had perhaps gone on long enough, so he followed.

He had assumed that Sil would head for the nearest bathroom, but he was wrong. The priest wasted minutes searching through the sprawling labyrinth of the hacienda.

Then he heard the sound of breaking glass, followed by a tearful cry from Mona Gallagher.

"What are you doing?"

Indistinguishable murmur in reply.

"I care because . . . well, because I do. You have too much talent, too much ability, too much *brains* to waste it all this way."

"I'm afraid!" Martin recognized his cousin's voice.

"All right, fine! So what? We're all afraid! Life isn't easy, it isn't pleasant, it's . . . hell. We just have to do the best we can."

"A pretty bleak attitude," said the priest softly as he leaned against the doorjamb.

Sil and Mona whirled, guilt tingeing both faces.

"Any evidence that it's not the correct one?" Mona asked with some acerbity.

"Yes. The two of you. The fact that you"—the priest glanced at Mona—"want to help him."

"You know," groaned Sil, who sat down hard on the toilet, burying his head in his hands.

"Ernie told me."

"Son of a bitch."

"He cares too."

"Well, he sure as hell didn't care enough to keep me from having to resort to the streets," Sil said bitterly.

"That was my doing. I told him to cut you off."

Mona gasped. "But he could have *died*. Who knows what they cut—"

"I thought it was worth the risk," Father Martin

interrupted. From her expression it was clear she didn't agree.

"So what are you going to do?" Sil's voice dragged with weariness.

"For starters, I think we ought to get out of the bathroom and retire into your bedroom. It'll be more comfortable," said Martin.

The trio arranged themselves into various corners of the room. Waited. Silvestre broke first.

"All right, so what do we do now?"

"I think that sort of depends on you," came the placid reply from his cousin.

"Oh, I thought you were the great puppetmaster here."

Mona spoke. "Sil, a few days ago you seemed on the verge of making a change."

"It's not that easy," he said.

"There are clinics—"

"Mona, forgive me, but I don't feel sanguine about going off to some psychiatric hospital that has to advertise. *Having trouble with your teenager? Send him to us! We'll get his head right!*"

Martin laughed. "I see your point. But, cousin dear, you've got a fine family doctor."

"I can't tell him this." Sil flung himself off the window seat and crossed the room in wide agitated strides.

"He's heard worse. Priests and doctors soon learn to be unflappable. That or they don't last," Martin said.

"I don't know. It'll be hard."

"Yes," Mona agreed softly.

Martin studied Silvestre's hands where they locked behind his back, spasmodically clenching and relaxing. "Sil, you've never been a coward. Sure, it will be hard—"

"But that's *just* what I am. Ask Mona why I started. Ask her!"

"I'd rather ask you."

It was a long moment before Silvestre could bring himself to answer. "Fear! Fear, that's why! It got so bad I couldn't climb into that saddle without a dose of my own private invulnerability.''

"You can regain the confidence," Mona said quietly.

"How? *How?*"

"By riding. I'll help you." There was something in her level gaze that leached the anger and tension from his slim body.

"You'd really do that?"

"Yes."

"Why?"

"Because I care about you. I'm your friend."

"I could just get off the junk, stay here, work for Franklin."

"You wouldn't be happy," Mona said softly.

His eyes closed briefly. "Why do you have to be right?"

"Believe me, it happens very rarely."

He looked up at the sad and slightly bitter tone in her voice. "Don't."

"What?"

"Don't run yourself down."

Martin spoke up. "Sil, you can't quit just because Mona and I want you to. It's got to come from inside."

"It does. I really am ready. I'm just whining about what I'll have to go through to get there."

The priest brought his hands down onto his thighs in a sharp slap. "Then let's do it."

"Huh?"

"Let's call Dr. Spector."

"It's Saturday."

"I don't think he'd want us to wait. You got any more of that crap stashed around?"

Sil walked to the bedside table, pulled out a drawer, held out a packet clamped between middle and forefinger.

"You'll clean up the spill in the bathroom?"

Mona nodded.

Silvestre crossed to her and looked down into the

delicate oval face. "You're sure you want to be a part of this? You don't owe me a damn thing."

"Friends don't talk about *owing*. Today I help you, next week it may be me. That's what friends are for."

He held up a hand, palm out. She pressed hers against it, and their fingers folded down tightly over one another's.

Nigel, silver hip flask firmly in hand, searched for Sil. Instead he came upon Mona kneeling on the cold brick floor of a back bathroom, wiping up a spray of white powder.

"You ought to be more careful when you're using. First, not to spill it, and then not to get caught. What if I'd been a policeman?"

She rocked back on her heels. "I'm not using, I'm cleaning."

"Oh." He frowned and scratched at his nose.

"You're drunk."

"Yep." He seated himself carefully on the edge of the bathtub. "Not much of a party, is it? Hope people are having a better time than we are."

"What makes you think I'm not having a good time?"

"You're hiding in a bathroom, using . . . er . . . cleaning. But I agree with your choice, bathrooms are my usual place of retreat. You run water, flush the john, nobody can hear your sniveling."

"What's wrong between you and Lexa?"

"Everything." His arm swung out in an unsteady arc. "We're a pair, aren't we? My wife doesn't want me because I'm not loyal enough, but your husband doesn't want you because you're too loyal."

Her hand tensed on the sponge. "What do you mean?"

"You stifle him. You don't understand him. That's what he tells Rhea. I, however, am very understanding."

Mona leapt to her feet and stared down at him. In a carefully controlled voice she asked, "Are you suggesting that I'm in the very humiliating position of the wife who's always the last to know?''

"Well, I wouldn't put it quite that way, but yes. But you needn't worry," he called after her fleeing back. "She doesn't really want Terry. She wants . . . me." The final words were an almost inaudible whisper.

The Sidewinder bar squatted peeling and unlovely on the very edge of the San Jose reservation. Three feet to one side, and you were on Indian land, dry and supposedly safe. Three feet to the other, and it was time to let the good times roll.

Inside, a jukebox blared. The fruity, vibrant country-western sounds mingled with the smoke haze and the stale odor of spilled beer.

Benny took a seat by the big picture window overlooking the gravel parking lot. He wasn't much of a drinker. Partly because of the taste—give him a Pepsi any day—but mostly because of the Indian curse. Some had tried to characterize it as a racial slur. But it wasn't, alcohol did have a deadly effect on people of his blood. Even so, tonight he needed a drink.

The afternoon ratcheted past in a series of tiny pictures like slides running through a balky viewer. Lexa, anger tightening her pretty features. Nigel, drinking and drinking until Benny and Sil had finally poured him into the front seat of the car. A scarcely overheard conversation between that pretty little trainer and her hosehead husband. Mona striving for calm, for rationality. *"Are you having an affair?"* Gallagher's voice, low and amused, tolerant and caressing. The voice of an adult to a temperamental child.

"No, of course not. Whatever gave you that idea?"
"Nigel."
"That lush."

Benny had burned with anger then. Not so much for Nigel's sake. For when all was said and done, he really didn't know Vallis very well, and frankly, Benny felt that he was too weak to be married to someone as fantastic as Lexa. No, he hurt for Lexa.

Then there was Paloma, upset because her favorite

law professor had declined the invitation. There was a girl who clearly had too much nerves and hair. How was she possibly going to survive in the rough world of the law? Yet he pitied her. The traditional Spanish and Indian worlds left little place for their women, but at least in the hidebound society of a Pueblo there was *some* role for women beyond wife and mother, and no aggressive Catholicism to tell them how sinful and useless they were.

Only Silvestre and Father Martin had seemed pleased with the day. Over and over their eyes had met. The priest's warm and approving. Sil's with a kind of manic joy. They had left shortly after folding Nigel into his car. Benny admitted to some curiosity. Despite his best efforts, he liked Silvestre. Sil had invited him to his home. And to give the rest of the C. deBaca clan their due, they had made him welcome.

Benny gave a small headshake and sipped at his Scotch and soda. There was a spray of gravel, and a big Cadillac Eldorado came slewing into the lot. It was hard to tell its color beneath the armor of mud that caked every surface. The young Indian sighed and briefly rested his head on a hand.

A moment later, the door burst open. In staggered Pepe Sena, youngest son of the lieutenant governor, and his friend and constant companion, Dan Varga. They were an odd pair. Sena was only twenty-three, and Varga, the former governor of the Pueblo, was a grizzled fifty if he was a day. Yet they were bosom pals, and no part of the 121,666 square miles of New Mexico was safe from their manic preambulations. In the Pueblo they were known as the Party Boys.

Pepe's bleary eye fell upon Aragon.

"Hey, Benny," he slurred.

They were *very* drunk, but since this was a normal condition for the pair, Benny met Sena's malodorous greeting with equanimity.

"Look, Dan. It's Benny."

"Uhhhh." The grunt faded off into a loud belch.

"Benny." Sena snapped his fingers. "We were looking for you."

"Oh? Why?" he asked cautiously. The Party Boys had a habit of trying to impress the "college graduate," and their ideas on that score had taken some pretty strange twists.

"We got a present for you."

"But you got to come out to the car to see it," added Varga.

"Pepe, the last time you brought me a present, it was a birthing sheep. I don't really want—"

"No, this is better. A lot better."

"That's what I'm afraid of." Benny sighed.

"Come on." Dan tugged urgently at his arm.

With a deep breath, Benny drained the last of his Scotch. "Okay."

"But wait. First we need a *drink!*"

"Pepe, don't you think you've had enough?"

"Nah, can never have enough."

Each of the rollicking pair bought a six-pack of Miller's and lurched out into the winter night. Benny picked his way daintily through the puddles in their wake. Sena and Varga were less fastidious. They plowed ahead like cows going to water.

Reaching the Caddy, Pepe triumphantly threw open the back door. Revealed in the harsh light lay a wizened figure. The light glittered on masses of silver jewelry and drew rich color from the deep purple velvet shirt. A scarf tied low over the forehead held back the long gray hair. The old man was curled in the fetal position on the back seat, mouth wide, breathing sonorously.

"That's a Navajo."

"Yes, I can see it's a Navajo," Benny replied.

"That's a *drunken* Navajo."

"Yes."

"Isn't that the most *disgusting* thing you've ever seen?"

"Close," averred Benny with a bland glance to the Party Boys.

"Well, he's yours."

"What?"

"We picked him up for you."

"Where?" Benny asked with a growing sense of alarm.

Pepe dug Dan in the ribs. "Where?"

"Huh, where?"

"Where'd we pick him up? You were drivin', Dan."

"Ummmmmm." And after this profundity Dan subsided.

"Pepe, think," Benny urged.

"He was sleeping on the side of the road," the boy offered brightly.

Better on the side than on, Benny thought wearily. Each year too many Indians, Navajo and Pueblo, died while walking along the side of New Mexico's lonely highways, or from sleeping on the asphalt for warmth.

"Fort Defiance," Dan suddenly announced.

"Fort Defiance!" Benny shouted. That was about two hundred miles away, on the Arizona border.

"You don't want him," Pepe said sadly.

"Well, it's not that, it's just . . ." Benny's voice trailed away.

Varga reached in and dragged the old man out. The old Navajo continued to snore even when propped against the back tire of a cranked-up four-by-four.

"Come on, Pepe, let's go."

"See if I ever bring you anything again," the younger man yelled as they fell into the Cadillac.

Benny stood for a long moment regarding his "present." The old Navajo's face was as dark and deeply lined as an ancient piece of oak. Even in a drunken sleep there was a dignity about him, and Benny felt a surge of fury that he should have been dumped in a parking lot, mud from a truck tire befouling his long silver hair.

Bending, he lifted the wizened figure and carried him to his car. His mother would give the old man a bed, and in the morning breakfast, and then they'd get him on a bus back to Fort Defiance. And doubtless somewhere along one of those lonely highways he would ask the driver to stop, and walk off into the desert, headed to a distant hogan and a family that had worried about him.

"Merry Christmas, Grandfather."

15

Mona was kneeling by a half-decorated Christmas tree, a string of glass garlands trailing from a limp hand. Floor-length tartan skirt, black sweater, the long brown hair braided with ribbons of green, red, and gold. The overt gaiety was offset by the black anguish in her eyes.

Silvestre hesitated in the doorway, the snow hissing softly about his feet. "I knocked," he said awkwardly, "but you didn't answer. So I tried . . . the door was unlocked."

She looked up, and what he saw in that white strained face pulled him across the room. Kneeling, Sil pulled her into his arms. After a moment of resistance, she clung to his shoulders, sobs shaking the slender frame.

"Mona, Mona," he crooned, his hand stroking her shiny hair. "What's happened? What's wrong?"

She gulped and wiped furiously at her eyes with the backs of her hands. "Why . . . why are you here?"

"You haven't come to see Favory for two days. It's Christmas, I knew you wouldn't ignore him."

She resumed decorating, pacing slowly about the tree, winding the garland like a druid priestess.

"Mona, talk to me."

She paused, stared at him, then said flatly, "Terry's gone."

"Gone?"

"He moved out yesterday."

"Yesterday!"

She gave him a watery smile and chewed hard on

her lower lip. "Yeah, he has great timing, doesn't he?"

"Oh, Mona, I'm sorry." She gave a tiny shrug. "Where did he go?"

"Can't you guess?"

"Not to—"

"Yes."

"Oh, Dios, what a mess."

"Well, everybody told me that Santa Fe was an incestuous little town."

There was silence, save for the rattle of tissue paper as she opened a box and removed a glass ornament.

"What will you do?"

"Stay. At least for the time being. Franklin's been paying me for four months. I owe him at least the loyalty of sticking around to see if I ever do get to do any of the work."

He studied his hands. "I'm glad you're going to stay."

"You're going to be the one who's leaving," she said with a sad smile.

"What do you mean?"

"You'll handle your fear, and that . . . other, and you'll go back to the circuit."

"You were going to help me with the fear part."

"I still will."

"Why don't you come back to the house? Mama's fixed a big dinner, and—"

She shook her head so violently that it set the heavy braid to thumping against her back. "No, I can't face . . ." She covered her face with a hand.

"Okay, I understand."

"The worst part of it is that he never even said anything to me. It was like holding smoke. I tried to talk. Needed to talk. He just kept smiling, and changing the subject, and reassuring me, and then he packed and left. How could he do that to me? Unless he never really loved me. Which makes me pretty stupid, doesn't it?"

"No, it just shows that you were always far too good for him." His hand gently stroked her hair.

Then the tears returned, erupting from her like an agonized cry. Swinging her into his arms, Sil carried her to the sofa, where he held her tightly, rocking her like a baby and waiting for the storm to ease. It was a long time in passing, but at last she lay limp and exhausted within the circle of his arms. Sil stared into the distorting surface of a large Christmas ornament, and saw reflected there a calvacade of ugly, violent scenes. Over and over Terry Gallagher lay dead at his feet.

With a jerk Mona came to life, twisted in his arms, and pressed her mouth feverishly upon his. He tasted salt, and coffee, and brandy, then his breath froze in his throat as she gripped his shirt, and yanked it from his pants. Her fingertips were cool against the warm skin of his belly as she ran a hand along his waistband. Her tongue darted past his teeth, fenced briefly, retreated. She fastened her lips on his neck, and bit down hard.

"Love me, Sil. Love me!"

"M . . . M . . . Mona."

"I'm so alone. I have to know . . ."

Her tears ran hot and sticky down his throat. Gripping her by the shoulders, he forced her head up and looked into her ravaged face.

"That you're lovable? That someone cares?" She nodded mutely. "You are, and I do."

She sensed his hesitation and drew back. "But?"

"You're reaching for me now because you're hurt and lonely and afraid. And I'm happy to be here for you. I just want you to know that if I . . . if we . . . well, it commits you to nothing."

"Sil . . ." Her voice was a mournful cry.

"You've said it many times, Mona, that we're friends. And we are. And friends are there for each other. But I don't want you to feel obliged to pretend that the love you feel for me is that more intimate emotion that exists between a man and a woman. If you really want me, I will joyfully make love to you. I just don't want you to feel trapped after it's over."

"What are you saying to me, Sil? That you really don't want me or love me?"

He gave his head an emphatic shake. "Christ, no! You're gorgeous. I've thought that from the first day you arrived. But I was thinking with my gonads. Then I woke up one day and realized I had a friend—a very close and dear one. I know we love each other, Mona. I just don't think we're *in* love with each other. This is not to say that when a very beautiful and very desirable woman—who just happens to be my friend—implores me to bed her that I'm going to say no—"

She laid a hand across his mouth. "I understand. What say we just cuddle in the bedroom, and let the chips fall where they may?"

"I prophesy . . . we will have a white Christmas. Our first in eight years," fluted Rhea. Her eyes were bright behind the nodding white feathers of her elaborate mask. Tiny crystal beads hung down from her temples and rang coldly each time she moved. "Are you all settled in?" she asked, leaning into Terry's broad chest and giving his mask an infinitesimal adjustment.

"Uh-huh." His grin held complacency as he eyed the shifting throng that filled the house.

"Isn't this better than stodgy religiosity?"

"Much, and it beats familial togetherness all to hell too."

"Naughty!"

"Huh?"

"I thought you were talking about Nigel. He looks so miserable, poor baby."

"No, I was thinking about . . ." But apparently speaking Mona's name aloud was more than he could bring himself to do.

"Now, don't you go feeling guilty, darling," Rhea scolded. "A person has to pursue his own happiness. You can't make yourself a martyr to other people's needs and expectations." She gave his arm a little shake. "We've talked about this."

"Yes, I know, and I agree. I just wish your really

irritating half-brother had kept his drunken mouth shut. If he had, I could have waited another few days—at least until Christmas was over—before leaving Mona, and people would have less ammunition. They're really going to rake us across the coals, you know that, don't you?''

"Yes, and I don't care. You're here now, and that's all that matters."

At the far end of the big living room Nigel paused in the act of refilling his glass from his hip flask. Elani and Em were drifting past, looking adorable in cat costumes. Elani trailed her mask in one hand, and her expression was anything but adorable.

"Elani, what's the matter?" Nigel asked.

She threw back her long blond hair with an angry flip. "Oh, it's *Mother!* I *hate* holidays."

"That's not the normal attitude."

"Most people don't have *her* for a mother." Her brother shot her a warning glance. "Oh, don't worry, Em. He's on our side. You don't like Mother, do you, Uncle Ni?"

Nigel goggled at his niece. Took a swallow of brandy. Squinted up at the blazing star atop the fifteen-foot-tall white-flocked Christmas tree.

"There are times when your mother's behavior disappoints me."

"That's a cop-out."

Nigel pinned his nephew with a stern eye. "You've learned better manners than that, young man."

"Why are you here? And without Lexa," demanded Elani, joining the attack. "Two years ago you weren't here. Last year you weren't here."

"Your mother had a special reason for me to come. I won't be here tomorrow."

"No, instead we'll be stuck with her latest walking penis." Elani jerked her head toward Terry. "I wonder what she's going to do when she's old and ugly and can't get them anymore."

As he gazed down into his niece's glowing, angry, beautiful face, Nigel suddenly understood why the twins were exiled to boarding schools. They would be fifteen in February. The years were passing, and Rhea didn't want to be reminded. Nigel's eyes sought out the tiny vivacious figure of his half-sister. Terry was at her side, and suddenly Nigel realized he hadn't seen Mona anywhere.

"Excuse me," he murmured to the twins, and pushed through the crowd to Rhea.

"Rhea."

"Nigel!" A cry of delighted surprise. For an instant he hated her for the fraud. She knew he would be here. She had made it impossible for him to refuse. "You are *not* going to leave yet. I insist that you stay."

"I'm not leaving. But I want to talk to you."

She flung open her arms in a quivering, overblown gesture. Nigel had seen her in these moods before—fey, manic, dangerous.

"How lovely. Excuse me, darling, won't you," she threw over her shoulder to Terry.

Nigel drew her out of the living room. "What are you doing?"

"What do you mean?"

"What's Gallagher doing here, and without his wife?"

"He will soon be *without* a wife." She gestured wildly, spilling champagne down his shoulder. Then she leaned in until he could feel her breath puffing softly against his lips. "He left her, Nigel. He loves me."

"Good God, he's maybe thirty, and you're what? Forty-five?"

She flounced away. "What has that to do with anything!"

"A damn lot!"

"You're cruel!"

"And what you've done isn't? His poor little wife adored him."

"He deserves to be happy."

"You mean *you* do." He grabbed her by the shoulder and flung her around to face him. "It's very simple, you wanted him, so you got him."

"Do you rank my seductive powers so high?" she simpered, but with a glitter in her blue eyes.

"Yes . . . oh, Christ, yes."

She averted her face and murmured into her shoulder, "He'll make me happy."

"You thought the other four would too."

"It's different this time."

"I've heard that before."

"Why are you being so hateful to me, Nigel."

"Because you're playing games with people's lives!"

"Don't make a scene!"

He covered his face with his hands. "Jesus Christ, you don't have any idea, do you? Or at least I hope you don't. If you did . . . do, you're the most viciously calculating person I've ever met."

"Nigel, no!" she cried, moving in on him.

Her hand was against his cheek, cool, soothing, loving. He wrenched violently away from her. The alcohol and his distress sent him caroming into the whitewashed wall.

"Don't touch me!" he panted.

He pushed slowly upright, edged past her. Her face had gone cold, expressionless, as implacable as death. His own emotions didn't bear scrutiny. Fear. Hatred. *Desire?*

"You're *not* leaving. I won't permit it. You know what I mean."

"I understand."

He resigned himself to the trap.

"Thank you."

"You're welcome. Anytime, ma'am," Sil added in a John Wayne drawl. "Always happy to oblige a lady."

"Even if we never do it again, I'm glad I satisfied my curiosity."

His fingers paused in their busy play among the heavy strands of her hair. "Curiosity?"

"I've never slept with anyone but Terry. And you're not the only one who's been attracted. I dreamed about you for days after I met you. You really are gorgeous."

"Thank you." A blush washed up from his throat and darkened his cheeks. "You're no mud fence yourself. You surprised the hell out of me."

"I'm pretty sexy, huh?"

"Yes, lady, I hadn't expected a volcano beneath that delicate, demure exterior."

"In another time, I think I might have made a grand horizontal. I really like sex."

His voice quivered on a laugh. "A grand what?"

"Horizontal. You know, courtesan. A lady who makes a living on her back."

"Thank you, I understand now. No need to spell it out for the moron." He pushed up on one elbow, the sheet slithering down to his waist. "Want to go look at luminarias before the snow ruins them?"

"All right."

The traffic was terrible. It always was. Tour buses filled with eager faces pressed to cold-and-breath-frosted glass. Cars filled with families. A time when the two faces of Santa Fe gave each other fleeting glances. Mercedeses, Cadillacs, and BMW's nosing their sleek front ends against the scratched and pitted bumpers of ancient Chevys or pickups or low-riders.

And it was magic. The light flickering through the brown-paper sacks filled them with a rich golden glow. Arches and curves of houses were outlined with these tiny fairy lights. The neighborhood Silvestre had selected was perfect. All the houses lay darkened, no electric Christmas lights festooned the trees or bushes, there was nothing save the shadow of houses, the trees tangling the stars in their bare branch tips, a keening wind which carried smears of cloud like silver pennants, and the mysterious wavering of the farolito candles.

Mona had wrapped a soft cashmere shawl over her head. Her profile was all shadows and ivory in the darkness of the Porsche. Sil kept one hand on the wheel, the other on the gearshift. Hers were folded quietly in her lap.

They slipped from the neighborhood, the red plastic tip of a policeman's flashlight showing them the way.

Sil turned back on the headlights, and they wound their way through the crooked streets of Santa Fe.

"Thank you, Sil. That was beautiful."

"I wish . . . well, I wish you could have appreciated it under different . . . circumstances. I just hope when you see them in the future they won't make you sad."

"No, that won't happen. This has been a terrible time for me, but you've given me . . . well, something very special," she concluded awkwardly.

"So what now? Do you want me to take you home?" A spasm crossed her face, and he added quickly, "On second thought, I've got a better idea. Ever been to a midnight mass?"

A quick headshake.

"Well, it's beautiful. We can go to the Cathedral and see it celebrated by an honest-to-God archbishop, or we can head over to the chapel and watch Martin celebrate. And later . . ."

"And afterward I could talk to him. Is that what you were going to add?"

"Couldn't hurt."

"Can't help."

"Hey, you were the lady with the faith."

"I seem to have laid it down somewhere, and I can't remember where."

"Look inside you, Mona, it's still there. Along with your strength and honesty and love. You're going to be fine. It's me I'm not too sure about."

"You'll make it, Silvestre!"

"Yes, ma'am," he replied meekly. "And so will you," he assured her as they entered the chapel.

Mona clung to Sil, rose and sat when he did, knelt and prayed. So much ritual. So alien, yet beautiful. She listened to the clear voices of the choir filling the tiny chapel. Candles and incense, the glittering gold surplice weighing down Father Martin's slightly stooped shoulders.

He didn't seem anything like the humorous, kind, approachable figure Mona had met three days before. His aspect was upon him: *A godly man,* she thought— and realized that she wanted to talk to him. She seemed

to be being drawn deeper and deeper into the
C. deBaca family. But how much more fortunate
she was than Terry. He had only Rhea. And what if
she tired of him?

He might come back to me!

The emotion struck her like a blow, and she doubled
over her folded hands. Sil's arm slipped comfortingly
about her shoulders. He urged her up and out of the
pew to join the other communicants. She thought it
wrong, but Father Martin's smile reassured her. The
long line of communicants shuffled forward. Sleepy
children cried and were shushed by their mothers.
There were coughs from the old, and overall, the quiet
murmurs of the priest. *Body and blood.*

Eyes tightly closed, she accepted the wafer from his
fingers. Allowed it to melt on her tongue. Sent up a
desperate prayer.

Oh, please, dear God. Let him come back to me.

Returning to the pew, she glanced up at the delicate
curving staircase linking choir loft to chapel. Legend
had it that St. Joseph himself had come in answer to
the nuns' prayers and built the stairs. Engineers
claimed that the stairs should not stand. Yet stand they
did. A miracle.

And gods walked in this arid land.

So perhaps her prayer too would be answered.

"I've come to be with Nigel." The words emerged
in tight little puffs, as if Lexa were loath to release
them.

Lexa remembered the fight that had preceded his
exit from the house. Nigel begging her to accompany
him. Her strident refusal. She had been trying to force
him to make a choice, and he had made the wrong
one. *Why?* What lay between him and his half-sister?

"I don't recall inviting you." Rhea gave her sister-
in-law a brilliant, brittle smile.

"You invited Nigel. Nigel's my husband. We come
as a package."

"Poor Nigel."

"Fuck you too, Rhea."

The tiny woman recoiled, the pleasure dying from her eyes. "You really are the most awful peasant."

Lexa pushed past her and strode into the living room. She froze when she saw Terry, then gave a shake of her head like a filly bedeviled by gnats and pushed on, searching for her husband.

She finally admitted defeat, and went back to her sister-in-law. "Where is he, Rhea?"

"Passed out on the couch in my office. You really should take better care of him."

Oddly enough, the twins were in the office. Elani was curled in the chair with her legs folded beneath her, Em seated sideways on the window seat, one leg swinging. Almost as if they were keeping guard over the stertorously breathing Nigel.

"He got sick," Elani said in a whisper.

"I know about this kind of *sick,* Elani, but thank you for trying to protect him."

"You're not going to be angry with him are you?" Em asked, pulling the mask from his eyes.

Lexa realized that there was much of Nigel in the boy's face. Her heart seemed to squeeze. *What would a child of ours be like?*

"He's not to blame," Elani insisted.

"You know who's to blame," Em told Lexa.

Two pairs of blue eyes, matched in intensity. A shudder ran down Lexa's spine. She hurried into speech, trying to turn them back into kids. Trying to banish the fear that their words had reawakened.

"What are you kids doing up at this hour?"

They stiffened, and threw up their heads with identical prideful gestures.

"We watched out for him," Elani said again.

"Against what?" demanded Lexa, but they were already drifting from the room.

She raised a hand to her face, and the fingertips came away wet. She felt like a fool for putting so much significance into the pratings of children. But her heart was pounding, and anxiety seemed to race along every nerve.

She leaned down and touched his shoulder. Surprisingly, he came awake at once and stared up at her.

"You came."

"I wanted to make sure you were all right."

"Help me." His eyes were bright, feverish in his narrow face. Lexa frowned down at him, sensing he was asking for something, but not understanding what. He flung an arm across his eyes, brushing away tears, then looked back up and said, "Take me home."

She helped him to his feet, supporting him with her shoulder as he groaned and swayed. Rhea was posed by the front door, the light through the stained-glass window shattering across her white gown in colored fragments. She still wore the feathered mask, and her fingernails were like red talons gripping the stem of her champagne glass.

They stood regarding one another.

She is an evil woman.

Lexa decided that the tumbler of bourbon she'd drunk had affected her more than she realized.

She and Nigel fought the wind to the Land Rover. Lexa clung to his shoulders, sobbing for breath while the snow threatened to smother her. Suddenly she was crying. He touched her lids with gentle fingers.

"Lexa, don't. I'm not worth it."

16

"Rhea, brace yourself, because you're not going to like my news," John Greer said.

Behind her Terry was whistling and Em was playing over and over a piano finger exercise. The droning growl of the vacuum cleaner put the final point on the drill bit that seemed to be eating its way into her head.

Covering the phone with a hand, Rhea spat, "Will you all be quiet! And, Maria, that can wait until later. Can't you see I'm on the phone?"

Terry gave Em a broad smile and jerked a head toward the door. With a look of pure loathing, the boy gathered up his music and left the living room. Gallagher then crossed to Rhea and began massaging her shoulders.

"All right, go ahead," she said into the phone. "Honestly, children and servants."

"Thank God for boarding schools, eh?" Terry whispered as he nibbled on her ear.

"Rhea, we've got the decision of the Secretary of the Interior. He's approved the lease of the land."

"What!"

"I knew this would upset you, but we're not down yet. The tribe could still vote down the lease."

"How did this happen? What about the environmental-impact statement?"

"It was prepared. I guess it looked all right to the Secretary."

"That can't be the sole explanation."

"What can I tell you? Obviously Pierce had bigger guns than we did, and was owed more favors than we were. It happens sometimes.'' The shrug translated across the phone wires.

"Easy for you to say. It's not your home that's going to be ruined.''

"Rhea, I don't mean to sound unsympathetic, but aren't you maybe making more of this than you need to? It's not as if they're putting a gravel pit next door. It's just a horse center, and whatever else Franklin Pierce may be, he's not cheap. Anything he does is always top-drawer. That center will probably be a real showpiece.''

"I take it that you don't want to represent me anymore. In any capacity.''

"No, no, no.'' Greer sighed. "I guess I'm just trying to prepare you for the worst. I think we've lost. But on to other matters. Tell Mr. Gallagher that I've filed the papers for his divorce.'' Rhea could hear the jealousy in the lawyer's voice. "I talked with his wife's lawyer, and it won't be contested. In fact Ms. Mandel said her client waives any claim on any of the property, and is not asking for support. As she put it, 'He couldn't support her when they were married. Why should it be any different now?' '' A fruity chuckle.

"Thank you, John. But now I'm a little busy so I'll talk with you some other time.'' Rhea edged her words with ice as she hung up. Then: "Damn! Damn! Damn!'' Short angry steps carried her about the living room. Furiously she seized a Waterford ashtray and smashed it on the brick floor.

"Bad news?''

"Yes. Franklin Pierce is one step closer to his center.''

"So?''

"So! I don't want this thing next door, and—'' She bit down on her lip in vexation.

"Yes, go ahead.''

"Your wife.''

"Ummm?'' The relaxed smile was still in place.

"If the center's built, she'll stay.''

"So what?''

She slid into the comforting circle of his arms. "Oh,

Terry, it's upsetting. I'm not used to being the other woman.''

"You're not the other woman. You're the only woman," he murmured into her fragrant hair.

A watery chuckle. "You make me feel so good. So safe.''

There was the ring of boot heels on tile. Rhea and Terry looked up as the twins entered. They were dressed for riding.

"And where are you going?''

"Riding," Elani replied with that teenager's drawl that held a wealth of contempt.

"I told you you couldn't take lessons from . . . her.''

"We're not. Silvestre is teaching us.''

"And how are you paying for it?''

"He's not charging.''

"I won't have it! I forbid you to ride there.''

"Why?" Elani asked, outraged.

"Because I say so.''

"That's not a reason," Em put in.

Rhea realized with a thrill of alarm that her son's voice was deepening. "All right, I'll give you a reason. Mona Gallagher is using you to strike back at me because Terry and I found that we were in love. She's trying to take you away from me, to steal your affections.''

Em's pale brows twitched together in a sharp frown. "That's silly. And it's also not true. And anyway, she can't steal what *you* never had.''

Rhea's mouth fell open in shock. In two strides Terry was across the room. The slap was loud in the silent room. Em's head snapped back on his neck, and a bright red spot blossomed on the white cheek. Without warning, Terry received a spitting, kicking fury on his chest. The assault by Elani took him by surprise, and he lost his footing and went down in a welter of arms and legs. Em followed her into the attack.

Rhea, hands clenched at her sides, screamed for them to stop. For a few violent minutes the fight continued. Then Terry, his face suffused with blood, ended it with a hammer blow to Em's jaw.

Elani knelt over her brother's still form. Eyes glittering dangerously, she screamed, "I *hate* you. When my father hears about this—"

Rhea bustled forward, seized her daughter by the upper arm, and gave her a hard shake. "He'll do absolutely nothing. He'll be shocked by your behavior. Now, you apologize."

"No!"

"Apologize."

"No!" Fury fled the girl's slender body, leaving behind a cold, deadly anger that was almost more frightening because it seemed so alien on her young face. "Don't you think we ought to call a doctor for Em?"

"He's not hurt," Terry blustered. He felt a bit ashamed for so losing his temper with a fourteen-year-old boy that he had knocked him out.

As if in response, Em groaned and pushed up on an elbow.

"Go to your rooms, both of you. You're going back to school just as soon as I can arrange for the tickets. Maybe they can teach you civilized behavior."

"Military school," Terry offered, his smile back in place. "They'll kick the pissiness right out of that kid."

With one final look of loathing, Elani helped her brother out of the room.

Rhea pushed back a loose strand of hair and sank into a chair. "Terry, let's not have any children."

"Suits me. Mona was always after me to have a brat. I never was very keen on the idea."

She stretched out a hand to him. "Why do they hate me? It frightens me when people hate me."

"They don't hate you. They're just at that age. Pack 'em back to school and forget about them. Actually, we ought to get the hell out of here ourselves. Let's run to the sun, what do you say? Forget about horse centers, and kids, and soon-to-be-ex-wives, and just go."

She shook her head. "No. I won't be a coward.

Besides, I'm about to break Nigel out of that terrible marriage, and he'll need me to get over those first rough months.''

"He's going to need a hell of a lot more than that. He's going to need a long stretch in a drunk tank to dry out.''

"Don't be mean.''

"I'm not. I'm being truthful.''

"It upsets me to hear you say things like that. Nigel and I are very close.''

He nuzzled her. "But not as close as us.''

"Oh, no, darling. Not that close.''

"Is this not an occasion for which we should all be happy? Is this also not a matter of our desire?'' intoned the elder in Tewa.

From all corners of the room came a resounding, "It is so.''

Lexa almost chuckled at the wan-faced young couple seated at the end of the long room. Marriages in a Pueblo were tough. The bride and groom were uniting two large groups of kin, and ceremonial sponsors were appointed to ensure the success of the marriage. Anglo couples had it easier. Didn't like the mother-in-law? Pack up the car and move to Anchorage, or Ankara, or Timbuktu.

Of course a Pueblo couple could do it too, but the ramifications went deep. Leaving a Pueblo was not like moving from your hometown to a new city. You left behind moieties—medicine, hunt, war, clown, and women's associations—kachina cults, and a kinship system that seemed unduly complex to outside observers.

The preselected elder Owha rose and continued to admonish the couple. Lexa spent a few moments in idle speculation over what role Owhas had played before the Spaniards entered the Southwest and Owhas had assumed the role of Catholic priest. The old man concluded, and hung rosaries around the necks of the bride and groom.

Benny suddenly leaned over and whispered, "Don't

you wish you had an arbitrator to take your domestic quarrels to?''

"No. I like to keep my domestic quarrels private." Lexa presented him with her shoulder.

"Are you trying to say, 'Take a hike, Benny'?" the Indian suggested.

"You got it."

The crowd was moving now, preparing to enjoy the banquet set by the bride's parents.

"I'm a good listener," Benny persisted.

"That's nice. Become a psychiatrist."

"Why didn't Nigel come today?"

"He was sick."

"The same *sick* he's been having all month?"

"Benny . . ." she warned.

"Lexa, what is going on with the two of you?"

"You don't take a hint, do you?"

"No."

"How do you do with out-and-out rudeness?"

"Ignore it. I've got a skin like a rhino."

"The sensitivity of one too." She sighed, and rested her shoulders against a wall. "Okay, to answer your question: we share a house and a dining-room table."

"How about a bed?"

"None of your damn business."

"Are you going to divorce?"

"I don't know."

The fact that the reply wasn't an explosive denial held him speechless for several moments. Finally, he managed a long, drawn-out, "Okayyy."

"And as long as we're asking nosy questions: what's with you? You've been getting the cold shoulder all afternoon. Did you diddle the bride or what?"

"Lexa . . ." he muttered, blushing. There was an oddly prudish streak in Benny. "I'm none too popular with a lot of the Pueblo right now."

"Why not? The center?"

"That and other things." He shrugged. "I'm viewed as a divisive element."

"I don't understand."

"You don't understand?" he mimicked broadly.

"Hey, gimme a break. I'm an archaeologist, not an anthropologist. I'm not one of those people you hide the TV from and lie to."

Benny giggled. "We ought to start a new association. The Silly Customs Moiety. We make up stories, and see how gullible the anthropologists can be."

"But seriously . . ."

"Seriously, I'm getting a rather strong message that I ought to take an apartment in Santa Fe and get the hell out of the Pueblo. I'm disruptive, and they're making it clear I'm not welcome here."

"Ralph Quintana and the Summer moiety?"

"And some members of my own moiety."

"But why? You've done so much . . . you're trying to do so much for them."

"That's part of it. Lexa, unlike you white folks, we don't put a lot of value on individualism. Our entire society is built around conformity. It makes sense when you think about it. When you've got a subsistence economy, everybody better pull together. When it's time to clean the irrigation ditches, or hoe the weeds, or harvest the beans, you can't have some asshole announcing that he'd really rather not do that this week. Well, I'm not too good in the conformity department, so . . ." An eloquent shrug.

Lexa gathered up her purse and wrapped her handwoven ruana around her shoulders. "Well, if you do decide to move into town, let me know. One of the science-fiction writers is headed to Hollywood to write for a new TV show, and he needs to rent his house."

"Thanks. I'll keep it in mind. But you don't have to rush off."

"I need to get home. Thanks for inviting me to your cousin's wedding. When will the church service be held?"

"Sunday. Some people wonder why we even bother with this native ceremony, but hey, we're traditionalists."

They stepped out into the blue-gray twilight of the February evening. A sliver of moon hung over the eastern mountains. With their boots crunching on the week-old snow, they walked toward the Land Rover, and Lexa made a face.

"Lousy weather. I've never seen this much snow. I hope we don't have a long winter. I want to get back into the field."

"Relax. Sit in your nice house in front of a fire and enjoy yourself."

"It's tough to enjoy yourself when the tension's so thick you can cut it with a knife. Damn! And I promised I wasn't going to do that."

"That's what friends are for." Benny stooped to mold a snowball. Tossed it. But the snow was too dry, and it collapsed in a powdery shower before it had traveled three feet. "Who would have thought that Franklin Pierce and I would cause so much trouble when we sat in the Compound last fall and cooked up this scheme? You and Nigel fighting. Your sister-in-law slamming you every chance she gets. Mona's husband taking up with your sister-in-law—"

"Yes, it's quite a little soap opera." She punched his arm lightly. "And it's all your fault."

"Yup."

They had reached the Rover, and Lexa offered her cheek for a kiss. "But don't regret it," she continued at his bleak expression. "In the words of my father, who was a notable philosopher: *you gotta do what you gotta do.*"

"Ha! Profound."

"Good night, Benny."

"Good night, Lexa."

Bouncing over the rutted dirt road, she glanced back in the rearview mirror. She raised a hand for a last wave, but Benny wasn't looking. He was talking with five young men. The body language reminded Lexa of circling dogs. A punch was thrown, and Benny doubled over.

Gravel sprayed as Lexa turned the Rover around. Jamming the vehicle into second, she came roaring and swaying down the road. Benny was no longer visible beneath a humping, thrashing pile of bodies. Lexa pointed the Rover at the brawl, and leaned on the horn.

There were yells of terror, and Indians flew like popcorn off a hot pan. Benny was on one knee, blood running from a split lip, one eye already blackening. Leaning across the seat, Lexa threw open the passenger door. Threats and curses came from Benny's assailants, and she saw that they had gathered up stones and fallen limbs from the big cottonwood trees.

"Hurry!" she screamed.

He lurched to his feet, and fell into the seat. She floorboarded it even before he had the door shut. A hail of stones whanged into the sides of the Rover, and one, connecting with the front window, put a spiderweb of frosted cracks across the glass.

"Say, you must be the cavalry," Benny said weakly, then began to laugh.

The blustery March wind almost blew Lexa through the door and into the shop. Nigel was carefully writing out a check for the stone-faced Indian on the other side of the counter. He finished his signature with a scrawl and pushed the check across.

"Here, Danny. And incidentally, I think these are your best bracelets yet."

With a nervous head-ducking glance to Nigel and then to Lexa, the Zuni man hurried from the shop.

Lexa chuckled, and hummed a bit of the theme from *Lawrence of Arabia*.

Nigel shook his head as he began arranging the intricately inlaid bracelets in the display case. "Worst time of year in New Mexico."

"You think any time of year is bad in New Mexico."

He tented his fingers before his face, considered. "Yes, I suppose that's true. And it does sort of bring up what I wanted to talk to you about."

"I thought we were going to lunch."

"In a minute."

He came around the counter, took her by the arm, and led her into the rug section. Seated her in a chair and squatted at her feet, his arms resting on her knees.

"Lexa, I've been doing a lot of thinking since Christmas, and I've made a decision."

She eyed him warily. "Okay."

"I want to leave Santa Fe."

"What?" She stared down at his golden head. "You're joking, aren't you?"

"No, I'm serious. Dead serious."

"Leave New Mexico," she said, stalling for time. "And go where?"

"I don't know. England maybe. I always thought I'd like to live there."

"And what am I supposed to do? Positions like the one at Cummings don't come along very often."

"I thought maybe you could teach, and I'd find something, and we could start a family."

"In the first place, I don't particularly like teaching. And in the second place, I only have a master's degree. I don't think some fancy British university is going to take me."

"You're an authority on southwestern Indian cultures. That's got to be unique."

"What brought this on?"

He stood, and took a turn around the shop. "A lot of things. Lexa, I want a family."

"I don't."

"Why not?"

"Because of you. You're not the man I married. You've changed."

"Because of this place!"

"Places aren't the problem, Nigel. Remember, wherever you go, there *you* are."

"It would be different somewhere else. I would be different. Lexa, I'm not happy here."

"Well, I am."

"Really, truly?"

"Okay, you want the truth, then I'll give it to you. Right now my life is almost perfect. The only problem we have is your sister and the fact that you haven't got the stones to tell her to butt out of our life. If you did that, everything would be fine."

"I can't." It was said so low that she had to strain to hear.

"And I can't leave. So I guess that settles it."

"Does your career mean more to you than I do?" The hesitation was slight, but it was enough to fill his gray eyes with pain. "I see. And if I give you an ultimatum?"

"If you were doing this because you were going toward some goal rather than running away, I might say yes. But I'm not willing to have my life, my career ruined because you're a coward." Anger was coursing through her. "No. I'm going to give *you* an ultimatum. Get Rhea out of our lives now, or you get out."

"What are you saying?"

"I can't live like this, Nigel." She stormed to the phone and held the receiver out to him. "Call her. Tell her. Tell her that she's an interfering, manipulating bitch, and you're not going to have anything to do with her anymore."

"I can't," he repeated, forcing the words past bloodless lips.

The phone gave a ring of protest as Lexa slammed down the receiver. "Then you can just get the hell out of *my* house. I'm sure Rhea will be happy to give you a place to live. After all, she gave you this shop."

"Lexa . . ." Anguish stretched his voice, and he held out an imploring hand to her.

"No! If you love her so much better than you love me, or owe her, or whatever the hell is going on . . . then so be it! I'm finished. I'm out. I'm going to a hotel. I want you gone in two days." She paused at the door, looked back. "And I hope you're very happy being Rhea's slave. It seems to be about all you're suited for!"

17

It was one of those spur-of-the-moment things. A brandy alexander, then wine with dinner, plus an eager planning session with Franklin, had left her with a pleasant buzz. Mona decided that she really wasn't ready for the romance of the ten-o'clock news and her empty bed, but what to do?

She had seen Lexa only once since that disastrous party at the C. deBacas'. They had had a tearful heart-to-hearter, with Mona crying and raging over Terry's betrayal. They had then settled down for three hours of blackening his character. The session hadn't done much to reassure Mona about the state of her soul, but at least she had felt less like a limp victim. Lexa had helped her release her anger, and Mona was grateful.

So now, humming lightly beneath her breath, she decided to drop in on the archaeologist. It was something she normally never did, but alcohol was a sure way to overcome inhibition.

The bell shrilled, and from inside the house Mona heard a loud crash. She counted heartbeats, growing more concerned by the minute as no one responded to the bell's summons. To the ring of the bell she added a frenzied knocking.

"Lexa," she bawled.

"Go away!"

"Nigel?"

"Go away."

It was obvious, from the faltering steps and thickened tongue, the state he was in. Mona's sense of foreboding grew.

243

"Nigel, open the door." She heard footsteps retreating.

With an angry shrug she started back to the truck, but something was tugging at her, slowing her steps, pulling her back.

If you walk away you will regret it for the rest of your life.

"Damn," she muttered aloud, and hurrying back, she boosted herself over the back fence and dropped down into the yard. Sucking at a long scratch, a gift from one of the forty rosebushes in the planter that ran the length of the fence, Mona crept to the sliding glass door. She felt like a perfect fool. What if Lexa came home and found her skulking on the back patio like a cat burglar? Or what if Nigel shot her as an intruder? He was in no shape to discrimi—

Shock sent her skittering back from the window. Nigel *was* holding a gun. Seated, head bent like a monk at his devotions, the man was contemplating the P-7 pistol that lay in the palm of one hand. His features had been blurred and bloated by the heavy drinking that had come to dominate his life. Dark circles hung beneath his eyes, stubble shadowed his cheeks, there was a large stain down the front of his sweater.

Her stomach seemed to be leaping in the back of her throat. Mona reached out with trembling fingers and tugged at the door handle. It didn't budge. The cold was biting into her hands and face. She tried again, desperately now, and her numb fingers slipped off the handle. She felt a fingernail tear, and thrusting it into her mouth, she sucked, and whimpered, and tried to think.

Go for help?

Yes, run next door and use the phone, call the rescue squad—

That will take ten minutes—what if he decides to act in the meantime?

Her eyes were locked on that huddled figure, so she saw when the muscles in his jaw bunched and tightened and the hand closed spasmodically about the pistol grip.

Whirling, Mona gathered up the large Mexican ceramic strawberry pot. It burst through the sliding glass door with a sound like a detonating bomb. Nigel jerked, and with an ear-ringing *Wham,* the P-7 discharged. The slug buried itself in the wall, as flakes of whitewash and adobe dust exploded out and spiraled lazily toward the floor.

Mona leaped through the broken door and flung herself on Nigel. Her hand closed viselike around his wrist. For an instant they struggled, and she was faced with the sickening sight of the gun barrel's black mouth waving evilly beneath her nose. Then he abruptly went limp, and she pulled the gun from his unresisting fingers.

With a touch she dropped the clip out of the pistol and pocketed it. Laid the gun aside. She was still keeping one hand on Nigel's shoulder while great shuddering sobs shook his slight frame.

"It's all right . . ." She pulled his head against her breast. "Everything's all right now."

She continued to hold him, murmuring silly endearments until the sobs subsided. His hands with their long slender fingers patted at his pockets. Mona ran to fetch a box of Kleenex. Nigel mopped at his streaming eyes.

"I'm . . . I'm sorry."

"You should be," she scolded gently. "For even *thinking* about killing yourself."

"There's nothing else."

"There's always something else. That's just the booze talking."

She snatched up an empty Jim Beam bottle and gave it a hard shake, as if she could somehow strangle the life out of its glass neck. The bottle landed with a sharp crack on the brick floor and rocked mournfully back and forth.

"Come on." She worked a shoulder under his arm and helped him out of the chair. "Where's Lexa?" she asked as she supported him down the hall toward the bathroom.

"Gone. She's left me."

"Oh." It took her a few moments to absorb that. Then with a resolute headshake she said, "Well, we'll talk about that later." With one hand she fished a bath sheet out of the linen closet and thrust it on him. "Take a bath, shave. I'll cook you something to eat. Then you can sleep."

"I thought you couldn't cook," he said with the first spark of interest she'd seen out of him since her precipitate entrance.

"I can't, but I can open cans. Now go." With a gentle prod she pushed him lightly into the bathroom.

While the water thundered in the shower, she pulled out clean clothes, unearthed a can of bean-with-bacon soup, discovered wieners in the freezer to add to the soup, set out crackers, and filled two glasses with milk.

He dragged into the kitchen, sniffed. "Smells good."

"Good that you noticed. You must be coming back to life."

She studied him critically, noting the pasty white skin, the slight tremor in the hands, the shadow of pain in the beautiful eyes. The crisis had only been delayed, it hadn't been averted, but for the moment he was safe.

Seating himself at the table, he rested his brow on a hand. "You never struck me as a particularly capable type."

"Sometimes I surprise even myself," Mona replied a little tartly.

"I didn't mean that as an insult."

She ladled out soup. "None taken."

He picked up a spoon and took a cautious mouthful. "It's amazing how much better I feel."

"I'll have to tell Madge that it works."

"Beg pardon?"

Mona wiped away her milk mustache and set down the glass with her hands folded lightly about the base. "Friend of mine. I went through some bad patches in my late teens. She knew I was borderline suicidal, and I remember once that she told me if I ever felt like I just couldn't cope, I should take a bath, put on clean clothes, eat something hot, and get a good night's sleep.'' Brown eyes met gray. ''Most people who commit suicide are dirty, hungry, and tired at the time they do it. Interesting bit of trivia.''

''How about miserable? Doesn't that count in the equation?''

''Oh, yes, but misery—just like hunger and exhaustion and dirt—can be dealt with.''

''That's damned easy for you to say. You haven't lost the person—'' He broke off abruptly.

''Yes, Nigel,'' she said softly. ''We do seem to have a lot in common.''

''Yeah. My wife. Your husband. My booze. Your cocaine.''

''What?''

''I found traces after you'd been in our bathroom at the autumn party. God, that seems a million years ago. And then again at the C. deBacas'.''

''I'm surprised you even remember that second time, drunk as you were. But as I told you then—I don't use.'' She nibbled at a hangnail. ''You're Silvestre's friend. I don't think he'd mind me telling you. Especially now.'' She jerked a thumb over her shoulder. ''That was Sil. Cocaine is very prevalent on the circuit, and very, very seductive. Sil had taken a couple of bad spills, and got lured.''

''How did you find out?''

''He told me.'' She gave a little bark of laughter. ''Oddly enough, I seem to invite confidences. Which is funny when you think about it, because I've always been unable to give any. Anyway, we talked with Father Martin, and Sil's been under the care of the family doctor. It hasn't taken him long to get it under control. Sil is a very strong person. He'll be back on the circuit by summer.'' She held up crossed fingers. ''I prophesy.''

''But the center?''

"You're Sil's friend. Could you really picture him as the business manager for Franklin's dream?"

"No," he admitted. "So we don't have as much in common as I thought. Less. Your husband is a bastard of the first magnitude. Lexa . . ." His voice caught. "Lexa was right to leave me."

There was a look on his face that wrung her heart. "Why, Nigel? What have you done?"

He began to shake uncontrollably. Frightened now, Mona gathered him in her arms and supported him as they made their way to the bedroom. She tucked him into the bed and piled on comforters.

"What's wrong with me?" he forced past chattering teeth.

"Shock."

"I could use a drink."

"I'll brew you some tea."

When she returned, the warmth of the water bed had eased the worst of his tremors, but he was lying on his side, knees drawn to chest while slow, silent tears squeezed from beneath his lids. She sensed he wouldn't want to be found that way, so she backed up, and with a great deal of noise, came back down the hall. He tried to take the cup and saucer, but his hand still shook.

"I'm weak as a kitten."

"Here." Helping him up, she steadied his hand as he sipped at the highly spiced and sugared tea.

"Enough," he said a minute later, and Mona set the cup aside. Nigel seemed to be making up his mind about something, and finally asked, "Does Lexa talk to you?" He began pleating a fold of sheet between long fingers.

"Some," she replied cautiously.

"You know that she thinks I'm not . . . loyal to her."

"Yes."

"I never wanted to come to Santa Fe, but the job . . . it was so good . . . for her. But I didn't want to come."

"Why not?" His grip on her hand was painful. She tightened hers, trying to give him strength.

"Rhea . . . Rhea was here," he forced out.

"I thought you and your sister were close."

"Close! *Oh, God!*"

"Nigel, easy. Easy."

She realized she was using the tone she used on frightened horses, and bit down vexedly on her lower lip. Emotions flashed across his face: fear, shame, an anger so deep and bitter that it frightened her.

"She hates Lexa, and Lexa's never known why. She keeps asking me, but how can I tell her?"

"Then you know why?"

"Yes . . . oh, yes," he whispered.

They were locked in an emotional whirlpool so strong that Mona found herself trapped in it. With her heart hammering, she took a tighter grip on his shoulders.

"Nigel, what? What can be so horrible that . . . that it left you in this state?"

"I can't."

"Please tell me." He cringed away from her. "Nigel, you've got to! You've got to face this—whatever it is—and deal with it. If you don't you're going to pick up that pistol someday when I'm not around—"

"Face it! I've faced nothing else for twenty-five years. Sometimes it's fainter, withdrawn deep inside me, but it's always there. *Nigel's dirty little secret.* Then we came here. Here! Of all places." He slammed his fists into the mattress. "Over the years, after our father's death, I'd only visited. That was safe. I was such a fool. I let her sink her claws into me again. Now she owns me body as well as soul."

Mona felt as if the room were tilting about her. It was hard to glean Nigel's actual meaning from this wild spate of words, but she was beginning to sense the dimension of his "secret," and it was horrifying.

"She loves me, Mona, and it's killing me."

"You should tell Lexa."

"No! She'd hate me. She'd never . . . come back. I can't talk about it."

"You're going to have to someday. You may as well try it out on me—it won't hurt as much."

His throat worked convulsively for several moments. Eyes closed, he leaned back against the headboard. "I was fifteen," he began softly. "My mother was Daniels's second wife. Rhea's mother had died when she was two. I think it really did shatter my father, and he doted on Rhea as that little piece of Susan that remained to him. A year later he met and married my mother. They never really suited. Mother was a shy, delicate lady who couldn't be the perfect hostess he demanded." He looked at Mona. "In case you didn't know, my father was a very wealthy man. He wanted a wife who would be a credit to him. An ornament for his arm. Mother was that, but she was too shy to have the dash and style that he demanded. She had several breakdowns, and finally they divorced when I was nine."

"And you stayed with him?"

"Oh, yes, Dad was not about to let his only son go. Somebody had to inherit and run his far-flung empire. I continued to see my mother on school holidays, but then, quite suddenly, she committed suicide."

"How old were you then?"

"Fifteen. Rhea was very . . . supportive." He looked up into Mona's face. "This isn't an excuse, but she is very beautiful."

"Yes."

"She was twenty, home for the summer from Paris. We had always been . . . close. Suddenly it became very physical." His voice was so low she had to strain to hear him. "We slept together—"

"Had you ever been with a woman before?" Mona abruptly demanded.

"No."

"I thought not. Go on."

He averted his face. "This is so sick."

"I'll let you know if and when I have to run to the bathroom."

A fine hand was run across his mouth, then with a deep breath he resumed. "This continued for over two months." He began to shake again, and Mona pulled him into a tight embrace. "Then one afternoon our father walked in on us. Rhea began to cry. She looked so small and vulnerable in that big bed with the sheet clutched around her. I stood there trying to hide myself, and she . . ."

"She what?"

"Nothing. Dad threw me out of the house and disowned me. End of story." He laughed bitterly. "But not, as you see, end of consequences."

"Whose fault was it, Nigel?"

"Mine."

"Fiddle! You men think you're the lords of creation, but I've got news for you—you don't get to first base with a woman unless she wants you to. We're in control in any sexual encounter short of rape. She was a *woman,* Nigel, playing games with an adolescent boy. And if you were like any fifteen-year-old I've ever known, you were ripe for sex."

"That doesn't excuse it."

"No, it doesn't, but I don't think she's as innocent in all this, as you make out."

An indefinable emotion briefly twisted his face.

"Ah! I'm right, aren't I?"

He stubbornly shook his head.

"Tell me! What did she do that day?"

Their eyes locked; hers demanding, his stubborn.

"I can't."

"Why can't you?"

"If I look at this . . . I'll kill her."

They were inches apart.

"I . . . won't . . . let . . . you."

The tension stretched between them, tighter, tighter, finally breaking as he began to speak. "She crawled off the bed dragging . . . the sheets . . . with her. Clung . . . to his feet." His voice was jumping wildly. "Wept, and begged for forgiveness. Told him she didn't know what I was doing until it was too late. She said I had . . . frightened her. She knew it was wrong, but she was too scared to stop. And she was no virgin!'' he cried, driving a fist into the bed. "If only I'd known that then."

"You wouldn't have said anything. You were too busy playing noble."

"He wouldn't have listened to me anyway. He loved her. More than he ever loved me."

Mona clutched and rumpled his hair. "Nigel, why don't you tell Lexa? It's shocking, yes, but bearable. You were a kid. She'd understand." She paused, and a grimace crossed her face as she chewed down on the thought. "Rhea . . . she's been threatening you with this, hasn't she? That's why you haven't supported Lexa. My God, what a malignant bitch she is!" Mona bounced off the bed, fell to pacing. "We'll go to Lexa and we'll tell her—"

"Mona, no. She thinks I'm a weak and useless son of a bitch. Hearing this sordid little story is just going to confirm that belief."

"Nigel, are you going to fight for your marriage or not?"

"Are you going to fight for yours?"

"That's not fair."

"All right, maybe it's not."

"I've about decided I'm better off without Terry."

"But it still hurts."

She sighed, sank down on the bed. "Oh, yes, it does hurt."

"And it's not just the center, and the shop, and Rhea that separate Lexa and me. We're having a very fundamental difference of opinion."

"About what?"

"I want to start a family. She doesn't. Her career is very important to her."

Mona laughed. "Goodness, what a pair we make. I quit the circuit because *I* wanted to start a family, and Terry didn't."

They laughed together. Nigel twined his fingers through Mona's. "Hey, want to start a family?"

"Sure, why not? Anything's better than a sperm bank."

"Probably even me," he laughed.

Their eyes met. Mona flushed and Nigel looked away—the joke had hurt more than it had helped.

Then Nigel cleared his throat. It transformed into a yawn.

"You're tired. Do you think you can sleep now? Remember, that was part of the cure."

"Yes, I think I *can* sleep now."

She rose, bent, and kissed his gently on the cheek. "I'll be in the living room if you need me."

"Mona, you don't have to stay. I'm all right now, really."

"Just the same, I'll stay."

Once, late in the night, he cried out, caught in the throes of a nightmare. Mona set aside the P-7, which she'd been quietly cleaning. She slipped into the bedroom and touched his face. It was wet with tears. She spoke softly—nonsense words, murmured reassurances—and he quieted. Then she realized that he hadn't undressed. Quickly she tossed back the down comforter and eased him out of his shirt and jeans.

Perched cross-legged at the foot of the bed, chin sunk in her hands, Mona studied his body. She felt like a voyeur, but excused herself, because aside from that one night with Silvestre, she had been weeks without sex, and after marriage with Terry, abstinence was hard to take. Deciding it was research, she eyed Nigel with the eye of a connoisseur. A grand horizontal indeed, she thought with a chuckle.

How different his body was from Terry's. Small, compact. The arch of his rib cage tapered down into the shadowed belly, a little slack now. The virtually hairless chest, so unlike Terry's thick brown pelt. Her eyes flicked across the gap in his boxer shorts. Then she abruptly threw the covers over him and strode with long strides back in the living room. Wind was rushing through the broken side of the glass door and she wondered again how she could close off that broken pane. The temperature in the house was plummeting.

Searching through the garage, she located a tatty blanket. Then, armed with blanket, hammer, and nails, she covered the broken door. It helped, but only a little. There was a fireplace in the master bedroom. Maybe best to retreat there.

Feeding twigs into the corner fireplace, she watched the burgeoning flames lick greedily at the dried pine needles. Each time they caught, there was a spurt of blue-green fire, and the pungent scent of evergreen filled the room.

Should she ignore Nigel's obvious distress, and tell Lexa what she had learned? Where did her loyalties lie? To the wife who had befriended her? To the husband whom she barely knew, but with whom she had shared an intensely emotional experience? *Barely knew?* Well that was no longer true. She now knew more about him than his own wife. Uncomfortable thought, that.

Sheets rustled as Nigel shifted and murmured in his sleep. She glanced over, watched the fire draw highlights from his tousled hair. *God, he was attractive.*

And how irrational was human chemistry. Why does life have to be so complicated? she wondered drowsily. It was her last conscious thought.

The smell of coffee pulled her from the depths of a confused dream. She was wearing only her teddy. In the bed. Nigel smiled down at her. A little wan perhaps, but a real smile. He held a breakfast tray complete with newspaper in the side pocket and an amaryllis blossom in a dainty vase.

She pushed back her hair. "Good heavens, where did you come by that?" she asked with a nod to the flower.

"Out of our greenhouse."

"Umm, smells good."

"I can cook too."

"Aren't we talented?"

"Yes."

"Aren't you eating too?"

"Ate already."

"What time is it?" Mona asked, starting in on the banana fritters.

Nigel pulled back his sleeves. "Ten-twenty-five in the mountain west."

"Dear God!"

"You were tired. Rescuing me was hard work."

"Pooh!" She looked away, embarrassed by the intensity of his gaze.

"Mona." His fingers closed about her chin, forced her face around. "I haven't thanked you."

"It's not necess—"

"Nonetheless, I thank you. For saving my life."

She applied herself to fritters, crumbled bacon. Nipping the amaryllis from the vase, Nigel twiddled it beneath his nose.

"I called a glazier. They'll be out this afternoon to replace the sliding glass door. Wouldn't do to leave it for Lexa to find."

"Huh?"

"She gave me two days to get out. Since I didn't peg out last night, I'll have to take a more ordinary course."

"Where will you go?"

"I don't know. Hotel, I guess." He covered his face with his hands, massaged at the hairline. "I still have that goddamn shop to tend to."

"Why don't you stay with me?" she heard herself asking, then dropped her fork and stared at him in comic dismay.

"Don't look so alarmed. I won't accept."

"Well, why not? I've got this big house—"

"Two bedrooms."

"Big enough."

"Mona, Sil would have my balls."

"No he wouldn't. We really are just friends. Now, Lexa might tear my eyes out—"

"No." His face had gone gray. "Lexa never changes her mind."

"How very foolish of Lexa," Mona said.

"I admire that strength."

"Strength is one thing, rigidity is another. Will you come? I'd like you to. I'm lonely. Maybe we can help each other."

"You don't need any help," Nigel insisted. "You're doing just fine. You're one of the strongest people I know."

"It's all an act. Inside I'm Jell-O."

"Inside you may be wobbly, but, lady, on the outside you're twisted blue steel and dynamite. I tried to lift that damn strawberry pot to get it back onto the patio, and I almost gave myself a hernia."

"Adrenaline," Mona said. "Now shoo. I'm going to get dressed—"

"I've already seen just about all there is to see."

"And so have I!" she shot back, and chuckled when he blushed. "Now, get packed."

"Yes, ma'am," he said meekly.

"That's what I like to hear."

> Lexa,
> I return your home to you. If you should wish
> to talk with me outside the confines of the shop,
> Mona has very generously offered me crash
> space.
>
> Love,
> Nigel

Benny watched Lexa's face undergo the most remarkable series of transformations. Lacing his fingers over his paunch, he leaned back and inspected the toes of his shoes. She reread the note, folded it a number of times, thrust it into the hip pocket of her blue jeans.

"Something wrong?" he asked mildly.

"I don't know."

She left the room, and he heard the scrape of hangers from the master bedroom. When she returned, her eyes were overly bright and her smile thin-lipped.

"Benny, I have the oddest sensation that I've made a very bad mistake."

* * *

"Hello? Anybody home?"

"Silvestre, come in."

"What are you doing? Playing chimney sweep?"

Nigel's grin glowed whitely in his black face. "Rescuing Barnaby. You are too adventuresome for your own good, little son," he admonished the kitten, who paddled the air with all four feet and tried to wriggle from the hand that held him. Then, to Sil, "Would you like something to drink? Tea, coffee, milk, or if you feel really daring, there's lemonade. It's pink," he added significantly.

"Whoa, that might be a little strong for me. Coffee."

"I heard all of that," Mona said a bit defensively as she entered from the kitchen.

Nigel rolled an eye to Sil. "She won't let me have a drink."

"She won't let me have a toot." Sil slipped an arm around her waist and kissed her on the cheek. "Mona's Halfway House for Wounded Ducks."

"This duck would have been a dead duck," Nigel said softly.

Pink with embarrassment, she wiggled free. "Stop it, both of you. *You* wash your face. And *you* come get your coffee and tell me what you've been up to."

"Been down to Albuquerque to Jerry's. He's got a hunter/jumper barn down in Albuquerque. I tried his new French mare."

"How is she?"

"Magic. Powerful, intelligent, fearless. A little inexperienced." He twirled the mug on the kitchen table, watching the tiny whirlpool that formed in the hot dark liquid. "He wants me to show her, get a few championships on her so he can sell her for a ton of money."

"Sil, that's wonderful!"

"Ummmm. I still haven't made up my mind."

"How high did you jump?"

"Five-seven."

Slipping out of her chair, she wrapped her arms

around his neck. "That's great. I'm so proud of you."

"Take a little credit for yourself. You're the one who got me over that first fence. You and your old gray baby-sitter."

"What's this about baby-sitters?" Nigel asked, entering the kitchen.

"Mona's old gelding, Favory. He's like riding a sofa. Safe, slow, comfortable. You see that big fence coming up between his ears, and you don't even care. He mumbles a little around the bit, flicks his ears back and forth a few times as if to reassure you, and just goes sailing over."

"Jerry's asked Sil to ride for him," Mona told Nigel.

"That's nice. But how does that jibe with being the business manager for the center?"

"That's the problem." Sil paused to sip coffee. "I feel terribly torn. Guilty about Franklin—"

"You should do what's right for you," Mona interrupted.

"—and not entirely sure I want to go back to the circuit. So until I make up my mind, I'm still on the team. Which is why I came by. Things are about to get hot." He tossed a day-old copy of the Albuquerque newspaper onto the table. An article had been outlined in blue ink.

Nigel frowned down at the circled story, then prodded the paper away with fastidious fingertips. "Oh, no."

"I don't understand," Mona said with a frown of her own.

"Environmentalists," Sil said patiently.

"I understand *that*. I just don't see the significance."

"There are two distinct camps out here in the scenic Southwest," Nigel explained. "Those who love environmentalists, and those who despise them. It usually breaks along economic lines—the rich whites loving, and the poor Hispanos and Indians hating."

"Though there is some slide in the latter group,"

Sil continued. "Indians tend to pay lip service to the various environmental groups when it suits their purpose. Like over the power lines through the Jemez Pueblo."

"Wait, wait, I'm lost," Mona complained.

Nigel picked up the explanation. "If a Pueblo doesn't want a particular project to go through, they usually issue the war cry of 'sacred Indian burial grounds.' If that doesn't work, they will sometimes join forces with the environmentalists."

"San Jose is about to make the final decision on the equestrian center," Sil explained. "So either Ralph Quintana or Rhea got the word out to the Protectors of the World, and they're going to picket the Pueblo."

"Which means we can expect some hot times," Nigel concluded.

"Franklin is of course going to be out there exhorting the faithful, and doubtless Rhea or that shyster lawyer of hers will be there too. Franklin would like us faithful troops to show support, so . . ." Silvestre shrugged significantly.

"I'm certainly willing to help. But just what is it that Franklin wants us to do?" Mona asked.

"Hang out at the Pueblo . . . talk up the center . . . look noble. Your guess is as good as mine. Benny can put us up," he added as an afterthought. "He's staying in his grandmother's house while she's having some surgery done."

"How long will we be out there?"

"Couple of days." Sil didn't miss the sharp glance that Mona threw at Nigel. Or how he kept his eyes focused firmly on the table before him. Was it fear of meeting Lexa? Perhaps he should tell him. . . . "Lexa's in the field," he blurted awkwardly. He watched Nigel blush. Watched Mona's fine eyes focus calmly, gently upon him. Realized that what he had suspected was true.

He lifted his coffee cup, preparing for a toast. It wasn't often that a person's two best friends in the world got together.

"Here's . . ." he began, then decided that the moment, the people, and the relationship were still far too fragile for his bluff and hearty congratulations.

God, I'm a noble son of a bitch, he thought ruefully as Nigel's hand closed unconsciously, tenderly, over Mona's.

18

"Weird."

"Very weird."

"Weirdest."

Mona, Silvestre, and Benny exchanged serious glances. Passed around the bottle of Cranapple juice. Watched the picketers trawling the perimeter of San Jose. New Mexico had done one of its odd weather shifts, and this early-March day was unnaturally warm. The yearly winds had arrived right on schedule, however, and Mona was ready to scream from their constant howlings. Her skin felt drawn and tight, and grit seemed to coat every surface.

"What are we accomplishing out here?"

"Showing our support."

Mona leaned on her sign. "We make a pretty poor showing against all of them."

"We make up for it in drive and energy."

"And the purity of our cause," Benny added with a cynical twist of the lips. "Seriously, what we're doing is a hose job on the media. Letting them know there are two sides in this fight."

Mona hefted her sign. " 'Progress, Choice,' " she read.

"Versus Preservation and Tradition," said Sil with a wave of his hand toward the serious-faced members of POW.

"I didn't know people like that existed anymore," remarked Mona, turning a fascinated eye on a fiftyish gentleman in patched blue jeans. A red bandanna confined his shoulder-length gray hair, and he sported love beads and sandals.

"This is New Mexico. A few communes still persist."

"I love the juxtaposition." Benny chuckled, gesturing toward the array of palatial RV's. An attractive woman, blond hair pulled back into a bouncy ponytail, hiking boots, safari shorts, and shirt came tripping lightly out of one of the vehicles.

"Sixties meets eighties. It's like some sort of demented wrestling match. See yuppies and hippies make common cause against the rapers and exploiters."

"Pendejos," Sil grumbled.

Mona seated herself on the tailgate of the pickup. "Why do you guys hate environmentalists so much? I have a Save the Seals T-shirt, but I'd be scared to wear it around you two."

Benny settled next to her and slipped an arm around her waist. "Mona, my sweet life, the environmental movement is a movement born of privilege. It's the brainchild of upper-middle-class whites who have the leisure to enjoy the great outdoors. The concept of 'less is better' doesn't get much play among people who've never had a chance to find out what *more* is all about."

"But you're an Indian."

He threw back his head and released his uproarious laugh. "Oh, dear, have you bought all that bullshit about how noble and in tune with nature we all are? The Apache are scared shitless by nature. Our entire ceremonial life is designed for controlling it. Because the sad truth is that nature can kill you."

"Anything can kill you," Mona replied tartly.

"True enough. Even your neighbors." His eyes narrowed as he eyed the group of young men who watched the trio from the central square.

"All this bullshit aside," Sil said, "which way do you think it's going to go?"

"Too close to call."

"If there's no center, I don't know what I'll do," Mona put in.

"Go back to the circuit."

"No, Sil. I really am finished with that. I want a home. And a family." She hugged her knees, glanced to Benny. "And as long as we're building air castles, what do you want?"

"To create an economic base for the Pueblo—"

"That's not wishing. Wishing has to be totally self-ish."

Benny laughed again. "All right. I want to make a ton of money, and travel, and be president of the Rotary Club."

"No family?"

"Hey, I'm young, don't rush me."

Mona shot a droll glance to Silvestre. "I think we've just been insulted."

"I think we have. Oh, God, speaking of marriages, I've got a great story."

"Wait, wait, let me get comfortable." Benny wriggled his back against the spare tire and laced his fingers over his paunch.

"I went to the wedding of a shirttail relative up in the Chama area last weekend. Mother insisted that I escort this crazy cousin of mine—"

"Not Ester?" Benny asked.

"Yes, Ester."

"The world's meanest Chicana—by her own definition," Benny explained.

"May I tell this story?" Sil asked.

"Go on."

"Anyway, it's real old-time Spanish up there. Four hundred years of isolation, and no outsiders allowed, thank you."

"If somebody offers you a great deal on a ranch up there, don't take it," Benny advised. "They'll burn you out."

"Really?" Mona asked.

"Really," confirmed Sil. "The problem is, after four hundred years you end up not only with the insular clan mentality but also with all the feuds that clans can engender. Some of these families have been fighting for generations, so the only time they all assemble is for a wedding or a funeral. The attitude is, hey, you got to grab the opportunity while you can, so they tend to settle old scores at these festive times.

"So," he continued, "Ester and I pull up, and here's the bride's party and the groom's party all milling around outside the church. I'm looking for a place to put the car when suddenly, *boom boom,* gunfire. Screams, hoots, you-name-it. Turns out that some of the groom's enemies had shot him down on the steps of the church."

"Oh, that's horrible!"

"That's not the best part. The best part is Ester. Naturally, there's no wedding, so we start heading back for Santa Fe, and she is in a tear. How *can* they have been so gauche as to shoot Manuel *before* the wedding? Now Juanita doesn't even get to be a widow!"

Benny whooped while Mona stared in outrage and disbelief at the laughing men.

"You mean she wasn't even upset over the shooting?"

"Oh, no. Just over the breach of etiquette."

Her lip quivered, and she sternly caught herself. "That is *not* funny. You're both awful. I'm going to go help your grandmother with dinner."

"She's a great girl," Benny remarked after Mona had left.

"Yeah."

"You never told your dream. What are you going to do, Sil?"

"Go back to the circuit."

"Does Franklin know?" Benny asked.

"I don't see any point in upsetting him until we know if there's going to be a center." He sighed, and Benny eyed him, carefully.

"I thought you and Mona would become an item once her slub of a husband was out of the way."

"You're damn nosy."

"Yep."

"It's funny. I didn't much like you that first night at the Compound."

"Ditto, rich boy."

Sil slapped his hands on his thighs and slid off the truck. "Well, even if we don't get a center, I've made two new friends and rediscovered a third."

"That sounds like one of those wimpy cop-outs to me."

"No. Mona really is my best friend. And I think— I hope—she always will be."

"You know who I really don't like?" Benny asked.

"Who?"

"Nigel."

"Don't let Mona know that. And by the way, I'm not too wild about that little remark. Nigel pulled me out of some tough spots in Nam. He's a hell of a man."

"Was a hell of a man," Benny corrected.

"He will be again," Sil said. "Because of Mona."

"If you say so."

"I say so."

"It just seems sort of dirty to Lexa."

"Hey, Mona is not a homewrecker. May I remind you it was Lexa who booted Nigel out."

"Okay, okay." Benny raised his hands, palm-out. "Don't get so hot. We all have our loyalties."

Moonlight glittered on the needles of the piñons and turned the bark of the cottonwoods into beaten silver. The car engine was loud in the night as Nigel drove toward San Jose. Then he quickly pulled off the road. It was too nice a night to violate it with noise. It was a night to walk.

He had just stepped from the car when he noticed several shadowy figures creeping up on the isolated house at the Pueblo's edge. His scalp tightened, and prickles ran down his spine. Quietly he leaned back in and removed the P-7 from the glove compartment. Crouching, he slipped from tree to tree.

There was the crash and tinkle of breaking glass, and a woman's shrill scream. *Mona!* Several of the figures were tossing things through the broken windows. A man popped up, worked the pump on a shotgun, and fired a blast through the cheap plywood door of the house. The muzzle flash silhouetted him against the night sky.

Nigel worked the slide, knelt, fired. The shotgun wielder gave a bleating cough and folded up. There were distant cries from the Pueblo now. Inside the house a dog was screaming.

Running footsteps from somewhere. Sil and Benny calling in panic.

Nigel leapt to his feet and ran for the house. The assailants were melting away, dragging their wounded companion with them. Nigel paused and fired two more shots after them, just to keep their minds right. He kicked open the door.

"Snakes," screamed Mona, transfixed on the bed. "They've bitten Skipper T. Oh, God!"

There was a quick-moving slither, then a thundering blast as Nigel fired and the nine-millimeter slug smashed the reptile's spine. "Hold still!"

Moving quickly, Nigel crossed over tô Mona, lifted her into his arms, and carried her swiftly from the house. Sil and Benny ran up panting.

"What in the hell . . ."

"Have you got a gun?" Nigel barked to Benny.

"Back at my folks'."

"Then take this one. You had some visitors who left snakes in lieu of calling cards. You'd better clean them out."

"Benny, they bit your grandmother's dog. I think he's dying." Mona was sobbing.

The Indian's round face seemed fallen in on itself. He nodded grimly, and stepped into the house. There was the spurt of a match, and then the warm steady glow of a kerosene lamp. Several more shots. Finally, a low whining that cut off abruptly at the crash of the pistol. Mona buried her face in Nigel's shoulder. Deep sobs shook her slender frame. He held her close, rocking and soothing.

"Why did you leave her alone?" he demanded of Sil.

"A fistfight had started between some of the protesters and a few hotheads. We went to try to cool things down. Mona was asleep, and we didn't want to disturb her. We never thought . . ." He broke off abruptly as Benny emerged.

"I think I got most of them. The others have probably gone to earth. We'll look in the morning. They must have really had to hunt to find rattlers this time of year. The poor stupid things have probably gone back to sleep. Mona, are you all right?"

"Yeah, Skipper warned me." Her voice caught.

"My granny had that dog for thirteen years. Somebody is fucking going to pay for this."

"I shot one of them, but I guess his buddies hauled him away. Do you think it's the same bunch who jumped you last month?"

"How did you know about that?"

"Lexa told me."

Benny grunted. "Yeah, probably. But how we'll prove anything . . ."

"One of them's got a nine-millimeter slug in his kidneys. He shouldn't be hard to find."

"And with a little persuasion he may want to talk," Sil added with a grim smile.

"I'm going to take Mona home," Nigel said.

"You'd better stick around. This happened on Indian land. Sheriff Mendoza will want to talk with you. I expect he's going to frown on a white man shooting an Indian in his Pueblo."

"You tell him I'll be back, but right now I'm taking Mona home."

"I'm all right now. I can stay," she said.

"No, Nigel's right," Sil said. "You go home. You can give your testimony tomorrow."

"God, what a nightmare. Poor Skipper T." Tears began to slide down her cheeks again.

Nigel swung her into his arms and walked away.

Nigel handed Mona the hot toddy, and she took a grateful sip. Then she glared suspiciously at his cup.

"What's in that?"

"Earl Grey, Madam Suspicion, and nothing else."

"I really didn't want you to stop at that liquor store."

"You've had a bad shock. You can use a drink. Frankly, I could too, but I'm sticking by our bargain."

She stared down into her cup. "Do you think you killed that man?"

"I might have. In fact, I rather hope I did."

"Why?"

"People who fire shotgun blasts through other people's front doors deserve whatever happens to them. They weren't trying to throw a scare into Benny; they were trying to kill him."

"Benny?" Her voice was faint with relief.

"Oh, poor darling." He relieved her of the cup and gathered her into his arms. "Did you think it was meant for you?"

"The thought had intruded."

"No, it was Benny they were after. They wouldn't have minded if either you or Sil had come in for some stray pellets, but . . ." His voice trailed away because she was shivering again. "There, there, you're safe now."

"I know." She laid a hand against his cheek, then caught his mouth with hers.

"Mona!"

"Don't sound so shocked. I was waiting for you to make the first move, but you haven't, and I'm cold and scared and lonely, and I want you."

"Mona . . ."

"I'm not a sixteen-year-old virgin. I've been married. I like sex. I'd like to have sex with you." Languorously she unbuttoned his shirt. Laid her palm against his chest. Felt the quickened beat of his heart.

"Lexa—" he began.

"Yes, I know. And Terry, and to a small extent, Silvestre . . . but, Nigel, I don't care."

"And Rhea. Don't forget Rhea." His voice was muffled.

"Her I would cheerfully forget. And so should you."

"Knowing what you know—"

"It doesn't make a penny's worth of difference."

He cupped her face in his hands. "God, you're beautiful, and it's been damn hard to maintain a brotherly mien around you."

"I just thought the booze had sapped your drive," she teased as she unbuckled his belt.

"Don't bet on it."

He rose from the bed and dropped his clothes in an untidy heap.

"Sheriff Mendoza," he put in. "I said I'd—"

"To hell with Sheriff Mendoza!"

She grasped his wrist and pulled him down to join her in the bed. Her hair formed a cloak for them both. His skin felt hot and dry, a welcome warmth after the clamminess that had gripped her ever since the shooting. Sliding a palm over the arch of her rib cage, he cupped one breast, rubbed the nipple between thumb and forefinger until it stiffened.

Mona measured her length against his. It was comfortable not to feel dwarfed by her partner. She pressed him back among the pillows. Straddling his thighs, she began a visual and tactile exploration of his body. An old scar lay like a brown weal across the skin over his ribs. She touched it lightly.

"Vietnam."

"Oh."

She massaged his belly with one hand. Tickled her hair across his stomach, darted her tongue into the hollow of his navel. He arched and let out a woof of surprise. She chuckled, and tangled her fingers in his brush. His penis thrust eagerly up from the golden hair, but she ignored it and slithered down the bed. Gathered a foot in one hand, and gave him a brief massage. Other foot. Slid her hands slowly up his legs, feeling the hairs catch on her chapped skin. She touched the head of his cock with a fingertip. Tiny moans emerged from between his parted lips.

Gently she rolled his penis between her palms. Kissed him on the inside of a thigh.

"Oh, Jesus!"

His hand closed on her shoulders and he pulled her

down into a desperate open-mouth embrace. Their
tongues fenced, teased, withdrew, met again in a
breath-stopping kiss. Releasing her, he set her to shivering with a series of tiny neck bites. Rolled over until
he had her beneath him. His cock was a vibrating hot
presence between them. He bit and sucked at each
breast. Reached down and brushed across her mons
with a delicate forefinger. Flicked and teased at the
labia. Grinned when she cried aloud.

Tongue replaced finger, and he brought her to a state
of quivering readiness. Mona came in a white-hot rush
that left her gasping. He began again to arouse her.
She tugged urgently at his hair.

He lifted his face, slick from her juices, and grinned.
"What?"

"Now, please. Love me."

He gave a throaty laugh and entered her. They
rocked, slowly at first, but with increasing intensity.
Sweat trickled between her breasts, and with each
thrust their skin parted with moist sucking sounds. He
was murmuring endearments, punctuating the words
with deep grunts. She cried aloud, hands scrabbling
at his sweat-slick back. He came within her, then fell
shuddering across her. Slowly the muscles of her thighs
relaxed their frenzied grip. Their breaths eased, met,
matched.

He threw back a sweat-matted forelock. "Dear God,
lady, I thought you were going to break my ribs."

"Equestrians do it with their thighs," she purred.

"Mona, you're the most amazing contradiction.
Meek and shy one minute. A virago the next. Bubbly
as a spring brook when you get the giggles, and a
volcano in bed."

They lay in silence for several minutes as she ran
her fingers through his silver-gilt hair. "Hello? Where
are you?" she whispered.

"I don't know."

"Feeling guilty?" Mona asked with a small stab of
alarm.

"Nooo."

"You don't sound very sure."

"I just realized that I can't keep drifting. I have to make a decision about my life."

"Oh, dear, does sex make you wax profound?"

He smiled into her eyes. "Not usually. It's you."

"Am I a weighty topic?"

"No, you make me wax poetic."

"Please don't. I had a lifetime of literary quotes from Terry."

"Poor darling. Then shall I tell you that I'm falling in love with you?" She folded her hands before her lips. "The shy doe is back. Is what I said so terrifying?" She shook her head. "Well, that's a relief. I thought I had blown it with—"

"Nigel," she forced out, "I think I'm in love with you too."

He fell back, a rueful smile on his lips. "Oh, Lord."

She levered herself up onto one elbow. "Now I've terrified you."

"No. It just makes for such an emotional . . . mess."

"How do we tell Lexa? When she comes back from the field?"

"I don't know. That's going to be very . . . very hard. Here, now, don't cry."

"I feel like I've ruined things between you and Lexa."

"No," Nigel insisted. "Things were ending long before you came on the scene."

"You seemed so close."

"Mona, relationships don't work too well when one member is so goddamn needy that he can't stand alone."

She looked guilty. "Like Terry and me."

"Like Lexa and me," he corrected softly.

She pressed her face into his neck. "Did I thank you for saving my life?"

He pushed her up, forced her to face him. "Did I ever thank you for saving mine?"

* * *

"Well, we found Dan Delgado." Sheriff Mendoza leaned back in his chair, the ancient springs crying under the stress.

Nigel leaned across, lifted the package of Camels from the desk, and shook out a cigarette. "May I?"

"Sure, help yourself."

"Talking to cops always makes me nervous," he said with a thin smile.

"You and everybody else. But you got nothing to worry about."

"Oh, really? Several of my Pueblo friends told me that I was going to get screwed for shooting an Indian."

"Hell, he didn't die."

"Are you going to charge him?"

"Us, hell no, we got no jurisdiction. He belongs to the feds, or maybe the state police will be in charge. Shit, I can never remember. No, I just wanted to go over your statement again before I pass it on upstairs."

"Where did they find Delgado?"

"The Party Boys picked him up, him and his good friend Rudy Maestos, and drove them over to Hopi. I figured that might happen when you told me you had winged one of them, and I had put out the word. You always carry a gun, though?" he asked with that disconcerting change of topic that is a policeman's stock-in-trade.

"Yeah, I drive a lot in the back country."

"Use it much?"

"Only when necessary."

"Like when?"

"Once against a hitchhiker—"

"You shouldn't pick up riders," interrupted Mendoza.

"Yes, I know that, Sheriff, but realistically it's about the only way a lot of poor people can get around this state, and I've only had one bad experience." Nigel paused and gave a quizzical little grin. "One of my hitchhikers brought a skinwalker down on me last fall. But I drew down on him and he . . . er, withdrew."

"Oh, them Navajo people. Superstitious, all of 'em. You don't believe that shit, do you?"

"Let's just say after that experience I'm reserving judgment."

"So you always got a gun with you?" Mendoza repeated.

"In the car, yes. I was coming up to join Mona and Benny and Silvestre when I saw several guys sneaking up on the house. I went back for my gun, heard glass shattering, Mona screaming, and then this puke fired a shotgun blast through the door. So I shot him."

"You didn't think to, like, come for me."

"Sheriff, that would have taken too long. I figured I could handle the situation."

"Four or five against one?"

"I'm a very good shot. Besides, these guys were punks. It's easy to fire on an unarmed person, a lot less fun when someone starts shooting back."

Mendoza covered his mouth with a hand and laughed quietly. "You're pretty cool."

"I did four . . . almost four tours in Vietnam."

"Man, you're a glutton for punishment."

"I liked the army." Nigel gave a modest little shrug. "And I seemed to have a knack for keeping my people alive."

"I was over there, one tour."

"Yeah? Where?"

The subject of the shooting was done with.

"How charming."

Mona flushed, then frowned and wiped her hands, covered with dirty saddle-soap lather, on her jeans.

Rhea pivoted, surveying the cluttered living room. The skirt of her rose silk dress fluttered softly about her, not a hair of her perfectly styled head moved, and her scent, a musky exotic fragrance, filled the room.

"This is a surprise, Mrs. Sheridan. Did you forget to knock, or am I just going deaf?"

Rhea continued to survey the small living room with a condescending smile.

"Did Terry forget something?" Mona asked, and she was startled by the bitterness in her voice.

"No."

"Then is this a social visit? I admit I'm not very sophisticated, but in my circle the other woman doesn't normally come calling on the injured wife."

A tinkle of laughter. "How cute you are. No, Mona, I didn't come about Terry." She seated herself and arranged her beautifully manicured hands in her lap. "I've come for Nigel's things."

"I beg your pardon?"

"I've come to pick up Nigel's things. Now that that marriage is mercifully over, he needs a place to stay—"

"He has a place to stay."

"—and I have rather more room than you do," she continued as if Mona had never spoken, "so if you'll just pop along into the guestroom and pack up his things . . ."

A blazing anger was tightening like a steel band about Mona's temples. Was it something personal with this woman that she couldn't let Mona have even a crumb of happiness? She shook off the irrational feeling. There wasn't anything personal about Rhea's actions. She was just undirected malevolence.

Mona stretched and leaned against the mantelpiece. Then, in a very tolerable imitation of Rhea's tones, she drawled out, "Nigel's not staying in the guestroom."

Two hectic spots of color flared in Rhea's cheeks. Her mouth tightened, and she suddenly looked every one of her forty-five years. "I'm not quite sure how I'm to respond to that. Is this some sort of attempt to lash out at me because of Terry?"

"Oh, no, I've become positively grateful that you took him. But you'll find out what he's like soon enough." Mona walked to the front door, opened it. "Now, if you'll excuse me, I have a saddle to finish cleaning."

"This would be so much easier if you'd just let me pack Nigel's things."

"But I don't want it to be easy. You're about to beat your head on a brick wall, Mrs. Sheridan, and I'm looking forward to watching you do it."

Rhea came out of the chair, her breast rising and falling in quick, agitated pants. "I'm going to talk to Nigel." Her heels clicked furiously on the brick floor.

Mona slammed the door, stepped in front of it, arms outstretched. "Oh no you're not! You are *not* going to bother and upset him."

"I would never upset Nigel. I love him, and I'm going to warn him that he's traded one controlling bitch for another."

As angry as she was, Mona couldn't control the laughter that bubbled out. "Controlling bitches? Lexa and I? Well, that's pretty rich, considering that you're the woman who could give lessons to us all." She sobered, and her eyes narrowed dangerously. "But I know what you're going to try. You're going to threaten Nigel the way you did when he was with Lexa. Well, it won't fly this time . . . because I know. *All* of it," she added with grim satisfaction at Rhea's horrified expression. "I know how an experienced older sister seduced her young half-brother, and then threw all the blame on him when they were finally caught. How you cost him his inheritance, and destroyed his faith in himself. Nigel's spent twenty-five years hating himself. That's what I really can't forgive you for. You add new meaning to the word 'slut.' " Her voice had spiraled higher until she was shouting.

Mona's head snapped to the side under the force of Rhea's blow. She blinked hard to clear the tears of pain that welled into her eyes . . . set her jaw . . . and backhanded the older woman.

Rhea fell back with a screech. Her hands flew to her face, and she shrieked again when she saw the blood staining her white fingers.

Mona jerked open the door. "Now, get out of my house. And don't come back."

"You'll hear from my lawyer!"

"I don't think that's very wise. We'd both look like fools."

But she was talking to Rhea's back. The other woman was running for her car.

Shaking with rage, Mona shut the door and leaned

against its welcome support. Nausea filled her throat, and she ran for the bathroom. A few minutes later she washed out her mouth, tottered into the kitchen, sat on the high stool, and called Silvestre.

"Mona, what's wrong?"

"Don't be so psychic," she complained.

"Not psychic, I just happen to know every nuance of your lovely voice."

"Sil, Rhea Sheridan was just here."

"Shit."

"Yeah. It got pretty ugly, and I'm still a little shook-up."

"I'll be right over."

"Thanks."

She occupied herself by setting out a lunch. The smell of the leftover roast beef assailed her nostrils. She gagged and ran again for the bathroom. Settled shakily onto the toilet after the spasms eased. Counted on her fingers. Figured, and refigured. Remembered throwing away her diaphragm shortly after Terry had left her. Claws seemed to close on her gut. She folded over, rocking herself.

The flat *brang* of the doorbell jerked her erect. She ran for the door.

Sil frowned down at her. "You look like hell."

"I think I'm pregnant."

"Oh, Christ."

19

"Why are you looking so stunned? I'm the one in trouble." Her voice broke slightly on the last word. "Oh, damn!" She furiously dashed away tears with the backs of her hands.

"Is it mine?"

"No. Don't be an idiot. I would have noticed if I hadn't had a period since December. *You* can rest easy."

"That is *not* how I meant that, and you know it. I was thinking of you. Of Nigel. How Nigel would have my butt if I'd gotten you pregnant. It *is* Nigel's?"

"Yes. Oh, God, the thing I most wanted in my life becomes the worst thing that's ever happened to me."

"Why?" Sil slipped an arm around her shoulders and guided her to the couch.

"Because I haven't got a husband. Eileen Mandel thinks my divorce will be final by the end of April. One short month away, and then . . . alone."

Sil did not question this outburst. He came from a traditional, conservative Catholic family. He found the fact that Mona was not sanguine about bearing an out-of-wedlock child perfectly understandable.

"You don't have to worry, you won't be alone. Nigel will be thrilled. He wants a family."

She turned horrified eyes upon him. "You don't think I'm going to tell him!"

"Of course you are. What else can you do?" It was his turn to look horrified. "You're not considering—"

"No, no, of course not. I could never take that route."

"So what, then?"

"I'll leave New Mexico. Go to live somewhere else."

"Going to sew a red A on your chest too, or are you just planning to put about that your baby's father was killed in El Salvador?"

"Don't be sarcastic."

"I'm sorry. I just don't understand why you won't tell Nigel."

"Because he'll feel obligated to marry me, and he and Lexa haven't even begun divorce proceedings, and maybe he doesn't even want to, and I'll have forced him to make that choice, and then forced him into marriage, and . . . and . . ."

She broke down and began to cry. Silvestre sat with a rueful look on his face and patted her shoulder consolingly.

"There is another option," he finally said.

"What?"

"Marry somebody else."

"Like who?"

"Well . . . like me."

"Sil!"

"You don't think you could bear it?"

"It's not that. I don't feel for you that way. It would be like marrying my . . . my—"

"Your brother, I know. But marriages like that have worked out before."

She scraped back her hair. "I don't know. I just don't know."

"Well, that's probably what you should have said first: you don't *know*—not for certain. Why don't you get tested?"

"True. All of these agonies might not be necessary. You won't tell Nigel, will you?" she asked in sudden fear. He hesitated, and she grabbed him by the collar. "Promise me, Sil. Promise."

"I don't know if I can. You two are my best friends in the world."

"You'll be betraying me if you tell."

"And betraying him if I don't. We males do play some part in this, Mona. He has a right to know. A right to choose."

She dropped her face into her hands. "Oh, God, why did this have to happen?"

He resumed patting her. "Martin would say that Blessed Father undoubtedly has His reasons."

"I think I'm going to be sick."

"I'll call and make you an appointment," he called after her fast-retreating back.

Father Martin brushed against a crooked stack of papers, and the entire mess went sliding onto the floor with a weary splat. A cloud of dust mushroomed up, and the priest rocked forward as an enormous sneeze shook his lanky frame.

"This should keep you occupied for a few days, Father," Monsignor Chavez said with a tight little smirk.

"A few centuries."

"I beg your pardon?"

"Nothing, sir. Sir." The prelate paused, one foot on the stone stairs leading out of the storage basement. "Is this really necessary?"

"The archbishop wishes to have the papers in these chests systematized. They represent valuable historical data."

"If they were so valuable, why wasn't this done earlier?"

"We were waiting for a man of your unique capabilities, Father. A real grasp of seventeenth-century written Spanish."

"I see."

"I'm glad you do."

They exchanged smiles. The door closed. Father Martin kicked at the scattered papers, then cursed as the explosion of dust set off another sneezing fit. This had nothing to do with his unique capabilities, and a lot to do with keeping him away from any kind of meaningful work. Fortunately, he loved God more than

he loathed certain of His servants, and by God, they
were not going to drive him out of the priesthood.
Sooner or later some of these old barnacles had to die,
and a fresh wind would sweep through the Vatican,
and out into her churches worldwide, and he would be
returned to Central America.

"So bear it with a cheerful heart," he instructed
himself, and threw open the first of the big hidebound
chests. Hours passed. He sipped water from his canteen, trying to wash away the dust that seemed to coat
his throat. Then he repositioned his Tensor lamp in an
effort to better see the spidery script with its faded ink.
Martin glanced at his watch. Almost five-thirty. He
would finish this last chest, and reward himself with a
large Scotch and a sixteen-ounce steak at the Valley
Forge. Then he would drive into the mountains and
take a short walk in this beautiful April weather. He
would—

"Holy God!" The canteen toppled, and water ran
across the dusty floor. Absently he wiped at the wet
patch on his pants as he rushed to go over what he had
just read.

They were the minutes of a meeting held in 1707,
appropriating funds for the rebuilding of the San Jose
church after the Apache raid that had devastated it.
Discussion had led to a decision not to rebuild in the
same location, but to move the church into the central
square, in conformity with most Pueblo churches.
Which meant the old church had not been in the center
of the Pueblo! Which meant . . .

Martin raced up the stairs to the library. Feverishly
he searched, forcing himself to move carefully so as
not to endanger the brittle parchments. At last he found
it—a sheaf of yellowing parchment adorned on the final page by an ornate gold seal and faded red ribbons.
He read the grant, reread the minutes, read the grant
again.

"Jesus! This is fucking wonderful!" he screamed at
the ceiling. He flung himself out of the Cathedral and
into his car to drive like a crazy man to the C. deBaca
hacienda.

The family was at dinner. They stared up at him in surprise and some consternation as he pelted into the room. His clothes were dust-streaked, and sweat had etched pale lines in the dirt that caked his face.

"Sil! We're going to make them sweat blood! Forgive the expression, but we're going to crucify them."

It was a council of war held at Franklin Pierce's old brick house on East Palace Road. Nigel, who had never been there, looked about with interest, and smiled a bit at the millionaire's choice of housing. Not for Pierce Santa Fe chic or adobe. He had purchased and renovated one of the old two-story brick houses from the 1890s, which had originally been built by white people trying to recreate the comfort and safety of their distant eastern homes. It was a deliberate nose-thumb, and Nigel chuckled appreciatively.

Inside, Franklin had assembled an impressive collection of nineteenth-century antiques. Tiffany lamps, a claw-footed settee, heavy red velvet draperies. Over the fireplace hung a portrait of his wife and daughter. An overhead light threw a gentle glow across the delicate features, and to either side sat a pair of elaborate Waterford crystal candlesticks. The candles in those sticks had been burned. This was obviously more than a memorial, it was a shrine. Nigel looked at the figure of Franklin Pierce with greater respect, and some pity. His rough exterior hid a sensitive soul.

Their host lowered himself with a grunt onto the sofa. "Okay, I got Benny here, and I got Mona here, and she dragged along Nigel, and now I'd like to know just what the hell is going on." He glared at Silvestre, who grinned back. "Call me up at nine at night all in a lather, and then not tell me what the hell is the matter . . ."

"I wanted Martin to explain, and I didn't want to have to repeat it a thousand times, so I called for this meeting. But thanks, Franklin, for organizing everything. You'd make somebody a great social secretary."

"I'm beginning to be sorry you ever got off the cocaine. Makes you smart-mouthed."

"You knew about that!"

"Shit, boy, there ain't nothin' I don't know about. Particularly when it concerns my interests." He lit a cigar. "But go ahead. Tell me this big news."

"Martin."

The priest opened a briefcase and carefully removed several pages of yellowing parchment. "It all begins with the minutes of a meeting of the archdiocese in 1707, authorizing a grant of money to rebuild the San Jose church. It had been burned in an Apache raid in 1705," he explained.

"So?" asked Benny.

"Yes, your skepticism is correct; in and of itself, that isn't very remarkable. A lot of old churches burned down and got rebuilt, but there is a mention in this report that the decision was made to *move* the church from its original location into the *center* of the Pueblo, as was traditional." Benny straightened in his chair, his brows climbing for his hairline. "I see you're with me." Martin smiled at the young Indian.

"Well, I sure as hell ain't," Franklin put in.

"Me either," echoed Mona.

The priest grinned. "Bear with me. This is so good that I just have to be a little dramatic. The fact that a church has been moved has very interesting ramifications—"

"For you maybe," Pierce murmured *sotto voce*.

"I went back to the historical archives and found this." He reverently lifted the thick sheaf with its gold seal. "This is a Cruzate grant signed on September 20, 1689, by Governor Don Domingo Jironza Petriz de Cruzate, granting to the Pueblo of San Jose four square leagues or roughly twenty-seven square miles." His voice dropped dramatically. "As measured in each of the cardinal directions from *the cross in the mission cemetery.*"

Sil unrolled the U.S. Geological survey map he had brought, and spread it on the floor. With a blue felt-tip pen he carefully drew the boundaries of the Pueblo, with its southern border reaching to Rancho de Palabra.

"Holy shit," breathed Benny.

"You get it," said Father Martin with satisfaction.

"Oh, yeah."

"Well, for those of us who don't, could somebody please explain?" Mona complained.

"The land grant runs from the location of the *original* church," Benny said. "So the subsequent measurements made in the nineteenth and twentieth centuries are incorrect."

Father Martin smiled like a satisfied shark. "And depending upon the location of that original church . . . well, let's just say that it might have a profound effect upon our friends in Rancho de Palabra."

"But that grant is ancient," Mona objected. She was puzzling over the seal. "And issued by a governor serving under the authority of a Spanish king."

"True, but the American courts have granted full faith and credit to these Spanish grants of Indian land," Benny cried triumphantly.

"Then if the old church was on the south side of the Pueblo, you could take away those people's homes?" Mona asked slowly.

Benny was up and pacing. "Yes. Or force them, or the United States government, to pay compensation. Either way, it's going to tie them up in court for years. But that's not what we're after—or I'm not, anyway. I'm going to use this as a bludgeon. Force them to drop their opposition to the center."

"Whoa, now," cautioned Franklin. "This is all just so much bushwah until we know *where* that old church was. And how we're gonna do that—"

"We get an archaeologist," Nigel said with a peculiar expression on his narrow face. Mona shot him a quick glance, and then forced her gaze away.

"And who—" began Franklin.

Benny shrugged an impatient shoulder. "It's obvious. We get Lexa. I'll go talk to her—"

"No, I will," Nigel said softly.

The Indian's gaze radiated hostility. "Yeah? Why you?"

"Because I'm her husband."

"Seems to me you've forfeited the right to use that title."

Waves of heat seemed to be washing through Mona's body. She swayed, clapped a hand over her mouth, muttered incoherently, "Please. Oh, please, don't," and bolted from the room.

Sil was on his feet, hands clenched at his sides, glaring down at Benny. "You son of a bitch!" A soft touch from Nigel silenced him.

"Please, I really think this is between Benny and me."

"What upsets Mona—"

"Yes, I understand that. I understand that you love her, Sil, but I do too." Benny emitted a rude noise. Nigel returned his calm gaze to the younger man. "So would you care to . . . step outside?"

"So it's going to be one of those, is it?"

"No, it was an infelicitous choice of words."

Franklin shifted his bulk irritably. "I don't mean to interrupt this private soap opera, but I've got an equestrian center to get built. So when are you gonna talk to your wife?"

"Tonight, Mr. Pierce."

A grunt was Pierce's reply. Benny had already slammed out the door.

Sil laid a hand on Nigel's shoulder. "What are you going to say to Lexa?"

The mobile brows arched up. "I'm going to ask her if she'll undertake the search for the church."

"This'll be the first time you two have talked since . . ."

"Yes, she's been in the field."

"That's not what I meant," Sil said. "Don't be obtuse. What are you planning to do?"

Nigel glanced back to where Pierce and Father Martin were talking. "Sil, why the third degree?"

"I need to know—are you planning to get things worked out between you and Lexa or . . . well, what about Mona?"

"Sil, you're a dear friend, and all that, but this really isn't any of your business."

"Nigel, there's something you need to know."

"Are you coming, Vallis, or not?" Benny demanded, sticking his head back in the door.

"I'm coming. Later, Sil."

"Yeah. Later may be too late."

Nigel frowned, shook his head, left.

Benny leaned hard on the low wall surrounding the tiny front lawn. The air was redolent of hyacinths. Nigel lit a cigarette. Followed the tiny arc of fire left by the falling match. Watched it die in the damp grass.

"Okay, Benny, I'm here. Have your say."

The young man turned, his plump face working as he struggled to find the words. "How could you? How could you treat her that way?" he finally blurted, and in that moment he seemed very young. Nigel found that the flicker of anger he had felt with the boy had faded with that anguished cry.

"First, Benny, Lexa asked me to leave. I didn't walk out on her. I would never have done that."

"But you did. That's just what you did. You emotionally walked out on her when she needed your support over the center, and the co-op, and all the rest."

"I guess you're right," Nigel admitted. "I did."

"Why?"

"The problems were so complex and so private that I didn't feel I could go into them with Lexa. That being the case, I'm certainly not going to go into them with you."

"You sure as hell could confide in Mona."

Nigel flipped the cigarette over the wall, and there was a shower of glowing ash as it hit the sidewalk. He stepped forward. He and Aragon were nose-to-nose, and despite Nigel's lack of height, there was something very commanding about him.

"If you *ever* use a tone like that again when you speak Mona's name, I will take you apart. Do you understand?" He bit off each word as if it were Benny he had between his teeth.

"Ye . . ." Benny coughed, tried again. "Yes."

"Good." Nigel walked to his car.

"Why are you suddenly helping us?" Benny demanded.

"Call it my way of atoning."

"But you never will have the balls to lay out that bitch sister of yours!"

"No." Nigel let out a sigh. "Probably not."

The house was cluttered with boxes of foodstuffs, a tent, a bedroll, a camp stove. How many years had he picked his way through such clutter after Lexa had returned from the field? His heart seemed to squeeze shut. He lifted his eyes to meet her level and somewhat hostile gaze.

"This is unexpected," she said.

"Yes."

"I'm going to keep unpacking while we talk. Do you mind?"

"No," he said mildly.

Silence yawned between them. Finally she asked in a carefully neutral voice, "How's Mona?"

"Fine."

This is absurd. Talk to her.

"I've just come from Franklin Pierce's. We . . . they need your help."

Lexa slid a box of cornflakes onto the top shelf, then turned and regarded him with her hands on her hips. "Mona is working wonders. For me nothing, but for her . . . you're suddenly involved."

"It's not like that."

"No? That's how it looks."

Frustrated, he paced away. "This wasn't supposed to go this way."

"What did you expect? Hugs and kisses and: Oh, honey, how I've missed you, and, darlin', won't you please come home?"

"No, not that."

"Nigel, what do you want? From me?"

"I don't know." He fiddled with the boxes, arranging them according to height. "You were right to boot me out."

She sank wearily onto the kitchen stool. "Wish I felt that way."

"Lexa—" The trill of the phone stopped him.

She snatched it off the wall, listened, held it out. "It's for you. It's Silvestre."

He took the receiver.

"Don't talk, just listen." Sil's words were clipped and nervous. "Mona's pregnant. She didn't want me to tell you, but I thought you had a right to know. And it could be important to your . . . calculations."

Nigel stared for a long time at the dully buzzing receiver. Slowly he returned it to the wall.

A child. The thing he had yearned for, the one thing Lexa had denied him.

"Nigel?"

He shrugged off her hand, then reminded himself that he had denied Lexa too.

"Trouble?" she asked.

He steepled his fingers before his mouth. "Depends on how you define trouble. God, I could use a drink."

"So could I. I'll pour us one."

"No!" He grinned crookedly, then moderated his tone. "None for me, thank you."

"About the center. You said you . . . they needed my help. To do what?"

He quickly outlined the situation with the Cruzate grant. An evil expression tightened her face. "Won't this be a poke in the eye for Rhea." She slid her eyes toward him, daring him to remonstrate with her for the venom that laced the words.

"Then you'll do it?"

"Is the pope Catholic?" She perched cross-legged on the rug before the fireplace and sipped at her Scotch. "The validity of some of these Cruzate grants has been brought into question, you know. The implication being that they're forgeries."

"Doesn't matter. As Benny said, we don't want to put people out of their homes, we just want them to lay off the equestrian center. Benny thinks that a chance to unite against their rich neighbors will remove the differences in the Pueblo too."

"As I said, Mona sure has you singing a different tune." Lexa took a long pull at the Scotch. "What's she got that I ain't got?" The tone was light, the pain evident. "I keep wondering if I ought to scratch her eyes out. Then I remember that I *like* Mona. Still like you too."

He dropped to his knees beside her, gripped her shoulders. "Oh, Lexa."

Panicked by his proximity, she leapt to her feet and plucked an envelope off the mantel. "I've had a job offer. In Guatemala."

"Will you take it?"

"That depends . . . and thank you for not asking *on what*."

"I'm brighter than that."

She set aside the glass, held him by the wrists, and stared deep into his gray eyes. "What do you want, Nigel? *Which* of us do you want?"

He lightly touched the back of her hand. "It's more complicated than you know."

Lexa stepped away and folded her arms protectively across her breasts. "Nigel, I've been doing a lot of hard thinking over the past two months, and I'm going to share the result of all that brain sweat with you. I don't think you're ever going to be happy—with me or with Mona or with yourself until you forgive yourself."

"That's the real trick, isn't it?"

"Nigel, you're drifting. You've got to take control, make a decision. Will you come with me? On this dig?"

"And do what?"

"Oh, I don't know. We'd find you something. You could work for the project."

"Forty is a little old to be pit crew on a dig," he said a trifle dryly.

"You've done it before."

"Lexa, you say I'm drifting. Well, maybe I don't want to *drift* down to Guatemala with you."

"Two months ago you issued me an ultimatum. Out

of Santa Fe, or else. Now I'm considering leaving, and you won't come.''

"Situations change. Two months ago I wanted to run from something—''

"What? What are you running from?''

He stared at her, expressionless, then resumed as if she hadn't spoken. "Now I want to build something. On my own, for myself, and for . . . someone else.''

"That someone being Mona,'' she accused.

"It seems likely.''

"Pretty goddamm tepid response!''

"Mona and I have something we have to work out.''

"But you won't work things out with me,'' she cried, and spun away. Laid a hand over her face and said huskily, "Oh, God, I'm so tired of these fights. Always the same fight. Back me, back Mona, back Rhea—''

"Lexa, I think I've got to start backing myself.'' He picked up his jacket, paused at the front door, and said, "I'll tell Benny you're going to work with him, and he'll arrange for the permits.''

She gave herself a shake, and looked over her shoulder at him. A gallant little smile curved her lips. "And then I and my grad students will run screaming into the desert brandishing shovels and trowels, and prepare to spread confusion among our enemies.''

"You and Benny—so warlike.''

"Nigel, some things in life have to be fought for.''

He smiled, and blew her a kiss. "You'll always manage to have the last word, won't you?''

"To my dying breath.''

20

Rhea was in the tower room sorting through the detritus left by the twins. She had received a frantic call from Elani howling for a book that she'd forgotten at Christmas, and Rhea couldn't depend on Maria not to just grab the first book she found, regardless of whether it was the right one. She didn't like to sound bigoted, but really, these people could be such children.

When she had designed the house she had added the round tower in a moment of whimsy. Circular stairs to a topmost room, stained-glass windows all the way around, an Austrian ceramic stove against one wall. Two little beds with trunks at their feet, a window seat that ran beneath the windows, with built-in cabinets for the storage of toys and books. A room built for children. No matter that the children spent nine months of the year in European boarding schools.

No, she thought as she knelt on the blue velvet cushion of the seat and pushed open a jewellike window. What the room really was, was her princess-in-a-tower-room. A place to rest, to plait dreams like a golden braid. To weave fantasies of love and heroic rescue and of living happily ever after. A place of safety.

The window gazed out over the high back wall of Rancho de Palabra and the scrubby mesa top beyond. Rhea froze, fingers still resting against the cool glass, for there were people on the mesa. A line of them marching slowly across the plateau. Eyes bent to the ground, boots kicking up tiny puffs of dust. One figure was unpleasantly familiar—Lexa.

Rhea watched as her sister-in-law bent, lifted something to her eyes, turned it between her fingers. Cast it away. Marched on. *Lexa*. That was Indian land. Projected site of the equestrian center. *Lexa*.

Rhea slammed shut the window and bolted down the stairs. The tower was no longer a place of safety.

"So that's it, huh?"

"Yes, don't sound so disappointed," Lexa replied as Benny frowned down at the stakes and string, shallow trenches, and faint dark lines forming a cross on the arid desert plateau.

"I thought there'd be something a little more dramatic."

"Your ancestors built with mud. The good padres learned the trick and followed suit, so not a lot remains. Foundation stones and charred remnants from the ceiling beams." She handed him a piece of blackened wood shaped rather like a knife blade.

Benny had grown pensive. "Funny to think of Apache hooting across this mesa and burning out a church. Gives me a creepy feeling."

"I know what you mean," Lexa agreed. "Sometimes when I'm digging in some remote location I imagine I can hear the voices of the dead murmuring on the wind."

Benny made a ward against evil, then recovered himself and said with a laugh, "Lexa, you're a romantic. I would never have thought it."

"I have a lot of surprises. Here." She handed him a folded cord.

"What's this?"

"The traditional fifty-vara cord used by the Spaniards for measurement. I thought you should have the honor of pacing off the correct boundaries of the San Jose Pueblo."

Benny squinted toward the wall of Rancho de Palabra. "It's clearly going to encroach on the development."

"Yes, and what's coming is going to be ugly. So

we've got to know *precisely* where the new boundaries
lie.''

"Okay.'' He tied the cord to a stake, played it out
until it pulled taut, tied that end, and staked. Lexa
loosened her end, and watched the stocky figure re-
cede into the distance, a bitter smile curving her lips.

"Hey,'' he yelled. "What do I do when I hit the
wall?''

"Climb over.''

"Very funny. And when I get arrested for trespass-
ing?''

"Then we get a lawyer, bail you out, and get an
injunction ordering them to give you access.''

"You're determined to land me in jail, aren't you?''

"No pain, no gain.''

"Stupid phrase.''

"No, Mrs. Sheridan, I'm afraid that the defendant won't be arrested. This alleged assault and
battery—''

"Are you doubting my word?''

"No, ma'am, but even if we catch a guy with a
smoking gun in his hand, standing over the body of
the victim, it's still an *alleged* homicide until twelve
people make it official. And as I was saying, this alleged assault took place weeks ago, and by your own
admission, you didn't suffer any grave bodily harm. In
such a situation, an arrest isn't justified. If you really
want to take action, I strongly advise you to take it up
in civil court, ma'am. You're going to end up there
anyway if the defendant files a countercomplaint
against you.''

"This is all very irritating. Why am I paying taxes
if the police won't act?''

The young Chicana's voice took on a decided edge.
"Ma'am, there are people in this town getting killed,
raped, and mugged every day. If we responded to
every little spat that arose, we wouldn't have time for
anything else.''

"So I'm to have no protection?''

"If you're that worried, hire a bodyguard. But you

can be sure that if this woman attacks you again in a manner likely to endanger public safety, she will be dealt with.''

"I see. So if she attacks me in public I can get some satisfaction. I just better hope she doesn't kill me in the privacy of my home."

"Oh, if she kills you, ma'am, you can be sure we'll get right out there."

The sarcasm in the young police officer's voice shattered Rhea's last thread of control. In a temper she slammed down the phone and sat glaring at the unresponsive instrument while she knuckled her chin.

Everything was going wrong. That lout Benny Aragon stumping across Rancho de Palabra with a cord, and that empty-headed twit Louise *letting* him. Didn't she realize that they were up to something? But no, she had just gone ahead and smoothed their way for them. Rhea's comments to her bridge and lunch partner had been caustic and to the point, and Louise had withdrawn from the bridge group after a copious shedding of tears. Good riddance. John Greer, to whom she paid enormous amounts of money, had proved himself completely inadequate to the task of blocking the center. It was only Ralph Quintana's pigheaded stubbornness in his fight with the Aragons and Barelas, and liberal amounts of promised pork barrel, that had thus far prevented the Pueblo from approving the lease of the land.

Then there was Nigel. For years she had prayed he would have the strength to leave Lexa and end that travesty of a marriage. And at last it had happened. But where had he gone? Not to his sister, who loved him, but to a useless little dab of a girl who couldn't even hold on to her husband, and Terry would never be half the man that Nigel was.

Rhea could be such a help to Nigel.

Emotions churned like a bad taste at the back of her throat. Malice seemed to be foremost among them. Everything was so wretched. Who could blame her if she wanted to strike out against the many problems besetting her?

And that useless little Mexican bitch at the police station. You just couldn't deal with those people. They were so bitter against anyone who had a few dimes to rub together. And they couldn't be depended upon to get anything done.

It just didn't seem fair that Mona was going to get off scot-free. Money wasn't the issue. Rhea didn't need any more money, and having a jury award her some token amount for the blow that had been dealt to her . . . no, that wasn't the answer. What Mona needed was a lesson.

Rhea remembered that she and Terry had seen Mona and Silvestre C. deBaca quite often at the Bull Ring. The food could be really uneven at the restaurant, but she could endure it for a few nights.

She just had to do something.

The calls went out.

Big meeting at the Pueblo tomorrow night. All the loyal troops should assemble for the final showdown. Ralph Quintana had to be convinced that it was more productive to poke rich Anglos in the snoot than continue his opposition to the center.

The faithful witnessed for their cause.

They would be there.

June had brought the tourists. Which meant Nigel was locked at the shop until six. Sil offered to buy Mona dinner, then they would swing by to pick up Nigel and head for San Jose. That was fine by everybody, and also gave Sil a chance to view the exasperating couple both alone and together.

He and Nigel had never alluded to the bombshell dropped over the phone that night at Lexa's. And Mona didn't know he had broken his promise to her about keeping the pregnancy a secret. He continued to work on her, urging her to tell Nigel. Thus far she had continued to refuse. And Nigel hadn't done anything either. Granted, one could consider his continued presence in Mona's house a positive sign, but Silvestre would have preferred something a little more concrete.

Mona was somewhere in the vicinity of four months along, and soon secrecy would no longer be an option.

There was a twenty-minute wait at the Bull Ring. So Sil suggested a drink. They stepped into the bar, its walls lined with the photographs of state legislators and former governors. The tiny round dance floor was filled with portly old government officials dancing with hot honeys in too-tight jeans and too-high heels. Sil wondered briefly if any of the hard-faced girls belonged to Ernie.

He pulled out a chair for Mona, settled into another and looked thoughtfully up at the grinning visage of one of New Mexico's more colorful governors. He had stripped the governor's mansion of its furnishings before departing from office.

"You know, it's always struck me that they shouldn't have omitted the social-security numbers from beneath those pictures."

"Sil, that's awful," Mona laughed. "Not all politicians are crooks."

"No, just most of them. And in New Mexico you get to add in cranks as well as crooks."

They placed their orders, and Mona leaned back and with a sigh surreptitiously opened the top button of her Levi's.

"Going to be time for fashions by Omar real soon now. How long are you going to go on hiding it?"

"I'm not trying to hide it."

"Oh, no, of course not."

She held the cold glass to her cheek in an effort to cool off. "Don't pick at me, Sil, please. I've got all these decisions to make, and I feel like I'm about to fly into a thousand pieces. I can't take any more pressure." She sucked down her Coke.

"I'm sorry, baby, I don't mean to nag. I just worry. And I care. About both of you."

"I know."

"Want to dance?"

"Sure, why not? May be my last time for quite a while."

"Nah, once you get real big, we'll rent the Elks

Club so you can maneuver without endangering the other dancers.''

''I *hate* pregnant-woman jokes. They are a really cheap shot. And it's always men who make them. They get us in this shape—''

''Or out of it.''

She slugged him on the arm. ''And then have the gall to crow about it.''

''Retarded development,'' he said, swinging her into his arms. ''Women are definitely higher on the evolutionary scale than men. Emotionally we're still swinging in the trees.''

The band had struck up a slow dance, and the floor was packed with swaying bodies. Mona's hair was floating with static, tickling at his chin, catching on his lips. It smelled *clean* with no overlay of shampoo scent. Sil's arms tightened around her, and he thought regretfully that human emotions and human chemistry were tricky things. Promising so much, and often delivering so little. Not that a friendship was to be despised—it wasn't—but with Mona in his arms he could find it in himself to be jealous of Nigel.

His eyes closed and he gave himself over to the music. Suddenly Mona staggered, falling hard against his chest, and his heels skidded on the slick dance floor. There was an anguished cry from somewhere near his feet.

''I'm sorry—''

''You knocked me down! You deliberately knocked me down!''

John Greer, looking acutely uncomfortable, was assisting Rhea to her feet.

Mona gaped. ''I didn't. You ran into—''

''Not content with striking me in the face, you now knock me down and hurt me.''

A crowd was gathering, the dancers ringing the combatants like spectators at a cockfight. The band stuttered to a stop, and in the sudden silence Sil could hear the spate of comments:

''. . . did knock her down.''

''Didn't look that way to me.''

". . . watching where she was going."

A scornful look crossed Mona's face. "Hurt you? A little fall like that? Must be a real trial to be that delicate."

Rhea shrank back against Greer's broad chest. He seemed bemused by this show of feminine sensibility. "John, she's threatening me."

Silvestre, eyes narrowing in fury, stepped in. "What are you playing at now?"

"Hey!" The lawyer's pudgy hand came up against his chest. "I don't like your tone."

"Get your hand off me."

"Sil, please, let's just leave."

Greer's big square face had begun to relax into lines of almost comic relief when Rhea said, "Not until I have an apology. And I think I'd better go to the emergency room. My hip is really hurting."

Mona, brown eyes glittering dangerously, said in a soft voice, "Yes, at your age, a broken hip is a frightening prospect."

Sil groaned. Beneath Mona's sweet tones he could hear the hiss of a cat. A sound of outrage burst from Rhea, and her hand lashed out. Sil, prepared for just such an eventuality, caught her by the wrist and forced back her arm. Rhea cried like a dying swan, and Greer, portly but determined, landed a hard if inexpert jab to Silvestre's eye.

I think I'm being stupid, came the thought, but it wasn't strong enough to prevent Sil from swinging back.

Mona darted for cover behind him, and Greer managed to land another punch. Sil gaped at the amazing sight of Rhea in hard pursuit of Mona, as if determined to force a physical fight on her.

Two uniformed cops suddenly pushed through the crowd. "Here, here, here. Let's break it up. Break it up. Now, what's going on here?"

Hortensio Garcia, the C. deBaca family lawyer, made their bail. Sil had instructed him to call Nigel, so he too was waiting at the desk as they recovered their personal belongings. Mona, her eyes glittering with anger and unshed tears, rushed past both Nigel and the elderly lawyer.

"What about the bitch and her shyster?" Sil asked in Spanish as he strapped on his wristwatch.

"There were enough people at the bar to swear that the two of you instigated the fight, so they weren't charged."

"That's just terrific. We were hosed. Set up by an expert."

"I'm going to take you home," Nigel said.

Mona set her mouth in a straight mulish line. "No, I'm going to the meeting at the Pueblo. We have to convince them. I promised Franklin . . ." The disjointed words trailed away, and a jagged sob shook her tiny form. "Oh, Nigel, I've never been hated by anybody before. I'm so scared."

Hortensio, gazing at the stained walls of the county jail, had taken on the aspect of a medieval saint contemplating the kingdom of heaven.

Nigel, holding Mona close, met Sil's grim gaze and asked in Spanish, "What happened?"

Tersely he explained.

Mona raised her head from Nigel's chest. "Don't treat me like a child."

"How am I doing that?" Nigel asked indulgently.

"By speaking Spanish."

"I've got to get out to San Jose," Silvestre said.

Nigel nodded. "I understand."

"Will you be coming?" Sil asked.

"Maybe later . . ." What looked like contempt flashed across Sil's expressive face. "I have another matter to attend to first," Nigel finished.

The frown cleared. "Ah, I think I understand," Sil said.

"I hope you do. I'm not as contemptible as everyone seems to think."

"What are you talking about?" Mona complained.

Nigel gathered Mona's hands in his. "Nothing, my darling. Now, let me take you home."

But once in the car, he didn't start the engine, but sat with bowed head quietly contemplating his folded hands. Then he sucked in a sharp breath. "Mona, we have to talk."

"Wh-what?"

"Don't look so panicked." He flicked a finger tenderly across her cheek.

"You're getting back with Lexa. I'm glad you know—"

"Mona, hush."

"You can level with me, honestly. I'm tougher than I look. I like to know where I stand."

"So do I." Her gaze faltered, and fell before his. "You haven't been entirely candid with me."

Her tongue shot out and moistened dry lips. "How . . . how did you find out?"

"I'm not unobservant." He excused the lie as being necessary to protect Silvestre.

"I didn't mean to trap you."

"You didn't." He turned the key and pulled out of the crowded lot—Saturday night was a busy one at the county jail.

Once home, he tucked her into bed with a tray on her knees and a stack of magazines.

"Where are you going?" she cried in sudden fear, shooting a hand out to him.

"To lay something finally and ultimately to rest."

"Nigel, please don't. It will blow over—"

"That's how I've handled it for years. No more, Mona. You deserve better."

"Better than what?"

"I'll be back in a little while."

"Nigel!"

He kissed her softly on the lips and pushed her back against the pillows. "Don't worry, I'll be all right," he promised.

His last image was of her two eyes, like darkened bruises in a terrified white face. It brought no answering echo of fear from his soul. Oddly enough, he was completely calm.

Maria opened the door to him, and without comment led him to the living room. Rhea, in a frothy confection of sea-green lace and satin, reposed in a corner of the sofa, bare feet tucked neatly beneath her. At the sight of him her hand fluttered to her breast, and fell away. She uttered a tiny cry, and with a rustle of material fled into his arms.

"Oh, Nigel, thank God you've come to me. I've been so upset, and frightened. Nothing like that has ever happened . . ." Her voice trailed away as his arms continued to hang stiffly at his sides.

He reached up and unclasped her hands laced frenziedly at the back of his neck.

"No."

"No what?"

"It won't do, Rhea, it really won't. Not anymore."

"Are you drunk?"

"Uh-uh. I've been sober for over four months now . . . thanks to Mona." There was malice in the tag.

Rhea shuddered. "Don't mention that woman to me. I think she's disturbed. This is the second time I've been assaulted by her. The first time I was willing to let it pass, but this—" She frowned, made uneasy by his impassive features and complete silence. "You do *know* about tonight."

"Oh, yes, I know."

"Well, my darling, I realize it must be terribly shocking to you—"

"It is. I don't think I ever realized before how frighteningly obsessed you were, and to what lengths your obsession would drive you. Lexa said once that you were a malignant bitch."

Her eyes widened, and the gasp of her indrawn breath was loud in the room. Rhea's tiny figure seemed to collapse in on itself, and for an instant he was concerned she would faint. Despite himself he took two steps toward her. Caught himself, jammed his fists deep into his pockets. She looked up at him out of eyes gone dark and vacant with shock. When she saw the implacable expression on his narrow face, she let out a despairing sob.

"Nigel, Nigel. What are you doing to me?"

"I'm escaping from you, Rhea. I have to. You've managed to destroy the past twenty-five years of my life. I can't—won't—let you have the rest."

"Escaping? Destroyed? What are you saying? How have they managed to turn you so against me? I *love* you, Nigel. I love you."

"That's the problem, Rhea."

"And you love me." She was back in his arms, the slender body straining against his. He threw her violently aside.

"No! You arouse a thousand conflicting emotions within me, but not one of them could be described as love. Maybe once, long ago, I loved you, but you've killed it the same way you've killed my strength and masculinity. I thought Lexa could give it back to me. She tried, God knows she tried, but fate—no, my own goddamm weakness—put us within your reach, and you destroyed us."

"I gave you the shop. I helped you when you couldn't find work. I—"

"You trapped me in a silken web! Poisoned me with love, and killed me with malice disguised as concern. You delighted in placing me between you and Lexa like a prize in some sick tug-of-war. You forced me to choose, then blackmailed me with our guilty little secret so I could never choose Lexa. By trying to protect her, I betrayed her over and over again. Well, it won't work anymore. You destroyed my marriage to Lexa. You will never touch what I've found with Mona."

"Because you told her!"

"Yes, I did. Everything, Rhea, everything. And she still loves me, so you no longer have any power over me."

Her lips went white as the blood drained from her face. Hands groping blindly for support, she clutched the arm of the sofa, and sank to her knees.

"Mona was right. I should have told Lexa years ago what lay between us, but I was afraid she would leave me, and I didn't think I could survive without her. So we drifted apart, and then Mona came into my life, and she'll never leave it. She's carrying my child,

Rhea, and I'm going to marry her just as soon as my divorce from Lexa becomes final.'' The anger that had lain coiled deep within his soul suddenly stretched and wakened. Bitter, sarcastic words rushed out, a flow of poison from a lanced wound: "Oh, I must thank you for one thing. If you hadn't taken Terry out of the way, I never would have found her.''

Rhea stretched out an imploring hand to him. He reached into his coat pocket and pulled out an envelope. "Here's the key to the shop and a tally of the value of my share of the business. You can either buy me out now or arrange to sell the business and pay me my share. Either way, I want the money quickly.'' He started for the door, paused, looked back. "Oh, before I forget. You won't press this complaint against Mona and Silvestre.''

"I will!''

"You . . . won't.'' The menace was implicit in the two words.

He reached the entryway. The patter of her bare feet on the flagstones pursued him, and she clutched desperately at his arm. "Nigel, don't leave me. Don't leave me!''

Looking down into her terrified face, he felt a stir of pity. For an instant he feared it was the return of the old, sick fascination. As he gazed down into that beautiful agonized face, he suddenly saw the network of fine lines etching the skin around her eyes and mouth, the roots of tiny gray hairs showing beneath the artful coloring job. And he realized it was no more than pity. Age and decay lay hidden just below the fragile skin. Soon nothing would hold them at bay. And with age came loneliness. Suddenly he understood her terror.

"Rhea . . .'' He took her icy hands in his. "Make it work with Terry. And reopen the lines to your children. Otherwise you will end up alone.''

Her mouth worked. Fury and fear crossed her face, warring for supremacy. The fury won. In a voice gone shrill with hatred, she snatched back her hands and cried, "I'll never drop the complaint. Never, never, never! I'll see her in jail, and you in hell."

"Rhea, I'm warning you."

"With what, you useless eunuch? I'll ruin that center. See how the two—three—of you like living on air!"

"And I'll turn this millionaire community into a nightmare for you."

"Fine words, *little* man."

His face had gone rigid, and bile hit the back of his throat as he struggled not to strike her. Spinning on his heel, he stormed from the house.

Clinging to the doorjamb, she screamed after him, "Run back to that little whore. You pitiful drunk. You'll never amount to anything. I *never* loved you."

The car door slammed, and he was gone in a squeal of tires. Rhea staggered into the living room and dialed the telephone, sobbing into the receiver, "Terry, you've got to come back from New York. I need you."

There was a pause as she listened, face tightening. "The goddamm book can wait! I *need* you."

Silvestre started at the expression on Nigel's face as he came striding into the nave of the San Jose church. He hadn't seen an expression like that since the night the VC had hit their camp in a surprise attack that left seven dead. Nigel, looking like a beautiful devil, had led them into the jungle on a retaliatory raid, and not one of the insurgents had been left alive to carry the tale back across the border.

Nigel paused, head thrown back, aristocratic nostrils tightening with distaste as he took in the situation. The droning attacks on the plan to use the Cruzate grant as the basis for a lawsuit. The sly, greedy looks as the opponents of the center counseled caution—after all, the rich Anglos were busy assuring a continuing gravy train for the Pueblo as long as the center remained unbuilt.

"That's fine if you want to remain a despised underclass," Nigel grated out. "How can you stand here and permit them to treat you like retarded children or ignorant savages? That's the bottom line of the message: those Indians are so fucking incompetent that all we can do is carry them along, providing everything for them. Why do you keep opposing progress and economic development? It'll just keep you poor and despised, and prove the truth of those contemptible stereotypes: drunken Indians . . . blanket-assed Indians . . . lazy, shiftless Indians.''

''Nigel, cool it,'' muttered Benny as he approached. But Vallis brushed him aside and continued advancing down the central aisle toward the altar.

''Or you can use the Cruzate grant, file suit, build the goddamm center, and bring an infusion of money into this community.'' Nigel turned to face the assembly, a sea of brown faces with black eyes impassive beneath woven headbands, stained cowboy hats, billed caps, and woven shawls clutched Madonna-like to the women's throats. ''How long are you going to let them sneer at you and keep you *quaint*? Their houses, their million-dollar mud palaces, are built on *your* land. What would they pay to have you relinquish title?''

''Lawsuits take years,'' came the flat reply from Ralph Quintana.

Nigel pinned him with an outthrust forefinger. ''True. So don't play fair. Set up fry-bread stands in front of their gates, and take families on tours to pick out their new homes. Scare the crap out of these people.''

Benny began to laugh, and said in an exaggerated Pueblo accent. *''Eh, great kiva, but you got it all fulla wadder. But no problem—we just drain it out and put on a roof.''*

There were a few answering titters from the usually unemotional Pueblo citizenry.

''This is crazy,'' snapped the Summer Chief. ''Why do we have all these whites here?''

''Because we care,'' Lexa began, only to be silenced by Franklin coming to his feet like a broaching whale.

''Because we're all gonna make a buck, Quintana. I don't blame you for makin' a face about all this carin' and shit. You've probably had a bellyful of white people *carin'* about you. You've got something I need—the use of your land for ninety-nine years or however long this crazy scheme of mine flies. I got something you need. I got money and jobs.''

''And a chance to poke those rich honkys right in the snout,'' added Benny. ''I don't know about the rest of you, but I'm tired of being patronized. I'm tired of being a tourist attraction.''

''We will lose our identity if we follow your way.''

''Maybe, maybe not. That's what you and Joe Martinez and the moieties and the ceremonial associations are there for. To see that we *don't* lose our identity. But I, as least, want a choice, a chance,'' cried Benny.

''It will take too long. We'll be arrested if we try these wild things,'' said Quintana.

''No.'' Father Martin was on his feet. ''We can get a ruling on the validity of the grant very quickly. Only the issue of compensation is going to take time, and if we take Nigel's crazy suggestions, they'll be begging to pay off.''

''My lawyers'll be happy to do the work,'' Franklin said.

''In exchange for what?''

''Drop your opposition. Give me the lease. Let me build my center!''

''This way you get it all,'' Father Martin added softly.

''Or lose it all,'' Franklin grunted.

''The world changes, Chief,'' Nigel said softly. ''People either take control and guide and monitor that change, or they get passed by and end up pathetic anomalies doomed to wither and die away.''

''So how about it?'' Joe Martinez, the Winter chief, joined his Summer counterpart at the altar. ''What do we do?''

''We vote,'' roared out Governor Barela.

''Vote, vote, vote,'' the crowd took up the cry.

''Only tribal members,'' Quintana said.

The non-Indians obligingly headed for the great hand-hewn double doors.

"What in the hell's gotten into you?" Silvestre asked as he fell into step beside Nigel.

"I'm paying back some old scores."

"How does it feel?"

"Great. Don't let anybody ever tell you that vengeance isn't sweet."

21

An amazing old crone sat in a rickety lean-to shack. In front of her a school-cafeteria table groaned under the weight of Indian bread baked in the traditional beehive oven. Nearby, two younger women poked with long sticks at the floating rounds of fry bread cooking in the hot oil. As Rhea paused in the car, waiting for the gates to swing open, the old woman came hobbling out from behind the table with a loaf of each kind of bread in her hands.

She wore the traditional married woman's whitened deerskin boots with folded uppers. Despite the heat of the late-June day, a brightly colored blanket covered her head and hung in folds over her cotton dress. She tapped at the window with a roughened knuckle. Rhea, recoiling, waved her away.

"Mom, let's buy some," Em said from the backseat of the Jaguar XJ6 sedan. "I love fry bread."

"No!"

Elani, staring out the passenger window at still more shacks selling pottery and jewelry, asked, "What's going on here?"

"Nothing that need concern you."

"We're not kids anymore," Em muttered rebelliously.

"I don't wish to discuss it. It's all very upsetting to me, and . . . just drop it, all right?"

"All right."

They wheeled up to the house, the big garage doors opening at Rhea's signal. Maria rushed out to help carry the luggage, and soon they were assembled in

307

the living room while the silent maid and old Eloy ferried bags up the stairs to their bedroom.

Terry ambled out of the library. "Hi, kids."

"Hello, Mr. Gallagher."

"All set for summer vacation?"

"I guess so."

Elani, who seemed to feel that something else was required, asked politely, "How have you been, Mr. Gallagher?"

"Great. I think I've sold my book. All I need is to make a few changes, and it looks like the editor will take it."

"Neat." Em knelt to relace his Reboks and cast his twin a droll glance. Elani choked back a giggle.

Rhea was running back the phone messages. Elani, suddenly drawn by a familiar voice, moved closer.

"Have you done it yet, Rhea? Time is running out."

"What does Uncle Nigel mean?"

Her mother whirled and let the telephone fall to the floor.

"Nothing! This is nothing that concerns you. Don't you have something you could be doing? Go outside."

With dragging feet, the twins headed for the door. They glanced back to see their mother sink into Gallagher's arms.

"How can he hate me so? Terry, you've got to stop him. Stop him from harassing me."

"I don't see what I can do. I don't even know what he *wants* you to do."

"Withdraw the criminal complaint against Mona."

"Well, do it. It's not such a big deal."

"Terry, she assaulted me! I thought Nigel would see what she was like, but he refuses to open his eyes."

"Hey, Moni's not that bad. A little immature and overly emotional, but basically okay. And don't look at me like I stabbed you. You know I love you. I just think you're making way too much out of this. Drop the fucking complaint, and let's go to Tahiti or something."

The children had reached the foyer and reluctantly opened the front door. Em stepped back, startled, and stared into the equally surprised features of Averell Prescott. Behind him were five other people.

"Is your mother at home?"

"Yes, she's in the living room."

The crowd streamed in. Em and Elani exchanged glances, and slipped in behind the adults.

"Rhea, this is an utterly intolerable situation. We just can't go on living like this. My nerves are a shambles."

The twins seated themselves on the bench of the white baby grand.

"I'm not feeling particularly wonderful myself, Averell. Nor am I happy to have the neighborhood association descending upon me without warning. It makes me feel like a criminal." Rhea gave a light and not terribly successful laugh. "Like those awful people who try to hold garage sales or whatever, contrary to the rules."

Louise spoke. "Well, Rhea, not to put you on the spot, but you really do seem to be at the center of many of our problems."

"And just what do you mean by that?"

Paul Weston, the temperamental American playwright, answered for her. "This whole mess with the Cruzate grant. Our lawyer's—"

"*My* lawyer, recommended by and paid mostly by me."

"Whatever. He's about to hammer out a monetary settlement with the Pueblo. One that's going to hit everyone hard in the pocketbook."

"The point is, none of this would have come about if *you* hadn't been so vehemently opposed to the equestrian center," spat out Prescott, his small mouth pursing into an angry bud.

"And now we're stuck with both the center *and* a hefty payment to the Indians to keep our homes. Besides that—"

"They're stomping all over my property," Averell cried, shrilly interrupting Louise. "They ruined my hyacinths, and your brother was with them. He's harassing me."

"Rhea feels that way too," Terry put in.

"I asked Nigel *why*, when we were about to reach a settlement, he wouldn't get those dirty Indians off the front gate, and *why* he and that . . . that Benny Aragon wouldn't leave us alone, and he said to ask *you*. He said he'd back off when you did. So I . . . we want to know. What is it he wants from you? And whatever it is, for the Lord's sake, *do* it."

"It's a private matter," Rhea forced out.

Weston slapped his palms on his thighs, rose. "Great, then keep it private, and keep the rest of us out of it. I'm getting pretty damn tired of being a laughingstock for the entire country. We even got picked up by *Time* this week. I am *not* happy."

"We want some peace and quiet, Rhea, and not to be part of a media event," Averell said.

"And if you can't see your way clear on this, maybe you ought to think about moving," Weston added.

"At least for a little while," Louise put in breathlessly, obviously disturbed by the blunt speaking. "Just until things blow over."

"Well, it certainly is easy to be critical after the fact." Rhea's voice was high and brittle. "You were all one thousand percent behind me last September. Oh, good work, Rhea. You're absolutely right, Rhea. We've got to stop this project, Rhea."

Weston replied to the bitter remark. "Rhea, your main problem is that you're a great deal too *busy*. You stick your nose in constantly. What's the big deal with this center? It's just horses. What if they'd wanted to open a gravel pit or an amusement park? Then we really would have had problems. But no, you've got to be little Miss Organizer. Even that wouldn't have been so bad if you'd let it rest after your lawyer presented our arguments to the Secretary of the Interior. But no, you wanted to play manipulative little games at the Pueblo." His eyes slid pointedly to Terry. "Naturally the Indians got pissed, and now we end up discovering that our homes are in jeopardy. Nice going, Rhea. You've been a big help."

Snatching up his battered Stetson, he slammed out

of the house. His companions made gobbling little apologies and meaningless noises of farewell and slunk away. Rhea sat rigid on the sofa, nails biting into her soft palms, eyes dry but a look of agony on her delicate features. Terry gave her a buffet on the shoulder.

"Hey, forget it, they're just assholes. Let them whine and snivel and pay off the Indians. What do you say we get away? Go down to Mexico."

"Mexico," Rhea said in total loathing.

"Okaaay, so you don't like Mexico. Well, some other exotic port of call."

"And who's going to pay for this, Terry?"

"Why, you are," he said in that bright impudent manner that always drew a laugh.

Rhea rose slowly. "My God, what a fool I've been."

"Surely you're not encompassing me in that remark?" Terry asked drolly.

Rhea just looked at him.

"Thank you for meeting me down here. I've got to get the merchandise packed up."

Lexa blew dust off the top of a kachina's head. "Why didn't the new store just buy you out?"

"They did, mostly. There were just a few items they didn't want. I figure I'll keep them as a reminder for the future—not to be so stupid."

"Then maybe I should take a piece too."

Nigel stuffed his hands awkwardly into his pockets. "Sure, take your pick."

"Why did you want to see me?" she asked.

"Lex, is that Guatemala job still open?"

"For you?" she asked, surprised. Then her cheeks flamed with embarrassment as she read the answer in his face.

"No, for you."

"Yes." Her fingers played nervously among the pile of turquoise and silver jewelry. "Yes, it is."

"Then maybe you'd better take it."

The heavy squash-blossom necklace clashed back onto the counter. "Just say it straight out, Nigel."

"Lexa, I want a divorce."

"God, this is ironic." She threw back her head, the tendons in her neck etched with the strain. "Five months ago I would have welcomed this. Unfortunately, Mona's turned you back into the man I married. A real slap to my ego having to face the idea that I emasculated you."

"You didn't." He gripped her arms. "The problem was with Rhea and me. It had nothing to do with you."

"I should have helped."

"You did your best, and . . . Lex, I'll always love you for that. But I love Mona too, and—"

A high tight laugh. "How would you feel about a ménage à trois?"

"It would have to be a ménage à quatre. Mona's carrying my child."

"Oh." She sat down abruptly on a packing crate. "What you've wanted."

"Yes. What she's wanted too."

"And the one thing I didn't want. Ironic, isn't it?"

"I think it's pretty surreal myself. Mona moves to New Mexico so she can have a normal home life and a family. My half-sister takes her husband away, you and I have our . . . differences, and I end up with Mona—"

"And I go off to Guatemala to dig up old Mayans. Yeah, pretty surreal."

"Do you hate me?"

"No, I hate myself for not seeing that you were in pain. For being so goddamn busy that I didn't see the danger you stood in. I let you down. I just thank God Mona was there to save you from doing away with yourself."

"Jesus Christ, can nothing be kept secret in this town?"

"I suspected something when I came home and found that bullet hole in the adobe. Finally Silvestre told me the whole story. And there *are* some secrets that can be kept. You and Rhea have shared one for years, one that poisoned our marriage."

"I'm sorry."

"Yeah, so am I." She paced away. "So what's going to make it work this time?"

"Mona knows that secret." Nigel sighed at Lexa's stricken look, took her hands, and sat her down on a crate. He took up a position opposite her. "And I think you deserve to be told. Twenty-five years ago Rhea and I began an . . . incestuous relationship. That's what got me thrown out of the house and disinherited, and that's what's lain between us all these years. It's also why Rhea hated you so much. She never stopped loving me, and she couldn't bear to think that you possessed what she could not."

"Oh, my God." Lexa's hand covered her mouth. Her eyes had gone dark with shock, and—Nigel saw sadly—with disgust. "And who . . . who initiated this . . . this . . ." She waved a hand, unable to say the word.

"I don't think that's very relevant. It's past and done with, and I've finally let it go."

"And did you . . . you and Rhea . . . did you . . . ?" Again her voice trailed away helplessly.

"No, I swear to you I have never touched her since that summer twenty-five years ago."

"Then Rhea . . ."

"Was blackmailing me, yes. I was trying to spare you because I loved you, and because I was afraid you wouldn't love me anymore if you knew." He stretched out a hand to her, and his eyes darkened with pain when she flinched away.

"I'm sorry . . . but maybe it's best that I do go to Guatemala." She paced away, then looked back. "And Mona really knows?"

"Yes."

"And doesn't care?"

"That's right."

"Well, she is fucking extraordinary. And I suppose you think I'm a bitch because I can't accept it."

"No, Lexa, let's have no mistake on that score. There's only one bitch in this whole mess, and that's—"

The bells had been removed from the front door, so they both jumped and whirled when Rhea said in a shrill, brittle tone, "Yes, and just who is this bitch, Nigel dearest?"

Lexa looked from one to the other, expecting the subtle cringe that had always marked her husband's dealings with his sister. Instead she read soul-curdling hatred in his gray eyes, and the violence and depth of the emotion frightened her. She also found herself unable to look at them together knowing what had passed between them. She was embarrassed and ashamed by her reaction, but she couldn't overcome the disgust that filled her.

"Why, you, Rhea," he purred. "Who else?"

"Nigel, please . . ." Rhea faltered.

"What do you want?" he asked shortly.

"We need to discuss the . . . matter that lies between us."

"Which one?" He smiled a little grimly at the surprised glance his sister shot Lexa.

"Well, I guess I'll be going," Lexa said in a too-casual tone.

"Do you want to take something?" he asked, walking her to the door.

"No . . . no, I think not."

"I'm sorry, Lexa."

"So am I."

Nigel folded his arms across his chest and leaned back against the closed door.

"You told her," Rhea whispered.

"Yes."

She shivered at his flat, emotionless tone.

"Nigel, I'll withdraw the complaint." She laid small hands on his breast. "Only *please* don't be angry with me anymore."

He set her aside. "Good."

"That's all?" she cried plaintively. "That's it?"

"Oh, yeah . . . we'll call off the fry-bread stands."

She gripped his arm and dragged him around to face her. "That's *not* what I meant."

"Oh? I thought that was the point of this entire ten-month battle—to protect your precious home."

She peeped up at him from beneath her lashes. He remained unmoved.

"Nigel, my whole life I've only been thinking of you. I suppose I'm just a typical protective big sister. I don't think any woman is good enough for my little brother, and when I saw Lexa making you so unhappy—"

"Very touching. Unfortunately, I'm not buying. We're not going to resume your little games, this time with Lexa replaced by Mona. You're going to stay the hell away from my wife and my family. Do you understand? This is our final meeting, Rhea. Better cherish it."

"*Nigel!*" She reached out to him.

"No! It's over." He stormed away.

Rhea pursued him, her hands clutching wildly. "I'll give you anything you want. Anything. What do you want?"

"I want you to leave me the fuck alone. I don't want anything from you! Can't you understand that?"

"Nigel," she whimpered.

"No!" He flung himself out of the shop.

"Emmerich, kindly take those things out of your ears," hissed Rhea as they entered the Meiter Gallery on Canyon Road. "We're here to see J.D.'s show, and it's rude for you to be listening to the radio."

"Why? You just look at art, you don't talk to it."

"Don't," she warned.

With a sigh he swept off the headphones and hung them around his neck. Elani cast him a sympathetic glance. He had been that way at school too, hating the field trips to galleries and museums. Obediently the twins followed Terry and Rhea into the artistically lit space.

The reception was already in full swing. White-coated waiters roved through the crowd carrying trays of drinks and canapés. Rhea straightened her elaborate seven-strand necklace of snowflake onyx, jet, and crystal beads and swept in on J. D. Michelson, who stood posed languidly near one of his attenuated sculptures. He had made the necklace for her, and she thrust her bosom forward for his inspection and admiration. Admiration was there for the necklace and the way it glowed against her white skin. The bosom didn't do so much for him. J.D. was not, as they say, a ladies' man.

"J.D., I'd like you to meet my children, Elani and Emmerich, and Mr. Terrance Gallagher. To borrow your phrase, he's my cave mate."

The artist appreciatively eyed both Terry and Em, and stretched out a large reddened hand. It was utterly incongruous with his pale and willowy good looks.

"Charmed."

"Mom, could we get a Coke?"

"Try a little champagne, Elani. You're old enough now for more sophisticated tastes."

"Okay." She and Em faded away. "But I don't like champagne," she added to him when they were out of earshot.

"Ugh."

"Well, it's not *that* bad."

"Not that, this." Her brother pointed at a mashed bit of clay set atop a slender column.

Elani giggled. "It looks like a pot that a baby sat on before it had a chance to harden."

Em eyed the two curving depressions that resembled the impressions left by tiny buttocks. "You know, you're right."

Other people had arrived to congratulate J.D. on his show. Rhea drifted away, following Terry's tall form with her eyes. How well he handled himself in company. He could discuss firing techniques with J.D., writing with her various literary friends, football with John, fashion with Louise. He was the perfect man for all situations.

Terry's eye was caught by a vivacious little figure standing with cocked head and puzzled frown before a sculpture of twisted steel and circuit boards with a pair of glass eyes peering out desperately. Her white dress curved lovingly over flaring hips and rounded buttocks, and a silk scarf bound her narrow waist. He stepped to her side.

"Interesting piece, isn't it?"

Aggressively outthrust breasts brushed his arm as she turned. Sparkling black eyes, a full pouting red mouth, all framed by a tumble of black curls. "But of a confusion . . . oh, of a greatness." Her voice was throaty and low, and overlaid with a fascinating French accent.

"Really? I think it's rather simplistic in its meaning."

"Then perhaps, m'sieur would be kind enough to explain to me?" The sultry glance she cast up at him from beneath her thick lashes was pure sex.

Terry threw back his head and laughed. "M'sieur would be delighted. But first, whom does m'sieur have the pleasure of addressing?"

"What is this 'pleasure of *undressing*'?"

"*Ad*dressing."

"Oh, I understand."

"I bet you do."

"I am Adrienne de Cressey."

"Terry Gallagher."

"Terry Gallagher . . . Bah, it is an impossible name for my mouth. But explain."

He took her arm, enjoying the touch of her flesh against his palm. Her figure was lush, and in later years she would probably run to fat, but right now she was a huggable armful. "Well, clearly this piece represents the confusion created by man's technological advances. How mechanism has covered man's soul."

She clapped her hands delightedly. "Oh, but yes, I see it now. How very clever you are."

"I've been an artist."

"But are no longer?" She pouted. "Me, I like artists. I am one."

"Well, so am I, only now I work in words, not paint and clay. And you?"

"I am my own art. I am a singer. I am here for the opera."

He frowned. "To attend?"

"But no, stoopid. To sing. I sing Violetta this season, and Pamina."

"Lovely." He tucked her arm beneath his, and they strolled. "Have you ever been in this part of the world before?"

"No. It is very beautiful and very ugly all at the same time."

"There are a number of sights you really shouldn't miss. Taos Pueblo, and Mesa Verde—"

"And cowboys."

He laughed. "Well, those are a little harder to find, but for you I'll arrange it."

"Really?"

"I don't mean to be pushy, but I do live here, and I would be happy to show you around."

"Right now we rehearse, oh, very much, but soon I will have time, and I would love to see around with you."

"Great, then it's settled."

Her eyes drifted to Rhea. "Your wife will not mind?"

"Oh, we're not married."

She nodded. "Good."

"And how did you know I was with her?"

"Oh, I noticed you from the first."

He nodded. "Good."

The heavy equipment rumbled across the rutted track that served as a road. A work crew, drawn almost exclusively from the Pueblo, followed. And as the first big blade cut into the clay soil, Franklin Pierce removed a handkerchief and gave his big nose a hard blow.

Mona, touched, patted his arm and had her hand gripped in a tight clasp.

"It's finally happenin'."

"I'm so glad, Franklin. I know how much this moment means to you."

"Hell, this ain't nothin'. Wait'll that barn goes up.

Red tiles, and white stucco walls, and big curving doors—"

"Sounds like a Moorish harem," said Nigel, walking up.

"Or like we're raising Arabians instead of event horses," put in Mona as Nigel bent and kissed her cheek.

"After all the screaming and scheming, it's hard to believe that it all ended with such a whimper."

"How so a whimper? You don't think fry-bread stalls were sufficiently dramatic?" Nigel objected.

"More like comic. I guess I just never expected the opposition"—Mona gestured toward the looming walls of Rancho de Palabra—"to collapse so abruptly."

"Yeah, I know what you mean, Moni. I really wanted to kick some butt," Franklin said.

"You're kicking it now," Nigel murmured dryly as a big earth mover rumbled past. "Neither environmentalists, nor traditionalists, nor politicians, nor rich honkies could your noble way obstruct."

Pierce rolled an eye to Mona. "Is he being sarcastic?"

Nigel patted the older man's arm. "Only a little."

"I got one problem," Franklin said.

"I should think that would be a relief after the past months."

"Hush," Mona chided. "You were saying, Franklin?"

"Silvestre ain't said nothin' to me, but I think it's pretty damn clear he ain't gonna be runnin' my center. You want the job?"

She backed up, hands upheld. "Oh, no. I'm hired to train horses and riders, not ride the books."

Franklin stared down at Nigel. "How about you?"

"How about me what?"

"You know how to keep books. You want the job?"

"No, thank you."

"You ain't plannin' to leave Santa Fe, are you?"

"Not at the moment."

Pierce's jaw thrust out aggressively at Mona. "And if he did leave, I suppose you'd go with him?"

"Of course."

"Hmmmph. So what are you living on?"

"Well, not that it's any of your business, but I received quite a substantial chunk of change from the sale of the shop. It gives me the luxury to sit back and consider my options."

"I've been trying to talk him into going to the university," put in Mona.

Nigel shook his head. "I am not going to have you trade one charming leech for another."

"You rate yourself pretty high," Mona teased. "Who says you're as charming as Terry?"

"*You* do."

She chuckled. "True."

"Ready to go?" Nigel asked.

"Yes. This equipment is kicking up so much dust I'm about to die."

"Uncle Nigel!"

He squinted at the two figures speeding over the brush and sand. "Em! Elani!" His arms closed tightly about his niece. "How are you guys?"

"Fine."

"Why haven't you called me?"

"It's . . . hard," came the slow reply from Em.

"Oh, I see. Then maybe you shouldn't be out here. I don't want to get you in trouble."

"That's okay. Mom's gone to town to get her hair done, and Terry's off with Adrienne." Em sucked in his cheeks and rolled his eyes significantly.

"Who's Adrienne?" Mona asked him, curious despite herself.

"Some singer from the Santa Fe Opera."

"My God. He's roving already? Now, don't look so miserable, Mona," Nigel said. "I think this is a real credit to you. After all he stuck by you for five years. With Rhea it's been a scant seven months."

"I can't help but feel sorry for her," Mona said to Nigel in an undertone.

"Don't. She doesn't deserve it."

"Hi, Mr. Pierce."

"Well, hiya, kids. We never did get that hot chocolate."

"You remembered."

" 'Course, I never forget a debt. So how about we go right now? Drive on down to the French pastry shop. Eat something gooey."

"Great."

"Mrs. Gallagher—" Em froze, embarrassed.

"How about just 'Mona'?"

"Okay, Mona," he agreed with relief, "Elani and I were wondering if you'd be teaching this summer. We'd really like to ride, study with you."

"Well, Em, I'd like to, but . . ." Her eyes met Nigel's. "There are just circumstances . . ."

Nigel said it for her: "Your mother and I aren't getting along right now, Em."

"What's that got to do with studying with Mona?"

"What happened to Lexa?" Elani asked abruptly.

"She's gone to Guatemala to dig for Mayan ruins."

"And you didn't go with her?"

"He's got the shop," Em offered by way of explanation.

"No, I don't, I've sold the shop."

Franklin took Mona's arm and guided her away, ostensibly to show her some factor of the building.

Nigel went on, "The truth is, kids, Lexa and I are getting a divorce, and I'm going to marry Mona."

"Wow, that's weird."

Nigel flushed. "Well, I don't know if that's quite the word I'd choose."

Elani chewed on the end of her braid. "Terry was married to Mona, but he left her for Mom. You leave—"

"I don't think we need to go into all that," Nigel said hastily. "Let's just say that it's certainly an unusual situation."

Em nodded. "I can see why you and Mom aren't getting along then. It would be really weird for all four of you to get together."

"Quite."

"But, Uncle Nigel, there's one thing I don't understand—"

"What say we go get that chocolate?"

"I hate it when adults get embarrassed," Em told his twin.

"Then don't embarrass them," his uncle growled.

Melinda Snodgrass

"I hate it when she . . . Are we getting embarrassed," Em told his twin.

"Then don't embarrass them," his uncle grow...

22

Nigel, hanging over the balustrade, realized with an eerie sense of déjà vu that he had been here before. He had stared down at these same tumbled rocks in the arroyo below, heard the murmur of people at intermission, the soft voice of the wind, the snarl of distant thunder. But there were differences too. It was Silvestre who had run the gauntlet for the drinks, Nigel's plastic glass held only Coke, and the silver hip flask was consigned to the bottom drawer of his dresser.

His eyes caressed the smooth curve of Mona's cheek. *There stood the greatest difference.* Lexa was gone, out of this scene, out of his life. There was a faint touch of melancholy, a brief flare of love. But it was all very distant, subsumed in the all-consuming passion he felt for Mona and their coming child.

Terry came bulling out of the crowd, his teeth very white in his tanned face. "Hiya, Moni. Nigel, Silvestre." Mona stiffened, and her male companions closed ranks to either side of her. "Whoa, I lost Rhea."

He plunged back into the milling throng, and emerged leading Rhea like a lost lamb. She seemed small and shrunken as she dangled at the end of Terry's hand, and again Nigel was struck by the changes. Last summer she had appeared out of the heart of a thunderclap, supremely assured, supremely confident of her power over him. Now it was all lost. She was beaten. And for himself? Fear had been replaced with a throat-closing rage. He took a big drink of Coke and chewed loudly on an ice cube.

The twins also appeared, Em with his headphones firmly in place.

Rhea reached out and swept them onto the ground. "I told you not to bring that!"

"I *hate* this kind of music."

"Strive for a little breeding."

"Do you like it?" The boy appealed to Nigel.

"Well, as loath as I am to disappoint you, yes, Em, I do."

"Fat ladies, and shrieking."

"Hey, Adrienne is *not* fat," Terry said, eyeing the boy with disfavor.

"Guess that depends on your definition of 'fat,'" Em said.

"Now, you look here, young man, I won't stand for that tone."

"You're not my father."

"He's going to be your stepfather soon enough, so you'd better watch your step," Rhea warned.

Gallagher's silence spoke volumes. Rhea reddened and stared imploringly up at him. His gaze drifted across the upswept struts of the stage roof. Nigel felt a stab of pity.

"Oh, you're getting married too, huh?" said Sil. "Must be something in the air. Nigel and Mona are tying the knot Sunday. When are you holding the ceremony?"

"We haven't gotten that far yet," Terry replied with an awful heartiness. "Hey, great opera, huh? Adrienne really broke my heart in that farewell scene. What an actress she is. I think she ought to try film. She's beautiful enough for it."

"How . . . how's your book coming?" Mona asked awkwardly.

"Oh, great. I should have the rewrite finished by the end of next week, then off to New York. You know, Moni, I think I've finally found my niche."

"What, as a gigolo?" Em muttered.

Nigel glanced quickly about, but only he seemed to have heard his nephew's ugly little remark.

"I'm glad, Terry, I really am."

"Yeah, and you're going to have a baby and a family, just like you wanted. I'd say that everything worked out for the best."

The little group stood in stricken silence until Silvestre finally spoke. "And I think you're an ass." He deposited his empty glass in Terry's hand and took Mona's arm.

Nigel followed suit, nesting his glass in Sil's and taking Mona's other arm. "I think we'll be getting back to our seats."

"Well, I certainly have been told how important I was to him. How much I mattered," Mona said in a muffled tone.

"Mona, it's his problem, not yours. We ought to be laughing. Can you conceive of anyone that unbelievably self-centered and tactless? If he does marry Rhea, I'll bet he'll expect us to spend Christmas together. Just one big happy family." Nigel's voice shook with laughter.

Mona covered her face with a hand. "Oh, God, you're right. I always thought he was so much smarter than I was, so much better adjusted because things never bothered him. Now I realize that they didn't bother him because he had the sensitivity of a rutabaga."

"Oh, Lord," Sil whooped.

They continued to snigger as the lights came down and the conductor returned to the podium.

"How could you? How could you?"

There was an indistinguishable mutter in reply.

"To so humiliate me. Stack me in a corner like so much old wood, and hold hands with her all night!"

Elani sat up in the small bed, pushed back her hair. "Em."

"Ummm."

"Wake up, listen."

"To what?"

"I think I hate you."

The boy pushed an arm from beneath the covers, squinted at the luminous dial of his watch. "Four A.M."

The sound of shattering glass followed by a muffled thud brought them both to their feet. Quietly they crept down the circular tower staircase until, hidden by the final curve, they could sit and eavesdrop.

"You don't suppose he hit her?" Em whispered.

"No. But what do we do if he does?"

Em's face settled into grim lines. "I'll just have to go down and stop him. Try to stop him," he amended as he considered Terry's inches and bulk.

The sharp tink of a bottle against a glass. "So you hate me, huh? That's pretty rich, considering you're the one who's been trying to maneuver me into marrying you."

"I don't *maneuver* men."

"Bullshit! Because, let me tell you something, baby, I'm sure as hell *not* marrying you."

"Terry!"

"Stop looking like I've killed you. We've had some good times. Don't spoil it all now by acting like the heroine in a Harlequin romance."

"It's her, isn't it?"

"If by *her* you mean Adrienne, yes, it is. She's invited me to return with her to Paris after the Santa Fe season ends, and I'm going."

"Then you can just get the hell out of my house right now! Let's see how you like trying to live without some woman to batten onto."

"Rhea, let's handle this like adults, like civilized people. Throwing me out on my ear just before dawn isn't going to do either of our dignities any good. Come on, babe, it was great while it lasted, but it's over. Let's remember the good times, and—"

There was a sharp slap.

Elani leaned in to Em's ear. "I think the hits are coming from the other direction."

"Good. He's a jerk."

"Okay, if that's the way you want it to be. But I'll always be grateful to you for introducing me to your publishing friends. Really."

"You'll never get that book sold! Frankly, Terry, it's a piece of crap!"

"If you say so. But even if this book ultimately doesn't sell, I'll be in Paris, where generations of writers—"

"Far more talented writers than you'll ever hope to be."

"—have worked and found inspiration. I'll do another book. Sooner or later I'm going to make it. I've got what it takes." Footsteps receding. "Oh, yeah, I'll be out in the morning."

"I'll have John fire her!"

"No you won't. Think how stupid you'll look when he refuses. Don't be petty, Rhea, it doesn't set well on a woman of your years."

The twins crept back up to bed.

The next morning Rhea sat with red-rimmed dry eyes and drank coffee. The twins eyed the empty place, each other, their mother. It was impossible to keep silent. They had to at least allude to Terry's absence.

Elani said brightly and too casually, "Where's Terry? He's out early this morning."

"Oh, uh, he's gone . . . down to Albuquerque . . ."

They all stared at each other. Maria brought in breakfast.

"Oh." Em ran his fork through his huevos rancheros, breaking the eggs and stirring the yolks through the green chili, beans, and hash browns.

Rhea covered her eyes with one hand. "Oh, God, I suppose it can't be hidden. You've got to know. He's gone. Moved out."

Em pushed back his chair, and stepping to his mother's side, slipped an arm around her shoulders. "It's all right, Mom, really. He was a jerk. Don't be up—"

"What do you know about it? Just what the hell

do you think *you* know about it?'' she yelled rag-
gedly.

"Okay, screw it! I don't know anything about it. He
was just great. So how come he dumped you?''

"Don't you take that tone with me! Don't you ever
speak to me that way! Neither of you has any manners.
You don't care about me.'' Voice breaking on a sob,
she flung herself from the table and ran weeping from
the room.

Elani followed and hung uncertainly in the doorway
to the office while her mother huddled by the window
sobbing into her hands.

"Mama, do you want me to call Uncle Nigel?''

"No! She mustn't know. She mustn't find out.'' She
was screaming into her daughter's terrified face, shaking her by the shoulders.

"Mama!"

Em ran into the room grabbed Rhea's hand, and
pulled her away. "Stop it! Leave Elani alone. Are
you having a breakdown or something? I'm calling Nigel.''

Her hands clutched frantically at his arm. "No! You
don't understand. He doesn't love me anymore. He'll
be glad.''

"That's not true. Nigel's great. He'll understand.''

Rhea fell back, suspicion tightening her features.
"You love him better then you love me!''

"Mother, don't be stupid,'' Elani cried.

Em dropped the receiver back into its cradle. "Love
him best? How can we love either of you? We hardly
know you. We've been in boarding schools our whole
lives. But at least Nigel seems interested in us, and he
doesn't play weird head games with us.''

"Nigel's *sick!* He did things to me—''

"I don't want to hear this! *You're* the one who's
sick! You're crazy! Come on, Elani, we're getting out
of here.''

"Em!''

"You can't go. I won't let you,'' Rhea screamed.

"You can't stop me. I'm calling Dad.'' Em took his

twin's hand, paused at the door. "And you're right about one thing. I *don't* care about you."

Mona, dandling Barnaby on her chest, sat up abruptly when she saw the expression on Nigel's face. The black cat let out a squawk of outrage as he got folded between her breasts and the swell of her belly.

"What's the matter? Who was that on the phone?"

"The twins."

"What's wrong?"

"What makes you think something's wrong?" he asked in genuine curiosity.

"I know your face pretty well. I've been studying it day and night for six months. I can tell when you're upset."

He sat on the edge of the bed and studied his hands. "Do you mind if the twins come here?"

"No, of course not . . . Oh, you don't mean for a visit."

"No, I mean for a few days until their father arrives or sends them tickets."

Mona threw back her hair, tossed Barnaby aside, and took Nigel's hand. "Better tell me the whole story."

In a few tense words he outlined the situation, then added, "I admit I wanted to be a coward and tell them no. I don't need any more battles with Rhea, but I am their uncle, and Elani was crying, and something Em said made me think Rhea might be crazy enough and vindictive enough to tell them about what happened between . . . us."

"You're right to say yes. They don't need that burden laid on them."

"I was also thinking of me. I love those kids, and I don't want to have them turned against me."

Mona leaned forward and kissed him. "You are the kindest man I've ever known." She threw back the covers and stood. Tapped thoughtfully at her teeth with a forefinger while she surveyed her wardrobe. "Nigel, I think you ought to call their father and tell him to pick them up. I don't think those kids should be traveling alone.''

"They travel alone all the time."

"Nigel, promise me that if we ever get really rich we won't treat our children that way."

"Mona," he said with a slight laugh, "I think I can confidently promise you that neither of those things will ever come to pass.'' He paused, and stared at his nails. "Because I've put in an application to the police department, and cops rarely become millionaires.''

"Nigel!"

"Do you mind?"

"Mind, no. If it's what you want . . ."

"It is. I've had a pretty adventuresome life, Mona. The boredom of running that shop almost killed me. I like people, I want to work with them, help them if I can.''

"Your age," she suggested softly.

"Is apparently no problem. They've got some fifty-year-old geezers in the academy. And I've got some pluses on my side. I speak Spanish, plus decent Navajo and a bit of Tewa. I told them I'd prefer to work with juveniles after I pay my dues, and again there's no problem. Sheriff Mendoza out at San Jose even put in a good word. He told them I was a real kick-ass kind of guy.'' Mona began to laugh. Nigel gave a rueful shrug. "So he hosed them.''

"Nigel, my darling. You *are* a kick-ass kind of guy. And I love you.''

He kissed her long and deeply, then set her gently aside. "Well, I'd better get up there and collect the kids. I just hope Rhea hasn't gone into her little-mother mode. If she has, it will look like a scene from *Uncle Tom's Cabin* with the wicked massa tearing de babies from her palpitating bosom.''

Mona was stretching for the zipper in the back of her maternity sundress. Nigel zipped her up, allowing his fingertips to caress the soft skin of her back. "I just realized," she said, "we don't have a bed in the guestroom.''

"I'll buy one on my way home."

She wrapped an arm around his waist and walked him to the door. "And it will be the final exorcism of Terry."

"Elani can have the bed, and Em can sleep on the couch or use my sleeping bag."

"We should have them in the wedding. I doubt their travel arrangements will be made by Sunday."

Nigel briefly crossed his eyes, and gave a tiny headshake. "This is such a bizarre situation. All we would need to make it truly surreal would be Lexa returning from Guatemala to attend."

"And my dad suddenly deciding to forgive me and attend."

"Hey, accidents happen. At least I'm making an honest woman of you. I don't know why he's being such a prick about this."

"Good girls don't get pregnant."

"Then how did you get here? Immaculate conception?"

"Nigel, I'm really glad he's not coming." She spun him around and gave him a gentle push down the steps. "Now, go."

Nigel, pausing between kitchen and living room with another basket filled with hot cheese sticks, considered the shifting reception crowd. The entire C. deBaca clan was assembled. Father Martin was searching distractedly for his stole. Franklin, a twin nestled under each arm, was talking business with Benito C. deBaca. Benny was laughing with Ernie while Jorge looked on glumly. Linda Gallegos was selling her therapy program to Mercedes. Smart girl to make a push for a donation from the C. deBacas. Equally smart to talk to the tenderhearted Mercedes. Kids tumbled on the rug, and the room was filled with the babble of voices in three languages.

As he continued to scan the room, Nigel realized that with the presence of some of his former artists, the Indians far outnumbered Hispanos and Anglos. All in all, it was a pretty damn unusual gathering.

It had also been a pretty damn unusual wedding. Never had a bride looked more radiant, or more pregnant. And never had a couple been so completely without family. Their friends had filled that role, Silvestre standing up for Nigel, Franklin giving away the bride. Elani was a flowerlike bridesmaid, and Emmerich, pale but composed, was ring-bearer. Nigel amended his earlier thought; he had had family in the slim persons of the twins and in the presence of his child swelling Mona's body. Father Martin had officiated, though Mona had been hesitant to ask him. Nigel had had no such scruples. He figured the priest was no hidebound stickler for propriety. And sure enough, the father had laughed and agreed to "make an honest woman of her."

It was all so different from Nigel's first wedding. He and Lexa had been married before a judge in Albuquerque's sprawling and ugly county courthouse.

Nigel's eyes sought Mona, and found her deep in conversation with Silvestre. The Spaniard squatted on the floor before her, balancing himself with an arm across her knees. For a fleeting instant Nigel felt a pang of jealousy, then with a rueful shake banished the emotion. Sil and Mona were going to continue to be close, and he would be an unmitigated bastard if he tried to harm that friendship.

The phone shrilled. Mona's eyes lifted to his, and he waved her down. Thrusting the now almost empty basket of cheese sticks into Governor Barela's hands, he hurried into the kitchen and snatched the receiver from the wall.

"Vallis residence. . . . Hello?" Silence, but it was obvious the connection remained open. "Hello? Hello!"

"Nigel." The word was a thread of sound.

"Rhea?"

"Yes."

Another endless pause. "What do you want, Rhea?"

"Nigel, I need you."

He frowned at the dragging quality in her voice, the slurring of the words. "Rhea, your timing is fucking surreal. I have a house full of guests, and I just got married."

"Yes, you've got people around you. You've even got my babies. But I'm all alone."

"And whose fault is that?"

She began to weep, a keening hopeless sound that raised the hackles on the back of his neck. "I have to be loved. I can't live if I'm not loved."

"Frankly, Rhea, you make it very hard for people to love you. You take and you expect and you demand, and . . . oh, shit, why am I having this conversation? Good-bye, Rhea."

"*Good-bye,* Nigel."

He slammed the receiver back into its cradle, the phone letting out a small ring of protest. Rested his forehead against the wall, fought to regain control, struggled to ignore the cold dread that gripped his gut.

It's not my concern. I don't care. It's another game. Another power play. Another invitation to psychodrama.

"What's wrong?" He whirled, and found himself staring down into Mona's concerned eyes. "Who was that?"

"No one."

Her fingers closed tightly on his arm. "Tell me." The color had drained from her face. "Was it Lexa?"

"No, of course not. Little fool." He gathered her in his arms. "Did you think she'd called to forbid the banns? If she had, she'd have been too late."

"I don't know. I was frightened. I get strange notions these days. Maybe it's being pregnant."

"Don't get notions. The only notion you need to have is that I love you."

"Who was it?"

"Rhea."

"What did she want?"

"To agitate me," he answered lightly. "But I didn't let her. She was trying to suck me into another game, but this time I refused to play." His eyes were flicking about the kitchen, unable to focus on any single point.

And if you're wrong!

Mona caught his face between her hands. "What has you so spooked?"

"She said she needed me. She sounded very strange."

"If you're worried, you should go."

He gaped down at her. "G-go? Mona, it's our wedding day."

She waved that aside. "Are you afraid of her?"

"Not precisely. But there's still *something* I can't pinpoint, can't face—"

"Then you need to. Face it. Lay it to rest." Mona leaned back against the counter and studied him. "Nigel, in the beginning you needed to hate Rhea in order to free yourself from her. But it's not in you to hate. You're the gentlest, most loving person I've ever known, and I think it will damage you in some fundamental way to have this hard, ugly knot eating at you. I think you need to make peace with her. Then you really will be free."

"My God, I love you." He took her by the shoulders and kissed her softly on the forehead. "I'll be back."

"I never doubted it."

He was shaking by the time he reached the front door. Deep within the house he could hear the ringing of the elaborate bell. Minutes passed. It was apparent that Maria was not in the house.

Concern flared like a nova, and Nigel dug out his key. Silence lay like dust over the house. His stomach retreated until it had formed a small hard ball pressed fearfully against his backbone. A pulse beat in his temple. He walked with ever-quickening steps throughout the lower floor. No Rhea. Breaking into a run, he flung open the door into the garage, expecting to find the engine of the Jaguar running, tailpipe blocked, Rhea slumped in the front seat. Just more silence.

He ran back through the kitchen and raced up the curving stairs to the tower room. Rhea was huddled on the window seat, her right arm cradled in her left hand, dark blood oozing sluggishly from several jagged wounds on her wrist. A puddle had formed on the floor at her feet. She was staring with empty-eyed fascination at the welling wounds. Behind her, the stained-glass window had been shattered. Obviously by a blow from her fist.

"Rhea . . . Rhea!"

She lifted her head, stared at him, let out a hysterical little giggle. Resumed her quiet contemplation. Tossing the coverlet onto the floor, he pulled a sheet off one bed, gripped the material in his teeth, and tore off a long strip. Knelt before her and quickly bound the torn arm.

She gasped and recoiled.

"It's all right. Easy, you're all right."

He was hoping to avert hysterics. In fact he was stunned that Rhea hadn't already collapsed. She had always been terrified by the sight of blood.

"*Nigel,*" she whispered, and lowering her lids as if they were too heavy for her, she laid her head on his chest. The smell of alcohol came off her breath in waves.

He forced himself to look down at her. The face held no allure. He tightened his arms; she remained just a slender woman of middle years, not a flaming presence. She was no longer a dangerous and deadly mystery. She had lost her power.

No, you've finally stopped giving *her the power.*

The realization was so profound that he almost sobbed with relief. The last small vestige of hate and fear melted away. He blinked back tears and raised his head to the wood-beamed ceiling. He would return to Mona with a soul that was free and a heart that held no secrets. There was a momentary regret that he couldn't have broken free while there was still time for him and Lexa, but that was over. The past was forever gone and buried. He had to look to his future.

"Come on, Rhea, dear. Let's get you to the hospital."

He rose and swung her lightly up into his arms.

She forced up her eyelids. "Nigel, you came."

"Yes, Sis, I did."

"Do you love me?"

"Yes."

23

There was a fierce grind of gears as the big yellow crane muscled up the wall of the barn. Dust drifted through the still August air, thrown up by the spinning wheels of the construction equipment. Hooves thudded as the seven horses circled at the trot in the white-railed arena.

Silvestre, hands resting lightly on his hips, spun in slow circles, watching his little class.

"Roberto, get your back up, and stop using the reins to post. Use your *legs,* not Favory's mouth."

"He's such a sweet boy," said Mona, leaning back into Nigel's arms.

"Who? Favory or Sil?"

"Favory, of course. I wouldn't call Sil a boy."

"I wouldn't call him sweet." He grinned down at her.

Franklin joined them with a smile of self-satisfaction on his round face. He gave his hands a defiant dust. "There, all done. The sign's up." His hand punched the words into the air. "The Denise Pierce Memorial Equestrian Training Center. And I see Sil ain't wastin' no time 'bout startin' the trainin'. Who are these rug rats?"

"The first students from the Pueblo," Mona replied.

"Have you ever noticed," Nigel broke in, "that when Franklin's insufferably pleased with himself, his accent gets thicker?"

"Do you think you should be pointing out derogatory things about my employer in front of my employer?''

"What's the worst he can do? Fire you?"

The old man grinned and folded Mona in a bear hug. "No, keep you workin' for me."

"Rosie, heels *down*."

"He's abusing my people," Benny broke in.

"Good God, redskin, quit creeping up on me!"

"Guilty conscience," Benny confided to the Vallises. "He remembers all those Indian massacres by his respected ancestors, and he figures I'm the Indian Nemesis."

"I'll be easier on them," Mona said, replying to Benny's opening statement. "But they're fortunate to have a chance to study with someone of Sil's ability. It isn't often you have a world-class equestrian teaching baby beginners. They should enjoy it while they can. He'll be gone soon." A little shadow of regret flickered across her face. Nigel tightened his embrace.

The class had lined up in front of Silvestre, and he was talking to them in low tones. With a proprietary look, Franklin wandered farther down the fence so he could hear.

"What do you do next, Benny? You've fought the big fight, won the big win. What now?" Nigel asked.

The Indian shaded his eyes and watched the kids. "I don't know. Franklin's thrilled, of course, and you guys have found your place—"

"And you haven't?" Mona asked quietly.

He shrugged self-consciously. "Once I've done a thing, I lose interest in it. I've had a couple of job offers back east, and I'm considering them."

"You'd leave all this . . ." Nigel gestured toward the distant walls of San Jose Pueblo.

"San Jose doesn't want me anymore. On some level I'll always want it, but I can understand why it's rejected me." He gave himself a shake, as if throwing off melancholia. "For the moment, though, I'm going to take a little vacation. Go down to Mexico." He slid his eyes toward Nigel. "And maybe even head on to Guatemala."

"Are you pursuing my ex-wife?"

"Who knows, I just might try."

Mona glanced anxiously up at Nigel, who gave her a reassuring kiss.

"Excuse me a moment, I have to help Sil," she said, wriggling free.

"Help him do what?"

"You'll see."

She hurried away with that distinctive tipped-back walk of the heavily pregnant woman. Benny dug hands into pockets and kicked at the dust. Abruptly he asked, "Would you mind?"

"Mind what?" Nigel pulled his attention from Mona.

"If I went down to Guatemala?"

"It's a free country. Go if you want."

"That's not an answer."

"What do you want from me? My blessing?"

"I guess the knowledge that you really have broken with Lexa."

"I have. Part of me will always regret it, but yes, there's nothing between us now."

"You don't like me, do you?" Benny asked.

"That may be too strong. I suppose in that deep irrational part that exists in all humans, I hold you responsible for much of what happened. But I don't dislike you. I'm just ambivalent about you." Nigel started away.

"I'll marry Lexa if I can."

Nigel smiled slightly at the defiant note in the young man's voice. "I wish you luck."

He joined Franklin Pierce at the rail, and they watched as Mona directed several of the grooms in setting up a jump course.

"What's going on?" Nigel asked the old man.

"I don't know, but the tension's so thick you could spread it on bread and eat it for breakfast."

Brick by wooden brick, a big wall went up. Sil walked into the ring leading a strikingly beautiful bay mare. Stooped and hugged Mona. Her face was tight with worry when she pushed her way in between Nigel and Franklin.

"What's going on?" Nigel asked.

"This is the final six jumps of the Paris course."

"Oh."

"He hasn't faced a wall yet, and he hasn't jumped anything over six feet." Her eyes were locked on Silvestre as he mounted and walked the mare in several slow circles.

"It seems very high," Nigel offered timidly.

"A little over seven feet."

"Jesus God."

The mare rocked into a collected canter. Circled one final time. Came in smoothly on the left lead for the oxer, and took it with an ease that made it seem contemptible. Sil was seated beautifully in the center of his horse, hands quiet, stretched forward along the mare's neck, body still and perfectly balanced. She landed lightly and made a flying lead change as they crossed the arena on a diagonal. A rather intimidating spread fence loomed before horse and rider. The mare dismissed it with a pert toss of her head, tucked her knees up under her chin, and sailed over. She went through the in-and-out with hardly a change in the rhythm of her stride.

"Oh, she's wonderful, isn't she," Mona cried with excitement. Then she sobered. They had negotiated the final bank and were riding for the wall.

Mona's fingers closed convulsively around Nigel's upper arm. He patted her hand, but like her, did not take his eyes off the man and horse. The mare's impulsion off her short stride was powerful, and rocked Sil into a perfect position for the jump. Calm seemed to radiate from that slim form. His eyes were focused between the horse's pricked ears as he gave her the freedom to break herself in two over the monstrous wall.

One impossibly slender foreleg took the shock of the landing, the other already outstretched for the next stride. The final fence was negligible. A spatter of applause rippled through the assembled grooms and students. Franklin cheered and tossed his cowboy hat high into the air. Mona was scrambling awkwardly over the fence, the swell of her belly making it impossible to slither between the rails. Nigel vaulted lightly over, and carefully lifted her down. Her eyes were bright with unshed tears, and she gazed past him to where Silvestre lay forward along the mare's neck, urgently hugging her.

"Oh, Sil, Sil, you did it! I knew you could!"

Silvestre leapt down and enfolded her in a rib-crushing embrace. "I owe it all to you! I could never have done it without you!"

"Attaboy, Sil!"

Sil and Mona disappeared behind Franklin's looming bulk. Nigel smiled softly and stepped back. He found himself seeking out the peak of Rhea's tower. He suddenly felt cold and a little bereft, despite the burning August heat. Then Mona was there, pressed to his side while Sil excitedly shared every nuance of the ride with Pierce.

"Don't look sad. What's wrong?"

"I can't help but pity her, Mona. She's so alone, and that's the thing she most feared in the world."

"Hey, come on," Pierce bellowed. "We're headin' out to the Sidewinder."

"Ugh, that dump? Why?"

"Governor Barela and old Chief Martinez and some of the other Pueblo honchos are meetin' us there for a steak dinner."

"Do the cockroaches come with, or do we have to order them special?" Nigel asked.

"So it's grungy, but they do the best steak dinner in Santa Fe," Pierce claimed. "Trust me."

Nigel cocked an eye down at Mona. "When Franklin says that, that's when I *really* start to worry."

"Hey, *pendejo.*"

"Whom are you addressing? There's a whole shit-load of *pendejos* seated at this table." Benny enunciated carefully, then giggled and clapped a hand over his mouth.

Ramon Dominguez was flanked by the Party Boys, Pepe and Dan. Behind him lurked Gilbert Gonzales and Fred Gomez and several other young men. Nigel didn't like the vibrations at all, and he wished that he and Mona weren't the only stone-cold-sober people at the table.

"So you're drinking with the white people, and you've got the rest of us out shoveling horseshit. Big man, college boy, big man," Pepe Sena growled. He and Dan were in their usual condition—totally pissed—and clearly spoiling for a fight.

"No, no," Benny began with a silly smile. "Sure, some of the jobs are for grooms, but we're gonna *train* people."

"To do what? Kiss white butt?"

Benny was still smiling, all ready to represent sweet if somewhat tipsy reason, but Franklin interrupted him.

"Hey, boys, this is a private party, so *fuck off*!"

"Asshole!" A glob of spit hit the table by Franklin's hand with a moist splat.

"Franklin . . ." warned Nigel, but the old man belligerently shook off Nigel's restraining hand. He came up from behind the table like a tidal wave and gave Ramon a hard shove in the chest.

Nigel kicked back his chair, grabbed Mona by the wrist, and swung her into Silvestre's arms.

"Get her out of here!"

Ramon kicked over the table—plates, silverware, and remnants of their dinner flying in all directions. He lunged toward Franklin, but Benny came between them, driving his fist into the Indian's belly. The falling table had clipped Ernesto Barela and tipped him and his chair over backward. The governor climbed groggily from beneath the wreckage. Blood ran from a shallow cut over his eye.

Joe Martinez bent to help the younger man, and Dan stepped in to kick him. He never completed the action because Nigel exploded into a spinning back kick. As the heel of his shoe connected with the man's knee, he felt the patella shatter. Dan fell screaming.

Nigel whirled as Gilbert Gonzales came lunging in low, the force of his body driving a hard right punch. Nigel stepped into the attack, stopped the punch with a folded arm block, then slammed alternating elbows into the man's head. Just for good measure, he ended with a front snap kick to Gilbert's groin. Gilbert joined Dan on the floor.

"Stay here!" Sil shoved Mona unceremoniously into the car and ripped open the glove box.

"Nigel . . . !"

"I'm going back to help him. *Shit!*" He flung maps and a flashlight onto the floor of the New Yorker, and finally unearthed the pistol.

"That's illegal in a bar!"

"Who the hell cares?" He bolted for the bar. In the distance he heard the rising wail of police sirens.

Hurry, please hurry! Sil prayed, and plunged back through the door.

Nigel crouched, ready for another attack. He saw Ramon pull a knife, saw Benny's unprotected back, and shouted a warning. Benny started around, but too slowly. Then Franklin was there, his big belly pushing between them. But Ramon was already committed to his blow. The blade slid into Franklin's body just below the short ribs. The old man folded his hands around the blade, and his fingers were cut as Ramon withdrew the knife. Blood seeped from between Franklin's fingers.

In a killing rage, Ramon closed with Benny, ready to finish it once and for all. Time seemed to be moving in slow motion.

Jungle all around. Slick mud beneath the boot soles. The dull thump as a grenade fell. Close. So close. The glare of white phosphorus as the grenade exploded. Sam, going up like a torch. The screaming.

"Sergeant!"

Nigel knew that voice. He froze, whirled. Saw the black pistol tumbling through the air. He caught it by the barrel, flipped it into his hand, cocked it.

"Freeze, asshole!"

Ramon eyed Nigel. Hefted the knife. Debated.

"Try it and die," Nigel warned.

"Fuckin' shit," Pepe whined. "No fair. Put up the gun, man. Fight fair."

"This is how a white man fights," Nigel raged. "You fuck with me, you fuck with a gun!"

Franklin gave a moist spurt of laughter. "You tell 'em, Vallis. Shit, and I always thought you were a pantywaist."

A bubble of blood seeped from his mouth. He was lying back in Benny's arms. The young Indian had a handkerchief pressed to the wound.

"How is he?" Nigel asked.

"I'll live," Pierce grunted.

Benny was white-faced.

"Ambulance! Somebody call for an ambulance," Sil yelled, then laid a hand on Benny's arm. "It's real tough to kill somebody with a knife," he said reassuringly.

"But—"

"Don't believe everything you see in the movies," Nigel added.

"He saved my life," Benny said brokenly.

The old man opened his eyes. "And I'll fucking never let you forget it, redskin," he whispered.

"May I have a sip of that?"

"The caffeine?" Nigel asked, glancing from the coffee to Mona.

"I think the baby can stand a little agitation. God knows, if he's picking up my mood, he's probably about ready to jump out of there."

"He'll be all right. Franklin will be all right," Benny said, passing through on one of his never-ending walks across the hospital waiting room. He sounded like he was trying to convince himself more than his companions.

"It has been a long time," Mona said softly as she leaned against Nigel's shoulder and sipped coffee.

"Surgery's never simple," offered Sil, but he and

Nigel exchanged glances over her head. They had a
better idea about how long it took to piece a man back
together than did the two innocents with them. And it
had been a long time.

"Why did I ever start this?" Benny flung himself
into a chair. "If I hadn't started this—"

"Don't be an ass," Nigel snapped. "Franklin
started this. You just helped him realize his dream."

"Some dream," the young man said bitterly. "I get
him stabbed in a barroom brawl."

"Franklin Pierce would have found a way to build
his center with or without your help. You're *not* responsible for what happened. Do you understand?"
Black eyes met gray. Slowly Benny nodded.

Quick footsteps on the tile floor. They all stiffened.
Mona's hand sought Nigel's and closed in a convulsive
grip. Dr. Ingram entered at his usual quick march, but
Nigel, searching the doctor's face, read the answer
there a fraction before the others. He had seen too
many doctors in Nam not to know that look.

"I'm sorry . . ."

"No!" screamed Benny. "You didn't try . . . you
fucked up!"

"Surgery is never simple," Ingram said gently.
"There's always a risk, and that risk increases with
the age of the patient. Mr. Pierce was not a young
man, nor was he in the best of shape."

"No! You're not going to get off like that. You . . .
you did something wrong."

Nigel caught Benny by his heaving shoulders. For a
moment the younger man stood stiff, resisting, then
allowed himself to be pulled into the hard embrace.
His tears scalded Nigel's neck.

Mona was staring at him dry-eyed, but with a face
the color of snow. She was so still that she reminded
Nigel of a marble statue, beautiful and lifeless, killed
by a few words. Silvestre slowly crossed himself.
Closed his eyes.

" 'Scuse me," snorted Benny, and breaking free,
ran into the bathroom.

"My grandfather used to go into the mountains and

wrestle demons into submission,'' Sil said softly. ''I guess he didn't get all of them.''

Nigel, his eyes on the closing bathroom door, said, ''Unfortunately, we each have to do our own wrestling with our own demons.''

There was a snarl of thunder, and the red-chili ristras hanging by the front door swayed and rattled in a sharp mountain wind. Nigel thrust the key into the lock and opened the door.

''Brandy,'' Mona said firmly, and went off after the snifters.

''None for me, thank you,'' Nigel said when she returned with four glasses.

''And I shouldn't. Never again.'' Benny swirled the amber liquid in his glass. ''It was a bunch of fucking drunk Indians who killed him.''

''Drink it. You need it,'' said Sil. ''We all do.''

''No,'' Nigel said. ''It's too easy, too seductive for me.''

Benny was standing with his back to the room, staring out the window at the black peaks of the Sangre de Cristo Mountains. Now they were touched by the lightning as the late-summer storm rumbled.

''What's going to happen to the center now that Franklin has passed . . . is dead?'' Mona forced herself to use the less pleasant word.

Benny turned to face them. He was grim-faced, and looked older than his twenty-eight years. ''*I* run it.''

''What?'' Silvestre blurted.

''I thought you were off to Connecticut or L.A. or some damn place,'' Nigel said.

''No. I'm here. For good. Franklin wanted that center not only for Denise, or because he loved a good fight, but for my people. He cared more than I did. I can't just go running off, trying to deny who and what I am. The Pueblo may not want me anymore, but I'm a part of it . . . forever. My Pueblo, my moiety . . . this land.''

''I heard a man at La Fonda describe this town as

black and sick," said Mona. "A theatrical set piece hiding its reality from the world. Art underscored with senseless random violence. A microcosm of hate—Indian, Anglo, and Hispano." She sighed. "Maybe he was right."

"No," corrected Nigel gently. "Take a look at this room. We're a microcosm of that microcosm. We're showing that people can put aside hate."

"Are you with me?" Benny asked, holding out his hand.

"For always," Mona replied, clasping it in hers. "We'll run that center, and we'll make it the best in the world."

"And I'll see to it that the world comes to it," Sil said.

"And I'll help keep the uneasy peace in this uneasy town." Nigel gave a wry little smile. "Until it can be a permanent one."

Suddenly Benny knelt, pulling the others down with him. They gripped hands, and Benny began a Tewa prayer. "Within and around the earth . . ."

"Within and around the hills . . ." Nigel picked up.

"Within and around the mountains . . ." Benny continued.

"Your authority returns to you," Nigel concluded.

And then the cleansing rain washed down.

About the Author

MELINDA SNODGRASS was born in California, but her heart belongs to New Mexico. Aside from a year studying opera at the Conservatory of Vienna, she has lived her entire life in that southwestern state. She graduated from the University of New Mexico School of Law and spent three years as an attorney before deciding it was not the profession for her. Then her best friend, Vic Milán, suggested she try writing. To date, she has sold fifteen books and can't imagine anything more rewarding than a career as a professional novelist. When not working, she spends her time with her Arabian horses and doing amateur theater. Her novel *High Stakes* is available in a Signet edition.

There's an epidemic with 27 million victims. And no visible symptoms.

It's an epidemic of people who can't read.

Believe it or not, 27 million Americans are functionally illiterate, about one adult in five.

The solution to this problem is you... when you join the fight against illiteracy. So call the Coalition for Literacy at toll-free **1-800-228-8813** and volunteer.

Volunteer Against Illiteracy. The only degree you need is a degree of caring.